Rebecca's Reward

Books by
Lauraine Snelling

A Secret Refuge
(three novels in one volume)

DAKOTA TREASURES
Ruby • *Pearl*
Opal • *Amethyst*

DAUGHTERS OF BLESSING
A Promise for Ellie
Sophie's Dilemma
A Touch of Grace
Rebecca's Reward

RED RIVER OF THE NORTH
An Untamed Land
A New Day Rising
A Land to Call Home
The Reaper's Song
Tender Mercies
Blessing in Disguise

RETURN TO RED RIVER
A Dream to Follow
Believing the Dream
More Than a Dream

LAURAINE SNELLING

Rebecca's Reward

BETHANYHOUSE
PUBLISHERS

MINNEAPOLIS, MINNESOTA

Rebecca's Reward
Copyright © 2008
Lauraine Snelling

Cover design by Koechel Peterson & Associates, Inc., Minneapolis, Minnesota

Scripture quotations are from the King James Version of the Bible.

Published by Bethany House Publishers
11400 Hampshire Avenue South
Bloomington, Minnesota 55438

Bethany House Publishers is a division of
Baker Publishing Group, Grand Rapids, Michigan.

Printed in the United States of America

ISBN: 978-0-7642-0202-5 (Paperback)
ISBN: 978-0-7642-0591-0 (Large Print)

Library of Congress Cataloging-in-Publication Data

Snelling, Lauraine.
    Rebecca's reward / Lauraine Snelling.
        p.   cm. — (Daughters of Blessing ; 4)
    ISBN 978-0-7642-0202-5 (pbk.)
    1. Norwegian Americans—Fiction. 2. Family—Fiction. 3. Frontier and pioneer life—Fiction. 4. North Dakota—Fiction. I. Title.

PS3569.N39R44 2008
813'.54—dc22
                                                                2008028308

DEDICATION

To my family, both in America and Norway
for my rich heritage and the beginning of my stories.
Who ever would have dreamed of all this?
To God be the glory.

LAURAINE SNELLING is an award-winning author of over sixty books, fiction and nonfiction, for adults and young adults. Her books have sold over two million copies. Besides writing books and articles, she teaches at writers' conferences across the country. She and her husband, Wayne, have two grown sons, a basset named Chewy, and a cockatiel watch bird named Bidley. They make their home in California.

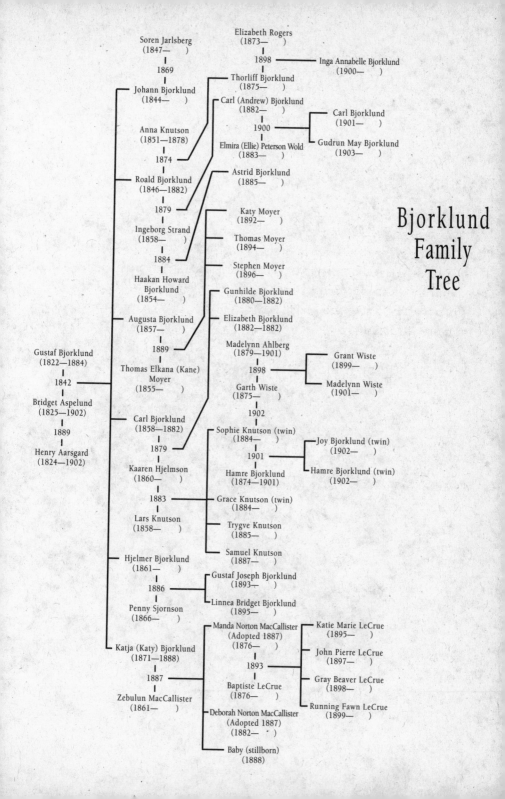

Bjorklund Family Tree

Gustaf Bjorklund
(1822—1884)

1842

Bridget Aspelund
(1825—1902)

1889

Henry Aarsgard
(1824—1902)

Soren Jarlsberg
(1847—   )

1869

Johann Bjorklund
(1844—   )

Anna Knutson
(1851—1878)

1874

Roald Bjorklund
(1846—1882)

1879

Ingeborg Strand
(1858—   )

1884

Haakan Howard
Bjorklund
(1854—   )

Augusta Bjorklund
(1857—   )

1889

Thomas Elkana (Kane)
Moyer
(1855—   )

Carl Bjorklund
(1858—1882)

1879

Kaaren Hjelmson
(1860—   )

1883

Lars Knutson
(1858—   )

Hjelmer Bjorklund
(1861—   )

1886

Penny Sjornson
(1866—   )

Katja (Katy) Bjorklund
(1871—1888)

1887

Zebulun MacCallister
(1861—   )

Elizabeth Rogers
(1873—   )

1898

Thorliff Bjorklund
(1875—   )

Carl (Andrew) Bjorklund
(1882—   )

1900

Elmira (Ellie) Peterson Wold
(1883—   )

Astrid Bjorklund
(1885—   )

Katy Moyer
(1892—   )

Thomas Moyer
(1894—   )

Stephen Moyer
(1896—   )

Gunhilde Bjorklund
(1880—1882)

Elizabeth Bjorklund
(1882—1882)

Madelynn Ahlberg
(1879—1901)

1898

Garth Wiste
(1875—   )

1902

Sophie Knutson (twin)
(1884—   )

1901

Hamre Bjorklund
(1874—1901)

Grace Knutson (twin)
(1884—   )

Trygve Knutson
(1885—   )

Samuel Knutson
(1887—   )

Gustaf Joseph Bjorklund
(1893—   )

Linnea Bridget Bjorklund
(1895—   )

Manda Norton MacCallister
(Adopted 1887)
(1876—   )

1893

Baptiste LeCrue
(1876—   )

Deborah Norton MacCallister
(Adopted 1887)
(1882—   )

Baby (stillborn)
(1888)

Inga Annabelle Bjorklund
(1900—   )

Carl Bjorklund
(1901—   )

Gudrun May Bjorklund
(1903—   )

Grant Wiste
(1899—   )

Madelynn Wiste
(1901—   )

Joy Bjorklund (twin)
(1902—   )

Hamre Bjorklund (twin)
(1902—   )

Katie Marie LeCrue
(1895—   )

John Pierre LeCrue
(1897—   )

Gray Beaver LeCrue
(1898—   )

Running Fawn LeCrue
(1899—   )

1

Late December 1902
Blessing, North Dakota

"GUS BAARD, YOU ARE the most stubborn brother a girl could ever have." Rebecca glared, hands clamped on her hips. Since she only had two living brothers, it wasn't much of a contest, but still, why could he never, ever see her point of view? To keep herself from launching a full attack, she slammed the kitchen cabinet door. The dishes rattled inside.

"You know we don't have any money for your silly dream, so quit wasting time on it. Destroying the cattle killed a lot of dreams."

"I know that, but if thinking about my soda shop makes me happy, what's wrong with a bit of happy?" What else could she slam, other than his head? "Besides, I have my graduation money." Every year each graduate of the Blessing school received one hundred dollars from Mr. Gould, a wealthy man in New York who'd been a friend of the Bjorklunds since the homesteading days.

"Money that should go into the bank to help replace our livestock." Gus shook his head. "Grow up, Rebecca. What's more important—our farm and keeping our heads above water or . . ."

She glared at him, anything to keep from bursting into tears again. Crying never did any good. All the tears she'd shed over the destruction of the cows, pigs, and sheep had only given her a headache. That and all the smoke from the burning carcasses. Hoof-and-mouth disease had decimated all the cloven-footed animals west of the Mississippi. They had gone for months without milk, cream, butter, and meat other than chicken, fish, or rabbit, unless they paid the exorbitant prices for that brought in on the train. With no milk to sell to Ingeborg Bjorklund's cheese house, they'd had no income until after harvest.

So what was wrong with dreaming? If only she could talk these things over with her mother, but Agnes Baard had died nine years earlier, leaving a hole in her youngest child's heart the size of North Dakota.

"You're not going to cry now, are you?"

The tone of his voice set her off again. "Gus Baard, you better get out of my kitchen before I . . . before I . . ." She started toward him, no plan in mind, but the look on her face must have convinced him that even though he was eight inches taller than she and a lot heavier, retreat was wiser than confrontation. She slammed the door behind him and collapsed on a kitchen chair. "Lord, I hate winter, I hate the cattle dying, and I hate all the sorrow around here. I just thought I could bring some people a little happiness, and look what it gets me. A never-ending fight with my brother. And the sad thing is, he's probably right. I hate it when he is right!"

At least Knute, the older of the two brothers, didn't try to boss her around all the time, but then, she didn't live with him, at least not anymore. Besides, he had his wife, Dorothy, and three little kids to worry about. Gus just had too much time on his hands.

Rebecca shook her head and, realizing her hair was about to tumble about her face, unpinned it, finger combed the thick mass, and twisted it into a coil to repin at the base of her skull.

Was she really being selfish, as he'd said many times before, or was keeping a dream alive important? Maybe she would ask the girls after church, or perhaps Gerald would have time to talk. It was a good thing she had friends, because it might be a week before Gus spoke to her after this round.

If only the wind would quit shrieking around the eaves and

sneaking through the tiniest cracks to freeze everything it touched. Her mother had said that when the wind got the better of her, she would get herself into the Word of God, because only God could order the wind about. The Bible didn't seem to make a whole lot of sense to Rebecca, at least not like it had to her mother.

The more she thought of what Gus had said, the madder she got. Did he think she was lazy? After all, he was the one for whom she'd been cooking and cleaning and washing, doing all the things that women usually do for husbands and children. Before she graduated last spring, she went to school and still managed to plant a full-sized garden. Her mor or far would have been disappointed with the spring housecleaning, however. Overbearing—that fit her brother. She stared at the table, seeing Gus. It wouldn't take too long for him to be married. Even if he didn't seem to notice how the girls looked at him.

He'd turned into one handsome young man—broad of shoulder, hovering right about six feet tall, with hair that nearly matched hers, a warm brown that glinted bits of fire when the sun hit it just right. Their mother had said the cleft in his chin was the fingerprint of an angel, put there when he was born. He was two years older than she but didn't get his full growth until the last few years, so some folks had thought they were twins when they were younger, a comment that always made their mother laugh. Agnes said she knew for a fact she'd never carried two babies at a time and thanked God for not sending them that blessing.

Best she get to the duties for the day. They were out of bread.

Rebecca had the bread dough rising on the warming oven when Gus returned.

"You've gone and ripped the knees out of those pants." She huffed a sigh. The mending pile was growing again, almost as if clothes were breeding in the basket.

He looked down at his pants, shrugged, and shook his head. "Can't help it. Maybe next time you can put double patches on 'em right from the beginning."

Amazing. He was talking to her. "You better marry some girl who loves to patch and mend, that's for certain sure."

After their parents' death, the two of them had stayed at the family home with their older brother Knute. Since the eldest, Swen, was already married to Dorothy, the couple helped as substitute parents. But life took another turn for the worse when Swen was killed by a bull, leaving a pregnant wife. Dorothy named the baby boy Swen, after his father, and nearly two years later, Knute married his sister-in-law. When Gus and Rebecca grew old enough to manage on their own, they moved back into their parents' farmhouse.

Gus stared at her until she put a hand to her hair to see if it was falling out of the rat she'd wound it around that morning. Wearing her hair in a pouf in front made her look older—at least she thought so.

"What now?" She knew her voice still sounded sharp, but he had started the battle.

"Nothing. I'm going out to work in the machine shed with Knute. If I can't fix that piece, I'm going to take it in to Sam. He said he thought he could make a new part."

"Couldn't you just order it?" She thought of the catalog she'd been daydreaming over, which was what had set him off in the first place. Only instead of machinery parts, this catalog had round tables with black iron pedestals, chairs with heart-shaped wire backs, and best of all, pictures of soda dispensers and refrigerated display cases. How she loved that word *display*, a place where she would show off her flavors of ice cream in the summer and scoop it out for everyone to enjoy.

No matter what some people seemed to think, Blessing really needed a place where people could come and have a good time eating and visiting, and perhaps young people could be courting there. And just maybe some stranger would walk in and she would fall in love and live happily ever after. Since she was the youngest child in the family and had always spent a lot of time alone, she'd always had a good imagination and invented fairy tales of her own. A shining knight on a white horse was all she wanted. Just liked the stories Mor used to tell her when she was little.

Onkel Olaf had already said he would build her display shelving and booths with gingerbread cutouts on the sides and pedestal tables for her soda shop. She'd had to cancel the order last summer when the great devastation hit. She heaved another sigh.

"You know we'd never spend the money on new parts if we can get it done cheaper here. Without the milk money, we have to be careful."

He stared at her as if studying the machine part to be fixed, but at least he wasn't yelling.

"Do you need anything from town if I should go?" He spit out the *need* as if daring her to ask.

"I'll start a list. I sure wish Penny still had the store. That Mr. Jeffers doesn't carry half the things we need." Besides, the man made her feel extremely uncomfortable when she went in there, as if he were sizing her up or something. She'd heard he was looking for a wife, but the thought of even being near him gave her the shudders. There was something about the man that just wasn't right. *I'd rather be a spinster than married to him.*

"Well, at least he carries men's pants. I'll get a new pair while I'm there."

"I thought you weren't going to spend any money."

He tipped his head back and closed his eyes. "I got to have warm pants." He motioned to the red long johns peeking through the rips. "You're the one who does the fixing."

"All right. Help me bring the sewing machine down where it's warm, and I'll do the mending instead." Instead of what, she wasn't about to say. As he'd said, mooning over the catalog and lost dreams sure wasn't going to get her anywhere. "If you fill the woodbox before you go out, I'll bake rabbit pie for dinner."

At least with the weather so cold, they didn't have to worry about what meat they had spoiling. Gus had shot and smoked a dozen geese, and the two Baard families had gone together and bought a dressed hog that had been brought in on the train. They were running snares for rabbits, and now that the river was frozen over, they'd be ice fishing.

All these years they'd had plenty to eat, but with the cattle, sheep, and hogs destroyed, the larder was pretty slim. Good thing she'd canned jars of chicken when she had so many roosters this year from the hatchings, along with all the vegetables that filled the cellar. She led the way upstairs to get the machine.

"Let's set it in the kitchen, where it is warmest." When they did, she went back to secure the blanket they had nailed over the bottom of the stairway to keep the heat from going upstairs. They'd also blocked off the heat register over the stove.

The wind tried to tear the door from his hands as Gus went out to bring in wood. Since the stack on the porch was dwindling, he took the time to haul some up to the porch from the stack along the side of the house. Even though they'd closed off the upstairs and Rebecca had shut the doors to the two bedrooms, keeping the downstairs even close to comfortable took a lot of firewood and coal.

She wrapped her shawl closer around her shoulders and gave the grate in the cookstove a turn before putting more wood in the firebox to heat the oven. Maybe this was why she was feeling like an old maid. She had all the responsibilities of caring for a home, but—

She cut off the thinking there. What was she complaining about? She had food enough to eat and a comfortable home, and now that winter was here, she even had time to read when she wanted to. Probably it was just the wind. Her mother had always said that the North Dakota wind could drive a person crazy if one didn't pray against it. Surely it was the wind making her morose. The party coming up would be just the thing to get her out of it.

Maybe the wind was ony part of the problem. She'd found her mother's prayer list, a small book actually, in some of her things, and reading through it had sent her into the doldrums. Life had been so much harder back in the early days. Her mother, Agnes, had been such good friends with Kaaren Knutson and Ingeborg Bjorklund that Rebecca had almost felt jealous. Here she was, no longer a girl yet not one of the women either. She'd always dreamed of being a shopkeeper like her cousin Penny, who'd started the general store, serving all of

Blessing and the area around it. She'd read so many notes about Penny in the little book and about her mother's praying for Penny's husband, Hjelmer, too. She had been a praying woman; that was for sure. And God had answered those prayers. The answers were written down too and the dates.

Why did she feel like God didn't answer *her* prayers? Like for her dream of having a soda shop? Or saving them all from the hoof-and-mouth epidemic, and most important of all, keeping her mother and father alive. She slammed the door shut on those thoughts and measured out the flour for pie crust. It wasn't just a figment of her imagination. God really didn't answer when she prayed. After all, her loved ones had died and all the cloven-footed animals had needed to be destroyed and thus her dream. Her dream that began with Mor's stories. A dream that would keep Mor close to her every day, not just sometimes. What would she do when Gus married?

She cut the rabbit meat off the bones, added potatoes, onions, and carrots, crumbled up several leaves of the sage she had dried during the summer, and added part of a jar of string beans, along with enough flour to thicken the liquid. After rolling the dough thicker than for a fruit pie, she fitted the crust into a cast-iron frying pan, poured in the filling, and rolled out the top crust. She sealed the edges of the crusts and slid the meat pie into the oven, checking the clock on the wall automatically. An hour and a half until dinnertime.

She rolled the remaining crust, lined a regular pie pan, crimped the edges, and slid that into the oven. She would make a chocolate pie tomorrow, using milk from the cow they shared with Knute and his family, thanks to the Bjorklunds. Gus loved chocolate pie; not that she didn't, but he was especially partial to that treat. Though why she would want to make him a special treat when he was acting so grumpy was an excellent question.

"You have your list ready?" Gus asked as he came in a while later.

"Couldn't get it to work?" she asked.

"No! Wish Far were here. He always knew how to fix the machinery."

"Along with everything else." She could feel moisture collecting in her eyes. One more memory to pile on top of the others nagging at her.

Gus turned from hanging his coat and hat on the pegs on the wall. He hesitated a moment, then blurted, "Maybe you ought to go with me and visit with somebody. Sophie or . . ."

"If I needed to visit, I could go over to Dorothy's." With the snow so frozen, she could easily walk across the small field to Knute and Dorothy's house. The person she'd really like to discuss some of these things with was working at the telephone switchboard. Now, wouldn't that cause a to-do if she strolled in and announced she wanted to talk with Gerald for a while? Perhaps she would see him on Sunday after church. He was so level-headed and such a good friend.

Gus's frown made her realize she'd been snappy again. "Maybe I should bring Sarah over here to play." Sarah was five years old and wishing she could go to school like her big brother, Swen, who would soon turn seven. She was not partial to staying home and helping with "the baby," as she called her two-year-old brother, Hans. She didn't yet realize that another baby was on the way.

"The kids all have colds again." He sat down at the table then, but at her look, he got up and washed his hands before sitting down again.

Rebecca set the steaming pan in the center of the table, the golden brown top crust making her mouth water. Shame they hadn't invited Knute over for dinner so that Dorothy wouldn't have had to cook too. She served both of their plates, then passed the bread and beet pickles.

Two more days until the party with her friends. Surely just thinking about it would perk up her spirits.

Gus swallowed a mouthful of rabbit pie. "Are you sure you don't want to go along?"

First he yelled at her, and now he was being too nice. *Make up your mind.* "No, I need to finish the dress I started for Sarah. She's growing so fast, we can't keep up with her." Rebecca picked up the pencil she'd kept on the table and added dark brown thread to the list. "Make sure you check for mail."

Gus rolled his eyes. "You'd think you were waitin' for love letters the way you go on about the mail."

"Just catalogs." At the look on his face she was glad she'd not mentioned the round tables and the red-and-white gingham.

"What a waste of time. Patching my pants would be time far better spent."

"Gus Baard, if you have some complaints about the way I take care of this house and us, you just get yourself a wife now, and I'll move into town and go to work for someone else." *The pay would be better; that's for sure.*

"I won't have you spending money we haven't got for a dream that might not work out."

"Oh sure, you can buy machinery when you need it, but if I try to do something, then it is only a dream." The ends of her hair sizzled. The nerve of him. Dreaming never cost a dime. And she wasn't stupid.

Gus glared at her and stabbed a slice of bread off the plate with his fork, daring her to comment on his lack of manners. "Besides, we haven't bought any machinery lately." He leaned forward. "Because there is no money." His voice cracked like a whip. He shoved his chair back, stomped to the stove, and poured himself some more coffee.

At the moment he looked so much like their father that Rebecca caught her breath. Back before Mor died, back when Far had been healthy and ordering his growing sons around. When there had been love and life and happiness in this house, in spite of occasional temper spells or blowups. She sipped her coffee and looked around the kitchen, deliberately not giving her brother the satisfaction of a fight. They'd had arguments before, but right now this felt more like a battle. Only she wasn't sure who was fighting and over what.

"Make sure you take the kerosene can."

He blew out a sigh. "I will. If a storm comes up and the north looks some black, I'll stay in town, so don't worry. But I should make it home before then."

"Don't take any chances." People died in blizzards, some just inches from the barn. He and Knute had strung ropes to the barns and across the field in case the blizzards were so bad they could get lost between the house and the barn.

Gus bundled back up, picked up her list, and headed toward the door. "I just don't want to see you hurt again," he said quietly before closing the door carefully behind him, in spite of the pull of the wind.

Through a film of tears Rebecca set about clearing the table and putting the food away. Any noise helped keep the wind at bay. But it didn't seem to help calm her thoughts.

Franny, her fluffy gray cat, rose from the box behind the stove, arched her back in a stretch, and wandered over to the door. "You need to go out?" A flick of her tail was the answer, so she opened the door. "Don't take too long, all right?"

A few minutes later she checked the door because the howling wind effectively drowned out any sound. She'd not even heard the jingle of the bells on the horse harnesses as the sleigh left the yard. Franny stalked in, nose in the air.

"Sorry. I wasn't sure how soon you would be ready to come in." Rebecca pushed the rolled rug tight against the bottom of the door to keep out the draft. She'd laid towels along the bottoms of the windows for the same purpose. Leave it to her hardheaded brother to insist on going to town in weather like this. It could get a lot worse before it got better, but at least the sun was still shining.

With the dishes done and knowing she had plenty of leftovers to warm up for supper, she pulled the rocking chair closer to the stove and sat down with her bound accounts book and a pencil to work on her lists again—in spite of Gus and his dire predictions. She had everything written down in there. She'd spent hours figuring and planning, putting it all away, then taking it out again, finding receipts and trying some of them out—her caramels had been a real hit at Christmas—so why did he think he had to keep reminding her of things like money? They'd talked it over more times than she could count.

If only her cousin Penny were here to give her business advice and answer more of her questions. It was probably about time to gather up her notes and send another letter to her. She knew she had to wait for the milking herds to build back up; at the moment there wasn't enough extra to make ice cream. But if she was ready then, she could save time.

After all, no one was looking at her like the girls did at Gus. Would he already be married if he didn't live with his sister? Even if her dream depended on a white knight, she could at least open the door for him.

It would help if Penny answered as quickly as she received the letter. Deep inside Rebecca had an idea Penny wasn't very happy living in Bismarck. But then, who would be happy at having to give up your business and move away from all your family, friends, and . . . well, life? Was marriage always like that? Maybe she was better off single.

2

"Far, Mor, did you hear about that dairy herd for sale?"

Ingeborg looked up at her elder son. So this was why Thorliff had skied out from Blessing in the middle of the day and burst through their door. They caught up on the news as she cut three pieces of apple cake and spread applesauce over the top, adding a bit of thick cream. What a treat it was to have cream again after those months without.

"The coffee will be hot in a few minutes. How did you hear about the dairy herd?"

"A letter from someone who knew of our plight here. It came to the newspaper office." Thorliff turned his backside to the stove. "It's cold out there, that's for certain."

"How's Inga?" Ingeborg set the plates on the table and brought the cups and saucers out of the cupboard. At the same time she checked to make sure there were sugar cubes in the clear glass sugar and creamer Haakan had given her after her surgery. Every time she filled them or noticed them, she thought again how much she loved this man of hers.

"I'd have brought her with me if the weather were better."

"Did you see your far at the barn?"

"He'll be right up. He wanted to finish fixing the stanchions he'd torn out." Thorliff rubbed his hands together. "Leave it to Far, fixing the stanchions even before he has enough cows to fill the barn again. He is always looking ahead."

"Ja. That is one of his gifts." Ingeborg smiled at her newspaper-owning son who also was partial owner of a family-owned company that built not only houses but had built and then rebuilt the flour mill after the explosion there. "That's something you both have in common."

"That would be a very good thing." He paused, thinking for a moment. "Elizabeth wanted me to ask if you are still concerned about his health."

"He seems better. But he is also not working as hard as he was during the summer and fall." Ingeborg checked on the coffeepot, then using a bundling of her apron as a pot holder, she poured coffee for both of them. "I've been praying for him every night after he goes to sleep. He says I worry needlessly, but I tell him I'm not worrying, just being observant and concerned, but"—she shrugged—"you know your far."

"And I know you. There is no one's faith that I admire and appreciate more."

"Takk." She smiled at the man who sat across the table and looked so much like his real father she might have thought Roald had come back to life and sat across from her. The differences? The smile lines around Thorliff's mouth and eyes, his ease of talking, and the fact that he was sitting in his mother's kitchen in the middle of the afternoon. She reached over and patted his hand. "I am so proud of you that I cannot begin to thank God enough. What a fine man you've become."

"Well, listen to us. Compliments flying like geese heading north." He pulled a letter from his pocket and handed it to his mother. "I think we should go buy the cows and do like we did with the last carload—let your milk families buy them at cost, and if there are any left, put them up for auction. Perhaps when Far and Lars go look at them, they might find other stock on nearby farms that could be purchased also.

I know Andrew would buy more pigs if he had a chance, and maybe you want a few sheep or goats."

"Not goats."

"Their milk makes good cheese."

"Ja. Just because I don't want any doesn't mean others might. I could do goat cheese if some got goats, but we'd need enough to do a batch." She had to rein in her imagination as it flew off to figure how to do even smaller batches of cheese to use the goats' milk. Here she didn't have enough milk to make any kind of cheese and she was planning on using goats' milk.

"I was teasing, Mor."

She brought her attention back to the laughter in his voice. "Oh. But it's not a bad idea." She could hear the sound of Haakan kicking the ice off his boots on the porch steps. Pushing her chair back, she returned to the stove to fill another cup.

"Temperature is dropping," Haakan said as he opened the door, "and the clouds to the north keep getting blacker. You better be thinking on heading home, Thorliff." While he talked he hung his outer clothes on the pegs.

"Trying to get rid of me before we even begin to talk about why I came?"

"No, never. But I don't trust those clouds." He nodded his thanks to Ingeborg as he sat down at his place and cupped his hands around the hot cup. "Ah, apple cake. That's what I thought I smelled. You going to send part of this home to Inga?"

Their granddaughter loved sweets of any kind, especially if made by her bestemor.

"I have ginger cookies for her." Ingeborg pointed to the round cookies with raisins for eyes, nose, and a smile. She knew Inga loved to pick off the raisins and eat them one by one, then nibble all around the cookie, keeping it in a circle until the last bite. Astrid had instructed her niece in the proper way to eat a ginger cookie.

With Astrid spending most of her time in the office and surgery with Dr. Elizabeth, Thorliff's wife, who was training her as her assistant, Inga and Astrid had more time together. No matter how busy the medical practice was.

"As soon as she sees those, she'll run with one in each hand to find Astrid. One day we found Inga giving cookies to two little children who were waiting with their mother. Next thing you know, she'll be running the whole house."

Ingeborg rolled her lips together to keep from laughing out loud. Their little Inga was indeed a busy little charmer. Shame that God had not seen fit to bring Elizabeth's last two babies to full term. But at least Elizabeth had gained her strength back. Ingeborg handed the letter Thorliff had brought to Haakan as soon as he'd eaten his cake and warmed his insides with hot coffee.

He read it, nodding all the while, then looked up at Ingeborg. "Looks to be a good thing. Holsteins. We'll need to find some Jerseys to add in enough cream. You show this to Lars yet?"

"No. It just came to the newspaper office," Thorliff said. "I would have sent it home with Astrid, but then she and Elizabeth decided she would stay overnight. They have a patient that needs watching." Since this happened so often, Astrid now had a room of her own up in the attic that Thorliff had finished for her, including a heating duct so she wouldn't freeze.

"When spring comes, we need to run the telephone lines out here," Thorliff said. "That instrument sure is handy. As soon as it rings, Inga runs for her mother. She even knows that two rings are for us. You need to come in and visit, Mor. Inga's different at home than out here."

"Ja. At your house she's a little tyrant, and out here she gets all the attention she wants."

"I know. We call her Queen Inga." Thorliff pointed to the letter again. "I can telegraph them that you want the herd, so they don't sell it. Then you can write to make the arrangements."

"I wouldn't want to ship them in this winter weather. We'd probably lose some." Haakan read the letter again. "But they say they need to sell soon. I wonder what the hurry is."

"You can always write and ask."

Ingeborg watched the two men. Haakan and Lars had brought back a train car of cattle in November to begin replacing the herds destroyed in the hoof-and-mouth epidemic the summer before. At least they had enough cows now to give everyone milk and cream again. Instead of hauling milk cans to Ingeborg's cheese house, those that had milk shared with the others. Ingeborg had only a couple of cheese wheels ripening in the cheese house. She'd sent the last shipment on the train eastward before Christmas.

She still had nightmares at times of the sound of rifle shots killing the animals and of the awful stench as they burned the carcasses. A pall of smoke hung over the entire Red River Valley for weeks.

They'd managed to stop the spread of the disease at the Mississippi River. The two new cows had yet to become pets like some of the others in their old herd had.

"I'll take this"—Haakan waved the sheet of paper—"to talk over with Lars, and we'll get a letter off. Thanks for bringing it out."

"Do you need money to help pay for them?"

Haakan shook his head. "But mange takk."

"We have another problem creeping up, I'm afraid."

Ingeborg motioned to his coffee cup, but Thorliff shook his head.

"What's that?"

"Harlan Jeffers at the store."

Haakan huffed out a sigh. "Now what? Thought sure he'd give in and close on Sundays like we asked, but he is some stubborn."

"This may just be gossip, since I've not seen it with my own eyes, but . . ." Thorliff paused and rubbed the side of his nose.

"Spit it out."

"I heard he is selling liquor under the counter."

Ingeborg closed her eyes. No matter how hard she'd tried to make the man feel welcome, he'd not fit in. And refusing to close on Sundays had set the entire community off. They'd talked to him politely and then boycotted. But he refused to give in, not that he had much business on Sundays anyway, other than folks off the train.

"He's carrying less and less stock. I've wondered how he can stay in business."

"I don't think he's ordered much new merchandise since he took over." Thorliff leaned back in his chair. "What do you think we should do?"

"What can we do?"

"Run him out on the rail?" Ingeborg adopted an innocent look to get laughs from the two men.

"Tar and feathers? At least he'd be warm for a while."

"You heard anything from Penny lately?" Thorliff asked his mother.

"A week or so ago."

"Did she mention if he was paying on the contract? Or if he was behind?"

Ingeborg shook her head. "She didn't mention anything about the store, nor even ask many questions about the goings-on in Blessing. The letter was pretty short."

"I thought she sold it outright." Haakan rose and went to the shelf behind the stove to get his pipe and tobacco.

"I did too until he mentioned something one day about business being hardly enough to pay the mortgage. That's why I wouldn't be surprised to learn he is selling hooch."

"Unless he borrowed from someone else to pay Penny off."

"True." Haakan used his penknife to clean the burned tobacco out of the bowl of his pipe, then tapped the blackened remains into the stove and returned to the table. "You know, I've said all along that we need to set some town ordinances in place. So far, we've all agreed on the way we want to run things, but with all the new people coming into the area . . ." He shrugged with his hands, pipe in one and tobacco can in the other. He set the things on the table, then lowered himself into the chair. "We need a town meeting."

"But how do we deal with Mr. Jeffers? Short of catching him in the act." Ingeborg wet a finger and picked up cake crumbs from the tablecloth.

"But, Mor, this is an unwritten law all you women forced into place. Nowhere is it written that there will be no liquor sold in Blessing. We just sort of agreed there would be no liquor at the dances and barn raisings."

"Well, we didn't all agree."

"But most everyone's gone along with the rule in order to keep the peace."

"True. Or the wives would take care of things." She rolled her lips together. There had been some rather loud discussions at the quilting meetings.

Haakan tamped the tobacco down in his pipe with one finger. "But not all the men are married or belong to Blessing Lutheran Church. And some of those young fellows like a drink or two. You know how they were after Sophie to put liquor in at the boardinghouse."

"So I suppose Mr. Jeffers should turn Penny's store into a saloon?" Sarcasm bled out of her comment.

Straight-faced as a judge, Haakan stared at Thorliff. "Probably not a bad idea, finance-wise."

"Haakan Bjorklund, what a thing to say!" Ingeborg glared at her husband, then caught the slight raising of his right eyebrow that always meant he was teasing. She huffed a sigh and shook her head, pushing at his shoulder. "Oh, you."

Thorliff shoved back his chair. "I better be heading on home before you two get into a fistfight." He fetched his long sheepskin jacket and knitted scarf and hat from the hat rack by the door and winked at his mother as he put them on. "I agree. We do need a town meeting, and we better make sure Harlan Jeffers is there. Maybe he'll get the message and this won't become an issue."

If he's as stubborn as most men, we have problems ahead. If only Penny were still here and running her store in the exemplary way she always had. "How's the flour mill doing?" she asked as she wrapped the cake and cookies in a cloth.

"Garth has it running well. He's a good man, that's for sure. We had them over for supper last Sunday, and Grant and Inga had a great time playing together. Bumping down the stairs was their latest trick."

"Ouch." She handed him the packet. "Where are you going to carry this?"

"Tucked inside my shirt. Should have brought a sack."

"You need any eggs or cheese?"

"I can't carry those too." He pulled on his gloves after tucking his scarf in around his neck. "Astrid can bring some in next time she comes."

Haakan and Ingeborg waved and called their good-byes from the porch as he skied off across the fields.

"Brrr." Ingeborg grabbed an armload of wood from the stack on the closed-in back porch and brought it in to dump in the woodbox. "The wind has picked up."

"Ja. Good thing he didn't stay longer. I'm going to milk early. Don't like the look of those clouds." He set his barely smoked pipe back on the shelf and bundled into his chores clothes. "Wish we had a way to tell Andrew to stay to home."

The sound of boots on the porch made him chuckle. "Speak of the devil."

"You mean the angel."

"Hey." The door opened and Andrew, their second son and a farmer at heart, stepped in. "Getting mighty cold out there."

"You go on back home, and I'll milk."

"No. I needed to come anyway. Mor, do you have any of that cough syrup? Carl is coughing again."

"I'll bottle some up for you. Stop in after you milk. Is he bad off?"

"Woke up from his nap, crying and rubbing his ears."

"Earache too. I'll get some things together and write down instructions."

"Good. Come on, let's get the milking over with."

The two men headed for the barn, and Ingeborg began gathering supplies. Sweet oil to be warmed and dropped into the ears, then

27

stuffed with cotton. She set the bottle and bits of cotton fluff into a basket, along with the cough syrup, shredded willow bark to make tea to help with pain, and goose grease with ground-up winterberries to rub on his chest. She studied the bottles of simples she had collected over the summer and some she had purchased from a company in Minneapolis. She sat down and wrote out the instructions, including a reminder on how to build a tent with a towel over a steaming kettle on the stove to help the little one breathe better.

Maybe I should go over there, she thought, knowing she could take care of little Carl and let her daughter-in-law get some extra sleep. With Ellie's due date drawing nearer, she finally admitted to being tired at times. Soon Ingeborg would have a third grandchild. They figured in February. All those years she'd wanted more children, but God didn't see fit for it to happen. Now there were babies in the house again, and Ingeborg loved every minute of it.

Please God, make little Carl better quickly. And keep us all safe if that is a blizzard bearing down again. The wind howling and shrieking around the house in a blizzard still brought back images of their first year on the prairie when so many had died. The wind had fought to blow them right off the land or at least out of their minds.

3

January 1903

"I AM NINETEEN YEARS old and not married or even being courted."

"That doesn't make you an old maid." Astrid stared at Rebecca in consternation.

"Or a spinster." Deborah MacCallister continued the thought.

"Then what does it make me?"

"Unhappy, it sounds like to me," Sophie Knutson Wiste said with a shrug.

"I am. And sometimes I'm jealous, and I don't like me very well when I feel that way." Rebecca stared around the circle of her closest friends, friends since her childhood, except for Maydell, who was Ellie's friend from Grafton. They were all gathered at the boardinghouse, ostensibly celebrating the new year but really celebrating Rebecca's November birthday. She gave Ellie, rounding with another baby, a half smile. "Look at you, married to the man you've always loved. You have the sweetest little boy, and soon you'll be having another baby. Far as I can see, you have the best of everything."

Her gaze moved to Sophie. "And while you had a terrible time what with Hamre dying, now you have a whole family and a wonderful business." She motioned around them. "Four children, including twins, and a man who adores you."

Sophie nodded. "I thank God every day for Garth and my family."

"I'm not married." Astrid, like the others, was sitting cross-legged on the floor. "I'm not even interested in any guy, so does that make me an old maid, since I don't want to be married yet?" She propped her elbows on her knees.

"We know all you want is to go to school and become a nurse." Deborah smiled.

"She's not just wanting to be a nurse anymore," Ellie said, shifting to get more comfortable. "She's becoming a doctor, thanks to Dr. Elizabeth's training her. All those years of sewing are coming in mighty handy."

Astrid gave Ellie a little shoulder nudge. "Remember our first samplers? Yours was nice and neat, and mine was all over the place. No two stitches matched."

"I was hoping Grace would be able to stay long enough for our party, but she had to get back to New York. She's sure not doing what she thought she would be, but far as I could see, she is really happy teaching at the Fenway School for the Deaf, even though she is far away from Blessing."

"Who would have thought Grace would leave Blessing and go so far away? All she wanted to do was stay here and marry Toby." Astrid sighed. "Life is strange."

"She never even told me she loved Toby until last summer." Sophie shook her head. "Guess I wasn't being very observant."

"Nope, you weren't."

Sophie poked Astrid. "You don't have to be so blunt about it."

"She's not married."

"No, but she sure is in love." Rebecca's eyes turned dreamy. "And with Jonathan Gould, no less."

Astrid wrapped her arms around her raised knees. "Grace is an amazing woman, and she doesn't even begin to realize who she is. I miss her so much. She was the closest I've ever had to a sister." She reached over and patted Ellie's arm. "Other than you. Of course, we did grow up together until Onkel Olaf moved you away. I cried and cried after you left. All those years of living so close." She tipped her head back to stretch her neck. "And Andrew. He turned into a grouch overnight. Took him a long time to get over that. I can still hear him saying"—she deepened her voice—" 'Someday I'm goin' to marry up with Ellie.'"

"And he did." Sophie passed the bowl of buttered popcorn around the circle. "Here, have some more. Mrs. Sam will be bringing in something else pretty soon."

"Something else?"

"It's a surprise."

"Well, I have an opinion, if you'd like to hear it," Maydell announced, tossing her hair back over her shoulder.

Ellie grinned at her best friend from Grafton, who had come to visit and help out for a while. "You always have an opinion, Maydell. I'm thinking you've been mighty quiet."

"I had to catch up on the news. You've not been the best correspondent."

"That's because I can't find the time to write, and when I sit down to do so, a letter to Mor is all I get done before I fall asleep. In fact, her letters take a couple of days to write. I don't know how our mothers did it all."

"They helped each other." Astrid reached for more popcorn from the crockery bowl in the center of the circle. "You know, we could sit on the chairs."

"But this is cozier." Sophie reached behind her and tossed Astrid a pillow. "Sit on that." She leaned back against the side of the bed. "I'll tell you, even with help, having four little children around all the time eats up the hours." She tipped her head back. "And energy."

"So two of you are married and have children, and the rest of us are single and sometimes helping you who need more help." Deborah looked around the circle. "Astrid knows what she wants to do."

"I know what I want to do too; it's the doing thereof that is difficult." Rebecca blew out a huff. "The one thing I want to do that I have some chance of doing is my soda shop. Now that we will have cows again, I am going ahead with my dream. First Gus said he'd help me"—she rolled her eyes—"now he's grumbling at me, and since Maisie Christopherson is selling out her dress shop . . ." She paused and glanced at Sophie, who shrugged.

"What can I say? Miss Maisie likes working here at the boarding-house, and she has a good head for business. Hiring her full time was one of my better ideas. Garth is happy that I am home more now. So are the children."

"So I am going to turn her shop into the Blessing Soda Shoppe with sodas, homemade ice cream, candies, cookies, and maybe even some gift items if this works well enough."

"Who's going to want ice cream in the winter?"

"I've been thinking on that. If any of you have suggestions, throw them in." Rebecca shifted and crossed her legs under her skirt so she could rest her elbows on her knees. "Maybe it will be a summer business."

"As if there isn't enough going on in the summer anyway."

"Maydell, you are looking mighty serious." Ellie tossed a piece of popcorn at her friend.

"I'm still thinking."

"And that takes a lot of effort for some." Sophie nudged Ellie with a giggle.

"Rebecca, isn't there someone in town that you've liked? Some male person, I mean."

"She always had a soft spot for Gerald Valders, even though he's lots older."

"He's always been my friend." Rebecca smiled inside at having met him just before the party. No matter what mood she felt, he always brought out a feeling like a warm hug.

"Like Toby was always Grace's friend?"

"This is different. She thought she was in love with Toby, but Gerald and I are just friends."

"Just friends make good marriages." Maydell munched more

popcorn. "That's a well-known fact. And if you're going to run a business too, you need someone you get along with."

"His mother ..." Astrid shook her head.

"You know, back when he first returned from the war and would get one of his malaria attacks, I'd take him something special I'd made, but his mother would never let me see him. 'It isn't proper,' she'd say."

"If Mrs. Valders had her way ..." Deborah let the thought hang.

"She'd run the town and everyone around." Sophie finished it. They all giggled.

"Remember how we used to sit in a circle and brush each other's hair?" Sophie made a sweeping motion with her hand. "Did you all bring hairbrushes?"

As they chorused assent, she stood. "Then let's do that. I'll be right back." She left the room as the others got up and dug in their overnight bags.

Rebecca sat back down and watched her friends laughing and returning to the circle, all taking down their hair as they sat down. Sophie wore hers in a bun now, but still kept the fringe she'd cut so long ago, shocking the whole school with her new look. Astrid usually wore hers in a single braid that she sometimes coiled at the base of her skull. She and Deborah pulled back the sides and let the hair ripple or curl down their backs, as the case may be. Sometimes they used the new rats. She had no idea why they were called that, but one wrapped the hair around it and poufed the front.

The daughters of Blessing, or at least most of them, had finally gathered together. All of them, but for Deborah and Maydell, had been born here and had grown up along with the town. Deborah and her sister, Manda, had arrived with Zebulon MacCallister, the man who'd saved them from dying in the family dugout along the Missouri so many years earlier.

"What are you thinking about so solemnlike?" Astrid whispered over her shoulder to Rebecca, who was brushing her hair.

"About all of us and how we've known each other since we were babies. And here we are all grown up...." At Maydell's choking laugh,

Rebecca giggled and added, "Well, mostly or sort of grown up. And who knows where life is going to take us. Or what will happen."

"My mor would add, 'It's a good thing we are all in God's hands.'" Astrid paused. "Your mor would be saying the same thing, and both of them would be praying for us like they did all along."

Rebecca smoothed the brush through Astrid's golden hair and fought the tears that surfaced so fast she could hardly contain them. She sniffed as one brimmed over and trickled down her cheek. "Sometimes I miss her so bad, I—I don't know what, but it's like the pain is new all over again. I mean, it's been nine years now, and you'd think it wouldn't hurt so much."

"I have a feeling we'd miss our mothers for the rest of our lives. I think of those who came from Norway and never saw their families again. Like my mor. She hardly ever talks about her family left in Norway. They write sometimes but not real often. Do you suppose it is easier that way, to lose touch so you don't think about them so much?"

"I don't know. I think of Penny. At first I wrote every week, then some weeks went by, and now I write more just because I want her advice on my shop idea. But she is busy and doesn't answer right away. You'd think she lives on the other side of the country, not just across the state."

"Thorliff says the telephone is going to change that for us. We'll be able to call up people anywhere when the lines crisscross the country."

"You think everyone will have telephones?"

"You watch. When spring comes and they can set poles again, all those in Blessing who want to will have telephones."

"He says eventually we'll all have electricity too."

"I'm going to put electric lights in the boardinghouse as soon as they get the lines in here." Sophie turned from brushing Deborah's hair. "There's talk of a coal-operated power plant going in near Valley City. I've been reading all I can about such improvements. Maydell, you ought to apply for the job of switchboard operator. We're going to need women to do that round the clock every day of the week."

"Why women and not men?"

Sophie rolled her eyes. "You think men want a fussy job like that?"

"Gerald's doing it, and he's not fussy." Rebecca bristled a little like a startled kitten.

"But he has a calmer outlook than most men, and besides, with his malaria attacks, he needs a quiet job," Sophie reminded her.

"So where is the switchboard going to be once it needs to be bigger?" Rebecca asked.

"The men are talking about putting up another building," Astrid answered. She ran her fingers through her hair, dividing it into thirds for a loose nighttime braid, but Rebecca pushed her hands away.

"I'll do that." So each of them plaited the hair they'd been brushing and tied a ribbon at the end.

"Can't you see me at a switchboard?" Maydell pantomimed a cartoon Thorliff had run in the paper, with something to her ear and a speaker in front. "Number please?" Her tone was even more saucy than usual.

"Number? Here we'll just say a name."

"No we won't. Each house will have a number." Sophie could speak emphatically, because she already had a telephone installed at the boardinghouse, one of five in the area. Thorliff and Dr. Elizabeth had one, the flour mill another, Pastor Solberg put one in his house, and the Garrisons had a public phone at the grocery store. Mr. Jeffers at the general store would have no part of it. He'd said it cost too much. "We already have our house number, but they didn't get the line strung to us before the winter hit."

"Do you really use the one at the boardinghouse?"

"Not much, but sometimes people call for one of our guests, like the company for the drummers. That kind of thing." Sophie lowered her voice. "Mrs. Valders isn't really very friendly when the post office gets busy and she has to stop what she's doing to connect a call, but so far it is working. Gerald does a fine job at night."

"Running water, no more outhouses, telephones, gas lights, electric lights—it's hard to believe all the changes that are coming."

"Don't forget automobiles." Sophie got a dreamy look on her face. "Just think how much fun it will be to go driving from town to town."

"We'll need roads first." Ever practical Astrid added her bit. "But when I am a doctor and we need to go to a patient, a car will surely be easier than a horse and buggy."

"Or to bring patients to you."

"If you can get it started. The automobile, I mean. You can always start a horse." Deborah locked her arms around her raised knees. "Manda and Baptiste make most of their money selling horses to the army forts. I can't imagine life without horses."

"I thought you were going to go visit them." Rebecca looked across the circle.

"I was, but then I got busy at the cheese house, and after the cattle had to be destroyed, I didn't care to go anywhere. It was just too sad. But Manda wrote to say they didn't lose a lot of cattle because they have mostly horses. Zeb is gone most of the time putting up windmills across the prairie. Besides the horses they breed and raise, they buy horses from the Indians, break and train them, and sell them to the army."

"Manda always was so good at training horses," Astrid said, reaching for more popcorn. "I bet she wears britches all the time too. Grace and I turned skirts into britches last summer, and you should have heard our mothers." She rubbed her tongue over her front teeth. "You'd have thought we went out naked. When I reminded Mor she'd worn britches when she was younger, she gave me a strange look. Said things were different then and left it at that."

"I heard she was a really good hunter back then too." Sophie narrowed her eyes. "Why do you suppose she quit?"

"Because it was scandalous, and Haakan didn't want her to offend other people moving in," Rebecca said.

"How do you know that?"

"My mor used to tell me tales of what it was like in the beginning. She and Ingeborg and Kaaren were such good friends, and they started the school and the church and everything."

"They had to be good friends. There wasn't anyone else."

"Other than Metiz."

Maydell thumped her fist on the floor to get their attention. "I think we need to get back to Rebecca's problem."

"Yes, ma'am!" Astrid saluted.

"No, really. She wants to be married, and I think it is our duty to help her."

"I'm sure you have advice for her."

"I have advice for all of us. Deborah, don't you want to get married? I know I do."

"Well, sure."

"Then here is what we do." Maydell motioned them to draw closer, as if someone might be listening in. "I think we should each make a list of all the eligible men and write down their good traits and bad traits and then figure out who will fit best with those of us looking for husbands."

"I think we need a shadchan. I read about it in a book. Families hire a matchmaker to find mates for their children."

Sophie groaned. "What's wrong with good old flirting and parties where people can get together and have fun?"

"No. Listen to me. Each of us who wants to be married must make a list of things she thinks are important in a husband, and then we can match up the lists. And we can study up on how to attract that certain man."

The others groaned. Ellie started to giggle. Sophie joined her, and soon they were all laughing.

"Make him tall and good looking," someone said.

"That's not hard here. They're all tall and good looking." More giggles, and the more they laughed, the harder they laughed until they were falling into each other and clutching their stomachs.

Rebecca flopped back on the floor. "This is crazy."

"I know, but . . ." Sophie tried to catch her breath. "If anyone ever breathes any of this to anyone else in town"—she stared hard at Ellie—"we'll have to deny it ever happened."

"Promise you won't say a word about this to Andrew." Astrid stared at her sister-in-law.

"But he's going to ask me what we talked about, and . . ." She rubbed her side where the baby was kicking against her ribs. "I must be carrying a girl, and either she's having a fit at what we're saying, or she's in total agreement."

"Ellie Bjorklund." Astrid tried not to laugh, but it got away from her. She pointed a finger at her friend. "You are not to tell Andrew. Promise."

"I promise." She held up her hands to ward off an attack. "I promise."

Mrs. Sam appeared in the doorway. "Are you young ladies ready for cake and tea?" Without waiting she carried the tray in and set it on the low table. "Sounds to me like you havin' a good time."

"Oh, we are. Thank you. Happy birthday, Rebecca. And happy New Year to all of us. Nineteen hundred and three. This is going to be the best year ever." Sophie got up to help pour the tea. When they all had cups, she raised hers. "To the new year and the daughters of Blessing." They all joined her, standing with their cups raised. "The women of the future."

Rebecca sipped from her cup when the rest did. Could she have her dream without causing a rift in her family? Maybe she could marry off Gus, and then he wouldn't be such a grouch. *But then where would I live? What does the future hold?*

4

Dear Rebecca,

How I love to hear from you, although if you would include more of the news from Blessing, I'd appreciate that too. We are getting by here in Bismarck, with the usual colds and runny noses for wintertime, but other than that, I must not complain. The children are doing well in school. Pastor Solberg gave them a good start. Hjelmer is busy with work, although I think he misses Blessing nearly as much as I do, even though he wasn't there a whole lot.

While I miss my store and all my customers, I have made this house a home and have joined the Ladies Aid at the Lutheran church here. It is strange to have so many churches. We live about six blocks from the church, this one built of cut stone and so large compared to our church at home.

There, I've done it again. Blessing is home to me. This is just where I live for the moment. I've heard that Mr. Jeffers is not doing well with my store. I am having a hard time forgiving myself for getting in a rush and selling to someone outside of Blessing, but with Mrs. Valders trying to buy it for nothing and Hjelmer insisting we needed to get moved—well, as they say, the rest is history. The moral of the story is, well, I'm not sure what the moral is.

So regarding you and your soda shop, I think you have a good idea, and of course you will be able to manage it. Don't listen to anyone who says you can't. I am sure the First Bank of Blessing will loan you money if you need to borrow. However, I am in agreement with Gus that you don't borrow unless you absolutely have to. I think you will soon find that the dress shop is too small and you will need to look for another place. Or be sure you can add on to it when time and money become available. If it were me, I would talk to Thorliff and his crew and see if anyone else is interested in another new building. The way Blessing is growing, they need to get some buildings built ahead, houses too.

It would be good if you could visit a similar shop somewhere else, like in Grand Forks. I'm not sure if Grafton has such a business or not. There is one here in Bismarck. You could always get on the train and come to see me, and we'll explore. In fact, I think that is a very good idea. Surely there is enough money in the family account for you to come to Bismarck. How I would love to see you. And the children would be overjoyed.

Regarding the bookkeeping, I always kept a ledger. You can buy a leather-bound one from the catalog, and you need to keep records of everything from the very beginning. Talk to Ingeborg if you have any questions there. She is the one who taught me how to do that. Mr. Valders, if you talk to him without Mrs. Valders around, will also give you good advice.

Rebecca stared out the window at a glittering diamond-crusted world. Asking Mr. Valders made her want to squirm inside. While he'd never been mean or anything, he was not the most approachable man. She'd rather talk with Ingeborg any day. Mrs. Garrison would be helpful too. And Sophie. When she thought about it, there were quite a few businesswomen in Blessing. But wouldn't it be fun to go visit Penny? But get on the train all by herself and go? What would Gus and Knute say? Maydell came from Grafton on the train by herself. Of course Bismarck was a lot farther away, but still . . .

Why couldn't she just do like her brothers said and be content to keep house until she found a man to marry? And if they had their way, her husband would want to work on the farm and just move into the farmhouse. When Gus got married, he could build another house.

She thought of Anji, her sister, now living part of the time in Norway and part of the time back here with her "Mr. Moen," as she always called him. The last letter said she was expecting again, and the new baby would give them six children, including the two daughters Mr. Moen had from his first wife. Anji had never dreamed of having a business. She always thought being a wife and a mother the greatest thing ever invented.

Rebecca returned to reading her letter.

> And so, my dear Rebecca, I will look forward to not only hearing from you, but seeing you soon, before spring comes and you need to start your seeds and spring housecleaning.
> All my love, Penny
> P.S. Linnea says she misses you and come soon. PB.

Laying the letter on the table, Rebecca studied the calendar on the wall, one Thorliff had printed and sent out with the newspaper to welcome in the new year. Dorothy would cook for Gus, so he wouldn't have to worry about cooking. Except there was the new baby coming, so when would be a good time to go? She didn't want to miss the birth. That wouldn't be fair to her family.

The thud of boots on the porch made her check the clock. Surely it wasn't dinnertime yet. When she heard three voices, she left her papers on the table and crossed to the stove, where the coffeepot always sat on the back staying warm in case someone came. Her mother had always done that, so the habit was ingrained. She slid a couple of sticks of wood into the firebox and brought the pot forward. Good thing there was still cake to serve with it.

Gus came in, and when she saw Haakan and Thorliff behind him, she was glad she had a fresh apron on.

"Good morning, Rebecca," Haakan said as he hung his hat on one of the pegs. "Fine day we are having."

She greeted them both and motioned to the table. "The coffee will be hot in a minute."

Haakan handed her a basket. "Some things from Ingeborg. She said you should come soon and spend the day. I know she has the quilting frame up and is always looking for another quilter."

"Maybe she would like to go to Bismarck with me." The words caught her by surprise, and the look that Gus sent her made her smile even wider.

"Bismarck? When are you going there?" Thorliff turned from hanging his things up.

"Soon." She indicated the letter from Penny, giving Gus, who was starting to say something, a look. "I never really thought of going until Penny said there is a soda shop in Bismarck and I should talk to the owners."

"That's a good idea," Thorliff said. "Sounds like you'll all be traveling."

Rebecca glanced at her brother, who looked a trifle confused. She pushed her papers into a stack and set them at the end of the table. "Would you rather have applesauce or cream on your cake?" It wasn't that often they had company. This was a treat. And from the sound of things, Haakan and Thorliff were here on an errand.

She kept an ear on the conversation as she cut the cake, put applesauce on some pieces and cream on the others, set those around, and poured the coffee, not bothering to offer cream and sugar, since all the men took theirs black.

"Sit down now so we can all talk," Haakan said with a smile. "This concerns you too."

"What does?"

"Remember when we went east this fall and returned with a cattle car of milk cows and some hogs?"

"Of course."

"Someone wrote to Thorliff and said there is a dairy herd for sale in southern Iowa. We wrote back to tell them we are interested and to see if they knew of any other stock for sale. So Lars and I will be going there at the end of January, and we wondered if Gus would like to go along. We'll be milking twenty head or more and hoping for some sheep and hogs. I wanted to wait until the weather warmed up, but the man who is selling needs to get this finished up. Sounds like he is in bad health." Haakan turned to Gus. "What do you think? Could you go along?"

"I don't know why not. We're working on machinery, but Knute can handle that. We only have the one cow, so that's no problem. Sure, I'd like to go."

Rebecca swallowed and ordered her heart to slow down. "And I could go to Bismarck at the same time."

All three men stared at her in unison. She sat a bit straighter and locked her fingers around her coffee cup. "How long do you think you would be gone?"

"Hard to predict that. I'll think we'll take hay and grain from here. That way we won't have to buy any."

"And we all have plenty of that."

"Right. Use the same cars both ways. I'll check with the railroad on that." Thorliff wrote himself a note on the pad of paper he always carried in his shirt pocket.

"Then you'll have an auction again like the last time?"

"I'll put an article about it in this week's paper. I'd love to go, but then we wouldn't have a paper for who knows how long."

"You need to train someone else to help with that." Haakan ate the last bite of his cake. "Very good, Rebecca. Mange takk."

"Would you like more coffee? Cake?" She'd almost forgotten her manners just thinking of all they were talking about. She and Gus both riding the train, only going in opposite directions. While he'd been to Grafton a few times, she'd never been farther than Ingeborg's.

"No thank you. We better be going." The two men pushed back their chairs. "See you in church on Sunday. I hear you girls had quite a party at the boardinghouse."

"We did. It was nice to be together, but we still missed Grace." What had Haakan heard? And how? From Andrew, of course, but what all did Ellie tell her husband? Surely she didn't mention the lists.

Mortified would be a good word to apply to the feeling that grumbled around in her middle.

"Greet Ingeborg and Dr. Elizabeth." Astrid would have told her mother some things about the party too, but they'd all promised not to tell anyone about the lists. She'd been very careful to keep hers hidden. Had the others started theirs?

"We will." They finished putting on their gear. "See you Sunday."

She shut the door behind them and then rolled her lips together to keep from laughing. She'd announced she was going, and with the other men here, Gus had just swallowed and not argued. All these years of her brothers telling her what to do and making sure she made no mistakes. *Hmm.* When she thought of it, did their being more than a little overbearing have anything to do with her lack of suitors? Or was she just not pretty enough, or . . . was there something wrong with her?

Should she go talk with Knute and Dorothy or let Gus do the talking? He would be so excited about going with the older men that he'd probably not say a lot about her. Why had Haakan and Thorliff asked Gus to go? She poured herself another cup of coffee and sat down to study her lists. One reason: he had no family to worry about. Two: no chores to do during the winter, and he was known to be utterly dependable. Besides that, he'd gone with the threshing crew the last few years, so he and Haakan were used to working together. Andrew had always made it clear that he didn't care if he never left Blessing. He'd much rather stay home and take care of things here. And be with Ellie and his growing family.

Rebecca had always thought it romantic that Andrew planned on marrying Ellie from the time they were really little. What would it be like to be loved like that?

❦

On the last day of January, Rebecca and the men caught the south-bound train in the morning to Grand Forks and then on south to

Fargo, where she would catch the westbound to Bismarck while they headed east. She'd made her first telephone call from the boarding-house and left a message for Penny at Hjelmer's office saying when she would arrive.

To her surprise Gerald had come to the station with a small pack-age for her. He had bought her a box of her favorite candy. "In case you feel homesick," he'd whispered. "Have a good time and try not to get into trouble." He'd winked but Gus had flushed. Rebecca hadn't been sure whether to laugh or cry.

After settling into her seat and tucking her bag under it and another in the shelf overhead, she stared out the window as they passed farms and endless drifts of snow.

"Your first train trip?" Haakan asked.

Rebecca nodded. "We're going so fast."

"Seems that way compared to driving a team. But Thorliff says we'll be building roads for automobiles pretty soon, and I expect many of them will follow the train tracks."

"Other parts of the country already have a lot of roads," Lars commented.

"Well, we do too. They just aren't very wide." Gus turned back from watching out the window. "You can drive to Grafton or Grand Forks or up through Drayton to Pembina."

"True." Haakan turned back to Rebecca. "Astrid says you are real serious about opening a soda shop."

She nodded. "This spring, I hope."

"You'd make your own ice cream?"

"And candies and other desserts possibly."

"You think there are enough people in Blessing to support a spe-cialized shop like that?"

"I know I'd have to keep the expenses way down, but you know how we all love ice cream as a special treat. Wouldn't you like to have a dish of ice cream sometimes without all the work of getting the ice, cranking the machine, and waiting for it to set up? Then once it is empty, it's all gone. I'll be able to make up several flavors and keep them frozen to dish out whenever you want. I'd like to serve sodas too and ice cream toppings. I saw an advertisement for some in a magazine."

The train stopped at every station, with the men pointing out various farms and points of interest, and before she expected it, the conductor was announcing, "Fargo. Next stop Fargo."

While the men got on their train east immediately, she had an hour to wait, so she set her bags on a wooden seat with a high back and walked around the inside of the depot to stretch her legs before sitting down again. She couldn't remember ever sitting so long without getting up. Even in school they'd not sat that long. After the men's train departed, it suddenly became very quiet in the station. And every time she looked up, she felt that someone was staring at her. Some men looked at her the way Mr. Jeffers did. When the time came to get on the train, she was exhausted.

The sun was setting, gilding the drifts, as the train headed west. She ate her supper from the basket she had packed and declined the offer of coffee from the pot on the stove that warmed the car. Several men were playing cards at the other end of the car, but the seats around her were empty. When the conductor came through, she raised her hand to get his attention.

"Please, sir, if I fall asleep, will you wake me when we reach Bismarck?"

"I'll make sure of that, miss, but most people have a hard time sleeping through my announcements. This your first train trip?"

"I left Blessing earlier today."

"You didn't get to see much of Fargo, then."

"No, just what's along the train tracks."

"Fargo's an up-and-coming town. So is Bismarck." He nodded to a call from someone else. "Have a good trip."

"Thank you." But gazing out the window only made her feel more lonesome. Once in a while she saw a light from a farm window, but there was a lot of empty land. They stopped at Valley City, Jamestown, and every small town on the western route. The conductor was right— she heard and felt every stop, even though she drowsed in between, too weary to take out the knitting she'd brought or the shirt she was sewing buttonholes in for little Swen. Astrid had told her to bring along things to do. And she had, but the lamplights didn't give very bright light, and the cigar smoke from the men at the other end of the car irritated her eyes. She wrapped her blanket around her and pillowed her head on the softer of her bags, letting her thoughts roam along with the weeping cry of the train whistle. She gripped the package from Gerald. Next time she took a train ride, she hoped to have someone else with her. Anyone else.

5

"Dear Astrid,

"I'm sorry it has been so long since I have written, but Mor assures me that she shares my letters with you and Tante Ingeborg. School here is going well. Because we have so many more students than the school in Blessing, I teach four to five classes each day and spend the rest of the time preparing for the next day. As you know, we teach all the subjects, so it is more like our regular Blessing school during the daytime, but like at Mor's, the children never go home.

"I am teaching the second- and third-grade combination class. When new students come, they have to be fairly proficient in sign language before they are moved into the regular classrooms. I have two women who assist me with my twelve students. I never dreamed I would love teaching in New York as much as I do. While I still get so homesick at times it makes my stomach hurt, I am so grateful to God for this opportunity that I cannot thank Him enough.

"In answer to your question, yes, Jonathan and I correspond regularly. I will be going to his family's house over Easter break for a week, and I am indeed looking forward to seeing him. You would love his little sister. Perhaps I should suggest she come to visit in Blessing. Jonathan has his father's permission to transfer to Fargo for school next year to study agriculture. He is working very hard to maintain top grades and spends as much time as he can with the school gardener, whom he says is as wise as Solomon.

"I must be ready for supper in a few minutes. I wish you could come here and visit, but I will be home for the summer in May. I'm glad all you girls had such a fun party and glad to know also that I was missed. We must do that again this summer.

"Love always,
Grace"

Astrid looked at her mother over the top of the paper. "And to think she was the one who didn't want to leave Blessing at all."

Ingeborg nodded. "We just never know what path God has laid out for us. When I was your age, I never dreamed I'd be living in North Dakota rather than in Norway." She widened her eyes. "And that I'd live in a flat river valley with not only no mountains but not a hill in sight."

"Do you miss Norway?"

"Not so much anymore. But those first winters in the soddy, the wind howled worse than the wolves. I know why people go crazy at times."

Astrid looked around the kitchen. "You can still hear the wind, but I'm glad we have this nice house and don't live in a sod house any longer."

"Me too." Ingeborg set the cooled flatiron on the stove, detached the handle, reattached it to one of the hot irons, then went back to her ironing. During the winter they hung the washed clothes out on the porch and, when they had frozen dry, brought them in and ironed them.

"You want me to do that?"

"If you like, but I thought you were studying." Turning the pillow-case, she folded the top half over the bottom and ironed it again. With one more folding, she set the iron on its end and folded the pillowcase in thirds to form a square. She set the next one in place on the wooden ironing board and started again.

"I am." Astrid tucked the letter into the back of her textbook and picked up her pencil to take notes as she read.

Ironing was one of Ingeborg's favorite chores. The fresh scent of newly ironed linens and clothing always made her grateful for the riches of her household. Sheets for the beds, warm quilts, pillows stuffed with the goose down she saved from all the geese hunted and eaten, feather beds to help keep them warm in the winter. Wool skirts and petticoats, stockings she knit from her finest spun wool, and sweaters and vests. Just like counting the jars in her cellar, ironing made her feel that she was indeed taking good care of her family.

Her lesson that morning had been from Proverbs, where she had read about the godly woman and all she did. Having servants would indeed make life easier in some ways, but then there would be more people to take care of. Her cheese house could be compared to selling purple dyes, and her husband was indeed a respected man in the community. They were for sure blessed in all ways.

She changed the iron again but took a minute to put more wood in the stove before continuing her ironing. The beans baking in the oven added another fragrance to the kitchen. When she finished the ironing, she needed to churn butter. Interesting how many things one took for granted until forced to go without. She had resolved to remember to be grateful every day for the milk, cream, butter, and buttermilk they now had again.

The sound of boots on the porch caught her attention. Must be Andrew coming to milk.

"Did Far and the others leave this morning as planned?" her younger son asked as he came through the door, scraping his feet on the rug.

"Yes, they did. What a long day they'll be having on the train."

"Do you think he'll call when they get there?"

Ingeborg pulled the coffeepot forward, *tsk*ing as she did so. "I can't imagine they would." To think one could make a telephone call. She still thought telegrams were amazing. "You have time for a cup of coffee? We made gingerbread men this morning."

"You know I can't turn down gingerbread men."

"I have some to send home for Carl."

"He always eats the heads off first. Did we do that?"

"You did and thought it hilarious. You had the most contagious belly laugh. Thorliff would make silly faces to make you laugh." She shook her head. "Listen to me. Today must be a day for remembrances."

While all the flatirons heated on the stove, she fixed a plate of cookies and set them on the table.

Andrew sat down by Astrid, who'd looked up to give him a smile then went back to her book. He tweaked the thick braid that hung down her back. "More tests coming up?"

"Always. Elizabeth is determined I will be so far ahead of the others that they will be embarrassed."

"And then they'll hate you and make your life miserable. You'd do better to just stay here and not go to Chicago at all."

"Therein lies the wisdom of Andrew. Will you let me operate on your arm so that I know how to fix it if you break it?"

"You really plan to cut up bodies?"

"Dissect cadavers? Yes. While butchering hogs and chickens has taught me a lot, the human body is different."

Andrew looked at his mother. "There she goes again. Think of all the people you helped, and you never went to school."

"Ah, but had I had more knowledge, I might have been able to help some of those who died." Ingeborg poured three cups of coffee and set them on the table. "But then, school isn't the only place to find learning. I always figured I did what I could and then depended on God to finish the job."

Astrid looked up from her book and took a cookie from the plate. "Do you miss being the doctor of Blessing?"

"I get to do enough with Elizabeth. I never chose to become the doctor here. It just happened. I was always interested in medicinal things—my mother kept simples too—and then Metiz taught me all she knew. Or at least as much as I could learn. Experience is an excellent teacher."

"But you have a gift for healing, Mor. Elizabeth always says that too." Astrid dunked her cookie in her cup of coffee and nibbled the soaked edge.

"I believe God gives the gifts that are needed to His people. He knew we needed medical help here, and He provided. Just like He provided a pastor when the time was right, and a schoolteacher."

"How's Carl?" Astrid asked her brother.

"Still coughing but back to being busy. Ellie was rocking him when I left, but there isn't much room on her lap for him right now."

"Soon there will be."

"Won't be too soon for her." He drained his cup. "I better get on to the barn. Did you already pick the eggs?"

"Ja. I didn't want them to freeze."

"True. I'll leave the milk in the springhouse, then?"

"Take what you need, and I should have the butter churned by then if you need some."

"Think I'll put one of the milk cans on the sled and take it over to Tante Kaaren. She must be needing milk by now."

"Takk."

He waved as he went out the door.

One more of the myriad things to be thankful for, Ingeborg thought as she ate the last of her cookie. *That son who takes care of all of us without being asked and always goes the extra mile.* She opened the oven door to check on the beans, gave them a good stir, and setting the lid back in place, closed the oven door. Baked apples sounded like a good idea.

❧

Bismarck, North Dakota

"Bismarck, miss. Our next stop."

Rebecca jerked away, not aware she'd really fallen asleep, even though it could only have been a few minutes since the last stop. "Th-thank you. How long?"

The conductor checked his gold watch, the chain looping from one vest pocket to the other. "About fifteen minutes. It is nearly midnight."

"Will someone be there to meet you?"

"Yes, my cousin."

"Good. I hope you have a good visit."

"Thank you." She reached up to touch her hat and, realizing it was askew, unpinned it and set it in her lap so she could smooth her hair back into its bun. Pinning her black felt hat back in place, she thought of the absurdity of the article. Too small to do any good to keep her warm and highly likely to get blown across the prairie, although Penny had written that there were rolling hills here, not flat terrain like the Red River Valley. She should have worn her knit stocking hat with the earflaps, but she'd so wanted to be at least a bit fashionable. After all, she was a young lady now, no longer a girl.

Feeling as if she were being stared at, she raised her gaze to see that one of the men a few seats away was studying her. She could feel squirmies wriggling up her back. Why was he watching her like that? She controlled the urge to touch her hat again and make sure it was still there. When he smiled slowly around the cigar between his teeth, she raised her chin slightly, narrowed her eyes, and turned to look out the window. At least there were a few lights out there now, not just expanses of white with a dark dot of farm places once in a while.

Sit still, she commanded herself. *Ignore him. No gentleman would be so rude as to stare like that.* The feeling reminded her of the last time she went to the store and Mr. Jeffers watched her like a cat with a mouse. She folded up her blanket and stuffed it into the bag behind her feet—anything to busy herself and keep from glancing back at him.

"Bismarck. We are arriving in Bismarck." The conductor's voice cut into her fussing. As the train screeched to a halt, steam billowed up, blinding the windows.

"May I help you with your bags, miss?" The man's voice grated on her already strung-out sensibilities.

She looked up to find him standing right beside her. The smell of his cigar made her wrinkle her nose. "No thank you. I can manage."

She waited, hoping he would take the hint and leave. But when he still stood there, she pulled her bag from under the seat and stood.

"This yours?"

Before she could respond, he pulled her other bag down from the overhead rack. Short of wrestling him for the handle, she had no recourse but to straighten her spine and comply with his gesture to precede him down the aisle. "Thank you."

"At your service."

At my service, my right foot. Where do good manners end and self-preservation begin? She took the conductor's hand as he helped her from the metal step to the stool and down to the wooden planking of the platform. "Thank you."

The man in a checked coat was so close behind her that she could feel the heat of him in spite of the blast of North Dakota winter that greeted her. *Is this what all the men from larger cities are like? Penny, Hjelmer, where are you?*

"They'll bring your trunk into the station, miss, in just a minute." The conductor glanced from her to the man behind her and then back to her valise. "I'll see that she gets inside. Thank you for your assistance."

Gratitude poured like warm water through her veins. She smiled to the man in the uniform who stood beside her, while the cigar smoker touched the brim of his hat and moved on. "Thank you, sir." She heaved a sigh that felt a heavy load lift from her shoulders.

"You are welcome. This way." He took her other bag and headed for the golden light that looked like the only warm thing in the blustery darkness. A blast of heat met her when he pulled the door open and ushered her in.

"Rebecca."

The sound of Penny's voice brought a lump to her throat. Rebecca turned and saw Hjelmer and Penny striding across the room. Never had the sight of anyone been such a relief. She forgot her bags and flew across the marble-floored room to be crushed against Penny's bosom, the wool of her coat cold and scratchy against her cheek.

"Sorry we weren't out there when the train stopped." Penny hugged her cousin again, then stepped back, hands on Rebecca's upper arms.

"That's all right. Oh, Penny, I'm so glad to see you." She hugged her again.

Penny turned to Hjelmer, waiting slightly behind her. "She grew up since we left, didn't she?"

"That she did." His deep voice hadn't changed, even though his face wore lines that hadn't been there before. "Welcome to Bismarck, Rebecca. I'll see to the bags and meet the two of you in front."

Penny tucked her hand through Rebecca's arm. "I am so thrilled you are actually here, that you came to visit us." Her eyes misted. "I cannot begin to tell you how much I miss everyone in Blessing."

"Even Mrs. Valders?"

Penny stopped and turned to look at her guest, then burst into laughter. "You are the one to tease me. But I tell you, I've been so homesick that even a good round with Mrs. Valders would make me happy." As they walked across the near empty room, Penny asked question after question, as if she were perishing from human contact.

"Haven't you made friends here?" Rebecca asked.

"Oh yes, but Blessing is my family." They pushed open the heavy double doors to be attacked by the bitter wind again.

Hjelmer waved from the sleigh as he pulled up in front of them. "I have all your things. Climb in so we can get on home."

"Where's your automobile?" Rebecca asked.

"In the barn. It doesn't do well in the snow."

Penny held up the robe for Rebecca to crawl in and then joined her. As they tucked the robe around themselves, Hjelmer *hupp*ed the team and off they trotted.

"This is a big city." Rebecca held the robe up to cover her nose but gawked from side to side at the three- and four-story buildings.

"It likes to think so."

"Those are gaslights?" She pointed to the lamp poles along the street.

"Yes, and we have gaslights at our house. It most certainly is convenient. And we have running water too."

"Really? All that?"

"Really. Life is easier here, but . . ." Her voice trailed off. "Tomorrow you have to tell me more about my store. Or rather, Mr. Jeffers' store."

Rebecca trapped a yawn with her mittened hand. "Excuse me, but I never stay up so late."

Sometime later, snuggled under the quilt that her own mother had made for Penny all those years before, Rebecca thought back to their conversation. Penny really didn't sound too happy—not like the old Penny before the move. And Hjelmer. He had the same look all the men in Blessing had worn when the plague had struck.

6

Blessing, North Dakota
February 1903

SOMETIME IN THE DARK of the night, Ingeborg heard a pounding on the door, and before she could get untangled from the sheets and blankets, an out-of-breath Andrew appeared in the doorway, calling "Mor" as he came.

"What is it?"

"Ellie is in labor, and she says the baby is coming fast. I ran across the field, but I'll harness the horse and sleigh for you."

"Call for Astrid too."

"I'm coming." The voice came from upstairs.

"Hurry."

Ingeborg dressed as quickly as possible, considering all the winter layers for warmth, and was lacing her boots when Astrid looked in her mother's bedroom door. "He sounded pretty upset."

"Andrew is calm with all the animals, but when it comes to Ellie ..." She grabbed a shawl off the bedpost and followed Astrid back into the kitchen. "My bag is in the cupboard."

"I know. I got it out." Astrid donned a coat and handed one to her mother. "Interesting that she didn't tell him about her pains earlier."

"Maybe this baby is in a hurry. Some are like that."

The two of them stepped out the door when they heard the jingle of the harness bells. The wind grabbed at their scarves and bit their noses, so both of them covered their lower face with a length of knit scarf. They climbed into the sleigh and were barely seated before Andrew *hupp*ed the horse and they flew across the frozen snow, not bothering with the lane, as all the fences were covered with snow.

"Easy on the horse," Astrid called, the wind whipping away her words.

"Hang on," Andrew called back.

He stopped right at the porch, and Astrid and Ingeborg, catching his urgency, didn't wait for him to help them out. "I'll put the horse in the barn and be right up."

"You better blanket him," Astrid called over her shoulder as she followed her mother into the house.

They could hear Ellie groaning and panting as they strode to the bedroom.

"Thank you." Ellie scrunched up her face and rode out another contraction. "For coming so quickly."

"You have no idea how fast we came. The sleigh flew from one drift to another." Astrid shucked her coat and stopped beside the bed. "Have you been walking?"

"No. I just woke up with one huge cramp. Andrew said to stay in bed because he had to leave."

"How close are they coming?"

"A couple of minutes perhaps, but—" She clenched the sheet in her fists. "Here's another."

"All right, let's get you sitting up. I'll wash my hands while Mor helps you."

"Andrew has water heating."

"It's boiling. Put the things in to sterilize while you wash." Ingeborg kept her voice calm and smiled to both her daughters. "We're going to have a new baby pretty soon."

"I was scared he or she was going to come when I was here all by myself."

"Good thing we live close by. You didn't have any contractions earlier?"

"Not that I knew of." Ellie took a deep breath and let it all out, clasping Ingeborg's hands so she could sit up. "I feel like a huge pumpkin."

Astrid returned to the bedroom. "Let me check on you, and then we'll get the padding on the bed." With Ellie lying back, she did a quick examination and grinned at her sister-in-law. "Let's walk. That will help you relax. This baby is coming soon."

With one woman on each side of her, Ellie marched across the room.

The sound of the door opening and slamming shut barely preceded Andrew's appearance in the doorway. "How is she?" He threw his coat toward a chair. "Here, let me do that."

"Ellie is doing fine, and this baby is in a big hurry to meet the new world." Astrid stepped back and let Andrew have her place. "We won't be walking very long."

Andrew put his arm around Ellie's back. "You can lean on me if you need to."

"Oh, Andrew, I always lean on you." She clenched her eyes and leaned in to the contraction. "Except for right now. *Ooh*. They're getting worse and closer together."

"Let's pray so. The sooner the better." Ingeborg waited while Ellie panted and they resumed the walk. She glanced over to see Astrid laying the folded sheets in the bed and making sure the blankets were warming in front of the stove. *Thank you, Lord, for this daughter of mine who is so capable and caring and for this daughter who is so strong and loving. Please let this be a normal birth and a healthy baby. So far, all is well, and let it continue to be.* She could feel the peace that filled the room, from the corners clear to the ceiling.

"Oh!" Ellie stopped walking and a puddle formed at her feet. "I'm sorry to make a mess."

Ingeborg chuckled. "Not a mess, my dear, just part of the process."

"That should speed things up." Astrid knelt to dry the floor.

"As if she hasn't been in a hurry already." Andrew stopped as another contraction gripped his wife.

"I . . . I think I better get to the b-bed."

Andrew and Ingeborg half carried her back to the bed. Then Andrew took his position with his back against the headboard of the bed, legs spread wide so that Ellie could lean against him. "You comfortable?" He pulled her back against his chest.

Ellie glared over her shoulder at him. "No, but . . ." Her words turned into a thin scream that she tried to bite back.

"You yell if you want to." Ingeborg checked on the process while Astrid scrubbed her hands again. "We have hair." Her voice broke, and she blinked around her smile. "I love to see a baby being born."

"*Ohh.*"

Astrid knelt between Ellie's raised knees. "You go ahead and push for all you're worth, Ellie. With the next one . . . okay, now bear down. Push."

"Ellie, dear, you are made for having babies." Ingeborg watched as Astrid slightly turned the arriving baby so the shoulders would slip through.

"*Now.* One more push, Ellie, and we're done."

With another cry and a groan, Ellie pushed her baby daughter right into Astrid's waiting hands.

Astrid grinned up at her brother. "You have one of each now, Papa." She laid the already yelling infant on her mother's chest. "And she's a determined one." Astrid wiped her streaming eyes with the back of her wrist. "What a beauty." When the afterbirth was delivered and the cord stopped pulsing, she tied it off in two places and cut between them. Then she massaged Ellie's now flaccid belly.

Ingeborg laid a flannel baby blanket over the baby while Andrew and Ellie murmured to each other and their new life. *Thank you, Father, thank you.* The words kept circling through her mind as she helped Astrid exchange the soiled sheets for fresh ones.

"You want to clean her up?" Astrid asked.

"Ellie or the baby?"

"The baby. I'll take care of Ellie."

Ingeborg smiled and nodded. Such a privilege to give her new granddaughter her first bath and dress her for the first time.

"Look at her. She's ready to nurse already." Andrew looked up at his mother, who nodded as she watched the baby rooting around, already seeking the breast.

"Let's get her washed and diapered. You help get Ellie cleaned up and then your daughter can have her first meal."

"The wash pan is on the reservoir," Astrid said. "It should be about the right temperature. I left the belly band and the diaper right there to warm."

Ingeborg wrapped the blanket around the baby and, after checking the water temperature with her elbow, unwrapped the little body and lowered her into the warm water. Holding her head with one hand, she used a bit of flannel to wipe the eyes and ears clean and smiled when the little one flailed her tiny fists. "You like this, don't you? I don't blame you a bit. Warm water after the shock you just went through. God loves you, little one, and I'm so thankful He sent you to us. What a gift. Maybe they will name you Delight, for that is what you are."

When she was finished, Ingeborg wrapped the baby in another blanket and took her to the table, where they'd laid a folded towel along with diapers, soakers, shirts, and gowns. After drying her carefully, she wrapped the belly band, diapered her, pushed the tiny fists into the sleeves, and tied the gown in the front. Then she laid her on a flannel blanket, wrapped her snuggly, and with a kiss on the tiny forehead, carried the baby back into the bedroom.

"Here she is, ready for her first meal." Ingeborg put the baby in Ellie's arms and smiled at Andrew, who stroked his daughter's head with one gentle finger.

"For a baby, she's right nice."

"Nice!" Ellie rolled her eyes. "She's beautiful, and you know it."

"Well, I guess." The twinkle in his eyes said he was teasing. "But if she was a calf or colt, she'd be up on her feet and bopping her mother's udder for milk. None of this lying around stuff."

"I'll bop you." Ellie settled her baby at the breast and held her nipple to the tiny mouth. The little one didn't need a second invitation. She latched on and started sucking immediately. Ellie flinched and stroked her baby's cheek. "You are one bright little girl." Looking up at Andrew, she asked, "So what are we naming her?"

"I thought you wanted to name her after your mother."

"I do, but we need a middle name too."

"She seems like a delight to me," Ingeborg said as she brought in a cup of tea. "Thought this might taste good to you. Then you can rest. I'll take Carl home with me, and Astrid can stay and watch over her patient for a while." She held the saucer under the cup so Ellie could sip without dampening the sheet.

Andrew yawned and eased himself from behind Ellie. "I know I didn't do any of the work here, but I'm tired. If you're ready to leave, Mor, I'll go get the horse and sleigh. Do you want me to drive you home?"

"Whyever would you need to do that? You sleep here for a few hours. The cows won't mind if you are a bit late."

Andrew stood and stretched. "Well . . . if you're sure you don't mind . . ."

"I'm sure. Now, you go and get some sleep."

He kissed his wife and daughter before heading out the door.

"I can't believe both Carl and Maydell slept right through all this," Ingeborg commented.

"Maydell's not here tonight. She's spending the night at Deborah's to work on the lists," Ellie murmured. "None of us thought this baby was planning to arrive tonight."

"What lists?" Ingeborg asked.

"I'll explain later, Mor, but you will be sworn to utmost secrecy." Astrid sat down in the rocking chair near the bed. "I have the cradle ready for her. That way you can sleep better, Ellie. I even warmed the bedding."

"She's sound asleep." Ellie handed the baby to Astrid. "Thank you for taking such good care of us."

"You made this one easy."

Ingeborg watched her girls and let her rejoicing prayers float heavenward. Such a difference between this one and poor Elizabeth, who had already lost two babies. She who helped so many others had trouble carrying her own. *Lord God, this isn't fair. Couldn't you do something about healing whatever it is that keeps Elizabeth from carrying her babies to full term? I know so well her heartache. Thank you for the ease of this one. Lord, I praise your mighty name.*

❧

Bismarck, North Dakota

Rebecca awoke to find a young girl beside her bed.

"You finally got awake," said Linnea, nearly eight, her dimples peeking out as she grinned.

Rebecca yawned. "Sorry, but I got to bed so late."

"Ma said breakfast is ready."

"All right. Tell her I'll be down as soon as I get dressed."

"She said to put on a dressing gown and come now."

"Where's your pa?"

"Gone to work."

"And Little Gus?"

"Filling the woodbox. Can you hurry?" Linnea, one front tooth missing, asked. "I'm hungry."

"Me too. I'll hurry."

"You know the way?"

"Oh, don't worry, I'll come find you. Now scoot." Rebecca waited until her young cousin was out the door, then threw back the bedclothes. Rather than taking time to wash, she dressed quickly, tying the ribbons of the layers of petticoats and fetching a wool serge skirt from the chifforobe where she'd hung the clothes from her trunk before she fell into bed last night. She added a waist that needed ironing and a sweater, bundled her hair in a snood, and hurried down the stairs, enjoying the fragrance of coffee, ham, and some kind of bread. And she hadn't had to fix it all.

The children were already at the table, and Penny turned from the stove. "Well, good morning. Sorry Linnea went and woke you."

"I don't mind. Little Gus, is that really you?" She grinned back at him. "You've grown a foot since you left Blessing."

"No, only four inches."

"Amazing, you both look so different." She turned to Penny. "Can I help?"

"No. Just sit down and pretend you are company, at least for today. I thought we'd go for a drive through town since the weather is nice."

"Couldn't we just stay here?" The thought of more travel was not appealing, much to her surprise.

"If that's what you'd rather. I thought seeing the ice-cream parlor would be at the top of your desires."

"It is, but do you know how long I sat still yesterday?" She thought a moment. "Maybe this afternoon?"

Penny set bowls of oatmeal in front of each of them. "True, you never have been one for sitting still." She set a bottle of milk on the table. "Pass things around now." When she opened the oven door, the smell of corn bread filled the room. "I should be baking bread today, but I can buy a loaf at the store. Another feature of life in the city." She returned to the table with the pan and set it down to cut it.

"You take after your mother in that—I mean having a hard time sitting still. Remember how she and Ingeborg would delight in sitting on the porch, but they were never without something to do with their hands. They'd be working away, talking a mile a minute. Those two, and Kaaren too, were my heroes. When I told them I wanted to start a store, they thought it was a wonderful idea. They even helped me get together enough money to open it up."

"Who built the store?" Rebecca scooped out a square piece of corn bread and set it on Linnea's plate. Linnea had insisted she sit next to Rebecca so Penny sat on the other side. "Pass the syrup, please."

"Everyone. They had a store raising, just like a barn raising. But I was in Fargo, working at the Headquarters Hotel while it was being built. Hjelmer promised to bring me back to Blessing when it was finished." Penny started the syrup pitcher around. "And he did. How I loved that store."

"I would have run it for you."

"Perhaps." Penny swooped over to mop up a glass of milk that Linnea bumped with her elbow.

"Sorry."

"You know better than to set that near the edge of the table. Get the rag from the back of the stove and clean up the floor."

Rebecca caught the sharp tone in her cousin's voice. Maybe she shouldn't be talking about the store. She poured the syrup over her corn bread and forked a bite into her mouth. At home Penny would already be at the store, and most likely she would have been the one caring for the children, although Little Gus at nine was pretty independent.

She turned to Linnea. "What would you like to do today?"

"Go to the ice-cream store."

"You should never ask her. That's what she always says," Gus said around a mouthful of mush.

"Don't talk with your mouth full," his mother admonished.

"Sorry."

"So what do you want to do?" Rebecca turned her attention to Gus.

"I want to go sledding." His voice picked up. "There are hills here, and you go down so fast you can't breathe." He flashed her a grin. "Pa bought us a toboggan."

"When he gets home, he can take you out there." Penny shook her head at his hangdog look.

"We could go over two streets and sled down there. All the kids are going there."

"You could, but it is too rough for Linnea."

"But—" At her look he clapped his mouth closed.

"Sledding down a hill. All we ever had at home was when the snow drifted up to the barn roof, and we slid down that."

"But remember hitching the sled behind the wagon?"

"Or Bjorklunds' mule."

"And ice-skating on the river."

"We have a skating pond here," Little Gus said, getting back in the conversation. "But I'm not very good at it."

"Then you need to skate more." Rebecca glanced over at Penny. "Do you still have your skates?"

"Ma does," Linnea chimed. "Ma is a good skater."

"So is Pa."

"All right." Penny raised her hands. "How about if we get the breakfast things put away, get dressed really warm, and go skating for a while. Then we go to Benson's." She turned to Rebecca. "It's Benson's Soda Emporium."

"It sounds like a perfect day, but I need a warm hat."

"I have one for you. Linnea, please clear the table, and Gus, you find all the skates. I'll use Hjelmer's."

With the chores done and everyone bundled up, they slung their skates over their shoulders and headed out the door. While it was plenty cold, the wind had died down, so the sun felt warm for a change. By the time they walked the four blocks to the skating pond, there was a group of boys at one end with hockey sticks, slapping a puck back and forth between two lines.

"I want to play hockey," Gus informed her, his eyes dancing, "but I don't skate good enough."

"Well," his mother said.

"Well, what?"

"Well. You don't skate well enough." Penny's voice took on the "I've said this before" tone.

"You don't let me come very often. That's why."

Penny rolled her eyes, and Rebecca almost laughed aloud. All the years in Blessing, Penny had been so busy that someone else was usually caring for her children.

They sat down on benches lining the pond, which had already been swept free of snow, and strapped the skates to their boots. Gus got done quickly and bent to help his little sister.

"I haven't skated for so long, I might fall down." Rebecca pushed herself to her feet.

"I'll help you," Gus said as he took her hand. "Come on."

Rebecca watched a man and a woman, their hands locked across their fronts, skating by smoothly, as if they were dancing. She wondered if she would ever find someone who cared for her. She sighed. "You and Hjelmer used to skate like that."

"They still do." Linnea stood beside her. "You can put your hand on my shoulder if you need to."

Rebecca allowed Gus to lead her to the edge of the ice. *Please, Lord, I don't want to fall and make a fool of myself.* She pushed off with one foot and followed with the other. She hadn't forgotten. Why had they not cleared the river ice at home and had a skating party? One year they let the cattle tank overflow and they had a pond right out in the pasture. Everyone had skated at their house. They'd built a bonfire and had a great time. But after Swen was killed, they'd not had parties at their farm.

Penny skated even with them. "For someone who says she hasn't skated for a long time, you sure remembered how quickly."

"You never used to get to do this at home except on some Sundays."

"I know. That is one of the good things of coming to Bismarck. I have more time to play."

"Look out!"

When Rebecca turned to see what the shout was about, a young boy, waving his arms and skidding out of control, slammed right into her. Her feet went out, and she slammed back on the ice, flat out, her head thunking against the hard surface. She lay there, trying to catch her breath and let the world stop spinning.

"Rebecca, are you all right?" Penny knelt beside her.

While Rebecca heard Penny, she opened her eyes to see a most charming pair of male blue eyes looking down at her. Was she dreaming this handsome stranger?

"Are you all right, miss, or do we need to take you to the doctor?"

Maybe swooning would be a good idea. If she knew how to swoon, that is. Was that something Maydell had talked about, or had she read it somewhere? *Please, let me be dreaming all this.* Anything would be better than the mortification heating her from skates to the top of her hat. Was she all right? How could she tell?

7

"WHO...WHAT...OH MY." Rebecca tried to sit up.

"You fell on the ice," Penny said as she took her hand. "Are you all right?"

"I-I think so." Unless feeling utterly stupid qualified as not all right. She turned her head. Yes, those blue eyes belonged to a real person, a real male person whose smile was as nice as his eyes were. Where had he come from?

"May I help you up?" His voice joined his other heart-pumping attributes.

She nodded. Her throat didn't seem to want to respond.

He took her hand and rose to his feet, taking her right up with him. "Are you dizzy?"

She swallowed again and cleared her throat. "I don't think so." *At least as long as I'm not looking into your eyes.* Was this the kind of thing that Maydell was talking about? She racked her mind. What had they all said to do? Nothing came, so she forced her quivering lips to smile. "Thank you."

"That boy! He ran right into you!" Linnea's eyes flashed.

Gus stayed by her side like a guard dog. "I'm sorry, I—"

"There was nothing you could do, Little Gus." Rebecca shook out her skirt and petticoats. "I'm not hurt. Just got the breath knocked out of me for a minute." She looked up into the deep-pool eyes. They were a deeper blue than the Bjorklund eyes, which were the bluest she'd ever seen, and set wide apart with straight brows. His nose was straight, and his smile made her heart turn over. Commas cut into his cheeks.

"My name is Kurt von Drehl, and I think we've already been introduced, in a way." He tipped his hat to Penny.

"This is my cousin, Miss Rebecca Baard, and she is visiting us. Are you by any chance related to Pastor von Drehl?"

"He is my uncle." He turned his attention back to Rebecca. "Do you feel like skating some more?"

She nodded.

He took her hands. "Ready?"

Talk, you ninny. Come on, mouth, work. "Yes." *That was brilliant. Didn't Maydell say to ask him about . . . oh, fiddlesticks.*

He pushed off slowly, taking her with him.

"Have you been here long?"

"No. I came last night on the train."

"Where are you from?"

"Blessing, North Dakota. It is a small town north of Grand Forks on the Red River." At least she could talk now—and make sense.

"And your cousin. Has she been here long?"

"No. They moved here last summer. Hjelmer was in the legislature but now is working for Carlson and Sons."

"Really? That is another uncle, only on my mother's side." He was increasing their stride and glide time.

"Do you know everyone in town?"

"Pretty much, I guess. At least the people who've been here a long time. Seems I'm related to half of them."

She almost stumbled when she looked up to see his smile again, but he gripped her hands more firmly and held her steady.

"How long will you be here?"

Were there other people skating on the pond? She felt like they were in an iridescent soap bubble, the rest of the world fading away. Her heart skipped a beat. "Um, what did you say?"

"How long will you be in Bismarck?"

Forever? She jerked herself back to reality. "I really don't know. Maybe two or three weeks."

"That's all?"

She shrugged. "I'll be needed at home." Stroke, glide, lean into the strokes, just like dancing. His hands were warm through their mittens, his shoulder firm against hers. Could they skate forever?

"Where does your cousin live?"

"A few blocks from here." She thought a moment. She had no idea which direction.

"Perhaps she will allow me to walk back with you. I mean, I would love to show you around Bismarck."

"Really?" *Just like that. Almost as forward as the cigar man on the train, except so romantic. Don't look into those eyes again, or who knows what might happen.*

"I'm attending the college here. Do you go to school?"

She shook her head. "I graduated from high school last May." Hard to believe it had been that long ago. "What are you studying?"

"I know this is a forward question, but are you . . . I mean is there . . . ?"

She almost smiled at his stammering and waited.

He slowed their skating and turned to face her, still holding her hands. "Is there someone at home waiting for you to come back?"

She almost gasped out loud. He was breaking almost every rule of etiquette she had ever known. And in Blessing they thought she was too forward speaking.

"My brother is off on a cattle buying trip."

"No. I mean . . ." He rolled his eyes and tipped his head back. He stared down into her eyes. "Are you spoken for?"

"Spoken for?"

"Betrothed. In love with, sought after." He shook his head. "Forgive me, I am handling this badly."

Her heartbeat picked up to double time. "This is not proper." Well, that was a brilliant thing to say.

"I know. I've never done anything like this before. My mother will have a fainting spell. But it's like you fell right into my life. And you're leaving almost right away."

"No. I fell on the ice. That boy ran right into me." *And no one in Blessing is going to believe this is happening to me. Me, the old maid of Blessing, the one who was asking for help in attracting a man.*

He turned and pulled her into skating beside him again. Their strides matched, and the rhythm took over.

How can he think he wants to know me better? This is happening so fast. My head is in a whirl. What will Penny say when I tell her?

Little Gus skated up beside her. "Ma says we should be going now."

"All right." Rebecca heaved a sigh. All good things had to come to an end. They skated over to the bench where Penny and Linnea waited, their skates already tied together.

Kurt held her hand until she was seated, then knelt in front of her to unbuckle her skates.

"Thank you." She stared at the wave in his hair, the deep blue of his scarf deepening the gold-streaked locks.

He handed her the skates and sat on the bench. "I hope you'll let me walk you all home." He smiled at Penny.

"Will that be out of your way?"

"It doesn't matter."

Rebecca caught her breath. What a romantic thing to say. Was this the way things really were, or was she living in some dreamland? She glanced over at Penny, whose eyes were twinkling. As they followed the shoveled path out of the skating area, Gus insinuated himself between Rebecca and the man who strolled beside her.

Rebecca tried to keep herself from staring at a streetcar that passed them. The streets seemed to be in constant motion between horses, sleighs, streetcars, and people. The houses here were so large that the ones in Blessing seemed like doll houses. But then, Thorliff said they would be building a lot of new houses come the thaw. Would Blessing one day look like Bismarck? And why was she thinking all this with a handsome man walking next to her? Maybe the dream was easier to handle than the reality.

Gus broke into her thoughts. "You know that boy who knocked you down?" He gazed up at her with question marks all over his face.

"Yes, Little Gus, I most assuredly remember. Do you know him?"

The boy shook his head. "No, but he goes to my school."

"What school do you go to?" Kurt asked.

"Bismarck Primary."

"That's where I went to school. Do you know Mr. Guthrie?"

"He teaches sixth grade."

"I know. He was my teacher for the sixth grade."

Gus slipped his hand in hers. "You could come to see my school on Monday."

"I'd like that."

"And I'm not Little Gus there. I'm just Gus."

Rebecca swung his hand. "I'll remember that." She'd always called him Little Gus so people would know she was talking about her cousin's son rather than her brother.

"Would you like to come in for coffee or hot cocoa?" Penny asked Kurt. "We're going to have some, and I'll be making fried cheese sandwiches."

"I'm sorry. I would be delighted, but I told my mother I would escort her during her errands this afternoon. Do you have a telephone?"

"Yes."

He turned to Rebecca. "Would you mind if I called you?"

She looked over to Penny, whose shrug covered laughter. "I would like that."

He repeated the number aloud, memorizing it, after she said it. "Good-bye, then. For now." He turned to Penny. "And thank you for the invitation." As they walked up the shoveled path to the front door,

Rebecca glanced over her shoulder to see him striding down the street. She could hear a whistled song floating back. A grin tickled her cheeks. What a shame that she had to fall on the ice to get his attention. That definitely had not been on Maydell's list of instructions on how to meet or entertain a man.

As they hung up their outer clothing, Linnea chattered about skating and how well she did, Gus gathered all the skates and hauled them out to the back porch, and Rebecca hummed a little tune.

"I know someone who sounds really happy." Penny picked up Rebecca's scarf and hung it back on the hall tree. She tapped her cousin's shoulder. "Hello in there."

"What?" Rebecca realized she'd been staring at the diamond-shaped leaded panes on either side of the door. And had no idea for how long. She turned to Penny. "What did you say?"

"Nothing important. Come along and we'll make dinner. Then we can go to Benson's."

"All right. Penny, are all the men in Bismarck so friendly to strangers?"

Penny started choking with laughter. "Most definitely not. And especially not Mr. Kurt von Drehl. According to church social gossip, no one can get his attention."

If her feet touched the floor, Rebecca was not aware of it.

Later that afternoon as they opened the door to Benson's, a bell tinkled over the door, announcing their arrival.

"Doesn't that sound just like the bell over the door at my store?"

Rebecca nodded, staring around the establishment. She was really here. Her dream was based on a real place with real people. *See, Gus, it is possible.*

A family of five took up one of the red-painted booths that lined one wall, a woman and child were being served at the counter, and two girls giggled at one of the round tables. A mural on one wall showed a man riding a bicycle with a huge front wheel, a brown dog barking at him, people strolling down a sidewalk, the girls wearing wide-brimmed straw hats and eating ice cream. The sign on the pictured store said Benson's Soda Emporium.

What a good idea, Rebecca thought. *I wonder who I could get to paint something like that on my wall?* She almost laughed to herself. Here she was planning the wall painting when she didn't even have the building for sure yet. Although Haakan had said she could have it when she was ready. She watched a young man behind the counter serving ice cream into a dish for the woman and one for the little boy. Freckles sprinkled his nose and dusted the tops of his cheeks, rosy as if he'd been outside in the cold. Strange that people were indeed buying ice cream in the dead of winter, something she had wondered about and many had also questioned. It didn't appear to be a problem here. But were there enough people in the Blessing area to support her dream? That was the question. Whether in winter or summer. And not just enough. Would her hardworking town see a stop at the soda shop as too frivolous?

Penny and the children stopped in front of the refrigerated glass-fronted case that held the ice cream in straight-sided metal containers.

"What can I get for you?" the young man asked the children. He glanced up to see Rebecca watching him, and his face turned as red as the stripes on his apron. Immediately he jerked his attention back to Penny.

"I want chocolate," Gus stated, as though he ordered one every day. At the clearing of his mother's throat, he added, "Please."

"One scoop or two? You can have two different flavors if you want."

Gus glanced up at his mother, who nodded. "Two please. One vanilla."

The young man slanted a look at Rebecca, who had now joined the others, and scooped out the chocolate. When he handed the dish to Gus, he leaned over the case and smiled at Linnea. "And what for you, miss?"

Linnea beamed up at her mother. "Can I have a bowl of maple nut, please?"

"Are you sure you want to try that new flavor?"

"If she doesn't like it, I'll take it." Rebecca grinned at the girl. "What do you think of the peppermint candy one?"

"If you get that one, we can swap tastes."

"Very true."

Linnea accepted the dish of ice cream from the man and tasted it. "It's good," she said, holding the dish up to Rebecca.

"Of course it is good. Benson's only makes good ice cream." The young man darted a glance at Rebecca and quickly looked down at the counter. "One scoop or two?" His voice cracked, making him blush again.

"One, I think. The peppermint candy, please." She watched him dip a metal scoop into a glass of water before digging into the ice cream. "Why do you do that?"

"Do what?"

"Dip the scoop in the water."

"Cleans off the other flavor and makes the ice cream slide off easier." He held out the dish and turned to Penny. "And you, ma'am. What flavor?"

Rebecca tasted her ice cream. Vanilla with smashed peppermint candies in it. How delicious.

"What flavors have you thought of serving in your shop?" Penny asked her after telling the young man to make hers peppermint too.

"I hadn't thought that far. I could freeze all kinds of berries in the summer to use in the winter. Keeping enough ice for ice cream on a daily basis seems like a mighty tall order."

"Are you planning an ice-cream emporium?" he asked as he took the change from Penny.

"I am. In Blessing."

"Where is that?" His voice seemed more stable, not hitting high notes like it had before.

"On the eastern edge of North Dakota."

"I've never been that far. Did you come on the train?"

"Yes. Last night." *Ask him if you can see the rest of the store. I can't do that. Of course you can. That's why you came.* "This is good ice cream. Do you make it here?"

"No, my pa makes it out at the creamery."

"You are a Benson?" *Talk about nosy. Rebecca Baard, mind your manners. This breach of etiquette must be catching.*

"Thomas Benson. My grandfather and two of his sons started the creamery twenty years ago."

"How many flavors do you make?"

"Five usually. The maple nut one is new. Ma tries different things, and sometimes we have contests to name new flavors."

"Do you run this store, then?"

"Me and my older sister." He cleared his throat. "You know my name now, but I don't know yours." The red flowed upward over his cheeks.

Rebecca smiled at him, tipping her head slightly forward. "My name is Rebecca Baard." She finished off her ice cream and wiped her fingers on her napkin. "Thank you, Mr. Benson. You have been most informative."

"Would you like to see the rest of our store? I mean, if you're not in a big hurry, or if you'd be interested?"

"That would be wonderful." She could hear Maydell in her mind. *"Now be demure. Act as if you're not interested."* Did that have to do with the ice-cream business also?

By the time he'd shown her the walk-in freezer—where a half a beef hung, since as he said, this was the biggest refrigerator in town—the various boxes of food that sat along the wall, the ice-cream containers, the closet with cleaning supplies and a mop, and pointed to the necessary, she realized how much work there would need to be done to open her own shop. Could she actually do it in Miss Christopherson's former shop, even with renovations?

"Thank you, Mr. Benson," she said with a smile. "I really had no idea what opening my shop was going to entail." She glanced at the counter and saw the cash register. Would she need one of those too? What was wrong with keeping the money in a box with divisions in a drawer? After all, she'd be the one behind the counter for the hours the shop was open. Penny would know.

"If you'd like, I could take you out to see the creamery one day." Thomas's voice dragged her attention from the cash register.

"Where they make the ice cream? That would be wonderful." She gave him her sweetest smile and watched the red flame his ears. "I planned to make mine in the back room of my shop."

"Do you have a telephone where I can call you when they are making some?"

"I do." She gave him the number and watched him write it down. Instead of no men in her life, other than Gerald, her best friend, now two men wanted to speak to her on the telephone? And on the same day? Maybe she wouldn't be an old maid after all. She smiled. And then she frowned. This attention seemed to appear only in Bismarck, not in Blessing. Still, it did give her hope, or at least a great story to share at home.

8

"WHAT ARE YOU DOING?" Linnea asked that evening.

"Writing a letter. Did you have your bath?"

"Yes. Will you read us a story like you used to?"

Rebecca smiled at her little cousin, whose hair was done up in rags so she would have curls for church in the morning. Had it not been for the white ties in her hair, she might have been taken for an angel in her white gown and robe. "I would love to do that. And Little Gus?"

"You aren't supposed to call him that, 'member?"

"It's hard to break a habit of nine years." Rebecca closed the leather binder that held her writing paper, envelopes on one side, and a tablet on the other where she kept her notes for her soda shop. At the top of one she'd written *Emporium*, because she liked the word. She stood and held out her hand. "Come, let's find the book. Which one is your mother reading to you?"

"Pa reads most."

"I'm glad to hear that." With Linnea at her side, Rebecca trailed her hand down the carved staircase rail. Compared to the house that was part of the store in Blessing, this one was a castle. Actually, considering most of the houses in Blessing, only Sophie's house and Thorliff's could begin to compare to this one.

But already she knew that Penny was not happy here. Her smile did not flash immediately like it had at home, and lines etched her eyes and forehead. Not that she had said anything, but Rebecca had known her too long and too well not to detect the changes. Perhaps tonight they would have a chance to really talk.

She and her little cousin cuddled in a big leather chair in front of the fireplace in the parlor, and Linnea handed her the book from the side table. "*Black Beauty*. I love this story."

"Me too."

Hjelmer strolled into the room carrying his overcoat. "Ah, I see you've usurped my place."

"I can move."

He shook his head and waved off her protests. "No. Tonight I get to listen." He folded his coat over the sofa back and sank down. "I marked the place we ended with a bookmark."

"I see. Do we wait for Gus?"

"He thinks he's too big to be read to, and Ma is busy." Linnea tucked her nightdress over her toes.

"So what does that make me?" Hjelmer asked.

"My pa."

He smiled. "Not Far?"

"Pa. All the kids here say pa."

"I see. So we have to be the same as everyone else?"

She nodded, her eyes looking serious. "Yes."

Rebecca watched the exchange. She was having a hard time remembering Hjelmer sitting down with either of his children. Or reading to them. Some things had changed. She opened the book to the proper page and began to read. When she closed the book half an hour or so later, Linnea was leaning heavily against her arm.

"That was sad."

"I know. Some of this book is really sad. I'd forgotten about this part."

"But Black Beauty tries so hard. How could that man be mean to him?"

Rebecca looked to Hjelmer. How did one answer a question like that?

"Some people do not know how to be kind to animals, or perhaps to people either," he said.

"Jesus said to love one another. Doesn't that mean animals too?"

"Yes. I think it does."

"Do you know that Rebecca fell down on the ice and a nice man helped her get up? He was kind, huh?"

Rebecca felt the heat creeping up her neck.

"Yes. Mor told me."

"He walked home with us. I think he likes Rebecca."

The heat reached Rebecca's cheeks and bloomed over the rest of her face. She wished the discussion had never started. "I think it's time you headed for bed."

Hjelmer stood and gathered up his overcoat. "Come along, Lin, before you embarrass our guest any further." He winked at Rebecca and said sotto voce, "Hear all, see all, speak all."

Penny stopped in the door. "Would you like a cup of tea, Rebecca?"

"Please."

"I'll bring it in. Hjelmer?"

"No coffee?"

She shook her head. "Tea."

"I suppose."

"Can I help you?" Rebecca started to get up but sat back down when Penny waved her back.

"So what did you think of Benson's?" Penny asked later when the tea was poured and the lemon cookies passed.

"I loved the mural on the wall."

"It is nicely decorated."

"And the ice cream is good. Not as good as we make at home, but good. I liked the different flavors."

"What did you think of Thomas?"

"He was nice, wasn't he, to offer to show me around like that?

When I saw the beef hanging in the freezer, I about jumped out of my skin. We don't have such a thing as refrigeration in Blessing. He said that was run by gas, like the lights."

"I'm sure Thorliff and his crew will be able to build you whatever you need." Hjelmer propped his feet on a footstool and rested his saucer on his chest, sipping his tea. "Of course, in the winter you can just set it all out on the back porch."

"I liked the glass-fronted display."

"That you can most likely order. I'm sure if we talk to Mr. Benson, he'll tell us where he ordered his supplies. You won't be competition for him, clear across the state like that." He reached for another cookie and, after a bite, held it up. "I think you need to have other kinds of desserts and things to eat besides sodas and ice cream."

"We've been talking about that. Cookies go really well with ice cream."

Rebecca sipped her tea and stared into the fire. So many things to think about. Deep blue eyes appeared in her mind. She nearly choked on her tea.

"Are you all right?" Penny asked.

Rebecca coughed and patted her chest. "I will be." She swallowed and coughed again. "Just swallowed wrong." *Kurt von Drehl. What a strong-sounding name.* She took another sip of tea. Skating with him had been more romantic than anything she'd done in her entire life. She could feel the rhythm flowing through her. Stroke and glide. "Ah, what?" She turned to find Penny studying her with an amused expression, and Hjelmer had left the room. "Did you say something?"

"Twice, as a matter of fact. You just floated off."

"Ah . . ." Rebecca figured they might as well douse the fireplace. Her face would warm the entire room. "Could you repeat it, please?"

"I asked if you've talked this over much with Ingeborg yet."

"No. We spoke some last summer, but then with the hoof-and-mouth disaster, I gave it up. The whole town was so sad."

"Strange to hear you say that—Blessing as a town. My store, the school, and the church were pretty much it for a long time."

"And the boardinghouse."

"True." Penny sipped her tea, then leaned her head against the back of the chair. "Sometimes I am so homesick I want to throw up. My heart just aches. I am doing my best here, but it never seems good enough."

Rebecca looked around the room. "You have a beautiful house here, and the children seem happy. They like having their pa around more."

"I know. I like that part too." Her sigh could be heard over the snapping of the fire. "This 'whither thou goest' principle is not always easy. Keep that in mind when you are thinking of marriage. What if the man you fall in love with either isn't in Blessing or for some reason wants to leave? I never dreamed I'd live anywhere but there." Sorrow weighted her voice. "And yet I know that I did the right thing. Your mor and Ingeborg would say that one must make the best of whatever happens. That is a woman's lot in life."

"They also say that time heals all wounds."

"Not sure it is time but rather the Holy Spirit. I've been spending more time in my Bible than ever before. I have to find the strength and the joy to deal with all this." She shook her head. "Joy is sadly lacking in my life right now." She smiled over at Rebecca. "That is why I am so grateful you came to visit. You have no idea what a help this is for me."

"I thought I was coming for me. To see the soda shop and talk with you about running a business."

Penny's smile didn't make it all the way to her eyes, but it was better than the somber look she'd been wearing. "That's one of the good things about God. He turns one thing into good for several. Think how happy the children are to have you here to show you around."

"Yes, and to watch me get flattened on the ice."

"I thought Gus was going to go after that other boy and throw him down on the ice."

"How will I ever get over calling him Little Gus?"

"It'll take some doing, I suppose."

Rebecca tried to stop a yawn and failed. "I should be knitting while I'm sitting here."

"Should." Penny rubbed her lips together. "What a heavy word."

"Idle hands and all that."

"Have you ever noticed that most men don't keep their hands busy all the time like we women do?"

"Maybe that's why some smoke a pipe. Others carve wood."

"Fix harnesses, do leather work. Hjelmer repaired one of Linnea's dolls. She thought he was God, but had I done it, she'd have taken that for granted. Mor can fix anything."

Should I tell her about our lists? The thought niggled. "If I tell you something, do you promise to not tell anyone?"

Penny raised her eyebrows as she stared at Rebecca. "Of course. Who would I tell?"

"Hjelmer maybe."

"Is this women stuff?"

Rebecca nodded.

"You learn early on to never tell men women stuff, even if you are married."

"Someone better tell Ellie that."

"She was in on this?"

"All us girls were. We celebrated my birthday late and New Year's at the same time. We all slept at the boardinghouse."

"A girl party. What fun. When I was your age there weren't enough girls around to have a party. We all had to become women too soon."

"By the way, Ingeborg said to tell you how much she misses you. She says the sewing circle isn't the same without you, and the store is a mess. Her words, not mine."

Penny chewed on her lower lip. "Tell me more about the party."

"Well, I told the girls I'm becoming an old maid, and I asked for advice on how to get a man."

"You didn't." Penny set her cup down and leaned forward, a chuckle dancing in the firelight.

"I did. How come none of the young men ask to walk with me or come to visit?"

"How can they with Gus and Knute guarding you like a stallion with his mares?"

"I was afraid of that. But I keep thinking maybe something is the matter with me."

"Has nothing to do with you. Look at the attention you received today. I need to give those two brothers of yours a good talking to. And it's time Gus got a wife of his own. He's how old now?"

"Twenty-one."

"Has he ever shown any interest in one of the girls?"

"No, but Maydell was flirting with him. She's Ellie's friend from Grafton. She said she'd give me advice."

Penny rolled her eyes. "From what I've heard, that is a place for good solid advice," she said sarcastically.

"She's like Sophie used to be. She likes to flirt. But I don't know how to giggle and tease like she does. Although Gus doesn't seem to notice or show that he does." Maybe that's why he'd been so grouchy with her lately. "So we all decided to make a list."

"A list?"

"Of what we want in a man."

Penny choked and patted her chest. "Why not just make a list of all the eligible men in Blessing and check off the one you want?"

Rebecca frowned. "You think that would be a good thing? There's not many right now."

"I am teasing you, for crying out loud."

"Oh." Rebecca stared into the fire. "What made you think you loved Hjelmer?"

"Oh, he was one dashing fellow. He made everyone laugh, and talk about good looking. There just wasn't anyone around that could hold a candle to him. Plus, my aunt Agnes, your mother, said he was dangerous, a bit of a bad boy, I guess you would call it."

"Like what did he do?"

"He made a lot of money gambling, smoked cigars, and those laughing blue eyes . . ." She shook her head. "He sure made my sweet little heart go pitter-patter." Penny took a turn staring into the fire.

"He was and is a wanderer and adventurer. He wants to see beyond the next horizon, but he's a good businessman with a keen sense of what is coming next. At least when he's the one responsible. I have to give him that."

"I think I hear a *but* in there." Rebecca surprised herself with her comment.

"Most likely. I never thought his adventures would include moving us all to Bismarck. Or how hard it would be for him to work for someone else." Penny heaved a sigh while Rebecca caught another yawn. Yawning herself, Penny stood and picked up the tray. "We have more time to visit another day. We don't need to do it all in one night. Do you have everything you need?"

"I most certainly do, and to think I don't even have to go outside to an outhouse." She stood, stretching and yawning again. "Do you bank the fire?"

"Yes, go ahead. Another thing I am grateful for is the coal furnace in the cellar. There are many good things about this house, but I'd still trade it for the one at the store any day."

"You could always have Thorliff build you a new house in Blessing."

"Maybe someday." She waited while Rebecca banked the fire and then turned out the gaslights as they left the room.

Snuggled under the covers a few minutes later, Rebecca thought back to their conversation. If she were to make a list of all the eligible men, who would she mark as the one she wanted? A new face floated through her mind, the one she'd seen when she opened her eyes after the fall on the ice. Kurt von Drehl. What was it about him that made her think of Hjelmer? An adventurer, Penny had said. And wasn't she always dreaming about an adventure? But look how unhappy Penny was now, no matter how much she loved Hjelmer. As Rebecca drifted off, Gerald's familiar face grinned at her with a teasing twinkle in his eyes, as if sharing in her exciting day. She didn't want to leave Blessing either.

9

"REBECCA, THE TELEPHONE IS for you."

"Thank you, Linnea. Whoever would be calling me?"

"Ma said it was a man's voice."

Something wrong at home was her first thought. *Gerald's calling from the switchboard.* But surely if it were that, he would have told Penny. She left her letter writing and followed Linnea down the stairs. Picking up the dangling black receiver, she put it to her ear and stood on her tiptoes to speak into the black trumpet. "Hello? This is Rebecca." She spoke slowly and loudly, as if she were hard of hearing herself.

"Hi, Rebecca, this is Kurt von Drehl, and you don't need to shout. I can hear you fine if you talk in a normal voice."

"Oh, sorry." She could feel the heat rising from her neck up. Now he must think her frightfully stupid. She'd pretty much given up hope that he was going to call her, since it had been over a week since they'd been ice-skating. Now he was calling her on the telephone, of all things.

"Have you talked on a telephone before?"

His voice sounded as if he were standing right beside her. She lifted the earpiece away and stared at it a moment before answering. "No, this is my first on my own." His laugh made the sides of her mouth lift, and she caught a giggle before it escaped.

"That's better. I was wondering if you might like to go for a sleigh ride."

"I—ah . . . um . . . when?" Now he would think her a dolt for sure.

"Now. I thought we might head west of town. I'm sure there will be a beautiful sunset this afternoon. We wouldn't be gone a long time."

Take a sleigh ride to see the sunset? All that for a sunset? She could hear Gus's snort of disapproval for wasted time. Surely it wouldn't be more beautiful than the ones from home. "Ah, let me ask Penny."

"Don't hang up. I'll wait for you."

"All right." She let the receiver dangle and headed into the kitchen to find Penny. "He's asked me to go for a sleigh ride to see the sunset."

"How lovely." Penny turned from adding coal to the cookstove. "He said he would call, and he has."

"You think I should say yes?"

"Well, why not?"

Rebecca shrugged and scrunched her face. "I don't know. I mean, I don't know him very well, and . . ."

"Do you want to get to know him better?" A hint of a smile curved her cheek. But she took pity on her cousin and crossed the room to give her a hug. "You go and have a good time. For a change your brothers aren't here to scare away any young man who might want to get to know you better."

"I thought about that."

"Go on now. Leaving someone hanging on the telephone line is considered rude."

"Oh no." Rebecca flew back down the hall. "I'm sorry I took so long."

"I was wondering if you might have forgotten me."

"Oh, I could never do that." Hearing her own words made her

close her eyes and shake her head. Sure enough, his chuckle came over the wire again.

"Then I will be there in a few minutes. Bundle up well. It is cold outside. Good-bye."

"Good-bye." She set the receiver back in its prong and clapped her hands to her hot cheeks.

"What did he want?" Linnea asked, leaning against the door-jamb.

"To take me for a sleigh ride."

"Can I go?"

Penny swooped into the hall. "No, you most assuredly may not." She took her daughter's hand. "Besides, I need you to peel the potatoes. Rebecca won't be gone too long."

Rebecca glanced down at her skirt. "Will this be all right?"

"Yes, but put a sweater on under your coat. I have a fur hat and muff you can wear. Surely he will have a hot brick or stone for your feet and a robe to break the wind. You have a long woolen scarf, right?" While she talked, Penny pulled the hat and muff out of the closet by the front door and handed them to Rebecca. "Don't worry about your hair. This hat will mess it all up anyway."

Rebecca took her coat from the closet. "I'll go get a sweater." Back by the front door a few minutes later with her coat buttoned up to the neck, she stood in front of the mirror while Penny set the hat in place and adjusted it at a slight angle.

"There. You look fetching." She draped the blue scarf around Rebecca's neck and flipped the long ends back over her shoulders. "Make sure you cover your lower face if it is too cold."

"Yes, ma'am."

"Oh, you. I am being a bit bossy, aren't I?" At Rebecca's slight nod, she laughed and continued. "That's what happens when you have children of your own. You tend to give everyone instructions like you do them." She kissed Rebecca's cheek. "Just have fun and enjoy the sunset."

Linnea turned from the long window by the door, where she'd

been watching. "He's here." Linnea squeezed her hand and grinned up at her. "You look nice."

Rebecca looked over Linnea's shoulder to peek out the curtain by the door. He most certainly was and tying the horse to the post with a metal ring for just that purpose. *Goodness me, but he is a handsome young man. And to think he has asked me to go for a sleigh ride.* The heat rising from her neck made the long scarf feel absolutely unnecessary. The top of her head felt like steam was rising from it. His breath circled him like the smoke rings she had seen Haakan blow from his pipe. She tried to think. Had she ever been on a sleigh ride with a young man all by herself? Nope. Only with her brothers, and that did not count.

She waited until the knocker fell before opening the door, even though she and Linnea had let the curtain assume its rightful place before he could see them peeking. Linnea giggled behind her, making Rebecca start to giggle in response. She forced her face into a proper smile and pulled the door open.

"Good. You are all ready." Kurt smiled. "We need to hurry, or the sun will go down before we get there."

Rebecca nodded. Did she appear too eager? Maydell had cautioned her against that in one of her instructions on flirting. *"A young woman must never appear too eager. It is better to let the young man think her more standoffish."* With Maydell's advice echoing in her mind, she closed the door behind her and took the arm he offered. Surely Penny knew more about proper behavior for a young lady than Maydell did.

Whatever was she doing going off on a jaunt like this at this time of day with a handsome young man she hardly even knew? She should be in the kitchen helping Penny cook the supper. What kind of guest went off on a sleigh ride instead of helping with the housework?

"You look wonderful in that hat."

"And warm enough too." In fact, she felt like she needed a fan, in spite of the cold biting her nose. *Say thank you, silly. Where are your manners?* The little voice that seemed to sit on her right shoulder sounded remarkably like that of her sister-in-law chiding her daughter.

Perhaps Mor would have sounded that way had she lived longer. Perhaps she had when Rebecca was younger. Sometimes she had a hard time recalling things her mor had said. It all was so long ago. While her mind was running faster than a North Dakota blizzard, her gloved hand felt even warmer tucked next to his side. *Say something.*

"Thank you for your help on the skating pond."

"My pleasure."

The smile he gave her made her heart rate pick up enough to catch her mind. "I usually skate better than that." *Another silly comment.*

"I'm sure anyone would have stumbled when rammed into like you were." He squeezed her hand to his side. "Besides, that gave me the chance to introduce myself."

To a nobody like me? But then, introductions were proper behavior. She'd read about that in a ladies' magazine that Sophie had passed around. How different Bismarck was from home, where everybody knew everybody, and if someone new came to town, they were quickly introduced to everyone, usually at church.

"Be careful now." He helped her step into the sleigh and settled the robe around her before going to untie the horse.

She held the robe up for him to slide under, and with a tightening of the reins, the horse backed up and then trotted down the street, harness bells jingling and the sleigh swooshing over the snow-packed surface.

He turned and smiled at her. "Are you warm enough?"

"Yes. This is wonderful. Thank you." *Help me, Maydell. What kind of ninny am I that my tongue is mired in glue with nothing to say or to ask?*

"Good. Tell me about life in Blessing."

"Well, we have a farm a mile or so from town. My parents died years ago, so one of my brothers and I live at the homeplace. Another brother and his wife and family built a house not far from the first one."

"I'm sorry. It must be terribly hard growing up without your parents."

"It was, sometimes still is. But my cousin Penny helped. That's why I miss her so since she moved here. I used to work in her store, and perhaps that made me think I want a business of my own too."

"She had a store in Blessing?"

Rebecca nodded. "A wonderful mercantile. She carried everything there. The man who has it now is letting it fall apart. People in town don't like him much."

"I take it from the tone of your voice that you don't either."

"Not really. When he refused to close the store on Sunday like it had always been, the people of Blessing boycotted him. No one went into his store on Sundays, and since the Garrisons opened a grocery store, lots of people don't go into his store at all. They order things from Grand Forks."

"Do you think you might stay in Bismarck?"

The houses were getting fewer and the road climbed a hill, making the horse settle to a walk instead of trotting. Shadows blued the land.

Rebecca shook her head. "No. I'm just here to visit and talk with the people who own the soda shop, since that is what I want to do."

"Perhaps we can change your mind, about staying here, that is."

She wasn't sure if she'd heard him right. But his smile made her even warmer. *Why would he say such a thing to me? Surely he is just being polite. After all, I'm not lovely like Grace, a good talker like Astrid, or bold like Sophie. I'm just plain, hardworking me, always taking care of Gus or someone, the house, doing what my mother told me to do. Afraid to dream, to want something else—like my store. I want to be like Penny.*

They topped the hill, and the western horizon glowed golden with the sun hovering above the rim of the land, mare's-tail clouds waiting for gilding. He turned the horse down a side road and found a place where they could stop and face the west. As the golden disc slid down, becoming a half circle, then a sliver, the clouds turned from gold to crimson and vermilion and all shades of pink and red and orange.

They sat in silence as the sun slid away and the clouds flung ecstasy across the heavens.

Rebecca sighed. "How lovely." She turned to look at him only to find him staring at her rather than the sunset.

"I think you are lovely."

Rebecca blinked. "Ah . . ." Her tongue refused to obey her command. Surely Kurt didn't mean what he'd said. He was just being polite. Or maybe he said things like that to all the girls. *I think you are lovely.* The words echoed in her head and sang in her heart. Her hands wanted to leave the fur muff and touch her face. Someone, a man, thought she was lovely. Her mother's voice whispered in her ear: "True beauty is from the inside out." But Kurt saw her outside. Her smile warmed even her toes. She wanted to leap from the sleigh and dance across the snowdrifts, run up one side and slide down the other. Shout to the streaks fading in the sky. I am lovely!

"Thank you," she whispered and cleared her throat. "Th-thank you. Ah . . . the hills. I think hills do make a difference."

His eyes twinkled. "You don't have hills at home?"

"No, the Red River Valley is as flat as a cast-iron griddle." *What must he think of me? Is this what flirting is like, what Maydell was talking about?* She felt like fanning her face in spite of the breeze.

"Really? No hills at all?"

"When you get away from the river there are hills, but the valley is miles wide from south of Fargo clear to Winnipeg in Canada. The only trees are along the rivers, but most of those have been cut down."

The colors slowly faded, as if saving their energy for another day.

"Hard to picture land that flat."

"Have you always lived here in Bismarck?"

"Yes. My grandfather homesteaded here and helped build the town. Now that it is the state capital, it has grown more. Well, I suppose I should get you back, since I said we wouldn't be gone long."

With the setting of the sun, the cold crept over the land, and an early evening breeze blew the chill right into her bones. What would Maydell do or say to do in this situation? Ask him more questions.

"Do you have brothers and sisters?"

"Oh yes. Two of each, and I am the youngest. Two of them are already married, and one is engaged to be married in the spring. Belinda and I are the only ones still living at home. She is going to college, like I am."

"My friend Astrid wants to be a doctor, and Grace is already teaching at a school for the deaf in New York, but I thought going to high school was enough. Unless I wanted to teach school, which I don't."

"But you want to own a soda shop?"

"I do."

He turned the horse and headed back the way they had come. "Do you mind if I ask you a personal question?"

Rebecca thought a moment. What would he ask? After what he'd said before, what could this be? "Umm, I guess not, but I reserve the right not to answer."

"Something like the fifth amendment?"

She mentally sorted through her history classes. What was the fifth amendment? "I don't know what the fifth amendment is."

"One doesn't have to answer a question on the basis that it might be incriminating."

Where did he learn all these words? Incriminating. She should know that one. "I guess." She ignored the flaming heat in her face, hoping he would think it windburn. "What did you want to ask?"

"Is there anyone special to you in Blessing?"

"There are lots of special people in Blessing. Most of them, in fact."

He laughed, a rollicking sound that made her smile again. He was a delightful companion.

"I guess I need to be more specific. Is there someone there . . . I mean a male someone to whom you have given even a piece of your heart?"

"If there were, I doubt I would be out seeing the sunset like this." Instantly, when she said the words, a picture of Gerald Valders flitted through her mind. But he was her friend, and this was different.

He laughed again. "Not one to mince words, are you?" Turning, he grinned at her. "Perhaps you could stay here and work at Benson's for a while. Learn about running the business firsthand. I could ask my father to look into that for you. If you are interested, of course."

Rebecca thought a moment. That might be a very good idea. But what would happen at home if she didn't go back? Was she really needed there? Dorothy would invite Gus over for meals, most likely clean house for him too. There wasn't so much work to do in the winter like this, which was why she'd felt free to come stay with Penny. Penny would be delighted if she stayed awhile longer. But then there was Dorothy's soon-to-be-born baby. She didn't want to miss being there for that. Too many possibilities too close together. In Blessing, Kurt would be considered too forward for making such a suggestion, but here his interest felt special. She smiled back at him. "Sorry. I was just trying to think this through. You caught me by surprise."

Kurt stopped the sleigh at the post in front of Penny's house. "No rush. I'll call you tomorrow."

"Call me?"

"On the telephone."

"Oh." She could feel the heat flowing up her neck. She was blushing at him like Thomas Benson had with her over ice cream. "Of course, how silly. I'm just not used to thinking of the telephone."

"That's okay. It took us some getting used to, but we've had it for a while now."

A silence caused her to glance up and catch him watching her. "What?"

"I'm glad you came to Bismarck. That's all." After tying the horse to the post, he returned to help her from the sleigh. "May I see you again?"

She placed her hand in his and stepped from the sleigh. As her skirt settled around her ankles, she smiled up at the man who still held her hand. What would Maydell do in this situation? She nodded. "I'd like that."

"Good." He tucked her arm through his and walked her to the door.

"Thank you for the sleigh ride. The sunset was lovely."

"You are most welcome. I'll call you." He touched a finger to the brim of his hat and opened the door for her. "Bye."

She watched him walk away until a giggle from behind her caught her attention. She was letting all the heat out of the house. Whatever was the matter with her?

Linnea pulled her inside and shut the door. "Did you have fun?" She reached for Rebecca's scarf and took her mother's muff.

"I did." She lifted the fur hat from her head and handed that to Linnea too. "I really did. He's very nice."

"Ma said we can eat in just a minute. Pa just got home. I already set the table."

Rebecca hung her coat in the closet and stamped her boots on the rug one more time. "Then let's go eat."

Linnea pushed her hand into Rebecca's. "There's a letter for you. We put it by your place at the table."

A letter? Who would be writing to her? Her life had definitely become full since she came to Bismarck. She'd come just to visit Penny and think about her soda shop. Now questions and possibilities seemed to crowd every thinking moment, leaving her almost gasping for air. It was exhilarating. So why did she feel as drained as when the wind kept howling around the windows in Blessing?

10

Blessing, North Dakota

"I CANNOT BELIEVE HOW much I miss Grace."

"You sound like Astrid." Ingeborg turned to smile at Kaaren, at the same time enjoying the shush of sleigh runners through the two inches of new snow. While she was more than ready for spring to arrive, bright sun on new snow was never a waste of beauty. Even the horse was enjoying the day, tossing her head and picking up a smart trot with just the tiniest flick of the reins. For a change Ingeborg almost wished the church was farther away. "Today I am thankful we no longer live in the soddies."

Kaaren stared at her. "What brought that on?"

"How much I enjoy the light. I know you miss Grace, and I know I will be saying the same thing after Astrid leaves. But right now Haakan and Astrid are at home, many farmers have more cows, the sun is warm, our world is gorgeous, and I feel like singing and shouting hosannas."

"I would too if I didn't miss my daughter so." Kaaren heaved a sigh. "Oh, all right." She raised her voice and shouted into the breeze caused by their speed. "Thank you, for this glorious day, for our warm and lovely homes, and that we can go to a warm church to quilt with our friends."

Ingeborg's laughter joined her. "And I thank you for our husbands, our friends, all our families. And that we have a horse and sleigh!"

"And fabric to sew with."

"And sewing machines."

Coming from the west, Mary Martha Solberg waved at them as she neared the church. Her halloo could be heard above the shushing and harness jingling.

"If she heard us, she will think we are nuts."

"No. She already knows we are nuts, and she'd join right in. After all, the Scripture says to shout praises." Ingeborg slowed the trotting horse.

"I know one thing. It made me feel better." Kaaren waved at Mary Martha and turned to look at Ingeborg. "You suppose that's why we are told to do that?"

"Well, it surely isn't because God has a hearing problem."

The two of them laughed again as Ingeborg climbed out of the sleigh to tie the horse to the hitching rail. She slipped the bridle off and draped it over the post, using instead the rope clipped to the harness.

"You two look like the cat that just cleaned out the cream. Care to share your secret?" The pastor's wife adjusted the heavy blanket she'd thrown over her horse, then reached inside her sleigh for two baskets, one of food and one of sewing necessities.

"I'll tell if you promise not to tell anyone else." Kaaren reached for their baskets.

"I promise."

"We were shouting praises." Ingeborg lifted out a pot of soup ready to be set back on the stove.

"I see. And have you taken up dancing before the Lord also?" Mary Martha's grin bespoke her teasing.

"Probably not in a sleigh."

The three of them laughed together and then looked around to see if anyone else was near enough to overhear. "I can see all of us dancing in front of the congregation on Sunday morning. You think they'd join us?" Ingeborg balanced the soup pot on the side of the sleigh to get a better grip. How good it felt to laugh like this. Due to a couple of snowstorms and blizzards, the women had canceled the last quilting meeting.

"Not ever. We'd be banished." The three shared another laugh and trooped up the stairs to the church door.

Ingeborg waited for Kaaren to open the door. Warm air, overlaid with the hum of female voices, bid them enter. Greetings from those in the room welcomed them, with Mrs. Valders turning and taking the pot of soup from Ingeborg.

"I'll set this on the stove while you get your coat off."

Ingeborg thanked her but stared a little disoriented after the portly figure on the way to the flat-topped cast-iron stove. Since when did the other woman offer to help, especially to Ingeborg? The relationship that had never been the best had nearly disintegrated those several years earlier when Andrew attacked Toby. Hildegunn Valders had a hard time forgiving.

"Did what I think I saw happen, really happen?" Kaaren whispered as she took Ingeborg's coat to lay over the chairs designated for such with her own.

Ingeborg nodded and then turned to answer a question from one of the other women.

"Is your Ellie coming today?" one of the women asked.

"No, the baby has been sleeping in odd time spurts. Only a couple weeks old and wants to be awake for all the activity. Ellie's pretty tired."

"Oh, too bad. I love holding the new little ones." Mrs. Magron's sweet smile blessed everyone. "Seems like so many years since I had a baby to cuddle."

"That's because it *has* been years." Ingeborg dug in her basket to find her shears. "Just think, of those of us here from the beginning, most of our children are grown."

"And some are giving us grandchildren." Mrs. Valders heaved a sigh. "I would indeed love to have grandchildren."

Ingeborg and Kaaren exchanged looks of surprise bordering on shock. Hildegunn actually expressing such a thing?

"Those two fine sons of yours will surely find wives one of these days," Mrs. Geddick said, her heavy German accent indicative of her homeland. She shook her head. "We need more young women here. That is for sure." Having four sons and one daughter, she had mentioned the need before.

Ingeborg kept the comment she wanted to make inside her head, keeping careful guard on her mouth. But one look at Kaaren's face told her she was thinking the same thing. There was not a chance in heaven that any young woman would be good enough for either of the Valderses' sons, not in Hildegunn's eyes, at least. Heaven help the girls they fell in love with.

"Perhaps friendships could lead to romance," Kaaren said. "I know that Gerald and Rebecca have been good friends for a long time."

"Huh," Hildegunn puffed out. "That one, no. Too giggly, and her head in the clouds. Wanting to open a soda shop—here in Blessing? What kind of an idea is that?"

The door opened, and Dr. Elizabeth blew through the doorway. "Sorry I am late. Even with Astrid there, I just couldn't get away."

"Did you bring Inga?" Kaaren asked.

"No, she is staying with Thelma, much to her dismay. But I think she is coming down with something, and I didn't want any others to catch whatever it is. Yesterday she was fussy, and today she has a fever and isn't eating."

While she talked, Dr. Elizabeth handed her food basket to Kaaren and removed her outer things. "This is such a treat to be able to join you all."

Ingeborg took her coat. "You being here is our treat."

"I told Astrid to send Thelma over here if there is an emergency she cannot handle. I am so proud of her, I could just burst my buttons. She knows so much more than I did, even when I first started work at the hospital in Chicago."

"That's because you are a good teacher, and you have given her so many opportunities to learn."

Mrs. Valders clapped her hands and raised her voice. "All right, ladies, let us get organized and get started. Take whatever places you want. We need six around each of the quilting frames. Mrs. Geddick brought another quilt top to be put on the frame. I brought an old wool batting that I thought we could use. When we finish this one, that will be five quilts we've made for the reservation, along with the hats and sweaters we have knitted."

Ingeborg sat down at the frame with the quilt already half tied. Since they were making quilts for the reservation, instead of quilting the top, batting, and backing together, they used yarn and tied them off, speed being more important than perfection. Early in the fall, they had sent a wagonload of supplies to the Indian agent who disbursed the quilts and clothing among the members of the tribe. Unlike the agents on some other reservations, the husband and wife who managed the Lakota site were honest and deeply caring people.

Ingeborg smiled at Elizabeth as she sat down next to her. "So good to see you getting a chance at something besides doctoring."

"And here I'll be knotting stitches. Could just as well have remained at the surgery."

"You could go cut pieces or use the machine to sew pieces together. I remember our first years when every stitch in every quilt was done by hand, and every little bit of fabric was shared and used. A red or yellow piece was prized. Now we can have so many choices and buy fabric just for quilts. So many changes these years have brought." While they talked, Ingeborg folded the yarn over the end of the needle to get a sharp fold and threaded the fold into the large eye of the darning needle. When she'd finished one, she handed it to Elizabeth and repeated the action.

"Thank you. You make everything look so easy."

"You do things long enough, and they better get easy, or you might want to find another way of doing it." She checked to make sure the batting lay smoothly between the top and the lining before taking the first stitch down through and back up an inch or less apart. Then she tied off the double knot and clipped the yarn. "Just make sure you tie a firm knot, or it will work its way loose one day."

"I see." Elizabeth repeated Ingeborg's actions. "I received an answer to my letter to Dr. Morganstein. She is so excited that she can offer that surgical rotation to Astrid."

"Now to convince that stubborn daughter of mine to take it."

"I know. Any suggestions?"

Mrs. Valders clapped her hands. "Ladies, ladies."

Everyone quit talking and looked up.

"Mrs. Knutson will now take suggestions for the Scripture reading for today. I will write them down."

The usual suggestions were made: First Corinthians thirteen, the Twenty-third Psalm, and Psalm ninety-one before Ingeborg requested John fifteen. Mrs. Valders busily wrote down the choices, including a later request of First John one and a couple other psalms. She handed the list to Kaaren.

"Now let us pray." Without waiting for any settling, Hildegunn commenced, "God in heaven, we ask that you bless our gathering today, comfort any who are sick, protect us all from the weather, and show us thy will. Amen."

I wonder if she ever thanks God for anything. The thought caught Ingeborg by surprise. She'd not noticed that of Hildegunn's prayers, but while Kaaren found her place for the first reading, she let her mind rove back through the years. Gratitude was not one of the woman's habits. For a long time Kaaren had led the prayers, and then everyone was invited to join, but in the years that Hildegunn had been leading the group, she'd offered short prayers, almost as if telling God what to do. Of course, she tried to tell everyone else what to do, so was this surprising?

The words *Love is . . .* washed over Ingeborg, seeping like sweet spring rain into the cracks and fissures of her soul and mind. *Patient and kind. Love is not boastful nor rude. Lord, I want to be all this. I know that only Jesus is everything herein, but please help me to love more deeply, more willingly, looking only for the good in people.*

Including Hildegunn? The name whispered through her mind, making her flinch inside. She sighed and shoved the needle through the fabric with a little more force than necessary.

Mrs. Garrison on her left leaned closer. "Are you all right?"

"Ja, I am," she whispered back. *Or at least I will be when I recover from the smart of that little prick in my heart. Thank you, Father. I will try to do better.* She concentrated on her stitching and tying, letting the age-old words flow around and through her. Such a pleasure it was to be read to. All of the women often commented on the delight of this part of their day.

After a while Ingeborg got up to stir the soup and put some more coal in the stove. Dorothy Baard was replacing her cool flatiron with a hot one.

"So when is our girl coming home again?"

Dorothy set the hot iron back flat on the stove. "She is having herself a fine time in Bismarck. We got a letter yesterday, saying that she wants to stay a week longer. I mailed her a note back and said she should do just that. She mentioned a young man she has met there. He's taken her ice-skating and sleigh riding, and he sat with her and Penny's family in church."

"My goodness, it sounds like she is having a good time." Ingeborg leaned closer. "No big brothers to act as watchdogs?"

Dorothy chuckled and nodded. "I try to tell them to quit acting like lawmen, but . . ." She shook her head. "Those Baard men, they don't take advice very good, you know."

Ingeborg smiled back. "I always thought she was rather sweet on Gerald."

"Did Astrid tell you about Rebecca's asking for the girls' advice about catching a fellow?"

"I'm not supposed to know, but Ellie let it slip the night the baby was born."

"I know. Me either, but maybe we should all put our heads together on how to help her."

"Help who?" Hildegunn asked as she stopped beside Ingeborg.

"Uh, Rebecca." *Help, Lord. How do I answer without . . .*

"I heard rumors that she was chasing after my Gerald, but you can believe I put a stop to that. Why, she's nothing but a girl yet and more than a little wild, if I do say so myself."

"Rebecca is *not* wild." Dorothy spun around and glared at Hildegunn. "She's the sweetest young woman and will make any man a fine wife. Gerald included, if he so feels."

"Running off to Bismarck like that, all by herself. Wanting to open a soda shop. Here in Blessing." Hildegunn shook her head until her chins wobbled. "She just better not come around sniffing after Gerald."

"Well, of all the . . ." Dorothy grabbed her flatiron and, despite being in the family way, stomped heavily back to the ironing board. She flung a glare over her shoulder that should have fried Hildegunn's hair.

" 'Blessed are the peacemakers,' " Kaaren started, picking up her reading again.

Ingeborg almost snorted. The Sermon on the Mount, including the Beatitudes, had not been one of the requested readings. Surely Kaaren had heard the interchange. The urge to light into Hildegunn subsided. *Lord, a heavy dose of wisdom would be a good thing right about now.*

"I thought I heard you mentioning that you wanted grandchildren," Ingeborg said to Hildegunn, keeping her voice low and gentle.

"Oh, I do, but . . ." A heavy sigh followed. "Gerald needs a lot of extra care. The malaria, you know." She paused to shake her head. "Not Rebecca. No, she wouldn't do at all."

Ingeborg bit down on the end of her tongue to keep from lashing out. When she could finally think of something gentle and loving to say, Hildegunn had moved on to the far quilting frame. *She is certainly a woman to try one's soul. How does Mr. Valders put up with her?*

11

"SHE DID IT AGAIN." Ingeborg flicked the reins, and horse and sleigh headed home.

Kaaren patted her arm. "I know. That woman has an absolute gift for setting people off."

"I had just prayed that I would be loving and not critical. I want to be like First Corinthians so bad, and then she disparaged Rebecca, and I wanted to dump the pot of soup on her, over her head, and—" She cut off an incipient tirade and heaved a whole body sigh instead. "Lord, please forgive me."

"He does. You know that."

"I know, but I get so tired of asking forgiveness for the same things over and over. All I can do is be thankful He says He forgets."

"As far as the east is from the west, He does. When I read those chapters aloud like today, the beauty of His love just pours over me all over again. There's something about reading aloud that makes His Word sink in more."

"Sometimes I think I should just stay home so she can't irritate me."

"You do know you are not alone."

"Uff da. Such goings on." Ingeborg looked to the north, where dark clouds were again building. She'd not needed to scan the sky; the bite of the wind warned her that the weather was changing again. "I have so enjoyed the sun and promise of spring, and now it seems another northerner is on its way."

"Oh, I wanted to go by the post office. There might be a letter from Grace."

"You want me to turn around?"

"Would you, please? Unless you think one of the men went to town."

"Neither Haakan nor Andrew mentioned it, and Astrid won't be home until later, I'm sure." While she answered, she turned the horse and headed across country. As more warmer days came, they'd have to stick to the roads, but for now the ice crust was still thick enough to drive the sleigh right over the fences and fields. She stopped at the hitching post for the post office and waited while Kaaren climbed out and went into the building.

"Get mine too," she called, and Kaaren waved over her shoulder.

With the moment of quiet, her mind jumped back to Hildegunn like a fox chasing a cottontail. Sometimes she wondered if the woman deliberately set out to be so irritating, or if it just came naturally. Surely she must be aware of how she drove people away. But then, why should she? People tiptoed around her, and she loved the importance that gave her. She'd noticed Hildegunn preen when she triumphed over one of the others. *Lord, you say for us to treat each other with love. Is it love that lets someone go on acting this way? You say to leave the fighting to you, that you will triumph, but I've tried to leave this with you, and nothing has changed.*

Ingeborg stared unseeing at the space between the horse's ears. Hmm . . . The women could all ignore her. But how would they bring that about without ending up in a gossip fest? And she knew what the Bible had to say about that. Something akin to murder, according to Jesus. There was even a commandment about it.

"So, Lord, what can we do?"

The horse's ears swiveled to catch her words. She stamped a front foot and snorted.

"Ja, that's what I think of it too. Just let it go, and let God take care of it."

She nodded as if she understood.

"That's about all you can do. Just nod and go on about your business. Maybe we should learn more of our lessons from our animals."

"So you're talking to the horse now?" Kaaren paused on the steps and glanced over at Thorliff's big house, which housed the surgery and what amounted to the local hospital too. "Sure is busy over there. Glad Elizabeth got away a bit."

Ingeborg looked over her shoulder. "So many people sick. This has been a hard winter for the little ones."

"Every winter is hard for the youngest and the oldest."

"You realize we are some of the oldest now that both Bridget and Henry died."

"Heaven forbid. Such morbid thoughts." Kaaren climbed back into the sleigh.

Ingeborg backed the horse and sleigh and turned toward home. "Did you get a letter from Grace?"

"I did, and you have one from someone in Norway." Kaaren showed her the envelope.

"Who is it from?"

Kaaren shrugged. "The envelope got wet, and I cannot read the return address, other than *Norge*. Gerald apologized for the postal service, as if it were his personal fault." She shook her head. "Such a fine young man. You have to admit the Valderses did a good job of turning those two young ruffians into sons they can be proud of."

"I know. Keep reminding me of the good things Hildegunn does or has done. I tend to get wrapped up in my feelings about her."

"She does manage to set you off on a regular basis."

"She doesn't bother you?"

"Not as much, but then, she hasn't been attacking my son either." She paused for a moment. "Or me."

"Today she made disparaging remarks about Rebecca. Can't she ever say anything nice about anyone?" She chuckled a little. "Dorothy hissed back like the hot iron she held." Ingeborg ducked her chin into the scarf around her neck and head. "Brr. That wind is making our ride colder by the minute." She flicked the reins to command the horse to pick up a faster trot. Clumps of snow rattled against the front of the sleigh. They flew by the lane to her house and on to the Knutsons'.

"I hope Pastor Solberg sees the storm coming and lets school out a bit early." Kaaren gathered her baskets, stepped down, and stepped back with a wave. "Forget about Hildegunn and have a good evening."

"I will." Ingeborg turned the sleigh and headed for home, not sure if the bits of ice flying by her were from the trotting horse or the coming storm. Haakan met her at the barn.

"Drive on up to the house. I'll put the horse away." He stepped on the sleigh runners behind her, and Ingeborg did as he said. He helped her out of the sleigh and handed her the baskets, along with the empty soup kettle. "We're going to milk early." He waved as the Knutson wagon, now on runners for the winter and filled with the deaf students and Trygve and Samuel, drove past their lane, heading for home.

"That's good. Pastor let the children out early. Is Andrew milking?"

"Ja. I told Lars to go on home, but he insisted he stay. I'll keep an eye on the weather."

"Good thing you didn't take the ropes down." Ingeborg stepped away so Haakan could turn the horse and head back to the barn. She trudged up the stairs. One good thing, Astrid would just stay at Thorliff's if the weather turned as black as it looked at the moment. She caught the frame of the izing glass–covered screen door when the wind tried to tear it from her hands and slam it back against the wall. "Uff da. I never have cared for wind like this." She stamped the snow off her boots in the enclosed porch, grateful for the buffer between the kitchen door and the snarling storm.

Stepping into her warm kitchen with the doors shut behind her made her breathe a sigh of relief. She set her baskets down on the floor and unwound her long natural wool scarf, removed gloves and hat, and unbuttoned her coat, already appreciating the warmth now tingling on her wind-bitten cheeks. Surely there was no place on earth as good as home. Even though she'd been gone only a few hours, coming back in the teeth of the storm made the warmth and lingering smell of Haakan's pipe, along with the rich fragrance of baking ham and beans, all the more appreciated. She hung her things on the coat tree and set the food basket on the counter, then made her way to set the other on the treadle sewing machine she'd moved into the kitchen, where it was warmer, for the winter.

The orange-and-white cat stepped out of her box behind the stove and stretched as only a cat can, revealing a pink tongue and white needle teeth. She chirped and came to rub against Ingeborg's heavy wool skirt.

"I sure hope you got that mouse I found in the pantry." Ingeborg picked up the cat and held her close while rubbing her head and ears. While the cat was officially Astrid's, she really belonged to the entire family. "S'pose we ought to start the biscuits, eh? I know you'd rather I sat down in the rocking chair in front of the stove and took up my knitting or something so you could have the lap." She set the cat on the floor. "Sorry, not right now. I need to work on supper." The cat stuck her nose in the air and strolled over to the rug to sit down and clean herself.

Ingeborg chuckled and retrieved the flour from the pantry, along with the buttermilk and other supplies. Using a spill, she lighted the kerosene lamps to drive away the early dark created by the storm. The wind pleaded for entrance and slammed the roof when denied. Ingeborg glanced up, grateful for the strength the men had built into the house. "Lord, keep everyone safe" had been her blizzard plea for years, even when she wanted to hide in bed with a pillow blocking the roaring wind. Years earlier she'd thought the stories of people on the prairie going insane with the wind and walking out of their house to freeze to death were myths until she knew a woman who did just that.

Now the only power she knew that was stronger than the wind was God himself. And so she prayed as she mixed the dough, kneaded it a few times, patted it out to a half inch thick, and cut the rounds. After sliding the pan into the oven, she paused to listen. Surely the men should be at the house by now. Wouldn't it be better for Andrew to stay overnight rather than cross the fields to his own house?

When she heard booted feet on the porch kicking off the snow, she let out a breath she didn't realize she'd been holding. But only Haakan came through the door, a bucket of milk in his gloved hand.

"Where's Andrew?"

"I sent him home earlier, before the storm got so bad."

Relief sloughed off her shoulders, and she stood straight again. "And Lars?"

"He is following the rope home."

"And to think I thought of taking it down the other day."

"Why would we take it down before May, when we always do?" He set the bucket on a stool and took off his outer clothing, then caught his heel in the boot jack and levered his boots off too. Padding over to the stove in his stocking feet, he held his hands flat over the heat. "It's been colder before, but that wind tears right through you."

Ingeborg set the bucket on the counter while she fetched flat pans to pour the milk into so she could skim off the cream that would rise to the top by the morning. "Supper is ready when you are. This is one of those times I wish we all had telephones. I want to know for sure Andrew made it home."

"He had the rope to follow if he needed it."

"He should have stayed here."

"And have Ellie worry herself sick all night?"

Ingeborg drained the last from the bucket and carried it to the stove, where she could wash it out with hot water from the reservoir. "So true. And she would worry. That's where the telephone would come in."

She pulled the pan of golden-brown biscuits from the oven and slid them from the pan into a towel-lined bowl, then set it on the table. The pot of beans she set in front of Haakan's place. The wind shrieked, but with Haakan in the house with her, it could shriek all it wanted. She had to take his word that Andrew had left early enough. Sometimes faith took a lot of prayer.

They sat down and bowed their heads. "Lord God," Haakan prayed,

"I thank you for this tight house, the good food before us, safety for all those we love, and most of all for your Son, who died and rose again that we might live. Mange takk. Amen."

Ingeborg joined him in the amen and reached to spoon out the beans onto her husband's plate. Such a simple thing and one more to be grateful for. She fought against the memories that the howling wind brought back, memories of winters in the soddy, the shortage of food, the loneliness, the despair. Slamming the lid on the box in her mind, where she stuffed the memories, she dished up her own plate and passed the bowl of biscuits to Haakan, then the butter and the strawberry-rhubarb jam. "You want pickles?" She held up the dish. At his nod, she forked several of the dill slices onto his plate and also several chunks of beet pickles.

After the first couple of bites, Haakan sighed. "This has to be the perfect meal for a night such as this. Ham we smoked, beans you grew and dried, pickles, flour from our wheat, butter and milk from our cows. All this from the hand of God."

"Helped along by our hands." She patted his arm. "Today has been a good day for thanksgiving."

"How was the quilting?"

"Good. We always accomplish so much. Elizabeth was able to get away to join us, and I managed to not dump the soup on Hildegunn."

He nodded with a slight smile. "Ah, I see. She's back to her usual tricks."

"If you mean her mouth, you are absolutely right." Ingeborg felt her shoulders tighten up.

"Ah, my Inge, let it go. You cannot change her."

"That's for sure. No one can. Of course, no one else is bothered by her so much as I am. I was thinking maybe all of us could get together and decide to ignore her when she starts her mean mouth."

"I think you'd do better praying for her. Safer that way."

"You think I haven't been?"

"Any news from Rebecca?"

"Dorothy said that she wrote and said she was going to stay in Bismarck an extra week. She must be having a good time."

"When we came through Fargo, Gus kept pacing, wondering if we would see her in the train station, even though we didn't make plans to meet her on the way back. She didn't mention how Hjelmer was doing?"

"Not that I know of. Oh, I forgot." She pushed her chair back. "We got a letter today, from Norge."

"From who?"

"I don't know. Water had blurred the return address, and I haven't read the letter yet." She crossed to the coatrack and dug the letter out of her pocket, waving it as she returned to the table to slice the envelope open with her knife. Drawing out the thin paper, she unfolded it and looked at the signature. "From my cousin Alfreda."

"Isn't she the one who wanted to come over some years ago?"

"Ja." Ingeborg leaned toward the lamp in the center of the table. Haakan pulled the lamp closer to her and returned to buttering another biscuit.

"Dear Ingeborg and Haakan,

"I am sorry I have not written sooner, but I still have the dream of coming to the new land. My husband, Thor, has passed away. Those traveling would be me and my two middle sons, the older of them being married. I have been saving for years to have enough money to come. Thor did not want to come, and that is why we did not.

"You mentioned before that there was land available, but I do not know if that is still true. But we are not afraid of hard work, as you know. I know that you have a cheese company, and perhaps you have need of someone to help you with that."

Ingeborg looked up to see Haakan watching her. "Just think, maybe this is how God is going to answer my prayers for more help after we get the herds built back up."

"Maybe."

She returned to reading.

"There will be four adults and two children. My daughter-in-law is pregnant again. We would hope to come as soon as the weather permits, if you are in agreement. Please write as soon as you can.

"Affectionately,

Your cousin Alfreda Brunderson"

Ingeborg glanced through the letter again before folding it carefully and sliding it back in the envelope. "Now, what do you think of that? All these years and no one has wanted to come."

Haakan nodded and rose to get his pipe from the rack behind the stove. Taking his pocketknife from his pocket, he pulled out the smallest blade and, opening the front lid on the stove, scraped the leftover tobacco into the coals.

Ingeborg waited while he went through the process of tamping the tobacco down in the pipe, lighting it with a spill, and returning to the table, where he leaned back in his chair.

"Would you like more coffee?"

He nodded and blew a smoke ring.

She fetched the coffeepot and filled both their cups, then brought a cake pan over to dish up squares of spiced apple cake and ladle cream over them. Peace reigned so supreme she'd forgotten about the storm. The cinnamon that flavored the apple cake made her taste buds dance. More family to join them in Blessing. She'd about given up that dream, although she'd thought of writing to one of her sisters or brothers with the same idea.

She waited for Haakan, knowing he'd speak when he was ready.

"I imagine you want to start writing the letter right now?"

As she pushed her chair back again, she patted his hand. "I knew we were thinking the same thing. You can help me."

Funny, she thought as she started writing, now it would be easier to write this in English than in Norwegian. What a day. Past and present all mixed up together, shifting in and out like the weather. She looked up as a particular blast made both of them glance at the window. *Lord God, please keep everyone safe from this beast of a north wind.*

12

Bismarck, North Dakota

LATER THAT NIGHT IN her room, Rebecca opened the letter. After glancing at the handwriting earlier, she'd known it was from Dorothy.

Dear Rebecca,

I miss you. I guess I didn't realize how much time we spend together until now that you are gone. Hans asks every day if today is the day you are coming home. I am glad you are having such a good time. You deserve to be out making new friends. Just don't forget the old ones.

And right now I'm feeling mighty old. Or just huge. My mind knows this baby is not that much larger than the others, but perhaps my body is feeling a bit worn. I brought out the baby clothes and got them all washed and ready. Thank you for those extra diapers you hemmed for me. Somehow I just don't find time to sit down at the machine, perhaps because every time I sit down, I fall asleep.

Gus was terribly disappointed, as were the other men, at the number of cows they brought back—half of what they'd been told and at twice the price. Some of these are bred heifers, and one was not old enough to breed yet. But at least all will be milking within the year, and that is more than we had before. Personally, I think Gus is lonely over there at the homeplace. He takes most of his meals with us and hangs around in the evening. He and Knute play cribbage after supper.

I guess that is all the news for now. Greet Penny and Hjelmer and the children for me. I'm sure they've grown a foot since they left here.

Your loving sister-in-law,
Dorothy

Rebecca laid the letter down on her folded-back sheets. Home-sickness blindsided her like a blizzard from the north. Her heart hurt and tears flowed. She should be home helping Dorothy. Neither of the men thought to help her much or at all, as far as she could figure. But then, they weren't the ones having the babies.

Was Gus taking care of the cat? Surely he wouldn't let Franny go hungry. But if he wasn't eating there . . . She reread the letter, mopped her tears, and looked around the room. This bedroom was nearly as big as the parlor at home. There was a bathroom down the hall, hot running water in the kitchen, and a basement furnace. She heaved a sigh. Would it be possible to put these kinds of conveniences in the house at home?

She thought to the arguments she'd gone through when she asked for water to be piped to the house from the well. You'd have thought she asked for a whole new house the way Gus carried on. But he'd appreciated the hand pump at the sink and even admitted one day that she'd been right. Well, almost admitted. Saying how handy it was had to do.

Rebecca laid the envelope on her nightstand to share with Penny in the morning. They were planning a sewing day, since the weather had turned blustery. She wondered if Penny would tell her what was really bothering her. Rebecca could see she was trying to listen to the Lord, but she also knew Penny well enough to sense there was more to her unhappiness than the move. Both she and Hjelmer seemed to carry a heaviness about them, like a secret they weren't allowed to share or the sludge in the river after spring thaw. Was living away from Blessing the cause, or was it something else?

She picked up her Bible and turned to the book of John, where she was reading. Finding time to read was easier here, where all the housekeeping chores didn't fall on her. Perhaps that's what Penny meant when she said she was searching for God's leading. If only Jesus' miracles were still happening today. But the Bible said God was the same yesterday, today, and tomorrow. Maybe she could ask Pastor Solberg some of her questions when she got home.

The sun came out the next day, and she and Linnea walked to Benson's Soda Emporium so she could talk again with Thomas. Since it wasn't busy, he sat down at the table to visit with her once he'd served their ice cream.

"So, how do you like Bismarck?" he asked, after jumping up to get them napkins.

"It sure is different from Blessing. So many people here. Do you know everyone?"

He shook his head. "My mother and father used to, but even they say there are too many families and businesses to keep track of anymore. They had to put on a third milk route this fall."

"Milk route?"

"We have horse-drawn wagons that carry the bottled milk, and a delivery man who sets the order on the front or back porch of those who have a standing order. They can order more if they want by checking off what they want on the delivery sheet."

"Well, I never. Sort of like the ice man who delivers ice in the summer?"

"Same idea. In the summer the milk is delivered really early in the morning, and blocks of ice in the milk wagon help keep it cool so it won't spoil. One year it got hot, and some of the cream got jostled around enough that it turned to butter before the last stop. When we started to get more new customers, Pa decided to have shorter routes and added a driver."

Rebecca took her list of questions from her reticule. "I've been thinking on things to ask you, but when I get here I forget." She motioned to the paper. "Do you mind?"

"Not at all." He leaned back in his chair and crossed his legs at the ankles. "Though maybe you should ask my pa."

She glanced down at her list. It was interesting how many lists she'd made lately. "Where did you buy your refrigeration machinery?"

"You'll have to ask Pa. I can get the information and have it here for you next time you come."

"That would be nice. I know I can't afford it yet, but after you showed me what it can be like, I know I'll need it eventually." She finished her ice cream. "Do a lot of people buy ice cream in the winter?"

He nodded. "We have a lot of parties here all year long."

"What a good idea." She made more notes to herself. Later, when a group of people came in, she put her paper and pencil away. "I can't thank you enough," she said as she left. "You have given me so much new information to consider."

Thomas blushed. "Come back again if you like. Would you like to work with me for a few hours to see how it feels?"

"That would be very nice. Let me check with Penny."

On the way home Linnea slipped her hand into Rebecca's. "I like him," she said, "and I really love going there."

"What makes it so special?"

"It feels like home." Linnea skipped a little.

Rebecca looked over at her, puzzled. "Like home?"

"Home in Blessing," Linnea explained. "And Mr. Benson treats me like I'm a grown-up."

Rebecca nodded. She'd noticed and smiled gratefully at Thomas when he'd answered Linnea's questions with courtesy. She remembered what that felt like. The first man who had treated her as nicely was Gerald. That was when they'd become friends. The end-of-school picnic when she was twelve and he was in the graduating class. All the schoolchildren were participating in the various games, but Swen and Knute decided Rebecca could get hurt and barred her from competing.

"You're too gawky," Swen said. "You'll just fall and be embarrassed."

She had been so humiliated and angry that she rushed off to hide at the bend at the river. As usual, her brothers didn't even notice she was missing, but Gerald did.

"There you are, Rebecca. I've been looking all over for you."

She quickly rubbed her apron across her red eyes. "For me? Why?"

"I know what a good rower and swimmer you are, so I need you to be my partner in the rowboat race."

"But my brothers said . . ." She hesitated. If she didn't tell him, then maybe she could. And they could actually win.

"Don't worry. They know you'll be safe with me."

Rebecca chuckled as she remembered their stunned expressions when she and Gerald swept over the finish line.

"What's funny?" Linnea asked.

"Oh, I'm thinking about a race I was in when I was young."

"Mr. Benson likes you. Do you like him?"

"I like him as a friend," Rebecca answered. She thought of her list of qualities she was looking for in a man: loves children, kind, good-looking, good Christian, strong character, good sense of humor, truthful, courageous. Thomas Benson had the first two, but she wouldn't be there long enough to know how many more qualities he had.

"He's nicer than Mr. von Drehl," Linnea said. "Mr. Benson acts real, and Mr. von Drehl just pretends."

Rebecca stopped for a moment in astonishment. What did Linnea see that she didn't? Well, it didn't matter. She wouldn't know what other qualities Kurt had either, unless he kept in touch. But did anyone have all those traits, or was she living in a dream, like her soda shop, according to her brothers? The same brothers who managed to keep all young men from spending time with her.

She liked the feeling of interest in her from Kurt and Thomas.

It was her first taste of freedom. Now with the miles separating her from Knute and Gus, for the first time ever, Rebecca realized her brothers had always been protecting her from dangers, real or imagined. But when she thought of the man on the train, she shivered and understood their concerns a little more. In their arrogant way they did care about her, she guessed, but they also never seemed to see her as a grown-up either.

Gerald always had. She mentally ticked off his traits and realized they were all on her list, although she knew some people didn't recognize the inner strength in him. Or his quiet humor. But she did. Ever since he had smiled his quirky smile at their rowing victory, she knew he was real too. A real friend. Now, if she could just find a real husband.

13

ROMANCE WAS SKATING IN the moonlight with one mittened hand held securely by Kurt's right hand while his left snugged her left hand against her waist. The warmth of his arm around her caused more heat than she expected. They started out skating with arms crossed in front, but when he switched to holding her closer to his side, they skated as one. The rhythm of their skate-shod feet made Rebecca feel like she was floating.

"Are you warm enough?" he asked, his breath tickling the tendril of hair that sneaked out from under Penny's fur hat.

She nodded and turned to smile up at him. Her breath caught in her throat. He had to be the best looking young man in all of Bismarck. And he was skating with her. In fact, he'd brought her to the skating rink. What was happening to her? If this fluttery feeling was what the girls at home had been talking about, no wonder Maydell was all in a dither about wanting a man in her life. Especially if the man looked and acted like Kurt von Drehl.

"Have you ever skated backward?"

The memory of ending up on her posterior more than once in her efforts made her shake her head. "I couldn't get the hang of it."

"How about if I skate backward first, then I'll help you?"

She flinched inside but nodded on the outside.

"Ready?" At her nod he took his arm from behind her and, with a smooth swoop was in front of her, skating backward and holding both of her hands. "Did you watch my feet?"

She shook her head, more mesmerized by the smile that curved his mouth and crinkled his eyes. Staring at him made her breath catch too.

"You want to try? We'll stop, and then I'll go behind you and put my hands on your waist. Then you just let yourself follow me, like dancing."

"Do we have to?"

"No, but I think you'll enjoy it. See? Like those two over there." He nodded to another couple skating in tandem.

He brought them to a stop and slipped behind her, and she felt herself easing backward. With his hands holding her up, her feet began the reverse rhythm, and she was skating backward.

"See, it's not so bad."

A giggle escaped as she swayed first to one foot then the other. "But I can't see where I am going."

"I won't let us bump into anyone."

At that moment her feet shot out from under her, and thanks to the impetus from two boys ramming into them, all four ended in a heap on the ice.

"I'm so sorry."

"Are you all right?"

The voices flitted around her, and ignoring the ignominy of it all, Rebecca started to laugh and couldn't stop no matter how sternly she ordered herself. She couldn't believe it had happened again. Somehow she attracted collisions. As they untangled themselves, others stopped to help them up. While Kurt scolded one of the half-grown boys, Rebecca grinned up at the two young men who pulled her to her feet.

"Are you hurt?"

She shook her head. "Not at all." It looked, however, like Kurt's pride had taken a tumble on the ice. "That's one of the good things about all the winter clothing. I'm well padded."

The tall blonde burst out laughing. "You are new here?"

"Fairly."

"Miss Baard is skating with me," Kurt told him, still sounding a bit put out.

"Well, if you get tired of skating with him, I'll be waiting." The young man skated off, his long red scarf trailing over his shoulder.

Wait until I get home and tell all these stories. No one is going to believe me. A pang of homesickness hit her with about the same force as the young skaters who crashed them all in a heap. A picture of Gerald flashed across her mind. He'd get a chuckle out of her stories, for sure. She liked to make him laugh, something he didn't do much of. Hopefully she'd have the opportunity to tell him when she got home. Mrs. Valders glared at her if she so much as smiled at her son. Maybe she couldn't recognize friendship, since she worked so hard not to have any friends herself. Hands crossed in front again, they resumed the swoops of ice dancing until the chill of late afternoon brought most of the skaters over to the two metal barrels where fires roared.

"I promised Penny I'd be home in time for supper."

"I suppose we better be going, then." Kurt motioned toward the benches. "I hope you've had as fine a time as I have."

She nodded. "Even the tumble was funny."

He rolled his eyes. "Don't remind me."

But the grin that tickled his cheeks made her smile in return.

"I can't see you tomorrow or the next day, as I have classes all day."

"Oh. I think I'll be leaving in three days or so."

"Really? Do you have to?"

No, but I want to, she suddenly realized. "I can't believe I've been here nearly a month already. Dorothy's baby is arriving soon, and I have a lot to do at home. I need to get seeds started for the garden, and spring cleaning has to be done before Easter. . . ."

"Is that a law?" He unbuckled her skates and then his.

"In Blessing it is. Besides, I already stayed on a week longer than I thought I might."

"I know, but it wasn't long enough. I was hoping you would stay here and go to school or something." They strolled up the sidewalk, which was framed by piles of snow.

How can I change the subject? "What classes are you taking?"

The rest of the way to Penny's house he told her about life at the college and how he didn't see any sense in taking more of the Romance languages and much preferred the sciences.

It all sounded like a foreign language to her.

"May I see you again before you leave?"

A lump in her throat made her only nod.

"We could write letters—or talk on the telephone." He held her hand as if she were about to fall down.

"I don't have a telephone, remember?" He sounded as if he really wanted to keep in touch with her. But why? His head was full of studies and her life was so ordinary.

"But you will eventually."

She shrugged. "If my brothers think it is necessary. I will write, though."

They both startled as the door opened and Gus stuck his head out. "Ma says supper is ready." The look he shot Kurt lacked any degree of hospitality.

"I'm coming." Rebecca smiled and nodded. "Thanks for the skating lesson."

Kurt touched his forehead with one gloved finger. "Anytime."

Rebecca allowed Gus to pull her into the house and turned to see Kurt walking backward and grinning at her.

"Gustaf Bjorklund, how rude," Penny scolded, just on the other side of her son. "I didn't tell you to drag her inside, just to say supper was ready." She looked to Rebecca. "You could have invited Mr. von Drehl in."

"That's all right." Rebecca divested herself of her outer things and hung them on the coatrack. "I skated backward for the first time." She grabbed Linnea's hand and twirled her around.

"I could teach you that," Gus said with a bit of a swagger.

Linnea smiled up at Rebecca. "You can teach me. Gus says I'm too little."

The three of them followed Penny into the dining room, where the table was all set and Hjelmer sat at the foot of the table waiting for them.

"You look like you had a good time."

"Oh, I did." Rebecca went on to tell them of the four-person tumble and about some of the other skaters.

"If I'd been there, no one would have run into you again," Gus declared.

That evening, after she and Linnea finished the dishes, she overheard Penny and Hjelmer talking in the parlor. She moved toward the room, intending to join them, but paused when Hjelmer said that he disliked his job more all the time.

"What don't you like?" Penny asked.

"It's not what I expected. He promised me things that are not happening, like an increase in pay, and the hours are getting longer instead of shorter. I guess I'm not cut out to work in an office all the time."

Rebecca could hear her mother talking against the evils of eavesdropping but couldn't tear herself away. When she heard Linnea call for her mother, she quickly left her listening post and made her way up the stairs to her bedroom. Did that mean they might come back to Blessing? Did she dare ask Penny? How wonderful that would be.

If only Mr. Jeffers wanted to sell the store. Tomorrow she would take Thomas Benson up on his offer to teach her how to make sodas at his shop. She needed to learn as much as possible over her last few days.

Sitting down at her desk, she took out pencil and paper to add to the letter to Gerald that she'd started two days earlier. She might make it home before the letter did, but she'd mail it in the morning anyway.

I went ice-skating with Mr. Kurt von Drehl today. There were so many people at the skating pond, some even dancing on skates. He tried to teach me how to skate backward, but thanks to two out-of-control skaters, we all ended up in a heap. I could tell Kurt was really embarrassed, but I thought it hilarious. No one was hurt. I am determined we will have a skating pond in Blessing next winter, even if I have to make it at our house. It's been too long without one.

Please don't tell anyone, but I've had a streak of homesickness the last two days, even though Penny is making sure I am having a good time. We sewed Linnea a new dress and a pinafore, along with a woolen jumper. So many things are more fun when you can do them with someone you both love and enjoy.

I feel like I am out of touch with everyone in Blessing, as if I am at the other end of the earth. I have received only one letter from Dorothy, and that was a short one. If I were going to be here longer, I would demand that you write to me. But I'll be home yet this week. I leave Wednesday.

She stopped and looked at the word *demand*. That was pretty strong. Should she cross it out? Shaking her head, she went back to writing.

I hope you have not had any malaria attacks recently and that you enjoy your job as the telephone operator. Tomorrow I will learn how to make sodas, no matter that Gustaf Baard himself thinks my dream of a soda shop is such a silly idea. Sometimes brothers who think they know everything can be a pain in the neck. Or some other place.

She stared at the last phrase. That was not very ladylike. What would her mother say? She would say to rewrite the entire page and delete what might be considered offensive. Rebecca heaved a sigh. *If only you were still here, Ma, to tell me things, to show me how to live the kind of faith you had. I know you would tell me to read my Bible, but I don't seem to find the wisdom there that you did.* Her second sigh was even deeper.

So I will see you in church on Sunday if not before.
Your friend,
Rebecca Baard

She folded the pages and carefully inserted them in the envelope. After addressing it, she propped it against the lamp. Maybe she should write to Gus and tell him what day she was coming home so he would come to town to pick her up. Snatching another sheet of paper, she dashed off a note with the minimal information, addressed the envelope, and set it with the other.

~

The sign on the window at Benson's Soda Emporium said it would be closed Monday and Tuesday. She turned to Penny. "Oh, I wanted to ask Thomas a few more questions. Why did I put it off?"

"You don't have to go home on Wednesday, you know. Thursday will be just as good."

"But I wrote and told Gus I'd leave Wednesday." *And Gerald.*

"But we haven't been to the post office yet. You could open the envelope and make the necessary changes."

Linnea clung to Rebecca's hand. "I don't want you to leave."

"I know, but I have a lot to do at home too. Maybe you and your ma can come back to Blessing to visit next summer, and you could stay at the farm."

"Do you have kittens?"

"We always have kittens." Even thoughts of the barn cats waiting for milk at milking time made her feel homesick. "Maybe we'll have a calf by then too."

"All right. Let's go to the post office, and I'll write on the back of the envelope."

"Then we can go home and bake cookies." Linnea tugged on both Rebecca's and her mother's hands. "I want to put raisins for the eyes and mouth."

With their other errands finished, the three stopped at the grocery store for eggs, milk, and cheese. When Penny motioned to buy a loaf of bread, Rebecca shook her head.

"If you have yeast, I'll bake bread this afternoon too." She stared at Penny. "Don't you bake your own bread anymore?"

"No. I've never been good at bread making. I always tried to talk Ingeborg into baking bread for me. Hers is the best anywhere."

"Ma baked good bread."

"She did. Agnes and Ingeborg were good at about anything they did. And such good friends. That's one of the many things I miss here. I don't have any really good friends."

"You haven't been here a terribly long time."

"It sure feels like it." She took out her money to pay the clerk. As they walked out the door, she continued. "It's like Blessing was another life entirely, like maybe I dreamed it all."

Rebecca slipped her string bag over her wrist. She and Penny each carried part of the groceries. "There's not a day goes by but I don't miss you, and every time people are together, they mention how much they miss you and the store the way it used to be."

Penny brushed a tear from her cheek.

"Hurry. I'm hungry, and I have to go," Linnea said, doing a small hop.

"All right. Why didn't you mention that earlier?"

"I didn't have to go earlier."

"Do we have to run?" Rebecca asked.

"Maybe partway."

The three set off walking so fast Linnea had to trot. Their breath billowed white in front of them, even though the sun was out and water was dripping off icicles from the edges of the roofs.

Some spots in the street were bare, showing the mud. The late February thaw was welcome, but no one dared hope spring was on the way. Not yet.

That evening when Kurt rang through on the telephone, Rebecca told him that she was leaving on Thursday.

A silence stretched for a bit before he said softly, "I wish you weren't going."

She couldn't agree with him, but the thought of not seeing him again made her shoulders slump. Shame there wasn't a way to have everything now that a young man was expressing an interest in her. Maybe it was her brothers' protection that kept them at a distance at home. But there were also definitely no Kurt von Drehls in Blessing.

14

March 1903
Blessing, North Dakota

WAITING WAS NEVER EASY.

Ingeborg stared at the calendar that Thorliff printed every year. Here it was the first of March, and Easter would be April 12. How could time fly by so fast on one hand and seem to drag on another? Would her relatives really come from Norway? She would have real family here in North Dakota—family of her own, not the Bjorklund side. Not that she didn't love them all dearly, but now her cousin Alfreda was coming.

Ignoring the wind that was spitting snow against the windows, she thought of spring coming to Norway, the snow-capped mountains beckoning all the young women to take the milk cows up to the high pastures, where the women would spend their days herding the cows, milking the cows, and making cheese. Nothing like the big operation she had built here, but they always had cheese enough to sell by the end of the summer when they brought the cows back down to the farmsteads. Oh, the stories she could tell of young women's dreams, discussions, and crushes.

Each year would pass with fewer of the older girls returning. Many left home to work somewhere else or got married and were replaced by younger girls. This happened to her until she was the oldest one left and people feared she'd never be married. Her mother had worried about it more than she had.

The smell of cookies getting too brown jerked her back to the kitchen in Blessing in 1903. "Uff da," she muttered. She grabbed a towel, drew open the oven door, and *tsk*ed, with a shake of her head. They weren't burned, but Haakan liked his cookies soft, not crisp like this. She set the cookie sheet on the table and, using a pancake turner, lifted the cookies to the wooden racks Thorliff had made for her so many years before, when Onkel Olaf was teaching the boys woodworking in his shop.

She rolled out the last of the sour cream cookie dough. She should make Haakan really happy by baking molasses cookies too. Little Inga would love to have a gingerbread man or two. She cut the cookies, moved them to the cookie pan, and sprinkled sugar on the tops. Moving the cookie sheet on the bottom rack to the top, she slid the third pan into the oven. Then she took one of the browner cookies and broke it in half. Munching it, she poured herself a cup of coffee and sat down for just a minute. For some unknown reason, her back ached sometimes now when rolling cookies or pie dough. Haakan said it was just a sign of getting old.

As if forty-five was old.

Times like this, letting her mind roam backward was too easy. What a treat it would be to sit here for a bit with Agnes. One didn't have too many friends like her come into a life. Kaaren was her other good friend, but she was busy with her school, especially the three children who were not adept enough with sign language yet to be sent to the Blessing school.

"Ingeborg Bjorklund, you will send yourself on a fast trip back to the pit of depression if you keep thinking back like this." She spoke firmly and forced herself to drink the last of the coffee, brush the cookie crumbs into her hand, and get going again. Sitting here feeling sorry for herself never did any good at all.

Why was it so easy to slip from rejoicing to fighting tears? *Lord, forgive me. I have so much to be grateful for. Just think of all I would have missed out on if I'd never known Agnes.* "I will sing praises instead, like David said. And Paul." She hummed a tune and put her own words to it. "Thank you, Jesus, I love you so," then segued into the children's song, "Jesus loves me, this I know." The cat arched her back, stretching from her nest between the stove and the wall, and wound herself around Ingeborg's skirts. Just singing the name of Jesus over and over to her tune made her smile. "Jesus, lover of my soul . . ."

The thudding of boots on the porch made her look at the window in the back door. Sure enough, Haakan was ready for dinner. And she hadn't even set the table yet.

"You sound happy," he said as he stepped into the warm kitchen. "It smells heavenly in here."

"Oh!" She flew to the stove and yanked another fairly brown pan of cookies from the oven. "Whatever is the matter with me today?"

"Burned?"

"No. Just crispy brown. The soup is all ready as soon as you wash up."

"I sent Lars home a while ago, just in case the weather became worse, but the wind seems to be dying, and the snow is letting up too."

She shook her head. "Spring has to be on the way. Maybe the old adage will hold true. In like a lion, out like a lamb." Just saying the word *lamb* made her swallow. For the first time since the second year they came to the prairies, they'd not had lambs. No sheep, thanks to the hoof-and-mouth epidemic that swept havoc through the farms. Haakan had asked her if she wanted sheep again, and she'd chosen not to. But this very moment she would give anything to see lambs gamboling beside the ewes, to hear the bleating of the flock that used to winter in the corral and shed off from the barn.

Haakan dried his hands and took his place at the table, snatching a cookie and winking at her. "I hope you plan to save some of these for Inga, even though you didn't do raisin smiles."

"If Astrid comes home today, she can take some back tomorrow."

Ingeborg dished up a bowl of chicken soup and set it in front of her husband. "Bread coming in a minute."

"Is there any of that corn bread left?"

"You'd rather that than sliced bread?"

"Please." He helped himself to another cookie. "I heard some sad news when I was at the post office. You know the Eldersons south of town?"

"Of course." She brought the pan of corn bread from the pantry. "What?"

"The missus had been crying a lot lately, the mister said, and left the house sometime in the night of the blizzard. He found her huddled against the barn two days later."

"Frozen to death." Ingeborg fought the tears that burned her eyes. "One more driven to despair by the wind."

"I know. Seems like we hear of at least one every winter."

"I should have gone to see her when they weren't in church lately."

"Ja, but not just you. Any of us could have, should have, gone." Haakan folded his hands, waiting for her to sit. "Come, let's say grace."

Ingeborg set a square of corn bread on his plate and took her seat. Poor Ida. *Lord God, take care of her mister.*

"I Jesu navn . . ."

She joined her husband in the Norwegian grace, but before saying the amen, he added, "And help poor Ernie as he grieves. This land is a hard taskmaster, so please remind us how to look out for one another. Amen."

Ingeborg wiped her nose and eyes with the hankie she always kept in her apron pocket. "I just didn't realize she was that bad off. We get so caught up in what's going on. . . . She should have . . ." She shook her head. "Maybe if she'd come to quilting . . . or if someone had gone to get her."

"Ernie said he is selling out. He didn't buy any cows to replace his, and he says he just hasn't the heart anymore to plant wheat when spring does come. Maybe his son will take over, but you know he went to Grand Forks to work." Haakan sighed. "I'm thinking we need a town meeting. There might be other people in trouble that we just don't know about."

"Has Rebecca come back yet?"

"Not that I know. Oh, that's right, Mrs. Valders said she wrote and is coming on Thursday."

"Gus told her that?"

"No, I think Rebecca wrote it on the back of her envelope." He rolled his lips together. "Now, don't go getting all het up. You know Mrs. Valders likes to know what is going on."

Ingeborg shook her head and blew on her spoon of soup. "The corn bread is a bit dry. Perhaps it would be good crumbled into the soup."

"It is just fine with butter and jam." He took another bite. "Oh, and Thorliff said to tell you that if your cousins decide to come, he'll get going on a house for them as soon as the melt comes. He's think-ing of building a couple of houses on that piece on the other side of the tracks. Two of the men working at the flour mill have talked to him about it."

"Blessing is growing, that's for sure. Did you go by the store?"

"Jeffers didn't have the thread you wanted."

"No white thread?"

Haakan shook his head. "He's moved stuff around so it looks like he still has stock, but that store is getting emptier. When I asked him, he said he'd order more thread. Just overlooked it."

The two exchanged a look that said concern.

A gust of wind caught their attention.

"Another blizzard?"

"I don't think so. Just a storm." Haakan glanced toward the stove. "More soup?"

"Of course." Ingeborg took his bowl back for a refill and set it in front of him, laying her hand on his shoulder in passing.

"Takk." He ate some more and paused at another gust. "Wish I had a way to tell Andrew to stay home. Lars and I can handle the milking."

"I was planning on cleaning out the cheese house this week."

"Andrew and I'll take care of it." He finished his soup, ate a couple of cookies, and then tipped his head from one side to the other, stretching but wincing at the same time. "Think I'll use this storm time to sleep awhile."

"Are you all right?"

"I will be." He pushed back his chair and headed to the bedroom.

Ingeborg watched him go while she cleared the table. This wasn't like him at all. Times like this he'd usually spend reading or fixing something, not sleeping. But then, as he'd reminded her, they were getting older, and actually a bit of a lie-down sounded like a very good idea. After she finished the dishes. "Well, Father, should I be concerned about this or just grateful we can rest when the weather is bad?" She glanced at the windows but couldn't see outside, because it had turned dark, like an early dusk. The ice particles screamed in agony when they struck the glass panes. She should have offered to rub his neck and shoulders. Uff da, how thoughtless.

With the dishes dried and put away, the cookies stored in the cookie jar, and the table wiped off, she looked longingly toward the bedroom, then headed for her sewing machine instead. She had cut out a spring dress for Astrid, and now was as good a time as any to put it together. Like most winters, she'd moved the sewing machine into the kitchen and hung a blanket over the doorway to the parlor. With the machine cabinet and their two rockers, the kitchen was a bit crowded but cozy.

After setting the kerosene lamp on the shelf above the machine, she lost herself in the steady thump of the treadle and the beauty and speed of machine-made seams. As the bodice came together, she pressed the seams open with the flatirons she'd set on the stove. Blue dimity sprinkled with white daisies helped her ignore the wind that scolded at the eaves and tried to sneak under the door and around the windows.

"Lord, I am so ready for spring to come. I've no idea why this winter has seemed so long, but I want to be digging in the garden. At least I'll soon be able to start the seeds here in the house. If anyone came in, they would think I am losing my mind, talking to myself, but I know you listen and that your grace is sufficient for everything. After all, you said so." She thought of the verses she'd read that morning. She was reading Proverbs for a change. Seeking wisdom. Searching after her, along with insight. "Lord, I so want to be wise, to be filled with your wisdom." One of her favorite verses reminded her that she had the mind of Christ since she belonged to Him.

Snipping the threads, she returned to the ironing board, humming as she fetched the flatiron. What was something special she could make for supper? After setting the iron back on the stove and adding wood to the firebox, she went to check on Haakan. He must be really tired to have slept so long. She could hear his slight snore clear from the doorway. Stopping beside him at the bed, she laid the back of her hand against his forehead. He wasn't running a fever, and he didn't sound like he was catching a cold.

She was about to turn away when his eyes fluttered open.

"Checking on me?"

"Appears that way."

"You worry too much." He stretched and rolled over to face her. "Feels sinfully comfortable to be safe and warm and ignore that old wind howling outside."

"Your neck still hurt?"

"I don't think so."

"I could rub it if it does."

"Ja, then it hurts. Hurts powerful bad."

Ingeborg slapped him on the shoulder. "Oh, you."

"I'm getting to be just a poor old broken-down man."

"Scoot over so I can sit." With strong fingers she rubbed his shoulders, up along his neck and at the base of his head. His sighs of contentment were all she needed by way of gratitude. "You need a haircut." She stroked up through the hair that curled over the top of his shirt collar.

"Hmm. Anytime you want to give me one."

Ingeborg continued rubbing his neck and shoulders. Did she dare question him further about how he felt? Every time she mentioned it, he brushed her off, saying she was worrying for nothing. She wasn't worrying, just concerned. If only she could get him to talk with Dr. Elizabeth, maybe have her listen to his heart. If only . . . Her hands slowed as her mind speeded up.

"Remember how you were so concerned when Dr. Elizabeth insisted I have the surgery in Chicago?"

"Uh-huh." He twisted slightly so she could reach another spot.

"Well, now it is my turn. I want you to see Dr. Elizabeth and have her give you a good checkup." There, she'd said it.

He sighed and rolled over. "There is nothing wrong with me that a little extra rest now and then won't take care of. You worry too much." His voice slipped into that I'm-being-patient-with-you tone that husbands sometimes took on.

"Then just do it to relieve my mind."

He rolled his eyes. "All right. To stop your nagging, I'll go see Elizabeth one of these days."

"Haakan Bjorklund, I do not nag. And if you insist on being contrary, I'll take all that back rubbing back." *Thank you, Father. It does relieve my mind.* "And for that, you get no more cookies."

"Try me, wife." He raised her hand and kissed the back of it. "Happy now?"

She nodded. "Just do it soon. All right?"

15

As Gerald stepped out from his front door, he took in a deep breath. Although the snow had stopped, a few indecisive clouds still hung overhead. He looked at the train station, still quiet this early in the morning, but a thin line of smoke showed that the stationmaster had started up the stove. He smiled at the thought of Rebecca's return the next afternoon and the opportunity to tease her about her letter. It reminded him of her as a young teenager and her laugh when something amused her. That memory had carried him through many a dark night during the war, knowing that in Blessing, joy and family would be waiting for him if he could just survive one more night. That and this familiar skyline—his every morning view.

"It never gets old, does it?" Anner Valders said, joining his son.

"No." Gerald pulled his jacket up around his neck as they turned to walk down the street. "Still pretty cold."

"Expect it will be for a while. How's the new switchboard doing?"

Gerald smiled at his father. He had always admired the way he asked direct questions indirectly. "Not as cramped, and we can take a little more time on the calls without feeling like we're news hawkers. I like the privacy. No reason for people to linger over their mail pickup now."

Mr. Valders nodded. "Good. With Blessing growing and new lines going in, we need to develop a professional atmosphere. Are you going to be too bored?"

Gerald patted his jacket pocket with his new book, which he hoped to read over a quiet morning. "Not until spring anyway. Or I run out of reading." He waved good-bye and stomped his boots on the boardwalk before entering the post office to hang his coat on the back wall. Then after he entered the switchboard room, he slid the bar in place, closing off entry. It shouldn't take long for everyone to realize they could enter from the street now.

"Thanks," he said to Toby, who'd taken the night shift. "Ma has breakfast ready."

"Good. I'm starving. Are you working two shifts again?"

"Deborah can't come in until early afternoon, so I'll sleep then and come back around ten."

"Feeling okay?"

Gerald stared at his brother. "Don't you start now. It's enough with Mother watching for every yawn."

Toby laughed. "I meant maybe if you're not too tired from all these extra shifts we could go to Grafton tomorrow."

"Maybe. Anything I need to know?"

"Some very elderly lady keeps calling and asking for Marjorie. It's a wrong number, but I can't seem to make her understand. And she keeps shouting like I'm deaf."

A few minutes later the woman called again and Gerald patiently explained the situation.

"Thank you, young man. The other person kept talking to me like I was deaf."

Gerald managed to smother a laugh as he hung up. There were two more random calls, and then the quiet set in. After the heavy snow, that was a good indication all was well.

In between calls he glanced out the window, enjoying his view of

Blessing and the folks who lived there. So far this morning, there had been little movement on the streets, except for Harlan Jeffers, striding from place to place instead of staying in his store. An early morning rooster strutted, and so did Jeffers, unusual behavior for the man who all these months had stayed as invisible as possible. What was he up to? Gerald hadn't trusted him since the day he arrived in town, and he knew Jeffers knew it. Sometimes Gerald thought that Jeffers deliberately avoided him, as if the man were afraid. He shrugged off the rank smell Jeffers always reminded him of. Memories he'd like to forget.

"When, O Lord, will the war memories end? Please give me your peace." He turned from watching Jeffers to a lit-up switchboard.

In fact, he became so peaceful that when his mother arrived to relieve him for lunch, he'd lost all track of time.

"Well, that young friend of yours certainly is full of surprises," Hildegunn said.

Gerald hesitated before answering. He never liked this tone in her voice, as it bode a level of gossip that bordered on pleasure. The odd thing was he knew she wasn't mean or cruel like the men he had heard use the same tone during briefing meetings when discussing the enemy. He often wished he knew what had happened to her while she was growing up that had left this mark in her. But maybe whatever it was also became the reason she took in him and Toby as orphans and, in effect, saved their lives.

"Mother, I wish you didn't pass on gossip to me," he finally answered.

"Not gossip. Mr. Jeffers himself told me."

Gerald stiffened immediately. That man was hiding something for sure. He knew his kind: mean and slippery as a snake. What could he possibly have to do with Rebecca?

"They're getting married," she continued. "As soon as Rebecca returns, they'll set the date."

"Mother, you know that all we hear is not necessarily the entire truth."

"He said the brothers gave their permission yesterday. So she'll finally settle down."

"Finally? Mother, she's only nineteen."

"I know. So getting married will help settle her flighty ways."

Gerald rose from his seat and fought to keep his voice calm. "She is not flighty, Mother. Far from it. Please don't spread false words."

"Well, it's not your concern anymore. Go for your lunch."

Gerald stood outside for a few moments. Should he go and confront the man? He could feel his mother watching him. Why was she always so negative toward Rebecca? A movement caught his eye, and he saw Thorliff wave before entering the store. Then Mrs. Geddick headed across the street toward Garrisons' Groceries. Reluctantly he turned away. Maybe a confrontation now was premature. Yet the thought of that man even touching Rebecca made Gerald's skin prickle. There was something definitely wrong here. But what? He heard the train whistle announcing the eastbound arrival. Her train tomorrow couldn't arrive fast enough for his liking.

16

"HAAKAN, WAKE UP. Is something wrong?" Ingeborg shook his shoulder once and then again. While he muttered, he didn't really rouse. "Haakan!" Fear slid a fillet knife between her ribs. "God, help us. Haakan." She patted his cheeks, leaning over him, then shook him again.

He mumbled something but she had no idea what. It was his muttering that had awakened her in the first place. Lifting the chimney from the kerosene lamp, she struck a match, and when the wick flared, set the chimney back in place. With the light she could see that his eyelids were flickering, but other than the mumbling, he was not awake. Would not wake up? Or *could* not wake up? The blade struck deeper.

She fetched her medical bag and, setting it on the chair by the bed, pulled out her stethoscope and listened to his heart. Dr. Elizabeth had insisted she buy one and then taught her how to use it. There didn't seem to be any irregularities, but did it sound sluggish? She listened to her own heart to compare. Yes, his was slower, but then, hers was probably faster due to the fear wrapping her in its slithery arms, the same fear that knifed through her again.

She forced herself to take a deep breath, all the while her mind screaming for God to listen, to take over, to make everything right.

"Haakan." She spoke in a stern voice, ordering him to pay attention. Surely the shock of that would wake him up. Keeping herself from screaming at him took every ounce of self-control. Clamping his cold hand between hers, she raised her voice again. "Haakan, if you can hear me, squeeze my hand." She waited. Was that just a reflex or had he squeezed her hand? "Please, Haakan, pay attention. Squeeze my hand." Sure enough, the pressure was faint, but it was there.

His eyelids flickered again and slowly opened. His brow wrinkled, and his eyes wandered before focusing on her searching gaze. "Wh-why? Y-yel-ling?" The effort of speaking made him suck in a breath.

"O dear God, Father, thank you. Thank you. Oh, Haakan, you didn't respond when I shook you. You scared me half to death." She clung to his hand, kissing his cheek, ignoring the tears that dampened the front of his woolen underwear. *Something has happened. He is not himself, and Astrid isn't even here.* While she had no idea what time it was, dawn had not yet begun to lighten the sky.

Her mind ran through all the diagnoses she could think of. Heart attack? It didn't sound like it, and he'd not complained of pain. Had it not been for his muttering, she'd still be sleeping. Heart attacks usually caused intense pain. Had he mentioned not feeling well after supper? No. He'd read some of the articles from Thorliff's paper to her while she sat knitting soakers for Ellie's baby. They'd had a cup of coffee, and he'd enjoyed a piece of cake, the last of the spice apple. And they'd gone to bed. There was nothing unusual she could think of.

"Are you in pain anywhere?"

He answered with a barely perceptible shake of his head. "C-cold."

She'd not have heard him were she not paying such close attention. "I'll get a quilt. Be right back." The extra quilts were stored in the trunk that had come from Norway with her and Roald. The freshness of cedar wafted up as she lifted the lid. Onkel Olaf had lined the trunk with thin slats of cedar so the moths wouldn't eat the precious wool quilts and knit sweaters and vests. She also kept some of her hand-spun wool yarn in the bottom of the trunk. Giving the quilt a shake she hurried back to the bedside and flipped it over her husband, all the while sending more pleas heavenward.

Haakan lay on his back, his gaze roving around the room as though he weren't sure where he was.

She took his left hand in hers. "Please squeeze my hand." The squeeze wasn't strong, but at least he could follow instructions. "Give me your other hand."

A frown creased his forehead. He looked at his right arm, then back at her. He lifted his head, obviously trying to raise his arm, but nothing happened. A whimper near to broke her heart.

"It's all right. Don't worry about this." She laid her cheek against his. "We'll get through this. I know God has a purpose." *God, please heal this man. Show me how to help him. Wisdom, Lord. We need wisdom.*

Haakan clenched his teeth and glared at his right hand, as if it were the worst of enemies. He flopped his head back on the pillow, sweat beading on his forehead from the effort.

"Haakan, please look at me. Fighting it isn't going to help. Not right now. I'm sure you'll be able to move your arm again, but it might take time." She couldn't understand his garbled response. Fear filled his eyes, and he squeezed them shut, his left hand clenching hers until she winced in pain. "Haakan, let loose. I'm not going to leave you except to go put more wood in the stove. I'll make some coffee, and we'll get you sitting up, see if you feel better that way. Please."

He nodded and let go of her hand.

She rubbed it to bring the circulation back, needles stabbing like a foot that had gone to sleep. "I'm going now, all right? I'll just be in the kitchen."

He nodded and closed his eyes.

If only we had one of those telephones, I could call Elizabeth. But coming in the night like this wouldn't be necessary. What kind of tea can I make that might help him? She let her thoughts roam through her simples, reminding herself what each of them did. Perhaps Dr. Elizabeth would have something. She could give him laudanum. That might help him sleep, but he didn't seem to be in pain. He needed something to help him relax. She filled the stove and left the damper wide open to get it burning more quickly, then poured warm water from the reservoir into the coffeepot.

Setting a small pan of water to boil, she crossed to the bedroom door to check on her husband. He lay as she'd left him, his eyes closed, but she could see the quilts rise with his breathing. Could this be apoplexy? Taking a lamp in hand, she stopped in the pantry to search through the bottles of dried leaves and roots, all her natural pharmacopoeia that she had gathered through the summer and fall. Willow bark could help for pain. Foxglove for heart, but the problem didn't seem to be his heart. Something that would be calming . . . Peppermint? Comfrey?

She checked on him again, this time stopping at the side of the bed and listening for any breathing problems. He seemed to be sleeping, his mouth slightly open. Was something wrong with the right side of his face too? Oh no. Apoplexy, then. But people recover from apoplexy, and he recognized her. Maybe this was just a little one, a warning. Haakan was right-handed, although he'd learned to use both hands fairly equally. *Dear Lord, you know he's never been a patient man with being sick. Thank you that those times have been so few. He's always been so caring, so ready to take care of others, but he doesn't like being on the receiving end.* Back in the kitchen she added the ground coffee to the boiling water and pushed the pot back from the hottest part of the stove. The clock showed four o'clock.

In all her years of doctoring, she'd learned that this was the hour that so many of her patients died. The time when the body's defenses were the lowest. If only she could ask Pastor Solberg to come pray with them. *Lord, I need someone, someone here to help me pray. Please don't let him die.*

Haakan's breathing was strong, and when she listened to his heart again, his eyes fluttered open. This time his vision was clear, and he looked more like himself.

"W-what?" He frowned and tensed again.

"I think you've had an attack of apoplexy. That means a blood vessel broke in your brain, but I don't think it was a big one. You have some difficulty talking, and your right arm is not responding. But it will come back. Can you move your right leg?" She watched as the leg moved, including the foot. "Good, very good. I'm going to send Andrew for Dr. Elizabeth as soon as he comes to milk."

"Lars."

"Yes, if he gets here first. He doesn't always come to the house like Andrew does. The coffee is about ready. I'll put some cream in it, and we'll see how well you can swallow."

A frown shaped a V between his graying eyebrows.

"I know. But all we can do right now is find out what all is affected." She patted his hand before turning away to get the coffee. *How do I help him sit up?* Her mind darted from idea to idea, not stopping, but like a hummingbird tasting every possibility. She poured the coffee, added cream, and sipped to make sure it wasn't too hot. Grabbing a spoon, she returned to the bedroom.

Haakan lay tipped to the right, his eyes narrowed in anger.

"You couldn't wait." She shook her head, forcing a teasing smile to her lips. "I've been thinking on this. I will help you from the right, and together we will get you braced against the pillows. But you must let me know if you feel any pain." Ignoring his glare, she set the cup down and walked around the end of the bed. She stacked their pillows against the headboard and knelt on the bed. "On three. Use your legs as much as you can. I'll be your right arm."

He nodded, his jaw tense, and planted his left hand against the mattress. When she said three, they both pushed. She lifted as much as possible and braced against his shoulder. They were both puffing when he sat fairly upright, leaning only slightly to the right. She pushed against him and stepped back.

"I'm going to start with the spoon, and let's see how your throat works."

He nodded and sucked in a deeper breath.

At least your lungs are working. She came around the bed.

He reached with his left hand for the edge of the mattress to counteract a tendency to slip to the side.

"I'll get another pillow for that later." She picked up the cup and, dipping a spoonful, held it to his lips. When he took it into his mouth, she watched his Adam's apple move down and up. "It went down?"

He nodded.

"Oh, thank you, God." She felt like collapsing on the bed and letting the tears roll, but held firmly on to her emotions. Instead, she held out another spoonful. After several more swallows, she laid the spoon down. "Do you want to try drinking from the cup?"

"Yes." His voice came stronger.

She held the cup for him and let him drink. "Once is enough for right now, I think."

He nodded and rested his head back, his eyes drifting closed. Ingeborg sat down on the edge of the bed and took his hand, lifting it to her cheek. He turned it and cupped her jaw, the gentle pressure speaking of years of love and caring.

"We're going to get through this," she whispered. "It could be so much worse."

"Ja."

"Do you need anything?"

He shook his head.

"Then I'm coming back to bed for a while and watch you rest. I know I should start the bread, but it can wait."

He nodded and sighed.

Ingeborg tapped a forefinger against her chin. "Let's get you prone first. I'm sure getting down will be easier than up."

Haakan nodded, his face slightly slack on the right side. He dug in his heels and scooted himself part way before listing to the right. Ingeborg went around the bed again and, moving his right arm, helped move him down. After rearranging the pillow, she pulled the covers up and tucked them around his shoulders.

"I'll be right back." The ticking clock sounded loud in the silence. The cat chirped once but didn't leave her box. Even she knew it was not yet morning. Maybe she should just stay up. After all, would she be able to sleep anyway? Or should she go for Andrew now? Something said she might need all the sleep she could get, so she refilled the stove, turned the damper toward closed, and moved the coffeepot to the cooler part of the stove. That's all she needed was to burn the coffeepot dry. When that had happened years ago, the coffee had tasted burnt for months. She lit a lantern and put it outside the door. If Lars arrived before Andrew, the light should bring him in.

Slipping back under the covers, she lay on her left side so that she could put her right arm over her husband's now steadily rising and falling chest. *Lord, you are our great physician. Please, I beg of you, see your way clear to heal Haakan of this infirmity. Restore the muscles and nerves so that he can use his hand with full strength.* The thought of the things he'd not be able to do with one hand pushed her down into the feather bed. She closed her eyes and inhaled and then released all the air in her lungs until she felt flat. Warmth started in her icy cold feet and moved upward. She breathed deeply again and saw in her mind Jesus sitting beside a creek in a grassy field. The smile He gave her made the sun seem dim. She could even hear his voice speaking gently, *Come unto me.* Tears seeped from the corners of her eyes. *Come unto me.* Was there anyplace else she would rather be? If only she could carry Haakan there. She fell asleep leaning against Jesus' knee.

"Mor."

The voice came from a far distance. Why was Andrew calling her? Andrew. *Oh, thank you, Father, it is morning.* As the memories of the night swept back, she kept herself from throwing back the quilt and instead slid out and headed for the door.

"You overslept. Are you all right?" Andrew stood on the rug by the door, removing his winter hat.

Ingeborg put a finger to her lips and glanced over her shoulder. "Is it Far?"

She nodded. "He woke in the night confused, and his right arm isn't responding."

"Can he talk?"

"With a bit of difficulty. But he can swallow, and he can move his leg. Is Lars at the barn yet?"

"I don't know. You want me to go get Dr. Elizabeth?"

"Yes, but let me check on him first to see how he is now. He went back to sleep about four o'clock." Andrew followed her into the bedroom and stared down at his father.

"He is breathing good."

"Yes. I think it is what they call apoplexy. A vessel ruptures in the brain, but this one doesn't seem to be a major one, because—" She stopped and leaned over the bed at Haakan's groan.

His eyes fluttered open. "It wasn't ... a dream ... was it?" His words were slightly slurred and slow, but he was talking far better.

"No. No, it wasn't. Andrew is here."

"Sorry."

"I'll talk to Lars, have him send Kaaren over, and then ski in to Thorliff's. You don't have to worry about a thing but getting better." Andrew's voice choked on the words. "Can I get you anything before I go?"

"No. Wind ... sound ... not good." Haakan forced the words out.

"The sky is clear this morning. I'll be back soon." Andrew touched his father's hand. "All shall be well."

Ingeborg sniffed at hearing those old, old words of comfort coming from her son. *All shall be well. All manner of things shall be well.* Pastor Solberg had read them from a book of famous early Christians one time. Juliana of Norwich was a devout Christian writer born in the 1300s. Grateful for the reminder of the words and the woman, Ingeborg followed Andrew back to the kitchen. "Have Thorliff telephone Pastor Solberg, please."

"I will." Andrew threw one arm around her shoulders and hugged her.

She closed the door behind him and leaned against it, feeling the cold biting through her flannel nightdress. She'd not even taken time to put her robe on. *Lord, protect my son. Let Elizabeth know what can be done.* She headed back to the bedroom to dress. *Let the worst part of this day be over.*

17

STARTING BREAKFAST WAS A good substitute for worry. And knowing that help was on the way eased Ingeborg's mind too. Truly God had blessed them all with one another. Andrew would have Lars send Kaaren over. He knew how much Ingeborg needed her.

"Inge?" The voice sounded faint, and she ran back to the bedroom immediately. Wiping her hands on her apron, she stood at the bedside. "What do you need?"

"To get up."

"I'd rather you wait until Elizabeth sees you. A bit more bed rest might be good." In case too much activity could cause a recurrence. But she hated to tell him that. Memories of the days he had been so sick with the mumps made her dread what lay ahead. But still, he was alive and had movement in his arms and legs. *Thank you, Lord.*

"If you help me . . . sit up, I can swing my legs . . . over the edge, and maybe . . . I can stand."

Had the incident affected his hearing? She started to say something, then recognized the steel clamping of his teeth together. "Can't we take this one step at a time?"

"That's what I want . . . to do. . . . Take a step."

"I'd rather Andrew were here to help pick you up if you fall. You are too heavy for me. Please. He'll be back any minute. He skied and left about twenty minutes ago."

"It seems longer."

"You fell right back to sleep when he left. Rest is healing."

A knock at the door caught her attention. "Promise me you'll wait until I can help you?" At his nod, she headed back to the kitchen in time to see Pastor Solberg closing the door behind him.

"How is he?"

"Wanting to get up."

"Good. Dr. Elizabeth called me, but I was about on my way over here anyway." He took off his hat and hung it on the peg, then his coat. "What time did it happen?"

"About three o'clock."

He shook his head. "Amazing. I woke at three with the absolute assurance that I needed to pray for Haakan. Like God gave me explicit instructions."

"I am not surprised. I've had that happen too, as you know. Thank you. Come and see him. Maybe you can keep him in bed until Elizabeth gets here." She led the way and motioned him ahead of her through the door. "You have company, Haakan."

"Good morning, my friend. You are looking better than I was afraid of." Solberg shook Haakan's extended left hand like that was the most normal thing in the world. He explained God calling him, and Haakan nodded.

"I–I'm glad . . . you came." While his speech was still slow, his words were more clear.

"Now, how can I help you?"

"I was about to bring coffee in. Would you like a cup also?"

"Of course." He smiled at Ingeborg and then turned his attention back to Haakan. "It affected your right side. Your arm, I see. How about the leg and foot?"

"I can move them."

"Good, good. Can you drink, chew?"

Haakan shrugged.

"Looks like you'll be using your left hand more for a while."

Ingeborg turned at the sound of the door opening. "Andrew?"

"Be right there," he called.

"I asked Haakan to wait to get up until there were men around to help. Just in case."

"Elizabeth will be here shortly," Andrew said as he came into the room and studied his father. "Thorliff was hitching the sleigh as I left." He greeted the pastor before returning his attention to his father. "Do you hurt anywhere?"

"A bit of a . . . headache. Thirsty."

"I'll get the coffee."

"None for me right now. I'll go help Lars finish the milking. Unless you need me here?"

"You go," Haakan said before Ingeborg could answer. He nodded to the pastor. "I need to . . ."

"You might shut the door on your way to get the coffee," Pastor Solberg said.

Ingeborg started to say something but quickly realized what the need was. So her husband was having a fit of modesty. That was far better than what could have been. Incontinency often happened with apoplexy. His pride would have a hard time with that. She figured that was one more hurdle to cross and was grateful they needn't. She did as asked and pulled the heating coffeepot off the front lid so she could add more wood. Perhaps oatmeal would be best for breakfast, something that didn't need chewing. Maybe she should run some of the rolled oats through the meat grinder to make the cereal even finer, as she used to do for the babies.

Praise that he wasn't worse dueled with worry about how Haakan would deal with this. *I know, Lord: Cast all my cares on you. I keep doing that, but they keep coming back. Would you please hang on to them a little harder?* After bringing the grinder in from the pantry, she set it on the table and unscrewed the crank until it would fit, then slid the grinder in place and cranked it down firmly. Fetching the rolled oats from the tin she kept them stored in, she dug out a cupful and poured it into the hopper while turning the hand crank. As soon as she had two cups she poured it into the kettle, where she had four cups of water and a dash of salt already simmering. Once the oats were boiling, she moved the covered kettle to the back of the stove, where it wouldn't burn, and went back to the grinding. Might as well do enough for several days now that she had the grinder out. Of course she could have used the coffee grinder, but it would be slower, and the oatmeal would have tasted of coffee.

The jingle of harness and bells announced both Elizabeth and Thorliff. He was quickly ushering her through the door as they both kicked the snow off their boots.

"How is he?" Elizabeth asked instead of a greeting.

"Better than at three this morning." Ingeborg swallowed. "It could have been so much worse. Thank God it isn't."

"Pastor Solberg is here?" Thorliff hung up both his and his wife's coat.

"Ja, he is helping Haakan with personal things."

"Well, his pride is a good thing." Elizabeth picked up her medical bag. "I'll knock first."

Ingeborg brought out a tray from the bottom of the cupboard in the pantry and set out coffee cups. While most of them drank theirs black, she added her cream and sugar glass pieces that Haakan had bought her and that had graced her table ever since. The cookie jar was empty, so she filled the cups and started to lift the tray.

Thorliff beat her to it. "I'll carry it. You take care of the door."

Tapping on her own bedroom door seemed as strange as serving Haakan coffee in bed. She led the way to the chest of drawers and pushed things to the side so Thorliff could set the tray there.

"I'll get chairs," Thorliff whispered in her ear.

While handing Pastor Solberg a cup of coffee, she watched Elizabeth moving Haakan's arms, hands, legs, and feet, instructing him to push against her hand each time. The left side appeared unaffected. That was the good news. How badly damaged the right was would still need to be determined.

When she'd finished, she stood studying him. "We'll know more when you sit up on the edge of the bed."

"We did that a few minutes ago," Pastor Solberg said, looking from Ingeborg to Elizabeth. "He listed to the right, but though shaky seemed pretty stable."

"He wasn't able to push himself up against the headboard during the night, but once we got him propped up, he did fine."

"But tired," Haakan added.

"Did you feel sick to your stomach?" Elizabeth took up her questioning mode again.

He half shrugged.

"Headache?"

"Some . . . but not severe." His Norwegian accent was more pronounced than Ingeborg had heard in a long time.

"Do you have pain anywhere?"

Another shrug.

She looked to Ingeborg. "Does that mean none or a little or he doesn't know?"

Ingeborg hoped that her puzzlement didn't show on her face. "I'm not sure. Haakan is never sick."

"Can you drink from a cup?"

"He drank some water earlier. I spoon-fed him coffee, and he could swallow just fine."

"How about trying yourself?"

He nodded and glanced to his wife, holding thumb and forefinger close together to indicate a small amount.

She handed Thorliff his, glanced at Elizabeth, who shook her head, and took a cup back to the kitchen to pour some out. *I should have thought of that. Of course he'd not want a full cup to start with.* She poured it back into the coffeepot and returned to the bedroom to add cream and a bit of sugar. At the look of disgust he gave her, she raised her eyebrows.

"Think of it as medicine." She sat on the left side of the bed and held out the cup. He raised his left arm, and while his hand shook, he was able to take hold of the cup and bring it to his mouth to sip. However, the effort sent him slowly tipping to the right.

"Your body will compensate as you do more things. Just be aware." Elizabeth propped a pillow next to his side and settled his right arm on his leg. "Finish your coffee, and then we'll see about getting you upright."

Elizabeth looked to Ingeborg. "Remember how we worked with Mr. Hedstrom from south of here? Massaging his legs and moving them for him until he could regain his strength?"

Ingeborg nodded.

"We'll do the same again. Thorliff can help you."

"As will I." Pastor Solberg crossed one leg over the other and rested his coffee cup on his knee. "You have a great number of friends who will be glad to do whatever you need."

"Good thing it is winter." Haakan lifted his cup again and drained it this time, then held it out. "Make it . . . black this time, please?"

"Let's get you standing upright first." Elizabeth beckoned to Thorliff. "You be his other side."

Thorliff slid his arm behind his father from the right side to brace him. "You can push against me."

Haakan gritted his teeth, and the effort furrowed two vertical lines in his forehead. He wiggled his body closer to the edge of the bed and heaved a sigh. But when he tried to stand using his left hand and arm as a brace, he half rose and slumped back down. When Ingeborg moved forward, extending an arm for him to grab, he waved her away. And tried again.

Ingeborg closed her eyes against the agony of watching his struggle. She could help him. Thorliff was trying to help him without doing the lifting for him. Was it better to let him struggle or to assist? *Lord, help us know what to do. Please. He needs strength, and I need strength, but of a different kind.*

She could feel Pastor Solberg praying beside her.

Haakan sucked in a deep breath and fought to rise again. His upper body strained against the weakness of his right side, but he couldn't stand all the way up.

"All right now, as your doctor I am taking over. I wanted you to see what it will take and to give me an idea of where we are." She paused and gentled her voice. "Please, now, let us all help you. It is not a sign of weakness or a crime to accept help. You would do the same for any of us if the need arose."

In spite of the chill of the room, sweat trickled down the side of Haakan's face. "I never thought . . . I'd be unable to stand up. . . . It has always been so easy."

"I know. But soon you will stand up on your own again. You will walk and use that right arm, but it will take some time."

"How long?"

"I don't know. But you have your own private doctor here who will do all that I tell her and then some. We don't know nearly enough about the brain, but we do know that nerves and muscles that are damaged heal themselves."

"God made our bodies that way, to heal and grow strong again," Pastor Solberg said. "Think about when you cut yourself, how that heals from the inside out and all without our assistance." He moved to sit down by Haakan. "This is a bump in the road, not the end of the journey."

"I-I can't be—" Haakan paused and slowly shook his head—"a cripple." He stared at his right hand. "Please, God, please."

"We're going to do all that we can to make sure that doesn't happen. Now, everyone, here are some things I learned." Elizabeth took Haakan's good hand. "Hang on to someone's arm here, above the wrist. You might also find that a cane helps. Something to assist your balance. We're going to help you stand now. Thorliff, help lift him but don't rush him. Pastor Solberg, stand in front of him, just in case. Ready on three. One, two, three." Between the three of them they had Haakan upright and, though shaky, standing on his feet.

Ingeborg felt like applauding. The relief on her husband's face brought tears and a clogged throat. "Thank you, Father God, thank you."

"Are you dizzy?"

"Some."

"Headache?"

"Some."

"Can you feel the floor with your right foot?"

"Ja. It is cold."

"Good. Can you move your right foot?"

Haakan nodded as slowly his right foot moved forward a couple of inches.

"That's wonderful."

He gave Elizabeth a look that screamed *Are you crazy?*

"I know." She shook her head at him. "You and I are looking for different things. If you couldn't feel the floor or move your foot, you would have a far harder battle to fight. This is good news. Can you move your fingers on your right hand?"

The others watched his hand. Ingeborg watched his face as he focused on moving. Slowly one finger shook and moved an inch or so. The sigh of relief was in unison.

"All right now, let's see if you can move your left foot. That means put your weight on your right. Thorliff, be ready to hold him."

"Here, let me take your place." Pastor Solberg moved Elizabeth away from Haakan's side and slid his arm around Haakan's waist. "Now let's see what we can do."

Thorliff braced his father with his left arm and held his right arm firmly. Haakan leaned against his son and shuffled the left foot forward. He leaned the other way and moved the right—not far but moved it. Sweat made him blink.

"Hot in here." He raised his head and sniffed. "Is something burning?"

Ingeborg sniffed and groaned. "The oatmeal. I let the oatmeal burn. Uff da." She hurried from the room to the sound of chuckles that turned to laughter.

"God be praised. We have something to laugh about. But now what will we have for breakfast?"

"Burned oatmeal isn't so bad," Pastor Solberg called. "Praise God, we have cream to put on it."

18

SAYING GOOD-BYE TO KURT was almost as difficult as saying good-bye to Penny. Was she throwing away the possibility of a real dream for an imaginary one? But to leave Blessing for good—that could never happen. Although, had it happened to Grace? Could real love do that?

Rebecca stared out the train window, hoping no one could see the tears that insisted on running down her cheeks, no matter how many times she mopped them away.

Penny said they'd try to come for a visit in the summer, but June or July seemed as far away as eternity. And while Kurt had promised to write, as had she, somehow their good-byes had had a feeling of finality to them. If she had stayed in Bismarck, could their friendship have developed into something deeper? She was almost certain he had wanted to kiss her, but with Penny, Hjelmer, and the children seeing her off, he'd just squeezed her hand and said, "Think of me."

She was sure Maydell would dub that little phrase *most romantic.*

Thinking of home dried the tears, even though she could most likely wring water out of her handkerchief. Trying to figure out all that might have gone on at home in her absence was about as useless as hanging out the wash in a thunderstorm. Would Gus have bought more than one cow? His diatribe about her wasting money on a soda shop when there weren't enough cows to supply milk for the cheese house, let alone cream for making ice cream, made her wonder if her dream was indeed frivolous.

Penny didn't think so. In fact, the night before, when helping Rebecca pack, she'd offered to be a silent partner with a loan that wouldn't need repaying for several years. By silent, she said she was available for advice but would not try to tell Rebecca what to do, quite unlike other members of the Baard family.

"Gus thinks my dream is selfish," Rebecca had said.

"Nonsense," Penny replied. "What is all the egg and butter money the women keep aside in sugar bowls and tins but a type of small business? And one that often helps the family financially. No one thinks of it as such, but it is. Everyone has a right to have a business if that is what they want." Penny laughed. "I'd like to see Gus tell Ingeborg her cheese is just a dream."

Rebecca had gasped at the thought and then joined Penny laughing.

Rebecca now took out the writing case that Penny had given her as a hint she wanted more letters and used the pencil to add to her lists of needed supplies. Her time with Thomas at Benson's Soda Emporium had opened her eyes to the real complexity of running such a business. And the amount of needed supplies.

But what if I fail? What a terrible waste of everything if I do. The argument buzzed again like angry bees barred from their hive. She sighed as she watched the countryside stream past.

Yesterday, as they sat over afternoon tea before the children came home from school, Penny had reminded her to pray about the whole matter, to lay it before the Lord, as Agnes used to say and Ingeborg still did. Saying it was one thing and doing so another.

"You can't let other people make up your mind for you," Penny had said.

"But your store was necessary to the people of Blessing. Where else could they buy tools and boots and spices and sewing machines and—"

"I took a real chance on the sewing machines, like you will with the soda shop. No one really needed a machine. They'd been sewing by hand since they were not much older than toddlers. But I believed that women were as entitled to machines to help them do better as the men were. You didn't see those men still plowing with a hand plow pulled behind a mule or an ox. As new equipment was developed, they bought it. That's why Hjelmer went into the machinery business."

"I think he wishes he'd stayed with that."

Penny's eyes took on a faraway look, as though she were watching another scene. She nodded slowly and sighed. "I wish he had. That's for sure. All those years when I wanted him home more, he was happy in the legislature. I should have just kept my big mouth shut."

"You didn't force him to take this job."

"No. Nobody can force Hjelmer to do anything. And I wouldn't want to do that, but he knew how I felt, and he was trying to do what was best for all of us." Penny heaved another sigh. "But here we are in Bismarck, and we have to make the best of it. So if I can help you with your business, maybe that will help me feel better too. I'll be glad when you can get a telephone and we can talk every now and then."

"If Gus has his way, the telephone will never come to the farm."

"I have an idea. You can put a telephone in your store, and people can use it and pay you for the service. Soon the telephone will become more and more a part of everyone's life, whether Gus thinks ahead or not." She grinned at Rebecca. "How'd he get to be such an old grouch anyway?"

"He doesn't want to spend any money, that's how. He said I should put my hundred dollars that I got from Mr. Gould for graduation into the farm fund instead of into a harebrained idea like mine."

The conductor walking through the car brought her back to the present. Cigar smoke filled the air because it was too cold outside to open any windows. Male laughter exploded from the group playing cards at the rear of the car. The woman in the seat behind her made a remark about the lack of manners of those indulging in such an obnoxious and smelly habit.

Gus had brought a cigar home to smoke one time. Seemed Mr. Jeffers had encouraged him to try it. She'd had to air out the house afterward and told him that if he wanted to smoke that stinky thing, he'd have to do so out in the middle of the wheat fields, where the wind could blow all the smoke away.

She'd noticed later that he looked a bit green around the edges but thought better of saying anything. She also wondered how her brother had allowed Mr. Jeffers to influence him so. That man made her skin crawl. Oh, if only Penny and Hjelmer would come back to stay.

Rebecca leaned her head against the back of the seat and closed her eyes. The first thing she wanted to do when she got home was have a talk with Gerald. He always treated her questions and ideas with thoughtful consideration. Like Penny did. What would he have to say about all her adventures in Bismarck? She hoped she could make him laugh at her skating stories. Gerald needed to laugh more. Penny had thought his bringing her the little box of candy before she'd left home was romantic. She'd not eaten it because she hated to open the box. She thought a bit. Perhaps boxes of candy like that would be a good thing to carry in her soda shop. Along with jars of candy like Penny used to have at the store. Oh, all the things she could do—if she ever got to start her business.

19

Blessing, North Dakota

THE SIGHT OF GERALD waiting for her on the platform made her heart give an extra thump. Rebecca thanked the conductor for handing her down the train stairs and the step and smiled up at her friend. She felt like throwing her arms around his neck but knew that would be all over town before she got home.

"What a nice surprise. How did you know when I'd be coming?"

He looked a bit sheepish. "My mother read the back of the envelope you sent to Gus." He took her valise. "Do you have more luggage? Your brothers just pulled up. I think they got stopped by the train."

"Yes, there's a trunk in the baggage car." She glanced down the platform to see her trunk being unloaded. "So, my friend, how have you been?" Wouldn't it be nice if she could just tuck her arm around his and go strolling through town? The audacious thought forced her to suppress a giggle.

"Very well, thank you. From your letter I think you had a good time in Bismarck."

"Oh, I did. I have so much to tell you. Do you like working the switchboard?"

"I do, although it gets a bit boring at times. I thought of taking up wood carving or perhaps knitting. . . ." She laughed along with him. "But I have plenty of time to read, and that's a very good thing."

Should I tell him about Kurt? The thought flitted on past. "I loved the box of candy." She wasn't about to tell him she'd not eaten it. She watched Gus approaching out of the corner of her eye. From the way he walked, she was pretty sure her brothers were in a hurry to get on home.

"I was hoping you would have time for a cup of coffee at the boardinghouse, but it looks like they want to go." They were walking slowly toward the hitching rail.

"That your trunk?" Gus asked without a hello or welcome home or any such pleasantry.

"Yes, and hello to you too."

He nodded to Gerald and continued past them.

"He seems a bit gruff." Gerald looked toward the sleigh, where Knute waited.

"I know. I hope nothing has happened with Dorothy." *Puzzling,* Rebecca thought. "Thank you for the offer of coffee. I'd love to talk for a while—very soon. Oh, by the way, Penny said to tell you hello."

"Good. Are they doing well?"

Rebecca shrugged. "Hi, Knute."

"We need to hurry." Knute kept his eyes locked on the horse's rump.

Well, how rude can one get? Rebecca turned. "Thank you for coming." She glanced toward her brother and shrugged again.

"I'll see you soon."

Rebecca nodded and settled the robe over her lap. Gus stuffed her trunk in beside her and climbed in front with his brother, who backed the horse almost before Gus was seated. What was going on with these two? After she tried twice to make conversation and all she got in return was silence or a grunt, she settled into flip-flopping between worrying and fuming, the latter of which was taking precedence.

"All right, what haven't you told me?" Rebecca asked as soon as they entered Knute's home. She crossed her arms, staring at her brothers.

She hadn't even greeted Dorothy and the kids yet, but she had to know what was up with her brothers.

Both men made slow work of taking off their coats and hats. Hanging them on the pegs on the wall took a great deal of precision. Exchanging looks raised the tension in the room so that even little Hans sat still in his chair, staring at the adults. When he started to whimper, Dorothy turned to the table and broke off a piece of bread for him.

"Sugar?" he begged.

"No, later."

"Sugar." His tone switched to demanding.

Rebecca refused to be distracted. Whatever it was, both brothers knew about it.

Gus sucked in a deep breath. "Someone asked if he could court you, and since you want to be married so bad, we—" he turned to include his brother—"we told him he could talk to you." The words came in such a rush that Rebecca felt like waving her hands to make him stop, or at least slow down.

Gerald. The name leaped into her mind, followed immediately by a no. Why would they be acting this way if it were Gerald? They knew he'd been her friend. Or they should have known. *Obtuse* was a word Penny had used in reference to the two Baard men. "Who? What *him* are you talking about?" One of the Geddick brothers? Someone new in town?

"Mr. Jeffers," Gus finally said. "At the store."

"Mr. Jeffers?" She turned to look at Dorothy, who was shaking her head, her face set like stone.

"I told them this was one of the stupidest things they'd ever done, but—"

"We didn't say you'd marry him or anything. Just that he could come see you."

Rebecca shuddered. "That man makes me want to wash my hands." Or take a whole bath. No wonder she'd felt him watching her the last time she was in the store. Shaking her head, she stared from Gus to Knute. "Do you hate me or something?"

"Now, don't go getting foolish or some crazy thing. He asked, and we said he'd have to talk with you. That we don't make decisions for our sister." Gus glared at Knute, waiting for him to agree.

"That's right." Knute kept his back to them, carefully stuffing his gloves into a jacket pocket.

Gus took a step forward. "If you hadn't been gone so long, this wouldn't have happened. I . . . we . . . uh, went to the store only two days ago, and he asked us then." He took another step forward. "We were only being polite."

"Oh, n-now you are blaming this on Mor's trying to t-teach you good manners?" Rebecca was even stuttering now, she was so angry.

"All you have to do is go tell him you don't want to see him, that's all."

"That's all? You go tell him you made a mistake and your sister is NOT interested."

Both men took a step backward, glancing at each other, then both staring at her. "But we gave our word."

Hans started to cry. Sarah stood beside Rebecca and sneaked her hand into her aunt's. "Please don't cry, Auntie Rebecca."

Rebecca dashed at the tears she hadn't realized were falling. "I'll write him a letter, and you can deliver it." She stared right at Gus, sure that her eyes were blazing. How could there be tears? Surely they'd turned to steam.

"All right, that's enough for now. Our supper is getting cold. Sarah, you sit by Aunt Rebecca, and Swen, you by Gus. Knute, please say the grace."

Without looking at Rebecca again, both the men did as told and quickly everyone was seated. Knute mumbled a prayer, they all said amen, and Dorothy started the serving plates and bowls around.

Rebecca stared at her two brothers, who were carefully not looking at her or at Dorothy. How could they even think such a possibility! Her mother always said to put the best face on what someone else did.

That's what the Bible said to do. Sometimes it was easier to do that than other times. This was one of the *others*. Thoughts chased each other through her mind like swallows darting for insects, leaving no track or pattern. How to figure like a man does. That was an impossibility. She hit on an idea.

"Would you like to have Mr. Jeffers for a brother-in-law?" How she managed to keep the rage from licking at the words, she had no idea. The question came out in an offhand way, something to congratulate herself for. She caught a nod of approval from Dorothy. The shock on her brothers' faces would have made her laugh at any other time.

"I suppose we could live in the farmhouse with you, Gus. After all, you seem to need someone to take care of you." Thoughts of the messy kitchen likely awaiting her narrowed her eyes. Again, she had to swallow a laugh. The look on his face told far more than anything he could say.

"But . . . but there is a perfectly fine place to live at the store." His voice squeaked on the last word.

"True, but then perhaps I should help you find a wife to do your laundry and cleaning and cooking. You don't seem to do so well yourself."

"I can find my own wife, thank you very much."

"But I can't find my own husband?"

Dorothy choked on her bread and had to leave the table.

Rebecca stole glances at the children. Their eyes were so wide, there was hardly room for their mouths. Never in his life had Knute paid more attention to his plate. Her focus returned to Gus and nailed him to the chair.

Self-righteousness melted like a snowbank in the spring sun. Gus's shoulders slumped. "Please pass the potatoes."

Rebecca let out a deep breath. They did mean well. She knew that. She could just picture Mr. Jeffers casually mentioning the idea of marrying her and then pushing until they agreed. He made the slime from a puddle in the cow pen look pretty. And smell better.

They finished supper without any more discussion. Sarah asked about her cousins in Bismarck, and as soon as they finished eating, Rebecca brought out the things she and Penny had made. The doll dress that matched Sarah's new dress was a real hit. Sarah ran and got her doll so Rebecca could help her put it on.

"Look, even buttons." She beamed at Rebecca as she hugged her doll. "Thank you. Know something else?"

"No, what?"

"My tooth is loose." She wiggled an upper tooth. "Ma says it will fall out soon, and a new one will grow in."

"That's right. Let's go help your ma with the dishes."

"Thank you for the new shirt," seven-year-old Swen said. "The sleeves are even long enough." He held his arms out to show her.

"You are growing so fast that I wasn't sure how long to make them." She patted his shoulder and dug down in her basket. "Think you can share these with your brother and sister?"

He took the brown paper sack and looked inside. "Hans is too little to suck on candy. But Sarah and me will like it."

"Perhaps you are right. Why don't you get Hans a cookie to make him happy too."

Swen held out the sack. "Don't you want one too?"

"Yes, thank you." Rebecca smiled at her handsome nephew and watched as he offered the candy to all the adults before taking one of his own. She should have brought more. What a generous little soul he was.

She rose and joined Dorothy at the stove, taking the dish towel that Sarah handed her.

"I'm so sorry," Dorothy muttered under her breath. "I just don't know what got into those two. I've barely spoken to Knute since."

"Maybe men don't see the same things in other men that women do." Being charitable took a strong act of will at this point.

"Maybe." Dorothy set a soapy dish in the rinse water. "But I think they should have to go back and make it right."

"Me too, but since I need to go shopping tomorrow, I'll just tell him I'm not interested. Otherwise who knows what other promises they'll make for me. I have to make it clear."

"Your letter mentioned a man you met in Bismarck."

Rebecca nodded. "His name is Kurt von Drehl. He is so handsome I couldn't believe he wanted to be with me."

"Rebecca Baard, haven't you looked in a mirror lately? Besides, what a romantic way to meet—on the skating rink."

"Ja, with me tumbled on the ice. Poor Little Gus was so mad at the boy who ran into me that he was ready to go slug it out. By the way, he doesn't like to be called Little Gus anymore, as he reminded me several times."

"Is Penny as homesick as she sounds in her letters?"

"Yes, but she says she will make the best of it. I got the feeling that Hjelmer is not as happy with his job as he thought he would be. But he is home more than he used to be. He didn't say so, but I think he misses everyone here in Blessing too."

"Hjelmer always liked the traveling."

"That's true." Rebecca dried a plate and set it on the table. "What all have I missed out on since I was gone?"

"Well, the big thing was the men not bringing back as many cows as they'd hoped. And being charged so much more than the man had originally said. Some folks just don't keep their word. He said he could have sold them for twice as much. There just aren't enough cows to go around. Nor pigs nor sheep either."

"What does Ingeborg say?"

"That she'll take as much milk as can be spared and God will provide for all of us. If we have a good wheat harvest, that will surely help."

If—always the big word for farmers. If the rain came, but not too much. If the sun shone, but not too hot. Let alone hail, tornadoes, grasshoppers, fire. Rebecca set the last plate on the table, and Dorothy put them all away in the cupboard. And Gus thought her shop was a risk.

"I did learn how pleasant it is to have a telephone in the house.

I know Gus will refuse to have one put in, but you could maybe talk Knute into it. Just think, I could have called you to ask what you needed from the stores in Bismarck."

"Uff da, that is too much. What will they think of next?" Dorothy looked around to find Hans curled up on the blanket kept for him behind the stove. He always hated to go to bed because he might miss something, so they had appropriated the warm space behind the stove. "I need to get the children to bed."

"We need to be getting home too. Thank you for the good supper."

"I was hoping to get over to your house to clean it up before you got home, but things got away from me." She patted the burgeoning mound under her apron. "Somehow this seems to slow me down some."

"How much longer?"

"A few weeks, I think. Dr. Elizabeth said I needed to get off my feet, but how does one do that with all this?" A sweeping gesture included the entire house and all those in it.

"I'll come over every day for a while and take care of things so you can rest. Why didn't you tell me that before?"

Dorothy shrugged.

Rebecca stepped into the parlor, where her two brothers sat talking. "We better be getting home."

"Oh. Is it that late?" Gus put down the newspaper and got to his feet. "See you in the morning."

"I'll help you get the horse."

"No need." Gus still didn't meet her gaze when he headed for the door to put on his things.

"You make a list of what you need from town," Rebecca told Dorothy, "and I'll get yours too." She reached for her coat. "Send it home with Gus in the morning."

"I will." Dorothy started to kneel to reach for Hans, but Rebecca stopped her.

"I'll do that." *What is the matter with that hardheaded man in there?*

Doesn't he pay attention that his wife is big as can be and he could help her a little? Maybe the baby sister needed to get her back up and get some changes started around there.

When they got home, again without a word, Gus filled the stove with wood, adjusted the draft so that it would burn slowly through the night, and headed for bed. He had taken over their parents' room on the first floor, and Rebecca had the one upstairs over the kitchen, so the chimney helped heat her room, plus a small grate in the floor let the heat rise. Rebecca took one of the bricks they kept warm under the stove and, wrapping it in a towel, took it and a kerosene lamp upstairs and slipped the brick under the covers of her bed to warm it.

At Penny's they'd had a furnace in the cellar, and heat came to every room in the house. Not so here. The windowpanes wore ice designs that turned to fire when the sun hit them in the morning.

Leaving her trunk for the morning, she undressed standing over the register and hung her clothes on the pegs along the wall, then pulled on her nightdress. She grabbed her brush and a ribbon and sat in her bed, pulling the quilts firmly over her legs.

She should have brushed her hair downstairs, where it was warmer. Thinking of the stove reminded her of Hans curled up in his special cave with his thumb and forefinger in his mouth. The dog used to sleep behind the stove like that, when they had a dog. How warm and cuddly Hans had been as she'd carried him into his bed, where Dorothy sat to undress him. Would the day ever come when she had a child to love and care for?

Thoughts of Kurt floated through her mind as she unbraided her hair. Would she see him again? Would she go to Bismarck again? No one but God knew the answers to her questions, and He wasn't telling. Brushing her hair always let her mind run free. Did she want to fall in love with Kurt?

Gerald took his place in her mind instead. At least they were good friends already, even if his mother didn't like that. Perhaps she would see him when she went to the post office in the morning, since the switchboard for the telephones was in the same building. She finished brushing and loosely braided her hair again, tying the end with a rib-bon. Thinking of Gerald was a pleasure. But what would she do about Mr. Jeffers? What would she need to say to him to make him take her decision seriously? Just the thought of him made her mad at her brothers all over again. Was she just livestock to be traded off?

She blew out the light and snuggled down under the covers, rub-bing her feet over the warm brick. Her mother would say to pray for wisdom. So she did. And thanked Him for a safe trip and a good home to come back to. Even if it was a mess. A mess made by the same brother who had gotten her into a worse mess. She glared into the darkness. "And I suppose you want me to forgive Gus and Knute too." Was that a chuckle she heard or just the wind worrying at the eaves?

20

Tears rolled as Ingeborg listened to Haakan whimper in his sleep.

Should she wake him in case this was just a bad dream or let him suffer, if that's what was going on. If it were a dream, most likely he would not remember it in the morning.

He'd spent much of the day sleeping, which wasn't surprising. At least then he'd not been so restless. She could tell that fear rode him like a phantom. And being the man he was, admitting fear would be like cutting off his arm. Although at the moment, if it were the right arm, he might not be too upset.

She'd done as Dr. Elizabeth suggested and sneaked some laudanum into his coffee to help him relax. Lars had brought him a cane for when he grew stronger, so hopefully he would be putting it to good use very soon.

The cry came again, like a small child lost or so terribly afraid he could not scream. *Lord, comfort this man who has been a comfort to so many. He's always there for those in need, and now when he needs me, I don't know how to reach him.*

My Word. The answer came softly through the night, not quite a whisper but insistent, demanding to be listened to.

You mean turn on the lamp and read aloud? Doesn't he need his sleep?
She waited for the conversation to continue. She'd been in this place
many times, needing the Holy Spirit and waiting for answers. Why
was it different this time?

Because it is Haakan. Her mind answered that one instantly. *Bone
of my bone and flesh of my flesh. Thanks to your mercy and grace, O Lord.
But, Father, we might be of one body, but one mind?* She had to answer
that one too. She was often amazed at hearing something she'd been
thinking come out of Haakan's mouth and oftentimes it worked the
other way too.

She rolled onto her side and laid her arm across his chest. Instantly
the small sounds in his throat ceased, and the tremors in his body
faded away.

"Inge?" His voice came softly through the darkness.

"Ja, I am here. Who else would have her arms around you?"

"Don't leave me."

"Oh, dearest Haakan, I never would." She laid her cheek on his
shoulder. "We'll get through this. God says so."

He turned his head to kiss her hair. "Tusen takk."

"Ja, indeed. I keep thanking God that He is healing you, restoring
you. He says worship and praise pleases Him."

He gave a small nod, and she felt him relax again, his breathing
growing deeper and more even.

Thank you, Father. Thank you a million times. Like a feather bed of
finest down, peace settled into the room and over their bed, wrapping
them in healing grace.

❧

She woke Friday morning to the sound of the stove lids rattling.
Haakan lay beside her snoring gently. Slipping out of bed, she slid her
feet in the moccasins Metiz had made for her those many years before
and grabbed her robe from the bedpost. She shoved her arms into the

sleeves and belted the robe as she crossed to the kitchen, closing the bedroom door behind her.

"Andrew?"

"Ja. Who else would it be?"

"One never knows with all the friends that have been in and out the last twenty-four hours. Why didn't you wake me?"

"I figured if you were still sleeping, you might have been up half the night with Far and needed the rest. But I didn't want you to freeze either, so I'm starting the stove."

"I stoked it before we went to bed but only woke when Haakan was restless. Actually he slept well."

"That's good." Andrew shaved small splinters from the hunk of sap wood onto the coals still alive under the gray ashes. When they smoked and burst into orange flames, he added larger pieces, then larger, and set the lids back in place. "That should do it. You could go back to bed, you know."

"I'm not sleepy now. How are Ellie and the children?" They'd been fighting colds, a standard wintertime dilemma.

"She wanted to bring them to see Bestefar, but we decided she could help cheer him tomorrow if they are better."

"She's giving them the syrup we made?"

"Ja, but the best thing that could happen is an early spring arrival. Let everyone out of doors again." He headed for the door. "I'll fill the woodbox after we finish milking. Tell Far to wait until I get back before he tries to stand."

"Ja. Right." She chuckled inside. As if anyone could tell that hard-headed Norsky to do something or not. When he made up his mind, he made up his mind. "I'll have breakfast ready."

"Burnt oatmeal again?" His chuckles followed him out the door.

As the stove heated and chased the cold from the room, Ingeborg returned to the bedroom to dress and brush her hair in the dim light from the kerosene lamp in the kitchen. Haakan snored on. With her hair braided and wrapped like a coronet around her head and then pinned in place, she donned an apron and tied it in the back. Leaving the door open for the heat to get into the bedroom too, she set about turning the sourdough she'd started the night before into pancake batter. It would raise some as it sat waiting to be poured onto the griddle. She'd made a double batch so that the leftover dough from breakfast could become rolls for dinner by kneading in more flour. Haakan loved what they called sourdough biscuits. Sometimes she grated cheese and onions into the batter before kneading to make something different.

When the water was boiling in the coffeepot, she added the grounds and set it to simmer. Pouring water from the reservoir into another pan, she set the syrup bottle in it to heat. As she moved from task to task, she found herself humming.

"Mor?"

Ingeborg turned with a start. "Astrid, I didn't know you were here."

Astrid scurried into the kitchen, her clothes over her arm to dress by the warm stove, just like the children always did when they were little. "I didn't want to wake you. Both you and Far were sleeping so soundly, so I sneaked upstairs and crawled into bed. Good thing I took a hot brick. It was cold up there." All the while she talked she was dressing under her gathered flannel nightdress.

"How is Far this morning?"

"Sleeping soundly. He was restless for a while but calmed when I was praying for him."

"Any time I have a restless patient, I want you to come and pray for them. For me too." Astrid settled her wool serge skirt over her woolen padded petticoat and slid into her waist, buttoning the front and the cuffs on the full sleeves.

"You can pray, you know."

"I know and I do, but I think God listens to you better."

"Did you hear Andrew come in? He was starting the stove when I woke up."

"No, and you were so quiet I almost slept through, like Far. I always sleep better when I am home. At the surgery I'm always listening for patients, I guess. Although last night you'd have thought I would listen for Far."

"God knew we all needed sleep."

"It's been over twenty-four hours, and he is no worse, am I right?"

"I think so. I mean, he hasn't tried to sit or stand yet today."

"I think this is good news. I read everything I could find about apoplexy, sometimes called brain hemorrhages, and most agree that the first twenty-four hours are the most dangerous. Some say the patient should get plenty of bed rest, others say get the patient up and moving as soon as possible. Sometimes they make me wonder about the medical community."

"I made a tea for calming. He said it tasted terrible, so I added honey. Does Dr. Elizabeth have any whiskey?"

"You might try Mr. Jeffers. We are sure he is selling liquor from under the counter, but short of searching for it, no one is positive. Those who might be buying are pretty tight-lipped."

"Maybe we should form a temperance league here in Blessing and go marching on the store."

"Mor! You come up with the wildest ideas."

"The women have done such in other places. Thorliff wrote an article about the women's marches."

"I'm sure he didn't think his own mother would start one." Astrid finished brushing her hair and bundled it into a crocheted snood. "I'll go check on Far."

Ingeborg laid aside the knife she'd been using to slice the bacon. "We'll both check on him. Put the cat out so she isn't tempted to snatch the bacon."

Astrid put the cat out on the back porch to go do her business while she and her mother went to stand beside the bed. Dawn lightened the window, but the sun had yet to clear the horizon. "His color is better?"

"Ja. He was pretty gray yesterday."

"I'm not sleeping. You can talk to me." Haakan's voice rasped, but his words were more clear.

"Good. Andrew made me promise not to burn the oatmeal today, so we are having pancakes. How does that sound?"

"Thorliff was laughing about the burnt oatmeal," Astrid said as she checked her father's pulse. "You've listened to his heart?"

"Not yet today."

"I'll get my bag." Astrid left the room, and Ingeborg sat down on the edge of the bed. "You were having bad dreams last night?"

"Ja. I was wandering in a terrible dense fog, and while I knew something was chasing me, I didn't know what it was."

"What happened?"

"I heard your voice, and it all went away. You were praying?"

"Off and on." She stroked his cheek with gentle fingers. "You need a shave."

"Perhaps I will grow a beard." He glanced at the limp arm. "I'd probably cut my throat shaving with my left hand."

"You use your left hand almost as well as your right. You always have."

"Just don't ask me to sign any papers."

"All right, I won't." She turned as Astrid came back through the door, black leather bag in hand.

"Elizabeth said the apoplexy affected your right side?"

"Mostly my arm and hand. I can shuffle the right foot along. And my speech is better today."

Astrid applied the stethoscope to his chest and listened. "Take a deep breath." She nodded. "Good, and another." She put her stethoscope back in the bag. "Your lungs sound fine, and your heart is ticking as steady as the clock in the kitchen."

Haakan nodded. "That's very good. So it was all in my head."

"In a manner of speaking. What happens when you sit up?"

"I fall over."

Astrid stared at him for a moment. "You mean sideways? To the right?"

"Ja, and it isn't a pleasant thing. My head doesn't ache like it did yesterday."

"You didn't mention that yesterday," Ingeborg said.

"You had enough to worry about."

Ingeborg rolled her eyes and heaved a sigh. "Uff da, what do we do with you?"

"I told Elizabeth."

Ah, that was why she gave him the laudanum. "And the tea helped?"

He nodded. "So let's get me up and into that chair. I feel as weak as a newborn."

"Andrew said to wait for him."

"Andrew isn't in charge here, no matter what he thinks and says." Haakan braced himself with his left hand and tried to push himself upright against the headboard. "I am stronger. I can tell. I was thinking during the night that if I had a bar to grab on to, I could move myself around better." He looked up at Astrid. "What do you think?"

She narrowed her eyes, thinking hard. "I wish I had more experience to offer here. I know we have to massage and move your arm and leg to keep the muscles from weakening. The problem is with the nerves. Wherever the apoplexy was, the blood clot is pressing against nerves. As that dissolves, we can retrain your body to work correctly."

"How do you know all that?"

"You know how hard I've been studying. In one of the textbooks, someone had dissected the brains of apoplexy victims, and the information agreed with what others had learned. We know so little about how the brain works, but more is being discovered all the time. Back to your question, Far. We can try anything. Muscles can atrophy quickly when they aren't being used, so if you are feeling up to it, we can start immediately."

"I want to do the chair first."

"You want to sit up on the edge of the bed first," Ingeborg put in.

"That too."

Astrid offered her right arm, bent at the elbow, for him to pull up with. Haakan grasped it with his left hand and pulled himself into a sitting position.

"See, that is where a bar would work, perhaps a pulley. Between Andrew, Lars, and me, we'll figure it out." His eyes narrowed again in concentration. He sucked in a deep breath and, using his left hand, pulled his right leg after the left until he was sitting on the edge of the bed, feet on the floor. "There, and I didn't even fall over, at least not all the way." He straightened his back and rolled his head from side to side. "Whoa. Maybe I won't do that again for a while."

"Dizzy?"

"Some."

"Tell me when you are ready to stand."

"Soon as I get my slippers on."

Astrid knelt and slipped them on his feet, then patted his knee as she stood again. "Now."

Astrid took his left side. "Mor, give him your arm."

"I thought I told you to wait until I got here." Andrew came through the door, still in his barn coat.

"Some things just can't wait," Haakan told his son. "Take off your coat now that you're here. You can save your mother's arm."

Andrew shook his head, his disgust evident. He offered his arm like Elizabeth had shown them and nodded to Haakan. "On three. One, two, three." He braced himself while Haakan tottered to stand upright, then moved to his father's side.

"Lean on Andrew when you are going to move your right leg."

"Left foot first." Haakan took one step and then shuffled the other.

"Good."

Ingeborg watched the three of them, wanting to close her eyes, praying for each movement. Was he stronger today? She watched the sweat bead on his temples. Or did they just want that to be the case so bad that they dreamed it? *Lord, forgive me for doubting. You promised healing, and I know you are doing just that. I know it. Lord, I believe; help thou my unbelief.*

21

SURELY GERALD WILL BE at the switchboard. I just wish it weren't at the post office.

The wind kissed her cheeks and lifted the horse's mane.

Rebecca flicked the reins, and the horse broke into a trot. He snorted and tossed his head, the harness bells jingling in fast time too.

"Ja, this is a beautiful day to be out." A crow answered her, and even his harsh cry sounded more like bells than a *caw.* "You can call all you want, but spring is coming. Can't you feel it?" The bird spread black wings and flew off toward the river. The icicles from the house eaves had been dripping when she left home, a sure sign that the sun was warm enough to melt snow. But the wind told the story. A south wind that brought light and life, not storm and darkness. How could one go to sleep with the north wind ripping at the shingles and wake to the south wind singing an invitation to come out and be blessed?

The smokestacks of the flour mill sent plumes of steam billowing white into the azure sky. The chimney of the boardinghouse puffed out gray smoke, telling her that Mrs. Sam was busy cooking breakfast or maybe dinner. Rebecca could almost smell the bread baking. At least when she left home, she had ham and beans baking in the oven, and

Gus had promised to keep the fire burning, even if he had to run in from the barn to do so. If he'd not agreed, she was sure she would have lambasted him a good one. She huffed a sigh. The nerve of those two who called themselves her brothers and claimed they were looking out for her own good. Still, she might be able to get some penance out of him for a while.

The last thing she wanted to do was go to the store and inform Mr. Jeffers of her refusal of his offer to court her. But she knew there was no way she could trust her brothers to make her position and desires absolutely, unequivocally clear.

"Think about visiting Gerald and dropping by the boardinghouse to see Sophie," she told herself. "Surely Astrid is at work with Dr. Elizabeth. The last thing you have to do is go to the store." She pushed out a sigh. Maybe Dr. Elizabeth would have some advice for her. Like how to maim her brothers, but not permanently. Just enough to get a tiny bit even.

Was Maydell still at Ellie and Andrew's house or did she go back to Grafton? So many questions. Who to talk to first and catch up on the gossip, or rather the goings-on, around Blessing. It felt like she'd been gone for six months rather than one.

The sleigh runners screeched as they crossed the railroad tracks, metal on metal, with the tracks poking up through the ice and snow. The heat of the passing trains kept the snow level down on the track bed. She debated whether to go to the boardinghouse first in search of Sophie, who would know everything, or give in to her desire to talk with Gerald. What had happened to her? Here she'd had such a good time with Kurt, and now all she could think of was Gerald. Had absence made the heart grow fonder, as the old adage said? Maybe it was just the need to talk to a real friend.

The horse slowed down at the post office, so she took it as a sign that picking up the mail and mailing what she'd brought in was the first order of business. She got out and flipped the tie rope around the hitching rail.

"Welcome home, Rebecca." Mrs. Solberg greeted her with a smile as she entered the post office. "We've missed you."

"Thank you. It's good to be home."

"So how is our Penny doing in Bismarck?"

"She's doing her best, but she misses all of Blessing terribly. Said she was coming to visit in the summer."

"Good." Mary Martha reached out and patted her hand. "Please pray a lot before you make any final decisions." With that she strode out the door, leaving Rebecca to wonder what in the world she was referring to. She thought a moment before going up to the counter to slide her mail into the slot that said *Outgoing Mail*. As if they'd put anything else in it.

Mrs. Valders glanced up from sorting the mail. "So you decided to come home after all?"

Rebecca smiled sweetly in spite of what she was thinking. "Yes. It is good to be home, thank you. Since that was my first trip on the train, it was an exciting experience."

Mrs. Valders leaned forward. "Did you tell Penny how much we all miss her?"

Rebecca stood quiet for a moment to absorb the shock that Mrs. Valders was actually talking to her like a real person. "I did. And she misses everyone and everything here. They have a lovely house, but Bismarck is really a big city. One could get lost there very easily."

"Hmm. I hear that congratulations are in order."

"They are?"

"Well, I shouldn't say anything. Wait until you make the announcement."

Rebecca glanced around. They'd moved the telephone exchange. The last thing she wanted to do was ask Mrs. Valders where Gerald was. "What announcement?" This was getting frustrating.

"Well, you know how news flies around here." She closed the door that covered the back of all the mailboxes. "There now. That's finished. You do have some mail. I should have just handed it to you."

"That's all right." Rebecca walked around the side of the counter to the wall of numbered post-office boxes. "In Bismarck all the mail is delivered right to the houses."

"Ja, well, they can do things differently in the cities. Here we are too spread out."

Ask her. I can't ask her. "Many of the people there had telephones too. Talking into a black mouthpiece and hearing a voice from the ear-piece . . ." Rebecca shook her head. "It took some getting used to."

"Mr. Valders says that soon everyone here will have them too. Then we will need a larger switchboard. That is why we moved it to a different room right away."

"Of course. That's what is missing in here. I wondered why the room seemed so spacious." She congratulated herself on changing the subject. Something to remember, Mrs. Valders liked to think of herself as one who thought up new things, stayed right with the times. "So where did you"—emphasis on the you—"move it to?"

"Right next door. No one else had rented the extra space that we built into this building. So now we have the bank, the barbershop, the post office, and the telephone exchange all in one building."

"And a fine building it is. I cannot tell you how good it felt to plant my feet back on the wood platform here in Blessing." *Oh brother.* She kept her eyes from seeking her eyebrows. She tucked the mail into her shopping bag. A letter for Dorothy was all they had. She'd been hoping that Kurt might have written to her right away, but she immediately realized that even if he had, the letter wouldn't have arrived yet.

She turned her thoughts back to Mrs. Valders. She'd have to ask Sophie what announcement the woman had referred to, although she'd never had such a pleasant conversation with the woman. "I better be about my errands. Good day to you, Mrs. Valders."

"And you."

Rebecca stepped back out the door and lifted her face to the warmth of the sun. That had been an unusual conversation. She'd not been glared at once. She turned to the right and, in a few steps, opened the door marked *Telephone Exchange.* Her heart took a little skip to match that of her feet.

Gerald looked up from the chair on rollers that faced a broad switchboard with holes, each of which connected to a member of the cooperative exchange. When a buzzer announced a call, he would ask whom they wanted and then plug a metal-tipped fabric-covered wire into the correct hole.

"Rebecca, how does it feel to be home again?" The smile he sent her warmed her clear to her toes. His dear face was so pale. Had he been ill again? His straight hair was slicked back with pomade, and his gentle brown eyes looked tired today. He started to stand up, but a call came in and he answered, "Operator. How may I help you?" He listened a moment. "Of course. Here you go." He plugged another wire in the correct place and spun his chair around. "You were rushed off so quickly yesterday, I didn't even have time to see what changes the big city had made in my good friend."

"Good friend." The words made her sigh inside. "No changes." *Other than I found out what perfidious brothers I have.* "And so glad to be home. Although I had a fine time." She crossed to stand at the wooden railing that separated the visitors from the machinery. "How do you remember who is what number?"

"Most people here just say the person they want to talk to. Sometimes the call comes in from somewhere else, like people calling the boardinghouse to make reservations. A lot of calls go to the flour mill or to the doctor. Thorliff says that this spring when they can set telephone poles again, most of the rest of this area will get telephones. By the way, if you go see Astrid, ask how her pa is doing."

"Haakan? What happened?"

"He had an apoplexy attack Wednesday night. But not a severe one, I'm told."

"Oh no." A pain stabbed her heart. They were fairly sure that was what finally took her pa, although she'd always believed it was a broken heart that gradually killed him after her ma died. So many of those she loved had died young. Although her ma and pa had not seemed young to her, others their ages were still alive and doing very well. And her brother Swen being gored by the bull . . . That was an accident that never should have happened.

"Sorry to be the bearer of bad news." He took care of another call, giving Rebecca time to think on the news and watch his hands plug the cords in securely. When a light flashed, he disconnected the earlier call.

"You like doing this, don't you?"

"I do. In most places women are the operators, but this is something I can do very well. I take care of the bookwork for the exchange also."

"So I don't suppose you could take some time to go have a cup of coffee with me at the boardinghouse?" *Rebecca Baard, what has gotten into you?*

"Are you sure you should do that?"

His question caught her by surprise. "Why not? I know young ladies aren't supposed to invite young gentlemen, but we're friends, and I want to catch up on what all went on while I was gone. If Sophie is there, she can have coffee with us too." Rebecca nibbled her bottom lip. No wonder his mother thought she was forward and silly. "I'm sorry, I—"

"You go on, and I'll meet you over there as soon as my mother can spell me. I'm about due for a break anyway."

"Oh good. I could wait."

"No, it might be better this way."

Rebecca got the feeling that something was going on, but again she wasn't sure what to ask. *"Are you sure you should do that?"* His question echoed in her mind. She held eye contact with him and smiled before turning back to the door. Leaving the horse hitched to the rail would not be a problem because it was warm enough and the boardinghouse was just across the street.

The planks of the boardwalk that surrounded the building echoed beneath her boots as she walked to the end, down two steps, and crossed Main Street to mount three steps to the porch of the three-story boardinghouse, painted gray with white trim edged with a dark blue.

They'd all helped to repaint the boardinghouse last summer. It had turned into one of the best parties of the year. She pushed open the right side of the double doors with etched glass panes, a bell tinkling her arrival. The fragrance of fresh baked bread and something made with cinnamon greeted her before Sophie looked up from whatever she was doing at the high registration desk.

"Rebecca, you are home!" Arms extended, she came around the end of the desk in a rush, and the two friends hugged in the middle of the room. "I was beginning to think you were going to write and say, 'Send my things, I'm staying in Bismarck.'"

She stepped back to give Rebecca a once-over. "You have a new hat." She touched the fur hat that Penny had given her. "And a muff to match. If you don't look stylish." She wrapped her arm through Rebecca's. "Come, let's have a cup of coffee, and I'm sure there are cinnamon rolls left from breakfast."

"Um, Gerald is coming too."

"Good. The more the merrier. Here, let me hang up your coat."

"Are the twins here?"

"No, they're at home with Deborah. She's been helping me for the last couple of weeks. When I work here, she takes care of the house. Other times she works here or at the switchboard. Between her and Miss Christopherson, things are working well." Arm in arm, they strolled into the dining room, where all the tables were set with white cloths, napkins, and silver, ready for the guests.

"Well, look who's here." Lily Mae, Mrs. Sam's daughter, turned from setting out coffee cups and saucers. "Welcome home."

"Bring us coffee and rolls, please, set for three."

"Sure 'nuff, Miss Sophie."

"Is Mrs. Sam feeling all right still?" Rebecca asked as they sat down at a table for four.

"Seems to be. Dr. Elizabeth has her on some kind of medicine that has made a lot of difference. Plus with the extra help, I make sure she doesn't work as hard as she used to." Sophie leaned forward. "But don't you ever tell her I said such a thing."

"I wouldn't. Oh, Sophie, I have so many questions to ask. Is Maydell still here?"

"Sure is, and you won't believe who she's been sitting with at church."

"Who?"

"Toby, that's who."

"Really?"

"Really. Now that you are back, we should have another girls-only party and see how the lists are doing. We could have it here at the boardinghouse again, just like we did before. What do you think?"

"I was hoping you'd say that. Otherwise, we can send Gus over to stay with Knute and Dorothy. Do you know what those two brothers of mine did?"

"You mean Mr. Jeffers?" She put a slight sneer on the *mister*.

Rebecca nodded. "I could quite cheerfully throttle both of them."

Sophie heaved a sigh of relief. "I admit I was shocked when I heard the news."

Rebecca felt her breath stop. "What news did you hear?"

"Why, Jeffers is bragging all over town that he is going to marry Miss Rebecca Baard."

Rebecca's jaw dropped. Openmouthed, she stared at her friend, then swallowed and slowly shook her head. "He isn't!"

Sophie nodded, sympathy sobering her face. "He is."

"No wonder Mrs. Valders was so nice to me. She thinks—" Rebecca tipped her head back and stared up at the lamp in the ceiling. "It's worse than I thought. I might die of embarrassment."

"If you want, I'll help you behead your brothers. No one ever died of embarrassment, however."

Until now. Rebecca slumped in her chair. *Maybe I better just get back on the train and return to Bismarck.*

22

SOPHIE WAVED GERALD OVER when he entered the dining room. "Have a seat while we try to help out our friend here." She filled his cup with coffee, motioned toward the cream and sugar, but when he shook his head, propped her chin on her hands. Contrary to what all their mothers had enforced, her elbows fit nicely on the table.

Gerald leaned slightly forward. "Have you heard about Haakan?"

"No. What?" Sophie set her cup back down.

"He had an attack of apoplexy Wednesday night that mostly affected his right side. He can speak, but slowly."

"Oh, poor Haakan," Sophie said.

Rebecca closed her eyes for a moment, fighting back the memories that threatened to swamp her. Haakan advising her brothers on farming questions through the years after their parents died. Haakan promising her that he and Ingeborg would take care of them no matter what. The friendship between her folks and the Bjorklunds. Haakan was never one to push to the front but could always be counted on to be there when needed. Haakan had taken Gus with him harvesting and to buy more cows. He was the closest to being an uncle of anyone in her life.

"Pastor Solberg said no visitors today, other than his family."

"I'll be glad when everyone has a telephone. Just think how quickly a call for help could be made." Sophie took a sip of her coffee.

"We'll be the last to have one if Gus has the final say." Rebecca shook her head. "Such a skinflint he is. I feel sorry for whoever he marries." She scrunched her eyes and heaved a sigh. "What am I going to do about Mr. Jeffers?"

"Confront him. That's the only way you'll get him to stop." Sophie patted her friend's hand. "Just go and tell him that your brothers had not consulted you before agreeing to the courtship and you politely refuse him permission to come calling."

"But I shouldn't have to do that. Knute and Gus should do it." She couldn't look at Gerald. He'd heard the gossip. The stories that Jeffers had been bragging about and spreading all over town. What must he have thought? "Besides, I don't even like to be in the same room as he is."

"Well, I'm glad this is cleared up. I was having a hard time thinking I should say how pleased I was when the idea of your marrying that man made me choke." Gerald's voice held such conviction that Rebecca dared allow encouragement to sit beside her. His smile made her think of summer evenings and a stroll with friends, especially one good friend. She tried to smile, but her lips didn't quite make it.

Then she planted her feet flat on the floor, lifted her chin, and sat straighter. "Let's change the subject."

"Good. How did you like being in Bismarck?" Sophie's eyes sparkled. "Travel is such fun."

"It wasn't Blessing."

"Of course not, silly. It's a big city with all kinds of exciting things happening. What did you do?"

"I went to an ice-cream parlor several times and learned as much as I could about having a shop like that. I could go work there for a while if I wanted to."

"You know, that sounds like a good idea. What else?"

"They have a frozen pond near where Penny and her family live, so we ice skated several times." She didn't bother to mention that she skated with Kurt most of the time. Somehow it seemed that had happened years earlier or to some girl she had read about in a book.

"We could make a pond here in town if we wanted," Sophie said. "That lot next to the surgery has a bit of a depression. If we dug it out some—"

"We could fill it with water from Thorliff's well." Rebecca grinned at her friend. "I would serve hot drinks instead of cold. That way I could keep the doors of my shop open year around."

Both girls turned to Gerald, waiting for his response. "You're being mighty quiet," Rebecca said.

"The pond sounds like a good idea. Safer than the river. I remember we used to make one by the Bjorklund barn. I wonder why we haven't done that recently."

"It's easier just to sweep the snow off the river, and then it can be any size." Sophie refilled all three cups. She looked up when Lily Mae set a plate of cinnamon rolls on the table. "Thank you, and you even heated them." She held out the plate for the others to help themselves. They each took a roll and visited some more while they ate the warm treats.

Finally Rebecca wiped her mouth with her napkin and gave a half shrug. "I need to get going. Gus promised he'd keep the fire burning, but for some odd reason, I'm having trouble believing his promises right now."

Sophie chuckled around a bit of roll. "You want me to come with you when you attack Mr. Jeffers?"

"I still think Gus and Knute ought to suffer the consequences of their rash behavior."

"Just tell him there has been a misunderstanding, and that will be that." Sophie peeled off a section of her roll and ate it. "I'd like to go with you, but Miss Christopherson can't come in today, so I need to be here over dinnertime." She smiled at Gerald. "And if you go, there might be fireworks."

"Could be." Gerald's jaw appeared to be a bit tight. "I need to get back to the switchboard. Thank you for the coffee and roll." He ate the last bite and wiped his mouth with the napkin. "I'll walk you partway, Rebecca."

"If you hear anything about Haakan, call me please?" Sophie said.

"I will."

The three pushed back from the table and headed for the vestibule, where the winter coats waited. Gerald held Rebecca's coat for her and lifted her hair from inside the collar.

Rebecca froze. Such an intimate gesture sent lightning bolts zinging up and down her back. When she glanced at him over her shoulder, she nearly fell into the warm pools of his eyes. His gaze touched her mouth, and she caught her breath. Something had surely changed since she went to Bismarck. And she'd not even told Sophie about Kurt and the times they'd had.

She and Gerald walked out together and paused on the top step while he drew his gloves on. In spite of the wind and sun, the winter cool had not left. Why all of a sudden was she having a hard time thinking of something to say? After all, she and Gerald had talked for hours sometimes. Although, now that she thought of it, rarely just by themselves. "I'm glad you like your job at the switchboard."

"It is better now that we have a separate space. I have a cot there for the night shift."

"Who else is working there?"

"Deborah. She helps Sophie with the children too, so she keeps really busy."

Things just felt different. She fished for something to say, the silence with their stroll growing. "You think we'll ever have as many cows again as we used to?"

"Oh, it'll take a couple of years, but yes. I'm just glad I don't have to milk them."

"Milking isn't hard."

"No. But I never cared much for it."

"You don't want to farm, then?"

"Not really. Although I've always done whatever was needed, I don't have that tie to the land like Andrew does. Maybe it's because I was born in a city, not on the land." He stopped in front of his building. "I'm really glad you are home and that you didn't agree to being courted by Mr. Jeffers."

"Me too." Her heart picked up the pace as she gazed into his eyes. "See you on Sunday?"

"If not before. I'll get someone to take a turn so I can come to church." He touched an index finger to the brim of his hat and headed for the telephone office, taking the steps two at a time.

She decided she would leave her list at Garrisons' Groceries first, then go confront Mr. Jeffers, and come back for the horse and sleigh when her groceries were ready. Just being out in the sunshine felt so good.

Mrs. Garrison was at the counter when she walked in. "Welcome home, Rebecca. I figured you'd be in today."

"Thank you. I take it Gus didn't come and buy groceries much."

"No, but you had stocked up before you left. Did you enjoy Bismarck?"

"I did. And I always love spending time with Penny."

Her dark hair worn in a coil on top of her head, Mrs. Garrison leaned against the counter, her dark eyes crinkling with her smile. "Does she miss us as much as we miss her?"

Rebecca nodded. "She's coming to visit this summer. They have a lovely big house, they attend a brick church, the children love their school, and she is making lots of friends. We spent part of the time sewing, and I got to visit Benson's Soda Emporium."

"Well, la-di-da. What a name." She shook her head. "I've read about sodas and how they make them. You planning on serving them?"

"Along with ice cream when I can, and I'm thinking of special desserts too. Perhaps candies, maybe gift items. We'll have to see." Rebecca dug in her reticule and pulled out her list. "Can you have all this ready in, say, fifteen minutes?" Surely that would be more than plenty of time to pick up the things on the list that Dorothy had given her and tell Mr. Jeffers she was not interested.

"Did you hear the news about Haakan?" Mrs. Garrison shook her head and dropped her voice. "That don't sound good for them at all. My father had a spell like that, and he didn't last a week."

"Oh, I'm so sorry."

"Ah, it was a long time ago. Anything else you want to add to the list?"

"Not that I can think of." Rebecca reread the paper. "Do you have any peppermint candy?"

"I do."

"Good. Give me some of that for the children." *Oh, I don't want to go next door*. Rebecca sighed. *Just get it over with*. Easy to think and hard to do. "Thank you. I'll be back soon." Her feet felt like Red River Valley mud was sucking them into the floorboards, each foot gaining weight as she slogged her way to the door. A crow perched on the peak of the train station roof announced her arrival outside. Ignoring the pull to go for the sleigh, she followed the boardwalk to the front door of what used to be the Blessing General Store, better known as Penny's Store. Feeling like she needed to get behind herself and push, she laid a hand on the door handle and pulled it open.

The same bell tinkled at the opening of the door.

The place did not even smell the same. No more cinnamon, sage, pickles, and peppermint. Now dust and despair colored the whole building, partly because the windows needed washing to let the sun in. She sniffed a bit of saddle leather, a touch of soap, and coal smoke from the round stove that used to be the host for farmers to sit around on a winter day and plan the spring planting. Even the coffeepot was missing.

She heard Mr. Jeffers talking to someone up at the counter, so she made her way to the sewing aisle. He'd sold the last sewing machine and not gotten another in. Heavy flannels and woolens, serges and corduroy hung in dark browns, blues, and blacks. The three bolts of cotton looked forlorn on a shelf where there had been fifteen to twenty.

By now the women would be sewing spring and summer dresses, and there was nothing to choose from. No bright calico prints, no plaids, no dimity. Just a bolt of cotton flannel for diapers, cotton with a fine strip of red on white, and a baby blue dimity without enough on the bolt to make a dress for Sarah.

Rebecca found a box with mixed spools of thread in it, dug out an off white, and searched for the half-inch lace to trim a pinafore. The only lace was black. No wonder it hadn't sold. She took the last packet of sewing machine needles and looked under the shelving to see if something was hiding under there. Empty boxes. How disgusting.

She straightened, sensing someone was behind her. She turned slightly to find Mr. Jeffers much too close and beaming as if he were the sun himself. Laying a hand to her throat, she took a step backward. "Oh, you frightened me. I didn't hear you coming."

"When I saw you come in, I wanted to rush right over, but a sale is a sale, you know." He stepped forward, closer, hovering.

She stepped back. "I-I was looking for cotton to make a dress for my niece. Where are all your spring dress goods?"

"Oh, that. Sorry, but the shipment is late. Should be here any day."

His apron looked like it hadn't had even a nodding acquaintance with soap since the first time he pulled it over his head. And what was that smell? She dabbed at her nose with the hankie she kept tucked into the wristband of her long-sleeved waist. It needed more than the fragrance from the sachet in her drawer to counteract the smell. *All right, tell him. Now, before another customer comes in.*

"Mr. Jeffers, we have to talk."

"Oh yes, indeed we do. I've been so looking forward to your coming home. I was beginning to think you planned on staying in Bismarck forever. We have a lot of planning to do. I mean, I know this is only a courtship, but I can't help thinking about our future. Why, when we get married, you can take over this part of the store and order what you want—within reason of course."

With each word he eased closer. His eyes darted all over her, as if he were touching her hair, her eyes, her cheeks. She wanted to scrub her mouth after his gaze rested on her lips. The nerve of him. Looking her over as if she were a side of meat.

"Mr. Jeffers." She shook her head as she spoke. She cleared her throat to speak more firmly. "I do not mean we need to talk about things like that. I am not interested in any kind of relationship with you. My brothers—"

He leaped in, interrupting her without even noticing what she was saying. "Your brothers, such fine young men. I had such a good talk with them, and they gave their word that I could come calling. *Courting* is what they said." His eyes narrowed slightly.

She caught her lower lip between her teeth, partly to stem the flow of words that thundered to be let loose. "Mr. Jeffers—"

"Oh, call me Harlan, and I will call you Rebecca. There now, don't that sound nice?" He reached for her hand.

She shook her head, hiding her hand behind her. Right now the muff would surely have come in handy. "No. You are not listening to me. Let me finish." She looked at him and caught something that flitted through his eyes. Whatever it was made her shudder inside.

"They said I could come courting, and here you are. I am so glad to see you, and we will get to know each other better, and . . ." He moved forward again.

Rebecca could feel something hard prodding her in the back as she stumbled against the implement section. She tried to move to the right, but he was there before her. Then to the left, as if they were dancing, but there was no music. Just a predator stalking his prey.

Wherever had that idea come from? She put her hand out, palm forward. "Mr. Jeffers"—she iced the words—"I am not interested in you courting me or even talking with me. Our discussion is over. Now let me pass."

Instead, as quick as a snake striking, he had his arms around her and his mouth searching for hers. Rebecca squirmed and fought to free her arms, which he had clamped to her sides.

"Ah, that's good," he purred. "I like a female with a bit of fight to her. Now, let's just kiss and make up, and—"

She stomped on the top of his boot, which had insinuated itself against her heavy wool skirt and padded petticoat.

"Ow! What did you go and do that for?" But he didn't back away, just pulled her closer.

Her nose pinched at the stench coming from his unwashed long johns. She twisted her head to the right and then the left, dodging that seeking mouth. "Let me go!" Finally freeing her arms slightly, she planted both hands flat against his chest and pushed with all her strength. At his chuckle, she stomped again and screamed this time. "Let go of me!"

"Rebecca? Where are you?"

"Here!" His mouth missed hers again. Gorge rose in her throat at the stench, the fear and the anger that raged from sole to hat. Her hat flew off, and his fingers locked in her hair. Pain shot through her rage.

"Miss Spitfire, you and me got some real learnin' to do."

This time she bit his lip.

At his curse she stumbled backward as a strong hand grabbed him from behind and propelled him down the aisle.

Rebecca bent over, fighting to catch her breath. She spit in her handkerchief and scrubbed her lips with a corner of it, anything to get the taste and the smell of him out of her mouth and nose. *Dear Lord, thank you for saving me.* Her upper arms ached from where he'd gripped her. If she'd not had her coat on . . . The thought made her retch again. *I will not vomit. I won't. And to think I was looking forward to my first kiss. Oh, dear God, what have I done? What did I do to bring something like this on?*

Thorliff hurried back to stop beside her. "Are you all right?"

"Where is he?" She closed her eyes against another roil of her interior.

"Headfirst in a snowbank. Swearing so hot he's melted a hole in the snow." Thorliff picked up her hat and dusted it off before handing it to her. "I'm afraid the feather is done for."

"If you hadn't come, I would have been done for." She closed her eyes and whooshed out a sigh. "I tried to tell him that I . . . I won't have him courting me, but he—"

"He won't be giving you any more trouble."

"He stinks."

"Yes, in many ways." Thorliff shook his head. "But now he's gone beyond what the people of Blessing will tolerate."

"Thorliff, you can't tell anyone what happened here. I-I'm mortified. If everyone knows, I'll never be able to hold my head up in this town again." She grabbed the lapels of his coat. "Please."

"Rest assured, Rebecca Baard, this was not of your doing, and you will not suffer from it."

Rebecca tried to listen to what he said, but her mind screamed louder. She squeezed the tears back. "What did I do?" She stared at the front of his coat, too ashamed to look him in the face. What would Mrs. Valders have to say about her now?

23

As Gerald returned to the switchboard, he found himself humming a song for which he could not remember the words, but it didn't matter, because the tune matched his mood. Although he had known all along that Rebecca would never have agreed to marry Jeffers, hearing her say so out loud removed all the nagging doubt from the past few days. Trust Jeffers to spread such a lie for his own benefit.

He caught a glimpse of Rebecca going into Garrisons' Groceries instead of heading directly to the general store. He knew she would take her time there. He kept an eye out for her on the boardwalk, but suddenly the switchboard became very busy, and he could only glance out occasionally. He wished he could protect her from the unpleasantness ahead. Suddenly a lull hit, and so did his heart.

He wanted to protect her from everything. His love for her had grown from friendship to her taking a place in his soul. And he could never let her know. He alone knew how cruel the grief was she carried from her parents' deaths and Swen's death and her sister, Anji, leaving for Norway. He could not add the death of a husband too, and if he married her, he would. Each attack of malaria reminded him that his days were numbered. And he loved Rebecca enough not to be selfish. Would he ever be able to see her married to another? He hoped the Lord would give him the strength when the time came, but not to a scum like Jeffers.

A quick movement outside caught him, and he stood up, astounded to see Thorliff tossing Jeffers into a snowbank. Thorliff! What happened? Where was Rebecca? Just as he prepared to help, the switchboard lit up like a cannon blast. He scrambled to make all the connections, but by the time he got outside, no one was there.

He returned to the now quiet board, certain something terrible had happened. If it had been Andrew, it might have just been bad temper, although he had tamed it considerably these last years, but Thorliff never resorted to violent action. He was always a man of words. Gerald needed Toby to come and relieve him. He went into the post office and tried to keep all emotion out of his voice.

"Do you happen to know when Toby will be back from Grafton, Mother?"

"No," she answered. "Why do you need him?"

"No reason. Just felt like a walk today. If you do see him, please send him over."

Hildegunn frowned a little. "You're sure you feel fine? Your voice sounds a little hoarse."

"I'm fine. Really."

Every call felt like an interruption as he tried to watch the street. Then a wagon pulled up in front with the new family he hadn't met yet. He couldn't even think of their names, only that they were blocking his view.

"Go take your walk, then," Hildegunn said.

"What?" Gerald turned. "Oh, okay. Thanks."

As soon as he reached the street, the littlest boy missed a step and fell from the wagon wheel, landing on his elbow, screeching up a storm. Gerald stopped to help him, the frustration boiling inside, then realized he had a reason to look for Thorliff. Through the gathering crowd he thought he saw Jeffers heading toward the livery, and he seemed to be staggering.

"I don't think his arm is broken," Gerald told the mother and the sisters, who were now crying, "but I'll carry him down to Dr. Elizabeth to be checked just in case."

As soon as he settled the boy in the waiting room, he looked for Thelma.

"Is Thorliff here?"

"No, sir. He took Miss Rebecca home in the sleigh. She looked as white as snow, and his face was thunder. Wouldn't want to be on that receiving end."

Gerald headed back to the livery, where a nervous stableboy answered his questions. Then he set out for the Baard farm.

What are you doing, Jeffers? What have you done? With each step Gerald's anger grew like an out-of-control river. It was the same rage that had driven him to sign up for battle, to get control over his emotions so that he didn't turn into his father, the father he and Toby had run from all those years ago. But in the army, his anger had turned to disgust under man's cruelty. Not just the enemy's but even those in his own troop. He had found with some relief that he despised the need to hurt or to kill.

But the training rose up again. He felt as if he were stalking prey, every sense attuned to the prints ahead of him. This was personal, and the fury burned. But he had seen firsthand the results of such bloodlust, and he didn't want to become like that. He wanted to turn his back on his own father's meanness. Did he have a choice? Was his life just waiting for the right spark to ignite his inheritance?

A mile later, as he approached the Baard property, the horse's prints in the snow seemed to crisscross, as though Jeffers couldn't decide where he was going or couldn't control the horse. Gerald stopped to think. Every bone in his body said he had to protect Rebecca, but he also knew he didn't have the right. And if he took things into his own hands, wouldn't he become the same?

But I can't control this, Lord. Please help me to do what is right and give me your strength to act with honesty. He took a deep breath. *First see if Rebecca is safe.*

Just as he reached the back of the house, he saw the Baards' sleigh crossing the field toward the barn without Rebecca.

Jeffers' horse's hoofprints continued toward Knute's. Gerald sighed with relief. God had sent him human boundaries. He could trust Him.

Should he go or stay? Rebecca wouldn't want to see him. But what if Jeffers came to the house looking for her? He decided to just wait and watch. In case he was needed.

How I wish I could have thrown that man in the snowbank myself.

Rage still made Rebecca shake, even here in her own house. She hung up her coat and set her poor abused hat tenderly on a shelf. Where could she find another black feather like that? She ran it between her thumb and forefinger, but where the break occurred, it flopped. If she snipped the dangling end off, it would still look mutilated.

Like she felt. She poured some warm water from the reservoir into a basin and, using some rose petal soap she had made the summer before, rubbed the bar over a soft cloth and gently washed her face. Her nose and cheeks stung where his foul-smelling stubble-covered chin had scraped her. She resisted the urge to scrub harder, for common sense said that would make it feel worse. Instead, she patted her face dry and applied some soothing lotion Ingeborg had made and given her. What she really wanted was a bath, but Gus would be back soon, and she hadn't the energy to haul enough water to heat for a complete bath.

Oh, to have a bathroom like the one at Penny's house. She closed her eyes and saw herself sinking into that glorious tub, with lovely smelling bath salts and enough hot water to cover her shoulders. Perhaps a trip to Bismarck was worth it just for the bathtub. Let alone Kurt von Drehl.

But why did she feel like she was looking through a spyglass the wrong way when she thought of him, his face growing smaller and farther away? In his place, she saw Gerald's smiling eyes.

She closed her own. What if he had heard the screaming and yelling coming from the store? The safest thought was that if he had, he would have come running to see what was wrong. *Thank you, Lord, that he didn't.* Having Thorliff see her like that was terribly embarrassing. What would people think? *I wish I could have kicked Jeffers a lot harder.* She reached for the toothbrush and tooth powder to scrub her teeth. Would chewing on the bar of soap remove the foul taste of him? She rubbed her upper arms, feeling the cold and finding tender places. Even though her coat was heavy, she'd have all kinds of bruises by tomorrow.

❧

"But what are we going to do?" Ingeborg looked from one son to the other. Thorliff had arrived a few minutes earlier after driving Rebecca home, skiing back to town, and driving out to pick up Andrew before showing up at his mother's house.

Andrew paced the kitchen from table to door and back again. "Run him out on a rail. Tar and feathers would be too good for him."

"The problem is he's not broken any real law. Yes, he frightened Rebecca, but he didn't actually hurt her."

"Thanks be to God that you arrived when you did." Ingeborg cupped her elbows with her hands. A shiver worked its way up her spine. After all they'd done for that man ... No matter how hard they'd tried to include him in family and community events, he'd insisted on staying an outsider. And now he'd attacked one of the town's daughters.

"She seemed to be holding her own. She put up a good fight. I wasn't even planning on going to the store, but something led or pushed me over there."

"Inge?" The call came from the bedroom.

"Coming." She made her way to the bedside, wishing they had shut the door so he couldn't hear what had happened. Haakan did not need one more thing on his mind right now, nothing but getting better. "What do you need?"

"I need you and the boys in here so that I can listen to what is going on."

"But . . ." Ingeborg closed her eyes, then tipped her head back. "This needn't concern you."

"If something happened to Rebecca, it concerns me. I told Joseph I would make sure his family was all right. A promise is a promise." While his words were still a bit slow, the determination in his eyes never faltered. "My right hand might not work so good, but my mouth and my mind are just fine."

He tried to push himself up against the pillows, and with Ingeborg's help, he succeeded. "And please bring the coffee too."

Andrew and Thorliff brought chairs in with them and sat down.

"Now, start at the beginning." Haakan nodded toward Thorliff.

"I was working on the paper when I felt I had to go to the general store. It was the strongest feeling. Strange." He glanced at his mother. "But I put on my coat and headed over there, no idea why, but before I walked in the door, I heard Rebecca screaming, 'Let go of me,' and while I couldn't understand what the man was saying, I charged in to find Jeffers had Rebecca up against the implements, trying to kiss her. He didn't even hear me coming. About the time I got there, she bit him on the lip, and he reared back to hit her. But I grabbed him by the arm, yanked it behind his back, and goose-stepped him to the door. He looked mighty fine with his head in the snowbank."

"And Rebecca?"

"Very shaken. But other than trying to scrub him off her face, the only thing really wounded was her hat."

"Thank God." Ingeborg closed her eyes and shook her head. "Thank you, Father, for sending Thorliff there, and thank you that Rebecca had the gumption to . . ." She shuddered. What was this world coming to? She turned her attention to Haakan. His left hand was clenching and unclenching on the bedcovers.

"She asked me not to tell anyone, but this has to be dealt with," Thorliff said.

"And Jeffers?"

"Mad as a whole nest of hornets. He was yelling something about marrying her and courting and her brothers. I have no idea what he was ranting about. He stomped his way back into the store after we left. Rebecca asked that we pick up her order at Garrisons', and after I got my skis, I drove her home. Good thing Gus wasn't there. I sure wouldn't want to explain to him what had happened, especially in the mood I was in. I'm thinking I should stop and talk to Knute on my way back to town."

Ingeborg sat on the bed next to Haakan and, picking up his right hand, began the gentle massage that Dr. Elizabeth said might help to restore the feeling. All the while a battle roared in her mind. Fury at the man for wounding one so gentle. Pleading that God would give them wisdom to handle this in the best way. Grateful that Thorliff had listened to the Lord's prompting.

"Do you think anyone heard him yelling?"

"Possibly the Garrisons, but with winter and all the doors and windows shut tight, perhaps not. I didn't see anyone else on the street." Thorliff crossed one ankle over the other knee. "The man doesn't impress me as too smart. I could smell the alcohol on him, so if he starts drinking, I've no idea what he'll say or to whom."

Haakan tipped his head back against the headboard and stared at the ceiling. "I think we need to bring Pastor Solberg into this and perhaps Lars, since I won't be able to go with you. Andrew, would you please go fetch Pastor Solberg? He'd be out of school about now, and you can catch him before he goes home."

"Ja, I'll go right now." Andrew paused. "You want me to tell Lars to come in? He's already at the barn."

"It's not milking time."

"No. He's fixing the ladder to the haymow."

Haakan nodded. "When he can take a break."

Ingeborg laid Haakan's hand back on the bed. "I better start a new pot of coffee. Can I get you anything?" She studied his face. The lines from nose to mouth had deepened since his attack, but at least there was no sign of palsy in his eyes or mouth. That was indeed something to be grateful for.

"Have you walked today, Far?" Thorliff asked.

"Some. Andrew helped me earlier."

"You want I should bring your rocking chair in here and you could sit in that for a while?"

Haakan nodded. "That would be a good idea. Better than the kitchen chairs."

Thorliff hauled the chair in and set it nearer the door than the bed.

"You want me to walk that far?"

"You want it closer?"

"Ja, but no." He heaved himself to the edge of the bed and, with a groan, swung both legs over the edge, hauling himself upright at the same time. He shoved his left foot into the slippers beside him and tried to make his right foot do the same. When it didn't happen, Thorliff knelt and slid the slipper over his father's foot.

"Takk."

"You've been practicing." Thorliff stood beside him on the right side. He grasped his father's upper arm with one hand and his forearm with the other. "Here we go." He counted to three, and they lifted together. "You are stronger."

"That's good to hear. It doesn't feel like it to me."

Ingeborg kept one ear tuned to what was happening in the bedroom and refilled the coffeepot with water at the same time. Surely if they needed her, they would call. Her mind kept walking around the problem, as if poking it with a long stick. In a town like Blessing, keeping secrets was nigh to impossible. Would there be some who might blame Rebecca? One name came immediately to mind: Hildegunn Valders. If only there were some way to get her on Rebecca's side, not that they really wanted anyone to take sides. But surely even she must acknowledge Rebecca's innocence. She herself couldn't stand Mr. Jeffers. Still, it would be much better if no one else knew about it. Was Rebecca a good enough actress that she could hide her turmoil from Gus? What a question. What a burden! And why should she? Her brothers needed to protect her too.

Please, Lord, we need your wisdom here. Thank you that she wasn't injured. That filthy old man. She knew he wasn't old, but he was too old for a nineteen-year-old woman. A thought crossed her mind. Surely there was more to this story than what they saw on the surface. Something told her she really didn't want to know it all.

What if she were to invite Rebecca to come and help her for a few days? Help her do what? Perhaps Astrid would have an idea when she came home from Elizabeth's.

Boots thumping on the porch told her Lars had arrived.

"Come on in," she said to the man who stepped through the door.

"Andrew said there is a problem."

"Ja, the coffee will be ready shortly. Go on in. Haakan is sitting in his rocking chair."

"Good." Lars hung his coat on the peg. "Kaaren said to tell you that she has a letter from Grace and you should come for coffee tomorrow to read it."

Ingeborg nodded. That was strange. Usually she brought the letter over or sent it with one of the boys. There must be more on her mind than just reading the letter. The jingle of bells announced a sleigh. Pastor Solberg. Why wouldn't he be on a horse? Ingeborg went to the door to look out just in time to see Andrew step out of the sleigh, skis on his shoulder. The two men walked up the shoveled walk together. Ingeborg checked her apron to make sure it was clean enough for company. Lars and the boys weren't company.

"And how's our man?" Pastor Solberg asked after a greeting.

"Better." Ingeborg glanced at Andrew, who gave a slight shake of his head.

"He said it would be better to wait for the news until we were together. It about busted my curiosity bump, I'll tell you." Solberg smiled.

She took his hat and coat and motioned them toward the bedroom. "I'll be right there with coffee and cookies."

As soon as they'd all found a seat, Thorliff told the story again. Ingeborg brought in the tray, and the men took the cups and a ginger cookie with a nod, keeping all their attention on Thorliff.

Pastor Solberg heaved a sigh. "Was he drunk?"

Thorliff shook his head. "He smelled of liquor, but he wasn't drunk. He was furious. He yelled something about courting and her brothers—it was all garbled."

"So the question is, what do we do now, if anything?" Pastor Solberg caught each man's eye around the circle.

"We can throw him out of town," Andrew said.

"But technically he hasn't broken the law." Thorliff tipped his head.

"So you are saying to do nothing?"

"Now, boys, let's not get in a lather here." Solberg leaned forward. "Do Gus and Knute know about this?"

Thorliff shook his head. "Not unless Rebecca tells them, and she was adamant that no one know."

Ingeborg sat on the trunk that had come from Norway with her and Roald, watching, listening, and praying.

"What might be some possibilities?" Haakan rubbed his left hand against the wool blanket that Ingeborg had put over his legs.

"Tell him he has twenty-four hours to get out of town." Andrew hadn't changed his point of view.

"We could offer to buy him out," Lars said, breaking his silence.

"That store isn't worth much now, save for the building." Thorliff rocked back in his chair, lifting the front legs off the floor. At a look from his mother, he set it back on four feet.

Ingeborg smiled inside. How many times had Haakan repaired the chairs because the men rocked them back? That's what rocking chairs were made for.

"Any idea how much he owes on it?" Lars continued his train of thought.

"Is he paying Penny?" Thorliff looked to his father, who nodded.

"Back to the situation with Rebecca. Jeffers should go apologize to her." Solberg studied his hands clasped between his knees. "That would be the best start to mend this."

Thorliff snorted and crossed his arms, his head shaking all the while. "He wouldn't do that. You watch. He's already told people some lie about it being Rebecca's fault. People like him never accept responsibility for their own actions."

"Offer him the choice: apologize or leave town."

"Andrew, you can't force a man to do that. This isn't the Wild West, you know, where the gun is the law." Pastor Solberg's half smile made Andrew nod.

"I don't think he should be allowed anywhere near her. And I'm sure she doesn't want to see him at all," Lars chimed in.

"Still, if it was my daughter, I'd—"

"I vote for calm," Pastor Solberg said, motioning gently with flat hands. "If we get this upset, you can see how easily mobs start."

Andrew sat back, nodding, but the glint in his eyes hinted at the anger that simmered below the surface. "So what do we do? Let a mob begin and take care of the whole thing?"

"Well, the Bible says if a man sins, the elders should go speak with him. I guess that needs to be our first step. Haakan, since you are unable to attend, I would request that Thorliff and Lars go with me. Andrew, I'm not shutting you out, but I think more than three would be too many."

"And I might not keep my mouth shut. Is that it?" While Andrew crossed his arms over his chest, one cocked eyebrow and a slight grin showed his acceptance. He eyed one fist. "I know. I promised to never use these again, and I will stay with that." He grinned at his brother. "You hit him."

Ingeborg let out a breath of relief. The anger had slithered out of the room, and calm reason shut the door behind it.

"So we talk with him, and then what?"

"It all depends on how he reacts. This might be the turning point for him. God can bring healing out of guilt and build a new man."

"When will you go?" Haakan asked.

"What about right now? If we wait, there might be further trouble."

"I'll take care of the milking," Andrew said, pushing back his chair.

"Let's pray about this first." Pastor Solberg bowed his head and waited for the others to follow suit. "Lord God, you know our situation.

First of all we ask that you bring healing to Rebecca; calm her anger and her fears. In regard to Mr. Jeffers, lead us to follow your way of resolution, always offering grace and forgiveness, as you do to us. Let him see the error of his ways and seek thy face. Father, we thank you for wisdom and the joy you give us in serving you. And while we have your ear, bring healing to Haakan. Restore the strength in his right side and protect him from anything further. In Jesus' precious name we pray. Amen."

"Someone want to help me back to bed?"

Andrew and Thorliff stepped forward as one, each taking a side and supporting their father as he wobbled to his feet. Step by shuffling step they returned him to the bed and, making sure he was stable, let him lie back down.

"I feel like I just did three days of plowing in an hour." He shook his head. "I've got to get out of this bed. It's turning me into an old man."

The others chuckled at his grumble.

"Go with God," Haakan told the others. "At least I can keep praying. That doesn't take good legs and hands."

Ingeborg blinked back the moisture that pride brought to her eyes. *Thank you, Lord, for such a man as he. He could be angry over this and instead he is making a joke.* She'd watched his eyes and well understood what this was costing him.

She followed the others out of the room and handed Pastor Solberg his coat. "Thank you."

"For what? We haven't done anything yet." He patted her shoulder. "God will bring good out of this. Remember, He promised to do so."

She nodded and closed the door behind them as they went about this business. Probably it was a good thing they didn't invite her to go along. She wanted to drive the man out of town, just like Andrew did. Maybe she should take their sleigh and go out and get Rebecca herself. Why hadn't she thought of that and suggested it? Was it too late? She hurried back into the bedroom to ask Haakan, but he was sound asleep.

He'd held up through the meeting, but look what a toll it had taken on him. So that left it up to her. Should she go after them, or should she stay?

24

HEAVING A DEEP SIGH, Rebecca stuck more wood in the firebox, checked the baking beans in the oven, added more water, gave them a good stir, and closed the oven again. At least Gus had kept the fire burning so they would have supper tonight. One promise kept. But rage at the position he and Knute had put her in flared in spite of her good intentions.

Rebecca poured water into a small pan and set it to heat for tea. Right now she needed the comfort of tea, a panacea her mother had taught her. Tears burned the backs of her eyes. If only she could bury her face in her mother's aproned lap and cry her eyes dry.

She would tell her mother how dumb her two sons were. But she had a feeling her mother knew that men didn't always think the way that women did. Or, as she sometimes wondered, think at all. Whatever made Gus and Knute think that she could or would tolerate Jeffers' attention? Didn't they see what pond scum he was? Or did they just want her off their hands?

That thought stopped her hand in midair, lifting the tea tin off the shelf. Was that the way of it? Was she more of a burden than a help? She surveyed the kitchen she'd spent a fair amount of time cleaning both yesterday and today. Gus lived a very comfortable life because she took over the house, garden, and the chickens. Were she not there, his life would be far different. And Knute? She knew Dorothy appreciated her care of the children, and as always, four hands made the work lighter, be it canning, spring cleaning, sewing, or cooking for the threshing and haying crews.

Before the revelation in Bismarck she might have believed she didn't pull her weight, but ever since then she knew she was not only capable but attractive. So why did they agree to let Jeffers court her? The thought still remained beyond her comprehension.

When the dog barked, she glanced out the window to see a man riding over to Knute's. He was hunched over, his coat collar up around his ears, hat pulled low. Surely that wasn't Jeffers. But who else looked like that?

The tree branches shielded her view of Dorothy's back door, but while she watched, the man mounted his horse again and rode down to the barn. Should she go see? What if it was Jeffers? She shuddered. Surely Gus would let her know what was going on. Surely. She ordered herself to believe that. While her tea steeped, she got out the makings for corn bread, including the cracklings that were nearly gone. If they had another hog to butcher, she'd render the lard in the oven again and have fresh cracklings to flavor corn bread, cornmeal mush, and other dishes. Another one of those losses due to the hoof-and-mouth disaster. Oh well, they didn't keep well over summer anyway.

Taking her pen and the writing kit Penny had given her, she blew on her hot tea and began a thank-you letter to her cousin. She tried to make light of the altercation in the store, but knowing Penny, she'd see right through it anyway, so she might as well be completely honest.

I have never wanted to physically damage someone as bad as I did today. I was too angry to even be afraid, which I guess wasn't very smart of me. I will forever owe Thorliff a debt of gratitude for hauling Jeffers away and booting him out the door.

She sipped her tea, inhaling the rich fragrance of real tea from China, not the dried leaves and stems of local plants, although many of those had medicinal value, according to Ingeborg. Was there a medicinal for a wounded spirit?

The dog barked again, and she rose to look out the window. Thorliff, Pastor Solberg, and Mr. Knutson? What were they doing at her house on a weekday like this? She opened the door at the knock.

"Come in, come in." Stepping back, she motioned them in. Her questioning gaze flew to Thorliff.

"It's all right. I . . . we . . . I mean, I felt I needed to talk this over with my folks. . . ."

"But I thought . . ." *Why? How embarrassing!* Mortification made her blink and want to run and hide.

"Please, we want to do what is best for you. And make sure he never repeats his behavior."

Pastor Solberg stepped forward. "Rebecca, you needn't be embarrassed with us here. All we care about is you and protecting you."

She nodded but still could barely look him in the eye. They all knew what had happened. And if they knew, how many others? If that was indeed Jeffers on the horse, had he told anyone else? Was he talking with her brothers? The thought that followed made her flinch. No, she did not want them to kill him. He was not worth anyone going to jail.

"Mor would like you to come stay with her a couple of days, if that would be all right with you. With Haakan laid up—"

"The apoplexy?" At his questioning look, she added, "Gerald told us. I had coffee at the boardinghouse with him and Sophie."

Thorliff nodded. "Mor could use some extra help."

But so could Dorothy. Rebecca nibbled her bottom lip. Maybe for just one night, and she could pretend Ingeborg was her mother. One night to feel cared for. "I could come tonight for a day or two. Let me get some things together. I don't have any coffee ready, but how about some tea?" She nodded to her mug on the table.

Pastor Solberg chuckled. "That's all right. Is Gus around?"

"He and Knute are over at Knute's doing chores."

"I think we'll go on over and see them for a bit."

"You won't tell him what happened?" *Please, please, just let this fade away like fog when the sun burns through.*

"We'll be back in a few minutes."

Rebecca hesitated. "I saw a man ride over there. It looked like Jeffers."

The men exchanged looks.

"Thanks for telling us," Pastor Solberg said.

As they filed out, with Lars touching the brim of his hat and giving her a comforting smile, she failed at keeping a smile in place. If her stomach hadn't been upset before, it surely was now. An awful taste burned at the back of her throat.

She put her letter writing back in the kit and tied the leather strip that held it closed. What else did she need to take along? Would Dorothy understand?

Gerald stepped out from the back porch as the men returned to the sleigh. He tipped his hat. "So there is some kind of trouble, then?"

Thorliff hesitated for a moment. "Why do you ask?"

"I saw you throw Jeffers in the snowbank earlier on but couldn't get out to help. Later I saw him staggering toward the livery. Decided I'd better check on Rebecca, since the boy at the stable said he kept swearing her name. Is she okay?"

"Yes, a little shook up but otherwise she's fine."

"May I join you?" Gerald asked.

"We're trying to find a way to keep this from escalating, Gerald," Pastor Solberg answered.

"Despite whatever it is he deserves, I agree with you," Gerald said. "Violence doesn't solve anything. That's one lesson I learned clearly in the war."

"All right, then, climb in," the pastor said.

"Do you have any idea where else Jeffers might have gone in town?" Thorliff asked.

"No, but he had a *Closed* sign in his store window, and I saw some people standing nearby in heated conversation," Gerald said. "The stableboy also said he was pretty drunk."

"I feel like a vigilante," Thorliff said as he drove the horse and sleigh across the snowy field.

"We are emissaries of peace. Keep that in mind." Pastor Solberg settled his hat tighter on his head and shrugged his scarf over his ears. "Whatever happened to that warm wind?"

"Sure would be welcome," Thorliff agreed.

"Go to the barn," Lars said as they neared Knute's house.

Thorliff did as suggested. After all, that's most likely where the men would be at this time of day. He stopped the horse and dug a blanket out to throw over him before the four men headed for the small door. Pastor Solberg had his hand on the wooden handle when they heard loud male voices from inside. He glanced at the other men, and all of them shrugged.

Thorliff groaned aloud. "No wonder Jeffers wasn't at the store. His *Closed* sign meant he was on his way out here. You were right, Gerald."

"Sure would have been a lot easier if he had kept his mouth shut." Lars shoved his hands into his coat pockets.

Solberg nodded as the voices grew louder.

They stepped through the door and let their eyes adjust to the dimness.

"You attacked my sister?" Gus grew three feet in stature.

"No, no. She attacked me! I was just tryin' to tell her we was to get married."

"You asked to court her, and we said it was up to her, but you could ask her." Knute took a step forward. "We didn't say she would marry you."

"It ain't my fault, I tell you." Jeffers staggered slightly on his step forward.

"What isn't your fault?" The roar from Gus made the cows shift their feet and turn to see what was happening.

"That Thorliff, he threw me outta my own store."

"What's that got to do with Rebecca?" Knute shook his head, obviously getting more confused all the time.

"Well, see, it was this way," Jeffers started. He shook his head and kept on wagging it.

"What happened to your lip?"

"The little she-cat, she bit me."

Gus leaped forward, hands reaching for Jeffers' neck.

Gerald's hands clasped into fists despite himself.

"That's enough!" Pastor Solberg roared. The action froze the three men as if they'd been doused in ice. "Knute, take care of your brother. Thorliff, you seem to know how to handle Jeffers. Feel free to do so again. Lars, let's you and I take the middle ground of common sense here."

Jeffers backed away from Thorliff, stepped in the manure-filled gutter, and stumbled against one of the milk cows. The cow shifted away from him, dumping him on the pile of dung. He scrambled to his feet and found himself backed against the wooden line of stanchions. Somewhere inside he dug out a bit of courage and came out swinging. Thorliff sidestepped, and the man kept going until he crumbled against the grain bin.

"Dunk him in the water tank?"

"No. He'd freeze to death before he got to town, and I'm not going to let Dorothy have to take care of him." Knute still held Gus's arms.

"Who else did you talk to?" Thorliff asked, taking a step closer. Jeffers tried to disappear through the wooden walls that held cattle grain.

"Nobody." Jeffers braced his arm on the lid and slouched to his feet. He paused. "I think. I'm not remembering too clear."

"Where'd you get the horse?"

"At the livery."

Thorliff shook his head, watching Pastor Solberg. Jeffers wasn't known for being close-mouthed. Mr. Sam wouldn't tell anyone, but who knew who else had been within hearing distance. By now half of Blessing knew there had been an altercation. He might as well have taken an ad out in the *Blessing Gazette*.

"Let me loose, I'll kill the—"

"Calm down, Gus. Rebecca is all right," Solberg said, his voice gentle. "We were hoping to keep this from escalating into a mob scene."

Knute released his brother. "Now, you going to calm down?"

"But he attacked our baby sister. Pa'll kill me."

"He can't. He's in heaven."

"When I get there, I mean."

Knute kept one eye on his brother and asked, "So what are we to do?"

"Well, there's no sense trying to talk to him until he's sober." Solberg glared at the mess of a man whimpering on the grain bin.

"We're hoping he'll leave town without any fuss," Lars said. "Wish we could put him on today's train, but it's long gone."

"We're taking Rebecca to visit Ingeborg for a couple of days," Thorliff told her brothers. "I'd suggest we put this disgusting thing on his horse, but the critter will take him back to the livery."

"Where he can spout off to the whole town, most likely." Gus took a step toward Jeffers but stopped when Knute grabbed his arm.

Pastor Solberg looked at Gerald and Thorliff. "How about you two escort him back to the store and his bed? Lars and I'll take Rebecca out to Ingeborg and Haakan's and then head on home."

"Maybe I'll tie him to his bed. Go let him loose in the morning," Gerald said. "We did that sometimes during the war when we didn't have enough men to watch captured soldiers."

Solberg and Lars exchanged looks. "Not a bad idea. He won't freeze to death that way."

"He's too stubborn to freeze to death." Gus's glare could melt the snow off the barn roof.

"And you two will just stay home and not talk to anyone about this?" the pastor asked.

Gus and Knute nodded.

"If Dorothy hears about this, I'll be sleeping in the barn." Knute shook his head. "How can something you thought to do right turn around and take your leg off?"

Pastor Solberg leaned closer and lowered his voice. "That's why the Bible says to seek wisdom and stay away from fools."

"So who was the fool in this situation?" Knute asked, grabbing the bucket of grain. "You start milking, and I'll feed."

Gus glared daggers in Jeffers' direction. "There's the fool."

Thorliff and Gerald each took Jeffers by an arm, hauled him out the door, and propped him up so he could mount. When he couldn't get his boot in the stirrup, Thorliff held the stirrup with one hand and pushed the foot in it with the other. "You need to be tied on?"

Jeffers looked at Gerald and shook his head.

Thorliff turned the horse around and, after letting loose of the reins, clapped the animal on the rump and sent him off toward town.

"Promise me, Gus, that you won't take matters into your own hands," Pastor Solberg said from the doorway.

"He won't," Knute hollered.

"I promise, but you're asking a mighty hard thing."

"We'll talk tomorrow." Solberg held out his hand. "You're a good man, Gus, and you don't want to go messing up your life."

"Just Rebecca's?"

"No. By the grace of God, Rebecca will be fine. One thing about tests, we come out stronger in the end."

Pastor Solberg and Lars climbed into the sleigh to take Rebecca to Ingeborg, while Gerald and Thorliff followed Jeffers to town, keeping a safe distance. Pastor Solberg was right, yet every bone in Gerald's body desired to pummel Jeffers to the ground. All the hunger for violence that had sickened him now seemed to crawl back inside him.

Together, Gerald and Thorliff managed to get Jeffers inside the general store and up the stairs to his bedroom. They dumped him onto the bed, covered him up, banked the stove, and went through the house and the store, dumping out the bottles of whiskey they found and leaving the empty bottles lined up on the counter.

"Can you stay a little while longer while I check in at home?" Thorliff asked, looking around the disgusting bedroom.

Gerald brushed off a chair and sat down. How could anyone live in this filth? "Of course I can. I just hope I don't catch anything while I wait. There must be fleas and lice everywhere." The two men shared looks of distaste.

Some time later, Thorliff returned to the store, carrying a plate of dinner for Gerald in one hand and a quilt draped over the other arm. He found Gerald in the combination kitchen/sitting room on the main floor. "I thought of asking Elizabeth to give him a shot so that he'd sleep through the night for sure, but I don't want her anywhere near him. Besides, her eyes were flashing when I told her."

"I didn't tie him down, but I sure thought about it." That had been the most generous of his thoughts. The rest weren't worthy of mentioning.

"I have bad news for you. According to Elizabeth, it's all over town already."

"Oh no. My mother, most likely." Gerald ran his fingers through his hair. "I'm sorry."

"It's not your fault, and considering Jeffers, it was probably an unlikely hope anyway, even though we tried so hard to protect Rebecca. Elizabeth heard it from Thelma."

"Someone might need to protect Jeffers now, much as I hate to suggest that."

"I think we have something on our side."

"What's that?"

"A storm is coming in. The north was as black as night."

"This would be the first time I'd be grateful for a blizzard."

"I decided I'd better spend the night over here." Thorliff held up the quilt he'd brought.

"Probably a good idea." Gerald finished his plate and set it on the sink. "I'll ask my father to come over to see you. He may have some suggestions that could remove Jeffers before a mob appears. He has a lot of experience with confidential situations."

"I'd appreciate that, Gerald. But I don't want to cause friction in your family too."

"Oh, it won't be anything we can't handle." For the first time in several hours Gerald smiled. "Especially to get rid of this vermin. I've never trusted him, no matter how hard people tried to help him. So anything that is good riddance, in my mind, is worth it."

As Gerald left the building, he glanced up at the sky. Good thing he didn't have far to go. The wind was trying to blow him across the tracks as it was.

25

"So good to see you here at the table," Ingeborg declared as she flipped a pancake over the next morning.

"I know." Haakan nodded to the young women on either side of him. "Thanks to you two."

Rebecca and Astrid exchanged smiles. "Your shuffle is getting closer to real walking."

"I was beginning to wonder."

"Far, it's only been three days. You really are doing well." Astrid laid her hand on her father's. "Like Mor said, it's a good thing you are so ambidextrous."

"Can you see me milking with one hand?"

"It would take longer, but then, calves only nurse with one mouth, so the cow shouldn't mind." Astrid smiled at Rebecca's giggle. "When you come right down to it, milking will most likely be good therapy." Astrid watched her hand as she squeezed and released her fingers. "Think of all the muscles it uses. Try it." She watched as all three made fists and released them.

"So saith Dr. Bjorklund." Rebecca grinned across the table.

"Because the other Dr. Bjorklund has been thinking of ways to help Far. And is pushing this future Dr. Bjorklund into the research."

"For which I am grateful. I can at least say grace without two good hands." Haakan bowed his head. "Thank you, heavenly Father, that the storm outside is over even though the one inside continues." He heaved a sigh. "Thank you that you have promised that you will not give us more than we can bear but will provide a way of escape. Thank you for this food and the hands that so lovingly prepared it. Thank you for sending your son to die that we might live. Amen."

Ingeborg blinked the moisture that clouded her eyes. *Thank you, O Lord, for this man. Bring him healing so that he can beat the discouragement.* She passed the platter of pancakes, holding it for him to help himself. Elizabeth had reminded her not to do the things for Haakan that he could do for himself.

He set his fork down and took the plate to pass to Astrid. "You never realize how important some part of your body is until it doesn't work right. So many things we take for granted, forget to be thankful for."

"I'm grateful I have teeth to eat with. Elizabeth and I treated that old man from up by where St. Andrew used to be. Not a tooth in his head. He says he gets so tired of only soft food. He'd give anything to chew meat again, not just gum it to death."

"Then enjoy the ham." Ingeborg started that plate around. "I'm grateful that Rebecca is safe with us and that Haakan is at the table." She glanced over to see Rebecca staring at her plate. Was her lower lip quivering? Should she say something or leave her be?

"Here's the butter for your pancakes." Astrid handed her friend the plate with a freshly turned molded butter circle on it.

"Thank you." Rebecca's voice wobbled a bit, but she sliced off butter and passed it to Ingeborg. "And here's the syrup." She sniffed but managed to keep the tears that sparkled at the base of her lower eyelashes from falling. Sucking in a shoulder-raising breath, she added, "Thank you all that I am here. I might have had to lock Gus out were I still at home. Sleeping in the barn would have been too good for him."

Ingeborg shook her head, a slight smile just for Rebecca.

"Sometimes being put on the spot makes one do crazy things. Wisdom comes more with age."

"And making mistakes." Haakan winked at Rebecca.

The sound of boots on the porch kicking off the snow caught all their attention. Andrew was done milking already? But when Thorliff opened the door, Ingeborg rose to get another setting for the table.

"Just in time for breakfast."

"Just coffee for me. I already ate." After hanging up his things, he joined his mother at the stove, rubbing his hands together over the heat. "Ah, this feels so good. The wind blew all night, and I think the temperature is still dropping. Good skiing weather, though."

"What brings you out so early?" Haakan asked.

"Thought I'd catch you up on the news." Thorliff took his regular chair at the table and held his cup for a fill of hot coffee. "I spent part of the night at the store, along with a certain person in town."

"Who?" Haakan paused with a forkful of pancake just before his mouth.

"Mr. Valders."

"Anner was helping you skunk-sit?"

"No. He was helping me write up a contract. After we finished that, he went home, and I stretched out on the floor by the stove with a quilt from home. I didn't want to take back any unwanted visitors, if you know what I mean."

Rebecca shuddered.

"Then Valders came back about six, and we cooked ourselves some breakfast. I had to clean up the kitchen first. Did I mention that I found quite a stash of liquor in the storeroom?"

"No, but I'm not surprised. That's probably why he never wanted any help there." Haakan leaned back in his chair. "What did you do with it all?"

"I took two bottles home for Elizabeth to use in emergencies should she run out of laudanum, brought one bottle here for the same, and poured out all the rest." He handed his mother a flat brown bottle. "Anyway, back to my story. Valders and I rustled up eggs and ham, and while he was toasting some rather stale bread over the fire, I had the coffee steaming away. Ol' Jeffers stumbled down the stairs, swearing like a longshoreman. He was some shocked when he saw us there. We made enough for him, but he didn't seem to have much of an appetite. Can't figure why."

Ingeborg rolled her eyes. "I've heard a hangover can be a mite debilitating."

"You could say that."

"So when we figured he'd drunk enough coffee to sober up, we laid our little plan before him." He paused and sipped his coffee. "You got anything to go with this?" He lifted the cup in his mother's direction.

"Stop teasing, Thorliff. What happened?" Astrid jumped up to fetch the cookie crock and set it in front of him.

"The whole crock? Don't I get a nice plate or anything?"

"You're going to have a bucket of water to cool you off if you don't continue."

Thorliff winked at her. "Can't let your older brother have a bit of fun, eh?"

"Thorliff Bjorklund, anything to do with that foul Jeffers is not a joke."

It was Thorliff's turn to roll his eyes, this time at his mother. "All right. Where was I?"

"You poured coffee into him." Rebecca leaned forward, her eyes pleading.

"I'd as soon have poured it on him, but I resisted. We laid our plan before him. He could sign the contract, take the hundred dollars lying on the table, and catch the train, or he could stay and address the mob—I mean the group of concerned citizens who were responding to flying rumors."

"Was there really a mob?" Astrid asked as she reached for a cookie.

"Well, how would I know? It wasn't even eight o'clock yet. But Mr. Valders and I figured there would be soon as word got around, especially after Jeffers himself had bragged about it the day before. . . . I'm sorry, Rebecca."

"I'm never going to be able to go to town or to church again." Rebecca formed both her hands into fists.

Haakan leaned toward her. "Yes you will, and you'll go with your head up. You did nothing wrong. He is to blame, and everyone knows it. You showed courage, and that part is getting passed around too."

Rebecca's eyes misted again.

Astrid patted her hand. "Why Mr. Valders?"

"He knows more about contracts than I do, and he has the keys to the bank. No one would ever accuse him of violence or misdeeds."

"Not that they would you either." Haakan looked longingly at his pipe on the rack behind the stove.

"Well, they might. After all, I am young and produce a newspaper, and my name is Bjorklund." He slitted his eyes. "And the contract said I would own his store. There are a few who might take exception to that."

"Mrs. Valders?"

"More than likely."

"I'm afraid Anner's never going to hear the end of this at home. But he was in total agreement with our goal of getting rid of Jeffers. And for a quiet man, his anger was as hard as a rock too."

"So what happened?" Astrid enunciated clearly in case her brother was hard of hearing, or listening, as the case may be.

"Well, he signed it. Several times in fact, mostly licking his chops over the cash money lying there in front of him. One of the paragraphs said he fully understood that he was signing this of his own free will, that there was no coercion, and while he glared at me, he signed that one too. Then he packed up his personal things, went looking for a bottle of whiskey, swore something fierce when he realized it was all gone, handed me the store's key after I reminded him a couple of times, and then we walked him over to the railroad station. Mr. Valders is sitting there with him until the train comes. Pastor Solberg is going to relieve him in time to open the bank. And that's that."

"So you now own the general store."

"Well, sort of."

"Sort of?"

"Well, at least for a while. I'll be calling Penny this morning to see if she wants to buy it back."

"And if she doesn't?"

"Then I guess I'll find someone to run it. I certainly don't have time nor the inclination. You want to run it, Far?"

Haakan glanced down at his arm. "I doubt it. I'm a farmer, not a businessman."

Both men turned to look at Rebecca.

She stared back at them, shaking her head. "I don't know how to run a store."

"Be good training for your soda shop." Haakan nodded slowly, eyes narrowed in thought. "In fact, what if you were to use part of the store for your soda shop even if Penny does want to buy it back? That way you could do both. Let one support the other. You'd probably need a couple of people to work for you through the summer months. You know, this could be an answer to all kinds of things."

"That place is filthy," Thorliff said.

"We'd need to do a cleanup," Ingeborg agreed. "But I'm sure others would help."

"Do an inventory." Thorliff looked thoughtful.

"And check Jeffers' books to see how much he owes and how much is owed to him," Ingeborg said as she got up to refill the coffee cups.

"I can't see Penny and her family moving back into that small house after the one they have in Bismarck. It's more like Sophie's house. Only with running water and an inside bathroom." Rebecca chewed on her bottom lip. Was all this really happening to her? Was she really ready to leave her home and live in town?

"Mor," Andrew called from the doorway. "Do you need some milk?"

"I'll get some later. I need to skim those pans out there first. Coffee is hot."

"Lars and I'll be right in. Looks like some kind of meeting going on here."

"Thorliff's just telling stories."

"You'll never believe him," Astrid said as she stood and began clearing the table, setting the plates in the pan of soapy water steaming on the stove.

Ingeborg watched as Thorliff stirred his coffee with a spoon, even though he'd not put anything in it. *So he has to figure out how to say something more? Or is he waiting for Andrew and Lars?* Her own thoughts refused any suggestions of control and skittered all over the place. Was Jeffers really gone? Surely this had gone too smoothly. He just took the money and left? Walked out and closed the door on his business behind him? Why did the feeling persist that there was something here that they didn't yet know? *We can't let Penny or Rebecca walk into trouble he might have caused.*

"Thorliff, have you looked at his books yet?"

He shook his head. "No matter what, that store is worth far more than a hundred dollars. There must be at least that much in inventory."

"But what if he is in arrears on all his debts?"

"I can't see that he's bought a lot since he took over the place. He just sold out the merchandise Penny already had."

"And we still have no idea where he got the money to buy it. He doesn't seem like the kind that has been saving for a long time."

"Anner gave him the remainder that was in his account at the bank. It wasn't much." He quit stirring. "Don't worry about it, Mor. I will deal with whatever happens. Let's just rejoice that he is leaving Blessing."

She could feel Haakan watching her. They'd talk more later. "Can I get any of you anything else?"

"Just sit down, and let's go on."

"You have more?"

"I do." He smiled at Rebecca. "So how do you feel about my idea?"

"I don't know. Would I live there like Penny did? Would it be safe?"

"I think it would be easier for you. And we'll make sure it is safe. We'll all help clean it up and get more stock in, so you have something to sell. I'll talk with Penny and Hjelmer today. Even if their decision is no, Penny might come for that visit earlier and help get everything back in shape or at least write us with her suggestions." He shook his head, small shakes that continued. "To think I can talk to them on the telephone over all these miles and not have to wait for letters to go back and forth. Or I could take the train and go see them." He rubbed the side of his nose with one forefinger, something that Roald, his father, used to do, but only Ingeborg would remember that.

He is like his father, trying to take care of everyone. And that is what took Roald. Ingeborg jerked her mind back from a trip down memory lane. They had to think of the here and now. Was that a sign that she was getting older, wanting to revisit the early years? Without being obvious, she studied Haakan. He was getting tired, the lines dragging at his eyes. But she knew he would resent it if she suggested he return to bed. *Lord, help us through this. Thank you that you hear and listen and fix things.*

Lars and Andrew let a cold draft in as they came through the door and shut it behind them, automatically kicking the rolled-up rug back against the bottom of the door to keep the heat in and the cold out.

"I'll take the milk cans to the cheese house later," Andrew said. "You have enough to start a batch of cheese."

"Good. I'll churn butter today too."

While Ingeborg poured coffee and rolled the leftover pancakes around butter and sugar and set them before the two men, Thorliff brought them up-to-date on what had happened.

Lars nodded, his eyes narrowed in thought. "This will be good, good for everyone." He picked up a pancake roll and ate it. "You are sure Gus and Knute won't make any more trouble?"

"That's why I wanted Jeffers out fast. They promised to not come into town."

"And they have chores this morning." He turned to Rebecca. "They were ready to pummel Jeffers, especially Gus. So much so that he might have ended up in jail."

"I think we'll be okay now." Thorliff reached for one of the rolls. "Rebecca needs to make a decision. Or another thing we can do is just lock the doors on the store until we hear from Penny and what she wants to do."

"I know what she'll want to do," Rebecca said quietly. "Take back the store. It all depends on what Hjelmer wants to do."

The thought of having Penny and her family back in town lightened Ingeborg's steps considerably. Was Hjelmer tired of Bismarck? Would he be willing to return here, or would he see that as a failure? It wasn't like he had nothing to come back to. While the sale of windmills had slacked off due to most of the farms in the area already having bought theirs, he still had the blacksmith shop and the machinery sales. If Haakan and Thorliff were right in their insight into the future, there would be more automobiles to sell and repair too.

"Dorothy needs to get off her feet, according to Dr. Elizabeth," Rebecca said, her brow puckered in thought. "Is Maydell still here? Could she help during the day?"

"Yes, I think she'd like to stay longer, and Ellie's doing just fine. I'll bring it up tonight." Andrew hesitated. "They keep talking about some list, though."

Astrid and Rebecca grinned at each other.

Rebecca laid her hands flat on the table. "Yes, I'd like to manage the store, and I think we should keep it open."

"Good girl," Ingeborg said with a wide smile. "One way to deal with hurts is to keep so busy you don't have time to stew on them. The store will indeed do that for you." She handed Astrid the dish towel. "Let's get these dishes done so we can go clean." *We? How can I leave Haakan here at home all by himself?*

26

"Pinch me. I must be dreaming." Rebecca grinned as Thorliff encouraged the horse to pick up speed.

Sitting beside her in the sleigh, Astrid chuckled. "Your life did indeed take a drastic turn. But think, what a great experience."

"I wish Penny were here."

"But if she were, then you would not be managing the store."

"I know, but she knows everything." Rebecca flopped her gloved hands to the sides, palms up. "And I know next to nothing."

"Well, you'll be learning quickly, and the first thing better be how to run the cash register."

"Oh, I forgot about that, but I did work at the store before, so I just need a refresher. Unless, of course, Jeffers messed that up too. And you know I don't like math very well. There'll be bookwork to do."

"There will be for the soda shop too, so this is just getting you in training."

"And all the stock to order."

"I was thinking. I'll bet Miss Christopherson will be able to help you with dress goods and notions, since she knows all about the dressmaking business. All you have to do is go back through the ledgers to see where and what to order. It'll be much easier now than when it included all the groceries too." Astrid tilted her head back so that the sun could shine full on her face. It had stormed all night and the warm wind was back by morning. "What unusual weather we are having."

"Maybe God did that so my brothers would have to stay home."

"Interesting thought. Wouldn't surprise me. I know my mother was praying, and God listens when she asks for something. When are you going to tell them?"

"When they come looking for me."

Astrid snorted. "You are paying them back?"

"You might say that."

Thorliff drew the horse to a stop behind the store and looked around. "Wonder where the woodpile went."

"He most likely burned it all and didn't bother to go out and cut more, or he was burning coal, and it is stored in a bin in the cellar." Astrid flipped back the robe and stepped out of the sleigh. She reached in the back for the buckets of cleaning supplies. Ingeborg had felt certain that Jeffers didn't have much in the way of cleaning things. Or else he had a lot, because he never used any.

Thorliff tied the horse to the post and led the way up the unswept steps and back porch. He unlocked the door he'd locked when they'd left earlier that morning and stepped inside. Since he'd banked the fire well, there was still some heat in the room.

Astrid and Rebecca looked around the kitchen that also served as a sitting room and then at each other and made a face. "Ugh."

"I agree. I think we better start with the store. Thorliff, how about calling the Solbergs and asking Deborah if she will come in and help? Let's see, who else?"

"I'm sure some of the church women would come if they knew about it," Astrid said. "This is all happening so fast."

"I'll ask Gerald to put out a call for helpers."

Has he heard what happened? The thought attacked Rebecca like a small bird dipping and darting at a crow or hawk to drive it away. Surely if he'd heard her screaming, he would have come to see what was happening. The possibility of keeping a secret in this town was like trying to drink from a sieve instead of a water dipper. And that was long before the telephone came. Shame ate at her. Surely there must have been something else she could have done to stop Jeffers. Or did she do something to cause it? Besides telling her to lay those ideas to rest, Ingeborg had gently reminded her to be grateful Thorliff came when he did. God had taken care of her. She needed to remind herself of that moment by moment.

She followed the others into the store through the curtain that hung in strips. Her attention automatically went to the dress goods aisle, and a lump lodged in her chest. The bruises on her arms reminded her of their presence. Sucking in a deep breath and letting it out was not a good idea. The store smelled of liquor, dust, and tobacco, with a faint undertone of leather and a heavy cloak of fear. In her mind, at least.

"This place stinks." She stomped across the room and unlocked the door, pulling it open and setting a brick in place to hold it open. She checked the windows, but they were painted shut. She turned around to the applause of her friends. With that, the heaviness in her heart flitted out the door and wafted away on the breeze. "I'll take the sewing section. I think I'll take the bolts of fabric out to the back porch and prop them on chairs. There aren't that many bolts. Shame we can't hang them on the clothesline to air."

"If there is a clothesline on the back porch, we could drape them over that." Astrid studied the area around her. "I think we should start by covering the stock and sweeping down the walls and ceiling. Then we can wash or at least dust everything as we put it back. What do you think?"

"The men can do that. We'll go drape the fabric. And Thorliff said we need to do an inventory. If we moved as much as possible into the kitchen, the cleaning would be easier."

"I hear you need help," Mrs. Geddick said from the doorway. "We clean this?" She made herself clear in spite of her heavy German accent.

"From top to bottom."

"Sehr gut." She wrapped her wool shawl a bit tighter. "We start the stove?"

"I just wanted some fresh air in here."

"I clean out the stove and start the fire."

While she did that, Astrid and Rebecca hauled the bolts of fabric to the kitchen. None of them were full bolts, so draping them didn't take long. They went ahead and used the clothesline in the yard, since the wind was gentle and inviting.

Each time they returned to the interior of the store, more people had arrived—Thelma from Thorliff's, Deborah MacCallister, and Mary Martha Solberg. Mr. Sam had joined Thorliff and Mr. Geddick, and Lars was removing things from the walls and sweeping down the dirt. Miss Christopherson came with the suggestion that they use her empty store as a storage place while they cleaned.

Rebecca received as many comforting pats and nods as she had at her father's funeral. But Gus and Knute were notably missing.

"I didn't go out to tell your brothers," Thorliff told her when they had a moment. "I figured to let sleeping dogs lie until after the train leaves."

Rebecca nodded. "Thank you." She glanced up when she heard footsteps in the doorway once again. Mrs. Valders did not look pleased. In fact, the thundercloud sitting on her forehead rolled over those around her.

She stalked over to Rebecca and Thorliff. "What is this I hear about Rebecca now owning the store?"

Thorliff shook his head. "No, ma'am. I own the store. I have the contract signed and sealed and witnessed. Mr. Jeffers was most agreeable. Rebecca will be managing the store for me."

Rebecca waited for him to mention Penny, but when he didn't, she kept her mouth shut.

"Well, why wasn't I told? I would have made an offer." Her clenched fists rested on her hips. "I tried to buy it before Jeffers did, but—"

"I know, but this was a bit of an emergency."

She glared at Rebecca. "You don't deserve this. After all, Mr. Jeffers was just operating on the permission from your brothers—"

Rebecca took a step back. "What are you saying?"

Mrs. Valders looked around to find all the volunteers silent and watching the show. "Well, I mean that old saying, you know, where there's smoke, there's fire."

"Aren't you needed at the post office?" Lars asked, taking a step forward. "I hear the train coming."

"I put up a *Closed* sign. I couldn't find Mr. Valders to have him watch the counter for me." She raised her chin and clamped her arms across her bosom.

Rebecca blinked back tears. *"Where there's smoke, there's fire."* Surely no one thought that she . . . But of course someone would, and who more likely than the woman before her. She straightened her back and clamped her teeth.

"I mean no disrespect, Mrs. Valders, but I want to clarify something. I tried to explain to Mr. Jeffers that my brothers had made a mistake. That I had no intention of engaging in any courtship or friendship or any other kind of relationship with him. I was trying to be polite when he attacked me." Rebecca trembled as she got the words out, but a stream of peace welled up inside her. She was not going to let that filthy man smear her life.

She heard the collective gasp of the others. Now everyone would know. But at least they would know the truth from her own lips, not a vicious rumor.

"Well, I never—"

"No, Mother, you never. You assumed."

Rebecca spun around at the sound of Gerald's voice. He stood just inside the doorway, and from the look on his face, he'd heard the whole thing.

"I believe you owe Miss Baard an apology, don't you?" he asked, his voice more gentle.

"No, I don't, and we will talk of this again in the privacy of our own home." She turned and, like a ship under full sail, sped out the door.

Rebecca swallowed, blinked, sniffed, and nodded at her friend. "Thank you." She knew what it cost him. Gerald did not like confrontation. Said he'd seen enough of that when he went to the war. As far as he was concerned, there was no good reason for people to get angry at each other and fight.

But he stood up for me today. And I was so worried he too would think I had somehow encouraged Mr. Jeffers.

"All right, show's over," Lars said, waving his hands like he was shooing chickens. "Let's get back to work."

Rebecca crossed the room and stopped in front of Gerald. "Thank you."

"You are welcome. I'm sorry Mother attacked you like that. She sometimes speaks before she thinks." He paused, peering into her eyes. "Are you really all right?"

"I am. I have plenty of friends who make sure of that."

"I'll come help as soon as my shift ends."

"Oh. Who is minding the switchboard now?"

"No one, but I had to come to make sure you were . . . I mean, you are . . ." He blinked and rolled his lips together. "I'll be back later." He reached out with one finger and touched her cheek, then turned and fled out the door.

Rebecca raised her hand to her face and touched the spot with her fingers. While they'd held hands when they were dancing—everyone held hands while dancing—he'd never touched her face like that before. She sighed.

"Rebecca, where do you want these?"

She turned at the call and waded back into the fray. What if Penny didn't want to buy the store back? Then what? How could she manage the store and build her soda shop? Or could the two of them be in the same building? She had so many questions. And why did anyone think that she should know where anything went? After all, it was Thorliff's store. She was just the manager. And Gerald was coming back to help, in spite of his mother. He was walking into a battle just for her.

The first step was rapidly becoming reality. Cleaning the place up.

Thorliff joined her as she started to move the display from the window and clean that. "I think we should just put things back where they were once we've cleaned," he suggested, "don't you?"

"Good idea." She handed him the divided crates and stepped off the raised area. "All of this merchandise here, these goods are so faded from being in the window that we can't sell any of it."

The bell chimed again. Every time it rang she was sure one of her brothers would be walking in and wondering what was happening. Just the thought of seeing one of them made her stomach churn. Anger had a habit of doing that.

"Rebecca?" Mary Martha's cheery voice helped Rebecca calm down again. "I'll set the food up on the counter for dinner if that's all right with you."

"Wonderful." Rebecca looked over to the counter to see many things stacked on it. "Let me clear it off first."

"You finish what you are doing. Is there fire in the kitchen stove?"

"Yes. That's where we're heating the water to scrub with. You could set the coffeepot on this stove. Mrs. Geddick cleaned and polished it before starting the fire."

"Coffee will save the day. Thank you." Thorliff left her and went to assist Mrs. Solberg.

Rebecca returned to the window. With everything out on the floor, she swept down the cobwebs and wall, then the display floor. As she turned and headed to the kitchen for clean rags and hot soapy water, she stopped, amazed at all the people there to help. You'd have thought they were having a party by all the visiting and laughter. The walls were already cobweb free, and the stock was being cleaned and put back in place.

Mr. Geddick was soaping the horse harness that would be draped again over pegs on the wall, along with bridles, halters, and even a saddle. Mr. Sam had the drawers that held hardware, such as nuts and bolts and nails and screws, all cleaned and was putting things back. While one spoke with a soft southern drawl and the other with a heavy German accent, their laughter transcended all language.

Astrid stopped beside her. "Sure wish Mor and Far were here. They hate to miss out on anything."

"I know. It seems strange not to have them here."

Thorliff joined them. "What seems strange?"

"Mor and Far not here."

"I thought of going out and getting them, but Far gets too tired too fast. Elizabeth and I talked about it, but she doesn't want him to overdo it. I know. We'll take the ledgers out to the house and let them go through those. That way they'll feel a part of all this."

Astrid looked at her brother with a nod. "You are one smart man, you know that?"

"As Mor says, by the grace of God. We all better be praying for wisdom to straighten this out. Mr. Valders came by a bit ago and said that Jeffers got on the train with a promise that he'd not get off anywhere in North Dakota. He reminded the man that the people of Blessing would not appreciate hearing from him or seeing him again."

Rebecca swallowed the queasiness that just hearing the man's name caused. She glanced over toward the household section of the store, almost expecting to see him there. "I'll be right back. I'm going to check on those bolts of cloth."

"You want me to help roll them on the flats again?"

"No. Let's use the counter for the food first. It will be easier to roll them on a flat surface like that."

With three boilers heating on the stove, the windows of the kitchen were all steamed up. Stepping out onto the back porch, even with the sun shining, the cold made Rebecca catch her breath. She held a length of fabric up to her face and sniffed to see if it still smelled like smoke and grime. While it did smell much better, she left all the fabric there and returned to the kitchen.

"Are you all right, dear?" Mrs. Solberg asked, concern darkening her gaze.

"Yes, of course."

"Not of course, considering what you've been through." She raised a hand. "Now, don't go getting upset. We've been praying for you, and nothing ever goes beyond our door, so you needn't worry about the rest."

"I think everyone knows anyway. Ingeborg made me promise to not stew about it."

"Easy to say, not so easy to do."

Rebecca nodded.

"Forgiveness is critical."

"I know, but how do you do that?" Rebecca stopped in her reach for the can of kerosene that she would dilute to use on the windows. "I mean, I can still smell him." She felt the bitter stomach fluid rise up in her mouth again. She touched her face. "And my skin still burns."

"Those things will fade soon. Forgiveness is an act of will, not a feeling. We choose to forgive others because Christ forgave us."

"Rebecca, I think you better come." Astrid beckoned from the doorway.

"I'll be right there." She squeezed Mrs. Solberg's hand. "Thank you. Can we talk more later?"

"Of course. Dinner will be ready in just a couple of minutes."

Rebecca pushed aside the curtain and glanced up at the rod that held the tattered fabric. The curtain would be the next thing to come down, and she would throw it in the fire for good measure. It wasn't worth washing.

Mrs. Valders once again stood inside the doorway with her hands on her hips. "I believe something underhanded went on here. I should have been told about the sale of the store. After all, I made myself clear before."

Oh no. I don't have the strength to deal with her again, Rebecca thought. *Why has she come back already?*

Thorliff stepped between Rebecca and her.

"Where is Mr. Jeffers?" the woman demanded.

"On the train heading east."

"Surely he wasn't guilty of what he was accused of. Why, no gentleman would act like that without provocation." She huffed herself up like an irate rooster.

"No one ever accused Jeffers of being a gentleman." Thorliff's voice steeled. "And I would suggest that you be very careful of accusing anyone by innuendo."

Rebecca wanted to hug him and slug Mrs. Valders. No wonder Ingeborg and her mother had had trouble dealing with the woman. Another case needing forgiveness. But right now, rage felt so much more necessary. *But that could hurt Gerald.* The thought put a clamp on her mouth. Gerald had stuck up for her with his mother. While the thought made her get all warm inside, she suspected that he would hear far more from her at home. Did she not realize what a fine man, no, what two fine men she had for sons? And that they were men now, not the starving little boys who had showed up on the train and stolen food from the store? Why were people so hard to understand? She blanked out thoughts of her brothers. Why were things becoming so difficult?

27

As GERALD SAT DOWN to the noon meal with his brother and parents, he could feel the chill in the room. His mother set the bowl of stew in front of her husband and took her place to his right. As soon as they'd said grace, she handed him the serving spoon.

"Thank you." Gerald took his filled plate from his father. "Bread, Mother?" Waiting for the blast that he knew was coming gave his hand a bit of a quiver. But this time she had gone too far. Whatever gave him the courage to speak to her like that, to back up Rebecca, was a miracle or a disaster, he hadn't decided which yet. As he passed the bread, he caught his mother's eye. No doubt, here it was coming.

"Please." Lips so tight the word could barely get through, she laid her napkin in her lap. "You had no right to speak to me like that today, especially not in public. I have never been so humiliated." Her lips quivered.

Gerald sighed. Talk about being caught between the kettle and the fire. He'd always been the dutiful son, but now he had to be firm. From the look on his father's face, he was staying out of it. "Mother, you were making accusations without knowing all the facts," he said softly. "And no matter what, that was not a kind thing to say."

"Kind? Why should I be kind in this situation?" She sat straighter, using her sternest face, the one she'd assumed when Toby needed scolding.

Only now it wasn't Toby. She continued. "Those young women today, such giggling all the time. What are people to think? So irresponsible."

Gerald closed his eyes for a moment and then let out a held-in breath. "Mother, Rebecca is one of the most responsible young ladies anywhere. She took over the care of the family home for Gus, and now that she was asked, she has stepped in to run the store. And she will do a fine job of it." *Please, Lord, give me just the right words to say here.*

"Most girls would either feel sorry for themselves or hide away after her humiliation, but she is standing up for herself instead of letting Jeffers smear her reputation. She needs the support of everyone who knows her, not more false accusations. If you weren't so upset over losing the store again, you'd be the first to tar and feather Jeffers for what he did. You've always suspected him of evil intent, and this time rightly so. Why are you taking it out on Rebecca?" His reasoning caught even him by surprise.

His father coughed, and Toby continued to eat as if nothing were amiss. His mother started to answer then fell silent. He could feel her stare upon him, so he looked up and gave her a slight smile. "I'd appreciate it if you spoke highly of her. I know you have a kind heart, and if I'm to marry one day, she is my only choice, and you will rejoice to have her as your daughter-in-law." Talk about taking coals to New-castle. His whole nature screamed *Run!* but he kept to his seat. The next bite of stew tasted like chalk.

He waited. She gulped air like a fish out of water. Did she need to be struck on the back? Something caught in her throat? "Are you all right?"

"She will be, son. Just give her some time to get used to the idea," his father said and then went on eating. "Pass the salt, please."

"But . . . but you said you would never marry. What about the malaria? Who would take care of you?" she stammered. He'd never heard his mother stammer in all the years of living in the same house. She made other people stammer, including him, for sure, back in the early years. How he wanted to reach out and pat her hand, her shoulder, something to show how much he cared and appreciated her love and concern.

He brought his mind back to her question. "I know. I'll be making a decision one day soon. She has no idea of my feelings. My point is,

I'd like you to show her the same compassion that you've given Toby and me since you took us in, regardless of what we said or did."

Gerald looked to his father. "What do you think?"

"I think you would be making a wise decision. Why, if the young lady's idea for a soda shop takes off as well as I think it might, it could eventually be expanded into quite an enterprise. I remember when Ingeborg started talking about a cheese business. Who would have imagined all the good things that have come from Blessing."

"Thank you, sir. I count on your advice."

"There are good things ahead for our little town. You mark my words." His father reached over and patted his wife's hand. "And you just might get your wish for grandchildren, after all." He wiped his mouth and tucked the napkin back into the ring. "I'll take my rest and then get on back to the bank. You tell Rebecca that if she needs some financing for her shop to come talk with me. We have excellent businesswomen here in Blessing, and I'll be pleased to help her become one of them."

"Yes, sir." He hoped he had kept his amazement from showing on his face.

He looked over at his brother scooping up the stew in a steady manner, shoulders shaking just a little.

Gerald stood and rested his hand on his mother's shoulder. "Thank you for dinner. Mother, you have given us so much, and I will always be grateful, but we're not little boys anymore, and some decisions are ours alone to make."

Hildegunn looked up at him with watery eyes.

He bent down and gave her a light hug. "Why do you try so hard not to let other people see your generous heart?"

Back out on the porch, he stopped to suck in a deep breath, hoping to calm the shakes that tried to attack him. Had he said the right things, done the best, or had he destroyed the family? He glanced over his shoulder. *Please, Lord, let her accept this in the manner I meant. You know how much I hate fighting or having people angry at one another. But Rebecca's been hurt enough. She doesn't need more.* He settled his hat on his head and strode toward the telephone exchange and the job he took pride in. Who knew what supper would be like.

28

"THAT WOMAN CAN CAUSE more trouble than a sky full of grasshoppers. Only thing is, she should know better."

Ingeborg watched her daughter stomp around the kitchen, smoke rising from her ears. "I take it you mean Mrs. Valders?"

"Who else would accuse Rebecca of flirting with Mr. Jeffers and inviting his attentions?"

"She didn't!"

"Not in those exact words, but the inference was there. I thought Thorliff was going to throw her into the snowbank. Everything was going so well, the store was getting cleaner by the minute. I never realized how hard Penny worked to keep that place looking good all the time." Astrid stopped and looked square at her mother. "Then *she* came in and the joy died in a heartbeat. She is determined that the store is going to be hers."

"That's why Thorliff had Mr. Valders help him write up the contract, so that she couldn't say there were any wrongdoings." Ingeborg rolled the bread dough over with a solid thump and kept on kneading. This would be the lightest bread they'd had in a long time. Kneading bread was always a good outlet for anger. She slammed the heel of her hand into the spongy dough and flipped the outer side into the middle, at the same time giving the mound a quarter turn. All of her actions were of such ingrained habit that she needn't think on the job at all. She could instead think of ways to discipline Hildegunn. Did she never listen to any of Pastor's sermons? Had she never thought that what the Word said about an evil tongue might apply to her?

Like forgiveness? The thought fluttered through her mind like a butterfly on a warm summer day, dipping and kissing the flowers. *Oh, Lord, there you go again. Why can I never be allowed a tantrum or three without you nosing in?* She slammed the dough over again.

"Maybe you better let me finish that, so I don't head back to town and scream at her."

"At the rate I'm going, I'll need to scrub floors or go split wood."

"Ah, Mor, you always know just the right thing to say to calm me down."

"I'm talking to me more than you. God just mentioned forgiveness to me."

Astrid rolled her eyes. "How come He never gets through to *her?*"

"I have to remind myself that He loves her just as much as He loves me. And that I am to love her in the same way." Ingeborg wiped her forehead with the back of her hand, leaving a streak of flour behind. She slammed the dough around again and straightened her shoulders with a heavy sigh. "Every time I think I have forgiven her and let go of the resentment—let's be real honest here—the all-out fury, she goes and does something like this, and there I go again."

"And you know what?"

Ingeborg looked at Astrid, while her hands spun the dough again. "What?"

"How are Rebecca and Gerald ever going to get together?"

"Are you sure he cares for her?"

"I think so, but he's very careful not to show it. I'm not even sure Rebecca knows."

"Uff da! Because of his mother?"

Astrid nodded slowly.

"How very sad. I thought she might be falling for that young man in Bismarck."

"She's always had a special place in her heart for Gerald." Astrid dipped her fingers in the bacon grease and rubbed the insides of the bread pans. "Were you planning on this for supper?"

"Ja. I got a late start what with all the commotion, and the yeast seems mighty slow." She thought a moment. "Sometimes that happens with the store-bought kind. Even though it is far easier than sourdough or potato water, like we used to use all the time."

"How's Far?" Astrid asked, dropping her voice.

"He was up much of the day, so he was really tired when we walked him back to bed. His walking gets better with every day. And he is able to move all his fingers. He's coming along." *That Hildegunn. How can she be so blind? Mean-spirited, that's what she is. And, Lord, you want me to forgive her—again. Uff da.*

Ingeborg slashed a hunk off the dough and rolled it into a loaf form, tucking the ends under to fit in the pan. "Did Thorliff talk to Penny?"

"He tried, but she wasn't home. He's going to bring Rebecca back out and all the ledgers, so you and Far can go through those if you want to. I told him you felt bad because you couldn't help out."

"Sure doesn't seem right not to be there." She tucked the second loaf into a pan. "How would you like scones for a treat?"

"Sounds wonderful. Far loves the fried dough too. Do we have any syrup?"

"In the pantry."

Astrid got the heavy iron skillet from the cabinet and set it on the stove to heat. "You cut them, and I'll pat them flat. We haven't had these for so long." She dropped a large dollop of lard into the pan and moved it to the hottest part of the stove.

Ingeborg cut off roll-sized bits of dough and went back to forming the loaves. It meant she would have five loaves to bake instead of six, but this would be a good treat. At least she could send fresh bread for the dinner at the store tomorrow. "You think they'll finish cleaning today?"

"No, especially not if they go to work on the living quarters too. That man was a real pig. No, I take that back. I don't want to insult our hogs."

"Inge?"

"Coming." She flipped a clean towel over the loaves, leaving them to rise while she checked on her husband. Behind her she could hear the sizzle of bread dropped into the hot lard to fry.

"Is Astrid home?"

"Ja."

"How did the cleaning go?" He'd pushed himself up against the head of the bed and was working on his right hand with his left, straightening the fingers and pushing against them with his other hand.

"I'll send Astrid in, and she can tell you herself."

"What smells so good?"

"That's a secret. You'll find out in a couple of minutes. How come you were sleeping so soundly, and as soon as something is cooking you wake right up?" She laid a hand on his shoulder. "Andrew should be coming to start milking anytime. Lars dropped Astrid off on his way home."

He leaned his cheek against her hand. "I feel so useless."

The sadness in his voice caught at her heart. "Not useless, only taking some time off for a bit. You'll be out and about within a week." *Please, Lord, let it be so.*

"Thank God spring is coming. I listened to the icicles singing outside the window before I fell asleep."

"You want to eat your snack in here or at the table?" Astrid asked from the doorway.

"Depends on what it is."

"You have to trust the cook. Here or the table?"

"Here."

"Make yourself comfortable, Mor, and I'll bring in a tray."

Ingeborg started to sit down in the rocker, but when Haakan patted the bed beside him, she went around and pushed another pillow up against the headboard. Then after untying her shoes, she sat against the pillow and tucked her feet up under the quilt across the foot of the bed. "Ah, now this is nice."

"You wait on everybody else all the time. Now this is your turn." He raised his head and sniffed. "Scones?"

She nudged him with her elbow. "Act surprised."

Astrid entered with a plate of the fried bread pieces, a bowl of warmed syrup, and three cups of coffee, along with napkins. "Where should I set this?"

"On your father's legs. That way we can all reach."

They'd just settled to dipping the bread in the syrup when a knock came at the back door, followed immediately by Andrew. "Hey, where is everyone?"

"In here. Bring a chair."

"And a cup of coffee if you want to join us."

Haakan ate his first bite and muttered around it, "Good idea." He licked a drip of syrup off his chin. "How come you never make these anymore?"

"I guess because the children are grown, and this seemed to be a treat for them."

Andrew set his chair beside the bed. "Having a party and you didn't invite me?" He dipped his piece of bread. "How did the cleaning go?"

"More important, how are your children?"

"Better. Finally. It seems one or the other has been ailing this winter."

"Tell Ellie to give them each a spoonful of blackstrap molasses. That will help. Penny used to stock cod-liver oil for a spring tonic. I don't suppose you found any such thing at the store when you were cleaning?"

"Nope. There was hardly anything in the medicinal section. Hardly anything in the entire store. Mr. Sam was grumbling about the hardware section. I think there were only five or six pairs of boots. Nobody better want new overalls or men's pants or needles, or plan on sewing any summer dresses. Or dresses of any kind, for that matter."

"It's going to take a lot of money to restock the necessities, let alone bring anything new in. Penny was so great at introducing new items for the women and our houses. I broke the last sewing machine needle today, and Jeffers told me a couple of weeks ago that he had ordered some and they should be in any day."

"There were no sewing machine needles, and Rebecca said she got the last of the hand-sewing ones. She's counting on you to locate suppliers when you go through the ledgers. Her voice quavered a little while we talked about it. I think she started to feel overwhelmed."

"She has a lot of emotions to work through, but she will receive strength as she needs it. I've been praying wisdom for her too, as for all of us."

Andrew dipped the last of his scone into the syrup, wiped his hands on the dish towel Astrid had slung over her shoulder, and stood, picking his chair up with him. "You need anything from the springhouse? Milk?"

"You want to feed the chickens and pick the eggs?" Astrid grinned up at him. The chickens had always been Astrid's responsibility, but since she spent so much of her time at the surgery, Ingeborg had taken over the hen house.

"What? And deprive you of your favorite chore?" He paused at the doorway. "You feeling up to a couple of small visitors, Far?"

"Anytime."

"Why don't you and Ellie come for supper?" Ingeborg swung her feet off the bed. "I'm making stew with dumplings. There's plenty."

"I'll take care of the chickens and go get them," Astrid said as she dipped her last bite into the syrup. "These are so good."

"Thanks. They'll like that."

"I hope Thorliff brings out the mail when he comes. And the newspaper." Haakan dabbed at a spot of syrup on his shirt front. "Eating in bed can be messy."

"You can always sit in the rocking chair. If you want to join us in the kitchen . . ."

"I think I'll read for a while here."

Ingeborg was cutting carrots to put in the stew when she heard harness bells announcing the arrival of a sleigh. As Thorliff ushered Rebecca, Elizabeth, and Inga in, Ingeborg spread her arms wide and the little girl ran into them.

"Gamma, I came to see you." She clapped her palms on Ingeborg's cheeks. "You don't never come to see me." After one more hug she wriggled to be set down. "Where's Gampa?"

"In the bedroom."

"He sick?"

"Go see him."

Inga charged across the room, leaving Ingeborg and Elizabeth to exchange smiles.

"Will you stay for supper?"

"I came to check on Haakan."

"I figured, but we'll have a family supper. Astrid is going to get Ellie and the children." She looked to Rebecca. "How are you?"

"A bit overwhelmed." Rebecca hung up her coat and took Elizabeth's to do the same. "There is so much to do there."

"And to think only a few days ago you were in Bismarck."

"Playing. And dreaming of my soda shop. Life was so simple then. Whoever would have thought things would change like this." Rebecca held her hands over the stove to warm them. "What can I do to help?"

"You can sit down and have a cup of coffee. The scones are all gone, but there are molasses cookies if you'd like."

Thorliff came back carrying a stack of ledgers. "These go back for the last couple of years. That should be enough."

"What did Penny say?"

"Before or after she cried?" He set the leather-trimmed books on a chest of drawers along the wall. A giggle from Inga turned his attention to the bedroom. "Sounds like a party in there."

"It is always a party when Inga is around." Ingeborg's smile brought one from Thorliff.

"I'll take the mail and the paper in, and Far will have something to keep him busy. How's he handling the forced rest?"

"So far so good. What did Penny say?"

"Oh, sorry. She said she'd talk with Hjelmer and see what they could do. From the excitement in her voice, I'd say she'll be the owner of the store again, even if from a long distance. I'll call her back tomorrow." He picked up a ledger too. "You have paper and pencil? Far can start finding the suppliers for us."

Sleigh bells announced more arrivals.

"We better bring in the other table from the parlor so everyone has a place to sit." Ingeborg handed him the writing box. "Full house tonight."

Astrid carried a basket and one-year-old Carl in from the sleigh. "Ellie brought an apple cake she'd just taken out of the oven." She set Carl on the floor. "Go find Gampa." She pointed to the bedroom, where Inga belted out another laugh.

"She seems to be entertaining everyone in there," Astrid said with a grin as she closed the door behind Ellie.

"Oh, the bread." Ingeborg opened the oven door. "Looks pretty brown, but at least it's not burned." As she pulled out the pans, she set them on the table, where Astrid had laid out the wooden racks, and tipped the bread out of the pans. Dipping her fingertips in the butter, she spread it on the tops of the loaves before covering them with another towel. While her fingers moved without thinking on her part, she asked Thorliff, now sitting at the table, "So is that what you expected from Penny?"

"I was hoping she would say she'll be here in a week and order whatever is needed, but that was pretty unrealistic. However, after I got Mrs. Valders to quit making nasty remarks, she was on her high horse, all right. . . ."

Dear Lord, here we go again.

"She offered to double my money. I don't think she knew what I paid for it. Her husband would be smart if he never told her his complicity in this deal, but she really wants that store. I told her Penny had the first rights to it."

"Did she stay and help clean?"

Thorliff shook his head. "She glared at me, snorted at Rebecca, and hightailed it back to the post office."

"How I pray that Penny and Hjelmer come back here. You have enough to do between the newspaper and the building, without taking on a store too."

"Penny was just about Rebecca's age when she started the store, wasn't she?"

"Close to it." Ingeborg tried to think back. "I'm not sure. Some things just don't come to mind as readily as they used to."

"Are you saying you are getting old?"

"Not necessarily, but older." *And hopefully, dear Lord, wiser. I need every smidgeon of wisdom you can give me. I have to keep remembering how you forgive me, or I might go in and let her have it with both barrels. And I've always known how to shoot well.*

❧

"You can't go, Haakan. Don't leave me!" *She felt the scream go on and on, but he walked away from her after turning once to wave good-bye. She fought to run after him, but something held her, no matter how fiercely she fought.* "Haakan!" *The wail echoed and re-echoed in her mind. And now she couldn't see him any longer, not even a shadow.*

"Inge. Wake up, Inge."

A warm hand on her shoulder shook her gently. "Don't leave me. Please, don't go," she mumbled, thrashing in her agony.

"I'm not going anywhere. You had a bad dream."

His voice. He hadn't gone and left her. She turned on her side and buried her face in his shoulder. She sniffed and the tears flowed.

"It was so terribly real." She struggled to speak without breaking into full out sobs. "You walked away and kept on going, and I couldn't go with you."

He stroked her hair with his left hand. "Hush. It is all right. I am here beside you, and God willing, I will be for a long time to come."

"If you leave me, I think the dark pit will devour me, and I shall not live either, even if I am alive."

"No, it won't be like that. God has said He will never leave us nor forsake us, and you know He won't. No matter what your dreams say. He has always comforted us, so why would He change as we grow older and need Him even more? See, He is even making my hand better."

She took his right hand in hers and stroked it gently, straightening the fingers that wanted to curl. "Sometimes it is hard to see Him."

"I know. My word, do I know that after the other night. But even at the worst, I could feel Him right beside me." He stroked her face with a gentle finger. "His rod and his staff, they did indeed comfort me."

"And you comfort me. Thank you for waking me. That was a bad one."

"Can you sleep now?"

"If I dare close my eyes." She sucked in a deep breath and heaved it out. "Mange takk."

He laid his hand across her eyes. "What do you see?"

"Nothing. I have my eyes closed."

"Now go to sleep."

She turned her head and kissed the palm of his hand. In her mind she began, *The Lord is my shepherd; I shall not want. He maketh me to lie down in green pastures: he leadeth me beside the still . . .*

29

I SHOULD GO TALK with my brothers, she thought as she buttoned her nightgown.

The thought plagued Rebecca. But every time she decided she'd go in the morning, she could feel all her insides tighten up and a red cloud wave around her. If they wanted to talk with her, they could come find her. It wasn't as if they didn't know where she was. A week since she'd spoken with them. Dorothy had sent her a small note with Maydell, but she hadn't mentioned them either. The only time she'd gone that long without seeing them was when they were off haying or harvesting or when she'd gone to Bismarck. And now Maydell had returned to Grafton for a while, so there was no one to help Dorothy. But then, perhaps Dorothy was doing much better.

She stared out the window of the bedroom at the Bjorklunds', even though there was nothing to see in the darkness. She needed to go get her personal things from the house. This would be her last night here. Tomorrow she would move into the store, and she would have her own place for the first time in her life. Just the thought of it made her stomach drop down around her knees. At least the place was clean now. She'd sewn a new curtain for the doorway on Ingeborg's machine one night after supper. Had she had her way, it would have been bright red or orange, but she had to use material from the store, so it was brown calico with small yellow flowers on it. Anything was better than the old rags.

At least if and when Penny decided to buy back the store, it was now looking more like when she'd had it, except for so much empty space. Hopefully the first shipment of goods would be on tomorrow's train. Opening all the boxes would be like having Christmas in the spring. She and Thorliff were talking about a celebration for a grand reopening. She knew that all she had to do was mention it to Sophie, and she'd make sure it happened.

She knew she needed to pray about all these decisions, but her requests and petitions seemed to hit the ceiling and bounce back. If only her mother were here. *God in heaven, I need my mother. I've needed my mother for years. It's just not fair.* But she knew Ingeborg and Mrs. Solberg were doing all they could to fill in.

What if she failed at this job, couldn't handle it? Returning to the farm with her tail between her legs was not appealing, much as she missed her house, with Dorothy and the children so nearby. Right now she had no trouble not missing her brothers.

A tap at the door made her wipe her eyes with the ends of her fingers and sniff before answering. "Come in."

Astrid peeked her head in. "Just me. Something told me you needed an ear or a shoulder or just another person."

"Ma would say God prompted you."

"Mine would say that too. You want me to go get her?"

"No. I feel guilty for bothering her when she is so worried about—"

"Mor would say she never worries. She just reminds God more frequently about whatever is on her mind." Astrid made herself comfortable on the bed. "You want me to go with you to pick up your things at home?"

"Would you?"

"Of course. We can get one of the men with a sledge if we need it. Lars or Andrew would help, I know."

"Well, I already have a table and chairs, a bed and chest of drawers. What more do I absolutely need?"

"What about bringing in your mother's rocker?"

Rebecca started to say something and then changed her mind, her eyes narrowing. "That's a good idea. I guess I'm hesitant to take things from home."

"Why?" Astrid tucked her nightdress around her ankles and pulled her shawl closer. "I'm sure Gus wouldn't mind."

Studying her fingernails, Rebecca didn't look up.

"Oh." Astrid set her chin on her bent knees. "I take it we are going out to the house when the men are sure to be at the barn."

Rebecca nodded. "They haven't even bothered to come to town to see how or what I am doing."

"You can be sure they know. The Blessing morning-glory vine has surely reached them. They're probably too ashamed to face you."

Rebecca let that thought roll for a moment then decided she couldn't follow it. "Morning-glory vine?"

"Sounds better than grapevine or gossip line. Works the same. I just thought it sounded prettier. Soon we won't need it if everyone gets a telephone installed. Speaking of telephones, have you seen Gerald?"

"Only for a few minutes yesterday. He said he'd come help unpack the supplies."

"Uff da. That's going to be a big job. Everything has to be counted, marked, and put on the shelves. I've done it with Penny before but never of this magnitude."

"Me too. Who'd have thought she was training us for running the store?"

"I think we need a girls' night like we had in January. What if we held it at the store?" Astrid reached for the brush and motioned to the bed. When Rebecca sat, she picked up the stroking. "You have such beautiful hair. It's got just enough red to give it spice."

"That's what I need, spicy hair." Rebecca tipped her head forward and let her eyes drift closed. After a stretch of silence, she cleared her throat. "That's a good idea. Thanks for thinking of it." A silence hummed while the brushing continued. "Umm." Another pause, this one longer. She clenched and unclenched her hand a couple of times, then said, "You have to be honest with me."

"Am I ever anything but? You want an opinion, just ask me, and you get it." Astrid kept on brushing.

Rebecca's faint chuckle would have been easy to miss. She cleared her throat again. "Do you think I did something to make Mr. Jeffers attack me like that?" She almost buried her whisper in the lace of her nightdress.

Astrid thumped the brush down on the bed and grabbed her friend by the shoulders. "You turn around here, Rebecca Baard, and listen up real good. Come on. Look in my eyes." When Rebecca was halfway around, Astrid continued. "Don't you let anything that anyone says make you feel guilty. That man was an animal of the worst sort. In fact, calling him an animal is too good for him. If anyone is to blame besides Jeffers, it's your brothers, because they set it up, even though I know they never meant for him to interpret it that way, but still . . ."

"That's the other part. How could they not see? Do they care that little about me? I am still so mad at them I want to scream."

"Me too. Take the buggy whip after them."

"But that isn't very Christian, so then I feel guilty about that too."

"You could talk to Pastor Solberg or to my mother."

"I know. But I hate to bother them. They've been helping in so many ways already."

"If they know you need them, they'll be hurt if you don't ask."

"Or they'll show up. Like you did."

"True enough." Astrid took up the hairbrush again.

"The only time anyone brushes my hair since my mother died, it has been one of you girls." Her voice took on a dreamy quality.

"Grace and Sophie and I used to do it for each other, but now Mor and I switch off sometimes too. Especially if we wash our hair in the rain. Everything smells so good after a rain shower, even hair."

"The way the snow is melting, we might have rain soon too. I saw a clump of violets yesterday when I was washing windows. The little round leaves were such a bright green, and bits of purple showed on the tip of the bud. They weren't open yet. I can't believe how fast they come up once the snows melts. Right off the back porch. Do you suppose Penny planted them there?" Her head drooped further forward. "I'm going to fall asleep sitting up. You want me to do yours now?"

"No. You rest. Get under the covers, and I'll blow out the lamp. I hope you sleep really wonderfully." She sectioned Rebecca's hair in three and braided a loose rope to hang down her back. "There, now."

"Thank you." Rebecca reached for the top of the quilt and the sheet and pulled them back, sliding under them without a protest. She turned on her side with a slight smile. "Night."

❧

The next morning Thorliff met Rebecca and Astrid at the store at eight. "Do you have any heavy things you want brought in from home?" he asked.

"I think my mother's rocking chair is all for now. I've got a list of things I need to get—bedding, clothes, things for the kitchen. That man got by with the barest of necessities. Thank you for taking the bed apart to make sure we got rid of all the bugs." She shuddered. "My ma would have had a fit at the filth."

"Mine too. Probably a good thing she wasn't able to help us."

"Penny took all of her household things with her, so the living quarters were pretty empty when she left. Interesting that that man had nothing with him when he came." Astrid spread a red-and-white checked tablecloth that she'd brought from home onto the kitchen table. "There, that looks better." She glanced up at her brother. "Did anyone ever mention things like that?"

Thorliff stared at her for a moment, then shook his head. "None of the men, but I heard someone say that he'd not been very friendly when we tried to welcome him into the community. But you know, you can't expect everyone to be like people we've known all of our lives."

"I guess." Astrid turned to Rebecca. "I have a feeling some of the women are bringing things in, so be prepared."

"I should box up some of the canning from home too. After all, I did it."

"Well, just in case, take the sledge rather than the sleigh. If you don't need me, I have plenty to do in the office if I'm going to get a newspaper out next week."

The two climbed up on the plank seat, and Astrid flicked the reins. In some spots they hauled through mud and in some through snow. They were in the between times, when it was neither spring nor winter, needing neither sleigh nor wagon. But they'd be moving the wagon boxes from sledge to wheels any day.

Everyone would stay off the roads as much as possible, as the land thawed out three feet down and turned to mud that clung so heavy the horses couldn't pull the wagons.

When they entered the house, the smell and feel of it announced no one was home. While the stove was warm, Gus had not kept a fire going in it for the day.

"He must be eating over at Dorothy's." Rebecca headed up the stairs to her bedroom. "Take whatever you think I need out of the cupboards and pantry. I'll get my things."

An hour later they were loaded and still no sign of the men. Rebecca stared across the field to the other house, where the chimney smoke said people were at home. To go over there or not. Surely they had seen the team and sledge. Why hadn't they come and offered to help? *Why should I be the one to make the first move? This whole mess is their fault, after all.* She shut the door and joined Astrid on the wagon seat. The other thing she'd brought of her mother's was the sewing machine, along with a box of notions and cloth goods. Gus would not be using that.

When or if Penny came back, where would she live? There wasn't room in the back of Miss Christopherson's empty dress shop for someone to live if she did end up putting the soda shop there. That was why Miss Christopherson roomed at the boardinghouse the years she'd had her dress shop. But maybe after living in Bismarck, Penny and Hjelmer would want a new house.

She could hear her mother's voice as if she sat right behind them, tapping her on the shoulder. *Let the day's own troubles be sufficient for the day.* She didn't have to decide what to do about her future living situation today.

"Do you want to go over to Knute's and tell them what is happening?"

"About like I want to stick my hand in a pot of boiling water."

Astrid giggled and headed the horses toward town.

Rebecca kept herself from looking over her shoulder only with the greatest difficulty. One day she would have to confront this, but not today. Perhaps the problem would just go away if she ignored it. Not that that had ever worked before.

When they got back to the store, the women had been there before them. A kettle bubbled on the back of the stove with the enticing aroma of beef soup. A loaf of fresh bread sat under a cloth on the table with its best friend, a mold of butter. White curtains hung in the windows, a braided rag rug lay in front of the stove, jars of canned beans, beets, pickles, apple sauce, and relish lined a shelf. Two large tins held flour and sugar. A new braided rug lay in front of the store door, and the bell had recently been polished.

"Who do I thank?" Rebecca asked, rolling her lips together to keep from sniffling.

"All of them," Astrid told her. "That has to be Mrs. Valders' rug, by the way; she has a special way of braiding them. I'm guessing that's her apology. The bread, butter, and cheese are from Mor. Tante Kaaren sent the curtains; they used to hang in her kitchen. If you are lucky, that is Mrs. Solberg's relish. She makes the best relish."

Together they unloaded the sledge, setting the chair and the sewing machine in the kitchen, which doubled as a sitting room. After lugging the bedding, including a feather bed, up the stairs to one of the three bedroom, they made up the bed and hung her clothes on the pegs along the wall.

"The way Mrs. Geddick scrubbed this room, no louse, flea, or bedbug would dare to remain. From the smell of it, she doused everything in kerosene."

"Just don't go lighting any matches in here for a while." Rebecca laid her hairbrush on top of the chest of drawers. "There. All done for now."

"I need to get on over to see if Elizabeth needs me. I'll leave the sledge there for Thorliff to take back." They both paused at the sound of the train whistle. "And then again, maybe I won't. Let's just go to the station instead and let the men load your supplies on it. Easier than wheeling all those boxes and crates with a dolly, muddy as the street is today."

Rebecca gave her new room another glance. One would never guess that Jeffers had lived here. The walls were whitewashed, there were more white curtains at the window and a braided rug on the floor, and now her own nine-patch quilt that her mother had made for her covered her bed. "Thank you."

"You're welcome. Just think. You have all your spring cleaning done before the middle of March."

Rebecca thought of the farmhouse. It would not get spring cleaned this year. And she wouldn't be there to help Dorothy either. Heaving a sigh, she followed Astrid out the door.

"Now to attack the next step. We have well earned tomorrow off. Good thing God declared Sunday a day of rest." The two tromped back down the stairs, through the kitchen and, snagging their coats, back outside.

A stack of boxes and crates awaited them when they arrived at the station. The conductor was already calling, "All aboard," and the train's wheels screeched as the train inched forward, then picked up speed to head north by northwest.

The two stared at the stacks of boxes and crates and then at each other.

"Don't worry," the stationmaster called. "Help is on the way."

Toby and Gerald Valders, Garth Wiste, Mr. Sam, Thorliff, and one of the Geddick brothers strolled onto the planked platform and began laughing and teasing Rebecca for ordering half of Minneapolis. They quickly loaded the sledge, then each carried smaller boxes and followed the team down the street. Some of the crates had to be left on the front porch, since there was no more room in the store.

Dark had fallen by the time they'd cleared the mess out of the store and left several crates unopened along the back wall. The shelves now had merchandise to sell: men's pants, boots, shirts, overalls, and hats, and the yardage department lit up the whole aisle. Mr. Sam whistled as he counted and organized the hardware section, while his son, Lemuel, hung the rakes, shovels, and hoes people might need to start their gardens. A display rack held packages of seeds, and rolls of twine, rope, and chains hung on one wall, ready to be pulled off and measured.

A roll of brown paper now filled the rack on the counter, with a spool of string to wrap with. The cash register had been cleaned and polished, and a feather duster hung on a hook behind the counter to be used to control the dust.

"I think you should come stay with us one more night," Astrid said as she shoved her arms into her coat sleeves. "Then you can come here after church and dinner."

"Thank you, but I want to stay here. I can get some more done after supper tonight."

"It's up to you, but if my mother scolds me, you have to defend me."

"You are welcome to spend the night if you want."

"Thanks, but I want to be there in the morning to help Far get ready for church. He says he's going even if we have to carry him." Astrid headed out the door to the horse patiently waiting with the sleigh.

Rebecca had just closed the door when she heard the bell over the store's front door tinkle, announcing a customer. "Surely everyone knows I'm not open yet," Rebecca mumbled as she pushed through the drape on the door. Her heart leaped at the sight of the man standing looking around. What was the matter with her? She'd never reacted like that before. "Hello."

"You have done miracles here," Gerald said. "I thought maybe you needed another pair of hands now that I am finished with my shift." He held out both hands.

"Astrid just left for home. She wanted me to go along. We'll finish the rest on Monday, even though the store will be open." She could tell she was talking too fast, but she couldn't seem to stop or even slow down. "Take off your coat, and I'll show you around."

"What a difference."

"Many hands make light work, to quote an old saying. And so many people have helped get this store back in shape, I can't begin to thank them all. You mother even sent me a rug. Please tell her how much I appreciate it. Astrid and I are talking about a grand reopening." She glanced over her shoulder to see him staring at her.

"Do you know that the lamplight caught in your hair makes it look like sparks of fire?"

Rebecca nearly fell over her feet, they nailed themselves to the floor so fast. "Ah . . ." *What do I say? This is Gerald, and he never says things like that. But then, who in Blessing has ever said such things to me? The party. Talk about the opening.* "We . . . um . . . we thought in a week or so. Maybe it will be dry enough to have it outside."

"You still have those to unpack?" He inclined his head toward some boxes.

"Yes. They can wait." Why did she feel like she was talking with a stranger? This was her friend Gerald. They usually talked comfortably to each other. After all, they'd even discussed religion and politics. Both of them truly admired President Teddy Roosevelt, and Gerald had even heard him speak one time.

"How have you been feeling?" she managed to force out of her closed throat.

"Lonesome. I missed you while you were gone."

Rebecca swallowed. "You did?"

"It sounded like you had a good time in Bismarck."

She turned to find him staring at her in that odd way again. She wished . . . But she couldn't wish that. Mrs. Valders would run her out of town if she so much as guessed that she and Gerald were . . . Were what?

"I did." *Can I ask him a really important question?* She rolled her lips together. "Gerald, if I ask you something, please don't get upset with me."

"I won't."

"Why does your mother hate me so?"

The question lay like a dead snake in the road between them. She stared at her fingers, watching them twine around one another as if they belonged to someone else. The silence stretched, broken only by a hunk of wood settling with a sigh into oblivion in the stove.

He sighed. "I wish I knew. I don't understand her at all, but she took Toby and me in when we were less than charming and has treated us like her blood-born sons all these years. I'll try to talk with her again. I know she hurt you deeply."

"She's hurt a lot of people through the years."

"I know. But then, she's done a lot of good for people through the years too."

"She brought me two braided rugs—one for the front door and one for my quarters." She paused. "Would you like a cup of coffee?" She was still amazed at the gift. But as he said, Mrs. Valders had done a lot of good through the years too.

"Yes, I would."

"It'll take a bit of time to make."

"Good. That'll give old friends some time to catch up."

Rebecca sighed. So they were back to old friends, eh? Well, at least that was better than not seeing or speaking to each other. And if his mother learned they'd had coffee together all by themselves, she would have a conniption fit. Maybe even take back the lovely rugs.

30

HE'D HELPED HER. GERALD had come to the store last night and helped her again—after everyone else was gone. The euphoria had floated her up the stairs to her new bedroom. Shame he hadn't stayed longer, but any visit was better than none.

Rebecca had recognized the signs, though. He was getting sick again. The gray tinge to his face had been a dead giveaway, especially after the bright flush. He'd grown quieter. Hopefully he'd gotten a good night's sleep to cut it off before it took hold.

This morning she had awakened to the winds again and ideas of a dozen things to be done before she opened the doors to customers on Monday. So much yet to do. Surely God would forgive her if she skipped church today. And though Astrid had invited her back to their house, she wouldn't be missed, for there would be people in and out all day. Besides, God forgive her, she still couldn't face her brothers, and somehow it seemed wrong to go to worship with so much anger in her heart.

Rebecca stretched and ordered herself out of bed. For the first time in her life, she had a place of her own with no one to tell her what to do or when to do it. Except the work list that she had written herself. If Penny decided to buy the store, so be it. It would be back in good shape before she would take over. If Penny decided not to buy the store back, then Rebecca had a good job and could possibly add her real dream to this one. The two would fit well together. It had to, because after all this she didn't think she could move back to the farm again.

Her mind played with one idea and then another as she dressed in a well-worn and thusly faded cotton dress, leaving off the padded winter petticoat for the first time this winter. She added a shawl to keep her warm while she started the stove. After brushing her hair, she braided it and wrapped both braids into a coronet to keep her hair out of her way. She glanced in both empty bedrooms, which had also been cleaned, as she made her way down the narrow stairs to the one large room that was kitchen and sitting room combined. While small for a family, the place was plenty large for her. If she stayed here, she could even let out a room, if necessary. So many possibilities.

Downstairs she could still smell a hint of the kerosene they'd used to clean the windows and scrub the dirtiest places, like behind the counter. Her mother would have been outraged at the amount of dirt they'd washed out of this place. Before starting the stove, Rebecca pushed aside the clean drape and strolled through the store. Her store. No matter that Thorliff had signed his name on the bill of sale, it was her store, at least for now. And Penny's.

She straightened the stack of men's overalls, righted a metal bucket that had somehow been overturned, opened a box that held women's shoes, size 5, and slid the lid under the box. When she came to the window display, she paused, one elbow in the palm of the opposite hand. And thought.

Shame she didn't have a wheelbarrow. Even a used one to set in the window to hold the hoes, rakes, shovels, and a bucket filled with seed packets. A yellow sun would look nice on the wall. She flew back to the dress-goods section, pulled off a bolt of yellow fabric, and took it to the counter to work. She made glue by mixing water and flour, smeared it on the back of a round piece of cardboard, and after cutting a bigger circle out of the cotton, glued it onto the cardboard. She now had a sun. Using a hammer and nail, she pounded it into the aging wood that framed the window display.

Streamers. How could she make streamers? Back to the fabric. She ripped some two-inch-wide strips, attached them around the bottom of the sun, and stretched them to where she decided to set a washtub instead of the wheelbarrow to hold the garden things. With the remainder of the display in place, she walked out the front door and around to look in the window. Not bad for the first time. Not bad at all.

She dusted her hands off and put away her supplies. She'd need to make some advertisements too, like the signs she saw at the store in Bismarck. Penny had pointed such things out to her. My, the things she'd learned in Bismarck for her soda shop were already coming into use.

⁂

"Are you sure you want to try going to church?" Ingeborg asked Haakan.

"Yes, I am sure. We'll have to leave plenty early so I can make it from the wagon to the inside."

"Much as I want you to be able to do this, the thought makes me really uncomfortable."

"So what could happen? I get there and the men carry me in on a chair. I walk in and I'm so worn out I fall asleep during the service. If that happens, I know you won't let me fall off the bench."

"True. I promise to keep you from falling." But would all the activity cause another attack? She refused to allow the thought to take over her mind, as well as refusing to voice her fears to her husband. If he felt going to church this morning was this necessary, she would do everything in her power to help him, including praying every minute. At least it was a beautiful day. The warmer air continued to charm the snow away, causing the water to soak as deep into the soil as the frozen ground permitted. As long as the melt continued like it was, the river would thaw slowly too. Heavy rains always increased the flooding, because the mouth of the river was to the north at Lake Winnipeg and was the last part of the river to thaw. She'd once mentioned that was poor planning on God's part, but He hadn't seen fit to change the river flow. She figured praying for protection was far more simple.

Andrew arrived and hitched up the lightest buggy, since the roads were now well cleared of snow. "I'll take you over and then come back for Ellie and the children."

Haakan nodded.

"Are you ready?"

"Ja, as I'll ever be." Haakan already had his coat and hat on and was waiting in the kitchen for Ingeborg to get hers. Then, leaning heavily on Andrew, he shuffled out the door for the first time since the apoplexy. They paused on the top step for him to inhale spring and new life. With Ingeborg on one side, Andrew on the other, and Astrid behind, he made it down the steps and out to the buggy. There they stopped. His right arm was not strong enough to help him in.

"All right, Mor, you get in the buggy and help pull him, and we'll give him a boost from the back."

"Ja, you be careful you don't boost me clear out the other side."

Ingeborg climbed into the buggy, praying for wisdom, strength, and anything else God figured they needed. "On three. One, two, and three."

Haakan twisted himself sideways so he landed on the seat instead of the floor and sat puffing. "Uff da. Never thought getting into a buggy would take every bit of strength I own. You think Pastor Solberg would move the service outside so I don't have to get out?"

"Everyone will be so glad to see you that they'd probably even do that." Ingeborg settled herself into the seat and turned to Andrew. "Let's get going so you can return for the others."

The rejoicing when they drove up exceeded her expectations. As she'd suspected, four men brought out Pastor's office chair, which had arms, and helped Haakan down into it. Then they picked it up and carried it and its passenger into the church. Ingeborg followed behind, grateful for the fuss being made over Haakan. Being on the receiving end of the outpouring was a new experience for him.

The Valderses stopped on either side of him. "Good to see you, Haakan." Mr. Valders shook the extended left hand.

"Praise God, Mr. Bjorklund. We are glad to see you here, in spite of all your difficulties." Hildegunn patted his shoulder.

Ingeborg kept her mouth shut, a feat that surprised her. She smiled instead, acting as if this were a regular occurrence. But then, she'd always been polite and proper with Haakan nearby. Ingeborg thought about it while the others milled around them. Hildegunn always called the men *mister*, even her husband. This bore more concentration. She'd think about it later.

As the congregation took their seats, she sat on Haakan's right and held the hymnal. *Please don't try to stand,* she thought. *Sitting all through the service is just fine, when standing is such an effort.* But she knew if she said anything, he'd probably make sure he stood. Men could be so stubborn.

But Haakan wisely chose the easier path and remained seated. She caught a glimpse of moisture in his eyes and reached over to stroke his hand. He covered hers with his left hand and didn't let her go, something so out of character that she had to fight tears herself. Just because he didn't say much didn't mean he didn't feel much. She tucked that kernel of wisdom away to be considered later as well.

"So, my friend," Pastor Solberg said after he pronounced the benediction and the final hymn was sung, "how are you now?"

"Mighty weary." Haakan shook his head. "I had no idea how tiring coming to church could be."

Solberg burst out laughing. "I'm just glad you didn't say I was boring."

"Never boring. Never wearisome, but I've never had to look at things from this point of view before." He patted Ingeborg's hand on his shoulder, another one of those out-of-character actions.

Perhaps things had shifted inside of him more than any of them knew. This seemed to be a day for Ingeborg to tuck things away in her heart like Mary, the mother of Christ did, to take them out and ponder them later and through the years. *Please, Lord, let there be lots more years.*

The same four men picked up the chair and carried Haakan back out to the buggy. With them assisting, he was settled on the seat with little effort on his part.

"You want to come home with us and do the same?"

"Ja, if that is what you need," Lars answered.

"I will come," Toby Valders said. He winked at Astrid. "If you promise not to practice your medicine on me."

"Why, Mr. Valders, I assure you I have enough to do with practicing on my father." She turned her chin slightly and gave him a sideways look that made him laugh.

"I'll ride with the Knutsons," Toby said. "They have more room."

"We would love to have you join us for dinner." Ingeborg leaned forward so she could see Toby's face. When his smile widened, she nodded. "And bring the rest of your family too."

"Thank you, but I'm sure Mother will go right home. Gerald is feeling poorly again. It came on suddenly in the night."

"The malaria?" Astrid shook her head. "Someday I hope they figure out a way of curing that disease. It can be so debilitating."

"Gerald tries hard to keep his spirits up. He's worried about his shift at the switchboard."

"Can Deborah take more hours?"

"Some, but it is easy to fall asleep at the post in the early morning hours. I should know. I did last night."

"Did you sleep through any calls?"

"Not sure how long one had been ringing. People should use the telephone only during daylight hours." He touched a finger to his hat brim and climbed into the back of the Knutson wagon.

The road was quickly turning to mire with the passage of the buggies and wagons. The men had to get out and free the buggy once and the wagon twice.

"I think we should develop a runner that slides over the mud, like the sleigh does the snow," Haakan said, leaning back against the seat. "We need to get out on the fields in the next few weeks too, but it's too wet yet." He clenched his good fist, then started working on the fingers of his right hand. "I have to be able to manage the lines." He pressed his fingertips into his thigh muscles and forced his right hand to stretch.

"If you keep working as hard as you have been with your exercises, we'll get you walking well enough to get to the barn in no time," Ingeborg said.

"I don't know. We might have to hire help this year."

"The cousins will be coming from Norway. That will give you two men."

"And women to help with the cheese house."

"I can go out and help plow," Ingeborg said, giving Haakan an arched eyebrow look. They all knew she could do it again, as she had in the past, but Haakan had pleaded with her to not wear britches any longer. Besides, she had plenty to do to keep her busy around the house and garden.

He mumbled something that sounded like "Over my dead body."

Ingeborg ignored him but wanted to remind him not to joke about such things. That could too easily have been the case.

Andrew dropped them off, then headed back to the church to pick up his family. They'd swing by home and bring whatever Ellie had prepared for Sunday dinner. While they'd suggested dinner at Andrew's, they decided it would be easier on Haakan to be at home.

"I think I'll take a quick nap," he said when he made it back into the house. "Those steps, I never realized how high the risers are." He allowed Ingeborg to help him out of his coat and took Astrid's arm to help him back to the bedroom. "I should be out shoveling the banking away from the house now that the snow is receding."

"Not on Sunday."

"But not tomorrow either. Uff da. The chores are building up." He sank down on the bed and watched her kneel to remove his shoes. Laying a hand on her head, he whispered, "You are such a good daughter. God has blessed us with such wonderful children."

She tucked the shoes under the bed and stood. "Thank you." She stepped back and let him fight to get both legs up on the bed. "You know I'd help you, but letting you do it is far better."

"I know." He flopped back on the pillows. "So if I bark at you, please forgive me. I feel more and more like barking the stronger I feel, which makes no sense."

"Sure it does. Remember all those years you reminded me of the importance of patience? You even gave me Bible verses to memorize, like Mor did."

"Why do I have the feeling I'm going to get my wise words thrown in my face?"

"Not thrown. Handed gently." She gave him a smile and headed to the kitchen. "Door open or closed?"

"Closed for now."

❧

"Rebecca?" a female voice called from the back door.

"In here. Come on in." Rebecca left the ledger she was working on at the counter and started toward the living quarters.

Sophie pushed the curtain aside. "I had to come and see the transformation."

"I'll go put the water on for tea and give you a tour."

"Forget the tea. I can't stay long." Her lips curved upward. "I just couldn't wait to see it."

Rebecca started walking her around the store, showing off the new merchandise. "And we have more coming, plus those crates back there to unload."

"Now I know why I couldn't stand to come in here. It was too dark and too dirty. This is wonderful."

"So many people came to help out. You should have seen them;

some would leave and others would come. Thanks for sending Lemuel over. He scrubbed half the walls, I think, up on the ladder. You wouldn't believe the dirt and junk we hauled out of here."

When they reached the window display, Sophie clapped her hands. "Perfect. How'd you make that sun?"

"Cardboard, paste, and yellow cloth. Penny took me around a couple of stores in Bismarck and taught me about displays and choices of merchandise. When we have some money ahead again, I want to put in washing machines, sewing machines . . . things especially for women like Penny did."

"Well, if Hjelmer comes back, I'm sure he'll be selling automobiles along with the farm machinery. You could carry oil and tires and rubber cement, all kinds of newfangled things. Anyway, I came to ask you to come for supper tonight. After all, we are neighbors now, and we want to welcome you to town living."

Rebecca chuckled. "This is me, Rebecca Baard. I'm not new to this town. I've known you since the quilting bees when we played under the tables while our mothers sewed quilts."

"I know, but come anyway."

"All right. Can I bring something?" She couldn't think of a thing to bring since she hadn't really settled into the living quarters yet. Her kitchen needed a good buying spree at the grocery store, but she didn't have any money for such a thing. Unless she tapped into her savings for the soda shop, and she refused to do that. She'd eat beans and canned goods first and whatever anyone brought her.

"Have you talked with your brothers yet?"

Leave it to Sophie to go right for the jugular. "No, they weren't at the house when I went to get my things."

"They weren't in church either. None of them."

Wonderful. Now I suppose it will be my fault they are staying away from church too. This is getting ridiculous. "Maybe I should write them a letter."

"I'll help you if you want."

"Sophie." Rebecca shook her head. "I was teasing."

"Well, I'm not. They need to realize what they did."

"How about if we have a girls' night again on Saturday, here at the store this time?"

"You don't have enough beds."

"No, but some may not be able to spend the entire night anyway. Everyone can bring an extra quilt for a pallet."

"Let's plan on it, then. I'll let them all know." She turned back. "You want me to invite Dorothy too?"

Rebecca felt her back stiffen and nodded. "Yes. I wish . . . but Dr. Elizabeth told her to take it easy. Do you think the baby came, and that's why they weren't at church?"

"No. Knute would have sent a message with someone." Sophie stopped at the draped door. "Did you know Gerald is down sick again?"

"He was looking a little tired last night."

"He was here?" An arch smile said the cat had caught a mouse.

"He came to help, since he'd not been able to during the day."

"I see."

"He left early." *Because he wasn't feeling well. Do I dare go over there and inquire? Only if I want my head bitten off. Or my reputation besmirched. Why does Hildegunn dislike me, no, hate me, so much? Should I ask Sophie?* The words were out of her mouth before the thought left her mind. "Why does she hate me so much?"

"Who?" Sophie blinked and immediately knew who Rebecca meant. "Mrs. Valders."

They nodded together.

"I don't think she hates you any more than any of the other young women who might be friends with her sons. None of us are good enough for them. Although, I believe that no woman walking this earth would be good enough in her eyes." Sophie thought a moment. "Probably even angels wouldn't be good enough."

Rebecca giggled. "Thanks for letting the girls know about our party. Shall we say seven o'clock? By the way, Gerald said he would come help me tomorrow when the store opens for business again."

"I wouldn't count on it."

"I guess." She watched as Sophie went out the door and shut it behind her. "I need a cat or a dog here, something alive besides me—and the mice. It better be a cat. There were kittens out at the barn. I'll ask Knute for one." There she was, talking to herself. The thought that Knute didn't seem to want to speak with her any more than she did him sent a dart into her heart.

Maybe the kitten would be a good reason to go see him. An excuse, at least. And she could check on Dorothy.

People came and went all day at the Bjorklunds', dropping food off or stopping to visit for a little while and then moving on. Ingeborg kept refilling the coffeepot, and Astrid kept washing dishes. The Bjorklund cousins played beside Haakan's bed, then snuggled down with him to take their naps. Thorliff helped with the outside chores, and Elizabeth put Haakan through hot and cold therapy she'd read about, then devised new ways to torture him, or so he called it.

"All in the name of regaining your strength," she blithely reminded him. "I thought you wanted to be ready to do spring work."

"I do."

After everyone but Astrid left and Haakan was sleeping, Ingeborg picked up her knitting and sat down in her rocker. Astrid looked up from the textbook she was studying.

"Can I get you anything?" Astrid asked.

"That's usually my line."

"I know. Just answer the question." She marked her place with a slip of paper.

"No thank you." The cat jumped up in her lap and bumped the top of her head against Ingeborg's chin. Her purring added to the feeling of peace in the room. Ingeborg stroked the furry back and, when the cat settled in her lap, returned to knitting soakers for Ellie's baby. She'd not had much time for knitting lately, nor piecing the quilt she was making for Inga's bed. So with all she had to do, why was the thought of riding the plow behind four up making her heart sing? She knew if she insisted, Haakan would agree. Instead, she would go out tomorrow and start forking the straw and manure, which they had banked up against the house to help keep it warmer for the winter, into a wheelbarrow and haul it over to the garden, where they would throw it on the snow or the dirt and plow it in when the ground was dry enough.

Perhaps she could start that when he was sleeping. Although each day he slept less, not including today.

"Rebecca didn't come today," Ingeborg commented.

"I know. She said she would, but I'm sure she got busy pricing things and getting ready to reopen the mercantile tomorrow. She talked about doing a gardening display in the window, like Penny used to do. Besides, I don't think she was ready to see her brothers."

"None of the other Baards were in church either."

"I noticed." Astrid kept her finger in the book. "I told Elizabeth I'd go help at the surgery for a while tomorrow, if you were agreeable."

"That will be fine. Although I thought you might help me shovel away the banking."

"I can do that too."

"What kinds of fabric did Rebecca get in?"

"She has ginghams, calicos, dimity, lawn . . ." She scrunched her eyes to better remember. "Lots of plain colors too. Word will get out, and all the women will be there stocking up."

"I hope she ordered plenty of needles."

"She did. I counted out the packets. Every size, for machines and for hand sewing."

"I'm glad Penny didn't see the way Jeffers let her store run down. Speaking of which, did Rebecca mention the attack?"

"Ja, we talked about it. She was doing fine until Mrs. Valders made her big speech. Mor, you would have been so proud of Thorliff. He stood between her and Rebecca, and with the utmost calm and fine manners, he eased Hildegunn right out the door. I feel sorry for those who live with her."

Ingeborg thought a bit, especially since Hildegunn had been so courteous at church that morning. "Maybe she's not so bossy at home. You know, she always speaks politely to Mr. Valders. And it sounds like he never mentioned his part in the sale of the store. So he doesn't tell her everything."

"Smart man. I know what the problem is."

"Oh, you do? Really?" Her smile took any possible sting out of the teasing words.

"She's jealous."

"Who? Hildegunn? Of what, whom?" The click of the needles picked up speed.

"Of you."

Two words that dropped into the pool and spread ripples across the placid water.

Ingeborg laid down her knitting, making the cat grumble and stretch before leaping to the floor. "Of me? Why?"

"I'm not sure. Let's think this through." Astrid propped her elbows on the arms of the chair and steepled her fingers, forefingers against her chin. "You have a good business, the cheese house. You have a lot of friends. You were the doctor around here for years. You have children of your own."

"But they adopted the boys."

"But they never had babies, little ones."

Ingeborg shook her head. "This is silly. Why me? Others have much the same. Kaaren has the school, others have lots of children. God has blessed us all in so many ways."

"Whose house do most people come to?"

"Well, ours mostly, I guess."

"As I said . . ."

"Oh, Astrid . . ." Ingeborg shook her head, and a frown wrinkled mouth and brow. "Kaaren's house is bigger."

"But all the deaf students are there." Astrid picked up her book again. "It's just something to think about and perhaps to help us understand her better."

"Who's the mother here?"

"You. I'm sure not ready to be one. I love being an aunt. Speaking of which, I need to get sewing on the pinafores for little May so she has something to wear this summer. I think I'll make matching ones for Inga and her doll."

"Surely Hildegunn hasn't let jealousy destroy her happiness all these years."

Astrid shrugged. "It was just an idea that came to me."

Ingeborg stared at her daughter, who'd gone back to her book on infectious diseases. Jealousy and bitterness, two things that God's Word said to rip out like quack grass, for they destroyed the soul. Leave no roots to grow. How difficult that was with quack grass.

31

Monday morning Rebecca woke when dawn was just a wish on the horizon. Standing at the bedroom window, she watched the horizon lighten, chasing the azure back with the gift that returned every morning. When the few cloud traces turned vermilion and rose, she went about her morning toilet, washing in the water from the pitcher and slipping into a clean waist and dark cotton skirt. Her white apron would cover it all, but she wanted to look nice for the day. Just in case Gerald did come. *And since when do you dress for Gerald?*

With her hair braided and wound in a figure eight at the base of her skull, she pulled a few wisps free and spit-curled them around her forehead. There. The slightly warped mirror showed a comely young woman with wide-set hazel eyes, hair with glints of fire like the sunrise, a pert nose, and lips that loved to smile. She'd heard those words describe her on the girls' night together and had filed them away for future reference.

Downstairs, she started a fire in the kitchen stove, blowing on the coals she'd carefully covered with ashes to keep them alive. At least she'd not started seeds at home, since she wasn't there to take care of them. Somehow she would manage to plant some here if Penny wasn't going to take the store back. So many *if onlys*. Fixing breakfast for just herself seemed a waste of time, so she toasted some bread and opened a jar of applesauce. That with a cup of coffee would have to suffice.

She checked the new ledger on which she'd printed the accounts of people who lived in and around Blessing. Collecting those would take some time, but she needed cash so she could order more merchandise. Thorliff couldn't be paying for all the stock. The store had to pay for itself. She glanced down the two lists she'd made of more things needed, the first list being the more necessary items and the second list less so. Considering how much they'd already ordered, the store was definitely in debt.

After breakfast she started a fire in the stove in the store to take the chill off the air and to make coffee. From now on there would be coffee for any shoppers who wanted a cup. Two chairs and a bench waited near the stove for those who wanted to sit and talk.

When she turned the *Closed* sign in the window to *Open* and unlocked the door, Gerald was already waiting for her on the porch.

"I thought you were sick."

"Good morning to you too."

"Are you sure you should be here?"

"I'm not contagious. And I promise to go home before I faint." He motioned to the door. "May I come in and help you?"

"Yes. Yes, of course." Maybe she had a fever; her cheeks felt on fire.

"You look lovely."

She coughed on the words she was going to say, whatever they had been. What had happened to him? "Did the fever addle your mind?"

"Hardly. What do you want me to do?"

"Do you know how to run the cash register?"

"I used to."

"It's the same one. I put money in it for change. The ledger book for accounts is right beside it." She glanced to the door. Maybe no one would come. Surely the word had gone around the area that the store was open again. She figured many would come out of curiosity, if nothing else.

She talked Gerald through running the cash register, explaining that two keys stuck sometimes, so he had to watch for that. Just being this close to him brought a flush to her cheeks.

She could feel his gaze on her hands, her face. Maybe having him help wasn't such a good idea after all.

The bell tinkled, and Mrs. Solberg peeked in. "Are you indeed open?"

"I am."

"Good. I really have needed needles for quite some time, and . . ." She followed Rebecca to the sewing section and clasped her hands under her chin in delight. "Oh, look at these daisies." She fingered the yellow lawn with white daisies. "May I have four yards of that, and—"

The bell announced another customer.

Rebecca measured and cut fabric, lace, and elastic, restocked the seed rack, and wrote down things that needed to be ordered. In between she found herself looking over to Gerald, and he would be looking back at her with a smile. Several women brought plates of cookies to go with the coffee, and she had to take time out several times to refill the coffeepot.

While Gerald moved the ladder over to get a harness off the wall, she rang up another customer. A dollar bill got stuck behind the drawer, so she gave a jerk, and the entire drawer flew out, throwing coins, notes, and paper money in every direction.

"Oh!"

"Are you all right?" asked Mrs. Solberg. "Here, let me help you." She came around the counter and knelt to help retrieve the errant money.

Rebecca picked up the cash drawer and stared at the bottom of it. "Look at this."

Mary Martha peered at the brown paper envelope that was glued to the bottom of the drawer. "What do you suppose it is?"

"I have no idea." Did Penny leave this and forget it? Mr. Jeffers? "There's no name."

"Well, you manage the store, so opening it must be part of your job."

Gerald joined them in picking up the money. "Interesting," he said when Rebecca showed him the envelope stuck to the underside of the drawer. "Open it."

Rebecca dug a fingernail under one corner and pulled up gently, trying to keep from ripping the paper. It wasn't terribly old, but smudges and some wrinkles showed the wear. Would it be money? What? Feeling like she did on Christmas when she tried to figure out what was inside the packages before they were unwrapped, she finally loosened the envelope and laid it on the counter while she and Gerald put the money and notes back in the correct places and the drawer back in the cash register.

Several customers waited, watching the proceedings and speculating on what might be in the envelope.

Rebecca took a letter opener from a wooden drawer under the counter and slit the brown paper. Inside were several pages, a form of some kind, and a picture of a man and a woman, which looked to be a wedding picture. She turned it over. Mr. and Mrs. Daniel Jeffers. The date read June 1, 1872. She opened the folded paper.

"It's a patent application and approval. Mr. Jeffers must have left this." She looked from Mary Martha to Gerald, who both shook their heads.

Mrs. Solberg studied the picture. "This must be Mr. Jeffers' parents, but he certainly bore no resemblance to them."

They looked like fine upstanding folk, but then, many families had a black sheep in their pen. Mr. Jeffers made even a dirty black sheep look good.

Rebecca slid the papers back in the envelope and put the envelope in the drawer under the counter. She would pass it along to Thorliff later.

"Next, please."

32

"THEY'RE COMING. THEY'RE REALLY coming."

"From Norway?"

Ingeborg fluttered the letter at Haakan sitting in his rocking chair, now moved back into the kitchen. "You want to hear it?"

"Of course."

"Dear Ingeborg,

"Mange takk for your fast answer to our letter. We are so grateful you are willing to help us with a place to live and jobs. As I said, there will be four adults and two children. We have our tickets to sail from Oslo to England on the fifteenth of June. We should arrive in New York on the twenty-fifth of June and then will take the trains to your town of Blessing. We have been learning to speak English like you suggested, but we do not know very much yet. I remember going to the setre every summer with you, those so many years ago."

Ingeborg looked over the top of the letter to her husband. "You remember that the setre is where we took the cows to the high mountain pastures in the spring."

"Ja, I remember. That is where you learned to make cheese."

"Whoever would have dreamed on those mountain meadows that I would marry and come to these flat lands." She shook her head. "How I would love to see mountains again before I go to heaven."

"Would you like to go back to Norway?"

"For a visit, ja. But to live?" She shook her head. "I am truly an American now. I want to live here." *With you for many years to come.* She returned to the letter.

> "Thank you for paying part of our fare. That generosity was far beyond what we had hoped. Please send as much information as you can so that we don't get lost along the way. I send you greetings from those remaining in Norway. Perhaps another time we can help bring more relatives to the new land.
>
> "Your cousin,
> Alfreda Brunderson"

Ingeborg read silently through the letter again, then looked to Haakan. "What other advice and information do you want to send? We need to write the letter and mail it soon."

"Let us think on it. Right now I would like to walk down to the barn."

"And back?"

"Ja. That would be a good idea." He shook his head. "What have you been doing out there and not wanting me to know?"

"Just getting ready for the garden. Andrew said he'll be plowing before too much longer."

"This sitting around with so much to be done." Haakan glared at his hand and stuck out his right foot. "Surely there are things that I can do; we just have to devise a way."

Ingeborg had been expecting this and was grateful he'd put up with things before now. "What might we work out?"

"Strap me onto the plow. The horses know what to do well enough that I don't need strength in that arm to guide them, especially if I drive the old team."

"But—" She bit off her words, finishing the sentence in her mind. *What if something spooked the team? Accidents happen so quickly. Lord, please give us wisdom and protection.* She knew that if she disagreed with him, mother-henned him, he'd get stubborn and go ahead no matter what. All these years of marriage had taught her that much, at least.

He flexed and straightened his fingers, forcing them straighter by pushing them with his other hand against his thigh. It wasn't for lack of effort on his part that the weakened limbs were still healing.

"Haakan, it hasn't even been two weeks."

"I know. Two of the longest weeks of my life." He stared out the window. "I know I could manage the plow."

"Let's walk on down to the barn." She let him navigate the back steps by himself, grateful they had a sturdy railing for him to hang on to. His stride was more even than the day before, but while she was pleased with his progress, each day it ate at him more.

She and Astrid had agreed to stay out of his way, let him do whatever he decided to try, but the doing thereof was more mountain than molehill. When he stumbled, she didn't grab him but managed to be where he could grab her.

He stopped to catch his breath. "I'm worse than an old man."

"That's your opinion." She raised her face to the sun. "What a glorious day."

When he started off again, she kept step. "Andrew said the sow would be ready for breeding any day."

"Did he put the boar in with her?"

"Let's go see." The three hogs were lying on their sides in the sun. Ingeborg and Haakan leaned on the fence. "Now, that's the way to spend the day."

"Not if the plowing needs to be done." He turned at the sound of metal pounding on metal. "I'm going to the machine shed. You can go on back to the house."

"Yes, sir." She snapped off a military salute.

Haakan swatted her lightly on her posterior and walked away.

"You could at least keep the cane with you."

His wave told her what he thought of that idea.

If he went into the machine shed, he would not be able to see her shoveling the banking away from the house. She sighed with relief and returned to her pitchfork and wheelbarrow. Pitching straw and manure did manage to work up a sweat and make her muscles ache. Spring work after winter's respite was always hard on backs and especially hands. Even though she was wearing leather gloves, she had hot spots on her palms after an hour's labor.

When her back screamed for relief, Ingeborg returned inside and drank a dipper of water without stopping. The kitchen seemed empty without him. After adding canned beans, tomatoes, and chopped cabbage to the soup she had left simmering, she went down to the cellar to search for more carrots. The few remaining were sending leafy sprouts through the layers of sand. She dug them out and, after grabbing a jar of raspberry jam for the biscuits and another of dill pickles, headed back upstairs. Soon it would be time to clean out the cellar too. But there was no sense in doing so until after the river thawed and they learned how bad the floods would be. While they'd built up a bit of a rise for the house, the cellar still flooded regularly.

She hummed while she measured the ingredients for the biscuits, added the buttermilk, and patted the dough into a half-inch-thick circle to cut out the biscuits. With that finished and the pan ready for the oven, she added wood to the firebox to heat the oven more and crossed to the door to let the cat in.

"No, I don't want a mouse in here. Ishda." She shooed the cat back outside. "You eat that out there." Thanks to their good mouser, she rarely had mice in the pantry, and those that got in never lasted long.

"Oh, today is the reopening of the mercantile. I was going to go there this morning." She swiped a lock of hair from her forehead with the back of her hand. "And here I am, talking to myself. Uff da." She kept on humming to keep her mind off worrying over Haakan. He would come back to the house when he got too tired. If only she believed that little story.

Stepping onto the back step, she rang the triangle that hung on a bracket by the door. Another first for this season. The call to dinner.

A few minutes later she returned to the door to look toward the barn. Haakan was walking slowly, but he wasn't leaning on Andrew or Lars, who were setting their pace to his. From her vantage point she could see his hands were greasy. He'd managed to do something, proving her wrong again. *Thank you, Father, for keeping him safe. And restoring his strength.*

The cat chirped from beside her, rubbing against the heavy woolen skirt. "Yes, you can come in now that you ate your mouse. Sorry, but I have a hard time appreciating the gifts you try to bring me." She bent over and lifted the purring cat, rubbing the furry head with her chin. She'd better get a basin of water ready for the men to wash.

They came in talking of plans like any other workday. Had she not recognized the exhaustion on her husband's face, it would have been easy to forget the last weeks.

He sank into his chair at the table and nodded when she placed a cup of coffee in front of him. She squeezed his shoulder as she passed and went to dish up the soup.

"Andrew, please say grace." Haakan nodded to his son, who gave him a look of surprise. Haakan always said the grace.

They bowed their heads and Andrew began the old Norwegian words. "I Jesu navn . . ." The others joined in, and after the amen, Ingeborg stood to get the biscuits out of the oven.

"So how did you do?" She took her place at the table and started the basket around.

"He did really good." Andrew grinned at his mother. "Might have slowed his hand down but not his mouth or his memory. Lars and I know exactly what to do now."

She snuck a peek at her husband's face. His smile said he knew Andrew was teasing. Her glance at Andrew earned her another smile.

"He did well, Mor. We're trying to figure a way to adapt the plow so he can drive it. We'll harness him up and send him out to the field as soon as the land is dry enough." He paused. "It'll be okay, Mor."

Ingeborg nodded and kept from heaving a sigh. This was worse than her two young sons trying to do men's work when they were still little boys. *Keep reminding me, Lord, that you carried them safely and will carry Haakan too.*

Later that afternoon Ingeborg and Kaaren turned to smile at each other as they approached the store in the buggy. A steady stream of customers was going up the steps to the store and others were coming back out, everyone with at least one package. While there'd not been this kind of business when Penny had owned the store, it had been some time since the community had had a fully stocked general store.

"We aren't the only ones out of things."

"At the rate this is going, Rebecca might be out of some items by now too." Kaaren glanced at the list in her basket. "And I ordered supplies for the school directly, like Sophie did for the boardinghouse."

The women climbed out of the light buggy and mounted the steps to the open door. The warm day felt almost like summer and time to pack away the woolen clothes.

"Look at her window display," Ingeborg said as she pointed.

"That child has good ideas. You'd think Penny was back. My favorite was the one with the sewing machine."

"The washing machine was better." The two entered the store and paused just inside. "A whole new world."

"How can I help you today, ladies?" Rebecca sang out. "We'll be right with you."

"We?" Ingeborg gave Kaaren a raised eyebrow look. Kaaren shrugged and pointed to the left, where Gerald, sleeves rolled back and a pencil above his ear, was waiting on a man they recognized as a farmer from south of town who rarely came to Blessing. "News gets around fast."

Together they strolled to the housewares aisle and picked up various packets of needles and thread, and then fingered the lace.

"Inga would love a dress out of this." Ingeborg held out a fold of yellow gingham. "I could smock the bodice."

"Add this narrow lace at the neck and sleeves, and won't she think she's the prettiest little girl ever?" Kaaren smiled. "I need to make something for Joy and Hamre. I haven't taken time to sew for so long. Perhaps when Grace comes home for the summer, she'll get some sewing done."

"Couldn't have anything to do with the curriculum you've been developing for the school for the deaf in New York?"

"I never dreamed that would take so much time. But when Mrs. Wooster wrote and asked if I would think on it, how could I say no?"

"Did you find what you needed?" Rebecca stopped beside them and leaned closer. "Wait until I tell you the news of today."

From the sparkle in her eyes, Ingeborg figured it was good news. She took two bolts of fabric off the shelf, added the notions, and carried the stack to the counter for Rebecca to cut and figure up. After telling her what she wanted, she found the bluing in another aisle for her laundry, as well as starch for her ironing.

As soon as Rebecca wrapped their packages and rang them up, she told Gerald she was taking tea with her guests and led them back to the kitchen. A fresh pot of coffee waited on the stove. "Would you rather have coffee, since it is ready? We've given out more free coffee today than I ever dreamed we would. I had to go next door and buy some more. The people of Blessing do like something that is free."

"Coffee will be fine." Ingeborg glanced around at the nearly empty room. "I see you brought in your mother's sewing machine."

Rebecca set two coffee-filled cups on the table. "Yes. I didn't think Gus would need it." She carried her own cup of coffee over, and they all sat. As she related the story of the cash register drawer, Ingeborg and Kaaren shook their heads.

"Well, I never. Strange that Jeffers never mentioned a patent. You'd have thought he'd have bragged on it."

"There was something strange about that man," Kaaren said as she set her cup down. "I have a feeling we've not heard the end of this yet."

33

Exhausted as she was, Rebecca still couldn't get to sleep.

A dog barked somewhere in town. With her window open, she could hear other night noises too. She wasn't used to houses being so close together. Thinking on that brought her brothers to mind. None of the Baards had come to the store today. Her first day in business, and they'd not come to wish her well. Did they hate her that much? Or perhaps they'd not heard that the store would be open again. She turned onto her other side.

Tomorrow night after the store closed she would walk out there and ask for a kitten. She who had always had a horse available or horse and wagon, whatever she needed, no longer had those services. She didn't have time for a horse here anyway. Besides, if she walked, she'd not get mired down in the Red River mud.

She'd given the envelope from the cash register to Thorliff. It wasn't her place to have to deal with that. But what did it all mean? She turned again, punching her pillow up in the process.

Gerald had spent his whole day off helping her in the store. Not that they'd had time for more than "Where is this," or "You need to order that." But she would not have made it through the day without him. The line would have been so long that some people wouldn't have waited. She had so much to learn about running a store. It wasn't as simple as just ringing up the cash register. But Gerald had made it seem so easy, and his smiles had lifted her tiredness all day.

She sat up and stacked her two pillows behind her. Lighting the candle took too much effort, and besides, the moon cast window squares of white on the floor. A kitten would be good company. Come Saturday, she would have a houseful of friends. What would she serve to eat? Talk about a bare kitchen; that's what she had. What kind of person invited people to a party with no food?

And no money to buy any. Thorliff had taken a lot of money from the cash register and put it in the bank today, but that wasn't hers. He had been both pleased and amazed. In the morning she would place her first order on the telephone. They would have new stock within the week. Oh, the convenience, the thrill of it all.

When she finally fell asleep, her dreams included the ringing cash register and Gerald watching over her.

The next evening, as soon as she turned the *Closed* sign on the door after another busy day, she threw a shawl around her shoulders and, with a basket on her arm, headed across the prairie to the Baard place. Strange to be approaching it on foot like this. She stuck her head in the door of the house she'd grown up in and called, but she'd already known no one would be there. She could just go down to the barn and pick up one of the kittens, but she headed on over to Knute's instead.

Her brothers were most likely down at the barn milking, not that three cows took much time. She tapped on the door and opened it. "Anybody home?"

"Auntie Rebecca!" Two small bodies barreled across the room and threw themselves at her knees. She hugged Sarah with one hand and Hans with the other, all the while searching for Dorothy. "Where's your ma?"

"In here," Dorothy called from the bedroom. "I'm not feeling too good, so I took a moment to lie down."

Rebecca swung Hans up on her hip, and with her other hand securely trapped between Sarah's, she made her way to the bedroom.

"Why did you move to town?" Sarah asked, her lower lip rolled out. "We never see you."

"I know. But you can come visit me at the store. I'm not hard to find."

"Unless you have a brand of stubborn that never ends." Dorothy rose up on her elbows. "I'd better get supper on the table. The men will be up in a few minutes."

"You stay right there. I can manage the supper. Sarah will help me."

The little girl nodded. "Yesterday I put Hans down for his nap and sang him to sleep."

"I'd hoped to see some of you at the reopening of the store yesterday. About everyone from all around showed up at one time or another, even with the roads being so muddy."

"I planned to go, but . . ." Dorothy shook her head. "I just couldn't face the ride in the wagon. The supper is in the oven in the roaster. Just put it on the table. Sarah, you set the table, please, for Auntie Rebecca." Dorothy shook her head again. "They are acting like spoiled children."

"I take it you mean Gus and Knute?"

"I most certainly do. They can't admit they made a mistake, and so they are blaming you."

"Now, isn't that a fine way for grown-up men to act?" Rebecca heaved a sigh. Stubborn did not begin to describe the Baard men, as she had known for years. Not that the women didn't carry the trait too, but somehow it wasn't the same.

"We are having pork roast. I saw Ma put it in the pan." Sarah looked up from setting the table, her cheeks creased in pleasure.

Rebecca raised her voice. "Do you have any bread or rolls?"

"No. I just couldn't bake bread today. My back is a mess." Dorothy leaned against the doorjamb.

"I thought you were going to stay in bed."

"I can't. There is just too much to do. Sarah, bring the pickles from the pantry, please."

"How long has this been going on?"

"A couple of days."

"Did you go see Dr. Elizabeth again?"

"No."

"Sit down in the rocker and put your feet up. I should be over here taking care of you, and now I can't leave the store."

"Don't worry. This will go away," she said while slowly settling her bulky frame in the chair. "It has before." When Hans asked to be picked up, she helped him crawl onto her knees, since her lap was now nonexistent.

The sound of boots on the steps made Rebecca suck in a deep breath. *Please, Lord, make this go well.*

"I brought—" Knute stopped and stared at his sister. "What brought you out here?"

"I came for a kitten." *And to set things right with the two of you.* Although she hadn't realized that part of her mission until just that second.

Gus shut the door behind them. Seven-year-old Swen stood by his father.

At least Gus had the grace to look ashamed. Rebecca sucked in a breath of courage. "I just wanted to say that I forgive you both." She caught a breath in surprise. That wasn't what she meant to say at all. "I know you didn't mean to have all this happen, and you were just trying to do the best you knew how."

Knute's jaw dropped. He blinked and turned to look over his shoulder at his younger brother. When Gus seemed as shocked as he was, he turned back to Rebecca. "We didn't mean . . . I mean . . . I thought . . . What I want to say is . . ." He held his arms out from his sides. "We never dreamed Jeffers would act like that."

"None of us did." *Best leave it at that,* an inner voice admonished. "I'm just sorry there have been hard feelings between us. Ma and Pa would be heartbroken to see this."

"Yes." Dorothy gave her husband a hard stare while Sarah glued herself to her mother's side.

"I . . . I'm sorry." Knute forced the words out.

"Me too," Gus mumbled.

"Then all is forgiven, and we can eat our supper in peace." Rebecca lifted Hans into the high chair, and Swen came to stand in front of Rebecca. "Do you want a black kitten or a gray one? I'll go get it for you." His smile widened. "I'm glad you are here. I wanted to come visit you during noon recess, but we aren't allowed to leave school without permission." He still spoke slowly, as he had since he was a baby. For a while they had been concerned about him, but he'd finally caught up with other kids his age, just slower.

"Thank you." She ruffled his hair. "But let's eat supper first." How she had missed these children, this family of hers. When they asked her the news of town, she told them about finding the envelope and how so many people had come to help clean up the store.

"Do you like working there?" Knute asked.

"I do. I always enjoyed helping Penny at the store. And these last two days, everyone who came in was so appreciative of what we've done. It was like one long party." She touched Sarah on the tip of her turned-up nose. "I have a feeling you might find something you like, for all three of you, in my basket." She nodded to the basket sitting on a chair by the door. "When we're done eating."

"You know, I wouldn't mind at all if you came home."

Leave it to Gus to invite her in such a roundabout way.

"In fact, he'd be glad," Dorothy added as she handed Hans his spoon again.

I'm sure you would be too, Rebecca thought. "Thank you, but I think for now, I'll stay in town. I'm even thinking of putting in a garden in that plot Penny used. The raspberries and strawberries are up."

"I see. Our house is mighty big for one person." Gus still didn't look her in the eye.

"Then maybe you should see about finding yourself a wife," Dorothy said, sharing a smile with Rebecca. "Your sister spoiled you something fierce."

"But right now Dorothy needs some help." Rebecca looked from brother to brother.

"You could take one of the horses into town and ride out every evening if you'd like."

"Or come home and ride to the store each morning."

"Or we could hire Mrs. Geddick to come out a couple of times a week and do some cleaning and baking. Or see if Maydell would come back."

"But why?"

"Knute Baard, don't you see that this coming baby is being hard on your wife? She should go see Dr. Elizabeth. You should go with her and ask what she recommends."

"But—"

"But nothing. I'll do what I can, and I'll let some of the other women know, but that's one reason so many women die in childbirth. The women are just too tired to—"

"Rebecca Baard, this isn't proper talk for a young woman or for our supper table." Knute sat up straighter. "Can I please have another cup of coffee?"

Rebecca almost said, "Well, help yourself," but thought the better of it. Instead, she smiled sweetly and got up for the coffeepot. But she whispered in his ear when she filled his cup, "You think on what I said if you want Dorothy here to raise your children."

After filling the other cups, she motioned for Sarah to get the basket. "I think there's enough for everyone to have a bit. Then, Swen, you get me a kitten, please. Gus, you get the horse, and I'll see you all tomorrow evening." She glared at both of her brothers. "And I sure hope someone has seen fit to make sure Dorothy takes a nap during the day."

"I think the gray kitten is prettier. She's fluffy with white paws." Swen came with a kitten in the basket and stood beside her.

"I think you are right," Rebecca said after peeking at it.

Sarah passed out the peppermint candies and leaned against Rebecca's knees. "Next year I go to school."

"I know. You are getting to be so grown up." Rebecca hugged her little niece.

"Do you need anything else?" Gus asked after he boosted her into the saddle.

"Not at the moment, but I do need some more kitchen supplies. Penny took all but the stove with her, and *that* man never cooked, so I'll make a list and get some each night." The scratching sound from inside the basket made her smile. "Thanks for the kitten."

"You're welcome. I'll bring in some hay for the horse."

She waved and set off toward town. Halfway there, she realized that God had indeed answered her prayer in ways she'd never imagined. She'd expected a loud confrontation, and He gave her a quiet peace. She was beginning to understand what her mother and Ingeborg meant about prayers. Looking toward the heavens, she whispered, "Thank you, oh, thank you so much. You do listen and answer."

When she got back to the store, after tying the horse in the shed, she found a note tacked to the door. *Sorry I missed you. If you need more help, let me know. Your friend, Gerald.* She felt a rush of pure happiness. After his long day he'd come to see her.

She set the basket with the kitten on the table and went to find a box to keep it in until she tamed it. While the children petted the barn kittens and played with them, they weren't well-mannered enough to be house cats. Hence the box with a lid, and in the morning she'd fill a small box with sand for the kitten to use. Maybe if she crocheted a leash and collar, she could keep track of it that way.

"You sweet little thing, what am I going to call you." She held the kitten in her arms and stroked her back and head. "Mischief? Miss Chief? After all, you're the only animal here. Mischief. That's it." Touching noses with the little creature, she cuddled her close. "You better grow up to be a good mouser like your mother. I hate mouse traps."

In the lamplight she made a list of things she needed from home and added to the order she would send in the next morning. The thought of doing that herself made her heart pick up speed like a sled going downhill. What if she made a mistake? Ordered something that never sold? Spent too much money? Couldn't keep the books straight? Although on that last, she shook her head. Anyone could keep better records than Jeffers had. Other than what people owed him. That was in detail to the penny. Which led to another question. How was she to collect that? Or should she just let it all go? But then, that decision was not hers to make but Thorliff's. After all, he was the owner. What would Penny do? The question sat in her mind, smiling sweetly.

It's not my decision.

So much hinged on whether Penny would buy the store or not. And if not? She closed her eyes and let her mother's voice answer the questions. *"Be not concerned for the morrow, today's own troubles are sufficient. Consider the lilies of the field, they neither toil nor spin, and yet your heavenly Father arrays them in beauty."* Soon the violets would be blooming and the bluebells. And they were beautiful. Surely she could trust God as her mother had. After all, He did indeed hear her prayers and answer them.

"Thank you, Lord. My brothers don't hate me, and I love them so dearly." The kitten in her lap stretched and yawned, its pink tongue curling between white needle teeth. "And I have a friend here." She thought back to the cleaning day and to Monday, the opening day. For certain sure, she had friends and blessings in abundance.

❧

By Saturday night she felt as though she'd lived three lives, between tending the store, riding out each night to check on Dorothy, and getting ready for the girls' party. At least Knute seemed to be taking a little more responsibility for his wife's health.

Saturday night Ellie was the first to arrive on the back porch, along with her baby, Gudrun May, and then Astrid, Sophie, and Maydell.

Rebecca stared at Maydell. "You came back. I thought you'd be gone for a long time."

"I couldn't miss out on this party. Besides, there is so much more to do here than in Grafton."

Sophie nudged Rebecca. "She means Gus. You want to bet?"

"Well, let me tell you, there is a lot going on. We sure would appreciate it if you went back out to help Dorothy." She paused, catching a funny look in Maydell's eyes. "Don't worry. The men are all right again. They just needed a dose of forgiveness to get over the grumps."

Maydell tipped her head to the side. "Well, if you are sure."

"Gus even said that house was too big for one person."

"You won't be going back?"

"I don't think so."

"So it all depends on how well you use your feminine wiles," Sophie said with raised eyebrows. "And how bad you want Gus, I guess."

The look on Maydell's face made them all laugh.

"Did you make your list?" Astrid asked Maydell. "Like we all agreed?"

"Oh, I made my list, but it only had one name on it." She put one finger to her chin. "Although maybe I should go visit Penny. That Kurt sounds like a real catch."

Not compared to Gerald, Rebecca thought. But this comment she kept to herself.

Everyone brought food, thanks to Sophie's putting out the word, so Rebecca hadn't had to think on that. As Sophie had said, "That's what friends are for." For Rebecca the term *friends* had taken on a whole new meaning. She wished she could tell them about all the things she'd learned lately, but it would take too long.

"We have to do this again when Grace gets home," Sophie said as soon as Deborah arrived. "She has missed out on so much."

"I think she loves what she is doing."

"I know she does, but Blessing is home and where all the important things go on." Sophie stopped and clapped her hand over her mouth. Eyes wide, she shook her head. "Can you believe I said such a thing? I was the one who wanted to see the whole world, yet I found it all when I came back here. God sure is amazing, is He not?"

Rebecca nodded. "He gave me all of you for sisters since mine went off and left so long ago."

"Speaking of Anji, are the Moens coming back here at all?"

"I don't know. They still have their house here, but Ivar seems to prefer Norway. Come to think of it, I haven't heard from her in a long time. I need to write to her with all the news here."

"So give us the grand tour of the store," Deborah said, locking her arm through Rebecca's. "Everyone is raving about it."

"Really?" She held back the drape. "Come and see." She showed them all the changes she had made and stopped at the cash register. "You should have seen the drawer fly out. It threw money everywhere. I swept up some more change this morning."

"Where is the envelope now?"

"Thorliff has it. We have no way of getting it to Jeffers."

Sophie made a face. "That skunk doesn't deserve getting it back."

"I know, but we will do the honorable thing." At least the thought of him didn't send her heart into high speed any longer. Although the night before she'd had a nightmare about him again.

"Did you hear from Penny?" Astrid asked, leaning against the counter, arms crossed. "This place looks so good again. I'm glad she didn't see it the way he left it."

"Me too, but we've not heard back yet. I know Mrs. Valders is pestering Thorliff. She wants very badly to buy it."

They all trailed back to the kitchen, where the quilts were folded and stacked against one wall. Rebecca lifted the kitten out of her box. "This is my latest friend. Her name is Mischief."

"Oh, so cute." Maydell reached for the kitten and cuddled her under her chin. "Did you talk with your brothers?"

"Yes, the other day. That's how I know all is well."

"Gus doesn't pay any attention to me, and I've tried everything," Maydell complained, fanning her cheeks.

"Well, perhaps you could cook him some special things. He likes good food."

They helped themselves to the bread and cheese, deviled eggs and pickles, cookies and coffee, and since there were not enough chairs, they all sat cross-legged on their quilts on the floor. Mischief scampered from one to the other, sniffing the plates and trying out her claws.

"Thinking back to our last party, Rebecca, your life certainly has changed. What happened with that man in Bismarck?"

"I don't know. Kurt said he would write, but I haven't heard from him."

"Did you write to him?"

"I did and thanked him for showing me such a nice time."

"Was he handsome?" Maydell asked.

Rebecca nodded. "And charming and—"

"I hear a *but* in your voice." Sophie leaned forward, eyes narrowed.

Rebecca studied the crumbs on her plate and then looked up. "But I realized he wasn't Gerald," she said in a soft voice.

Sophie threw her head back and stared at the ceiling. "But does he love you?" She paused and looked at Rebecca again. "Do you *really* love him?"

"I think so."

"But …" Sophie looked around the circle. "What about his mother?" They all nodded and groaned.

Rebecca nuzzled her kitten, who'd decided to sleep in the lap she knew best. What about his mother? How could she ever win Hildegunn Valders over? Surely the debt of gratitude he felt for her taking him in as a child would not take precedence over his feelings for Rebecca. That is, if indeed he felt more than friendship.

"You need to find out if he loves you before you go pinning all your hopes on him." Maydell got up and brought the plate of cookies back to pass around.

"What am I supposed to do? Go up to him and say, 'Say, Gerald. Do you love me? Not just as a friend, but in a romantic way?'"

The girls giggled.

"You could mention you had a letter from Kurt." Maydell had a cookie in each hand, taking a bite out of one, then the other.

"But that would be lying."

"Only a little fib."

Rebecca shook her head. Surely she wouldn't have to stoop to that. She couldn't. Then she'd be twisting the truth, just like Jeffers had. Besides, Gerald was her best friend, and friends don't lie to each other. She'd rather follow the way her mother had and do some more praying. Lots more praying. After all, look at the miracle with Gus and Knute.

34

"Penny's coming back," Ingeborg announced at dinner a few days later. "She says she and the children will come as soon as school is out, and Hjelmer will finish out his job the end of June. I guess she will go back to help move." Ingeborg thought a moment. "She wasn't clear on all the details."

"That is good news." Haakan sat down with a groan. "I never knew plowing took so much strength. It just seemed so much easier with the horses pulling the two bottom plows than it was with the walking plow."

Ingeborg read the note again then stared at her husband while she put it back in the envelope. Though he'd washed off most of the dirt, the gray around his eyes and mouth gave him away.

"Well, the first couple of days you couldn't make it to noon. Now you have. I'd say that is great progress." The fatigue showing on his face tore at her heart.

"I've . . . never been this tired . . . in my entire life." Each word came slowly, as if with great effort. "I don't think I can even eat."

"You don't have to do this, Far. We can manage for a while. After all, we're not usually out in the field this early." Andrew shook his head. "Give yourself a few more days. You are getting stronger every day."

"Say the grace."

Several minutes later, Haakan laid down his knife and fork. "Andrew, help me get up, will you please, and into bed? I can't eat any more."

Ingeborg rose and went into the bedroom to turn down the covers. When Andrew and Haakan got there, he started unbuttoning his shirt.

"Just lie down."

"I can't in these dirty clothes." He ripped at the buttons on his shirt. "Please. Help me."

They helped him, and she was sure he was asleep before he hit the bed. Ingeborg covered him with the quilt and watched him for a moment. *Lord, protect him, please. Surely this is not good for him to be so exhausted.*

"He is so stubborn." Andrew sank back down in his chair at the table.

"I keep praying for God to protect him."

"If only I could depend on him to quit before he gets so tired. He wanted me to tie him onto the plow."

"That might be safer."

"No. Safer is quitting while you are able." He looked up at her. "You'll have to talk with him, Mor."

She tipped her head forward and shook her head slowly and gently. "Maybe if all three of us, well, four including Lars, try at the same time, he might get the idea."

"If something happens to him out there, I'll never forgive myself."

"Tell him that. He would not want you to feel that responsibility."

Andrew chewed slowly, narrow eyes focused on the table. Ingeborg watched him, seeing Roald in this son of his. He used to do that same thing when thinking deeply.

"How about this? We say for the next two days, he needs to limit himself to two hours of plowing. If he can handle that, then we can add another half hour every two days until he is working till noon. When he gets stronger, he can come back out later in the afternoon after a rest."

"All we can do is try."

"Good. We'll all talk on this again this evening. I don't want to go through another time like this." Andrew buttered a slice of bread. "Trygve said he'd gladly stay home from school to plow."

"I remember you offering the same thing." She passed him the meat and gravy. How she longed for the first of the new potatoes, and they were not even in the ground yet. Good thing she had canned so many of the smaller ones. "Maybe Astrid will be able to take a break and go looking for dandelion greens pretty soon."

"Those south of the barn are usually the first up, but they're not big enough to eat yet. Give them another week."

"Next year I am going to make a cold frame on the south side of the house, you know, like I saw in that magazine."

"What? You'll be out tending it in the snow?" he asked.

"If I have to. What must it be like to live in a climate where the snow doesn't last into April."

"Or May. Remember last year the frost got the beans in mid-May." He leaned back in his chair and stretched his arms over his head. "I don't know how Far is doing it. I'm tired and achy, and I'm young. Spring is always like this. Time to get your muscles and hands toughened up again." He pushed his chair back. "I heard Lars go by, so I better get out there. I'll send Ellie over with the children in case Far gets restless. Carl thinks Gampa's stories are the best."

Ingeborg watched him go out the door. It seemed like only yesterday when he'd been sapling thin, and now his shoulders were as broad as Haakan's, and he stood an inch or so taller. She hoped Roald was able to look down from heaven and see his fine sons.

She'd just slid two dried-apple pies into the oven and cleaned up the mess when she heard the jingle of harness and male voices. What was Thorliff doing here this time of day? She didn't recognize the other voice. And here she'd just emptied and washed the coffeepot.

"Coffee will take a bit of time, but make yourselves comfortable." She poured more coffee beans into the coffee grinder without looking over her shoulder till she finished. Then she saw the two men who had just walked into the kitchen.

"Mor, I want you to meet Daniel Jeffers." Thorliff motioned to the young man beside him.

"Glad to meet you." She crossed the room with her hand out. "Welcome to Blessing. Are you related to—" She stopped, looked at Thorliff, and substituted one thought for another. "Related to the man who used to own the store here?"

"I thought I might be until Thorliff described the man. And when he showed me the photograph, I knew. The man in the picture is my father, Daniel John Jeffers. I am Daniel Jacob. There is no Harlan in our family. And my father is missing."

"Missing." She stared into his dark eyes.

"Yes. I came west searching for him. When he left home, he had this envelope with him."

Ingeborg backed up until the chair hit her skirt and sat down. "But what about—? I mean . . . He couldn't . . ." Her thoughts wouldn't wrap around this fund of knowledge.

"Is Far sleeping?"

"Not anymore" came from the bedroom.

"Good. I wanted you to hear this." Thorliff turned to the young man. "You have a chair while I go get him. Like I said, he's been sick. I'm sure Mor will have the coffee ready very soon."

"Oh, pardon me. Of course." Ingeborg rose on a long exhale. "This is too much. If there was some skulduggery going on, no wonder Mr. Jeffers was so secretive." She shook her head and commenced to making the coffee. "Please, Mr. Jeffers, have a seat."

She snuck quick glances at him. He had dark unruly hair that tumbled down on his forehead, a square face with a straight nose—the girls would dub him good-looking—hands that had not seen a plow, slender but not as tall as her sons. His clothes were of good quality but not of great wealth. He also looked very tired, perhaps not from hard work but more from worry.

"Where are you from, Mr. Jeffers?" She stumbled a bit on the last name.

"Iowa. My father worked for a farming machinery company and

invented things on the side. He applied for patents on several ideas and received approval for this and one other. Deere and Company wanted to buy this one, but Father left on a trip north to Minneapolis with a list of possible partners to produce the new seeder himself, and he disappeared along the way."

"What happened?"

"We don't know. My mother is sick with worry. My father had set off with such high hopes. He'd been turned down by one company and thought to find someone who would work with him on bringing the patent into production."

"Wait," Thorliff called from the bedroom. "We'll be there in a minute, so you don't have to tell everything again."

Ingeborg smiled at her guest. "The pies won't be done for some time, but I'll get something else out to go with the coffee." She set a plate of sour-cream cookies on the table. "Help yourself."

When all the men were around the table and Mr. Jeffers was introduced to Haakan, Thorliff asked him to tell his story again from the beginning.

He ended with, "My father visited two companies in Minneapolis and was turned down. I visited the third company on the list and found he'd never made it there. I met a salesman from another company, and he said he'd heard of a Jeffers who owned a store in Blessing, North Dakota. I came here to meet him, just in case." He motioned to the envelope that lay on the table. "And was given this." A silence grew as all of them stared at the innocuous brown envelope, dotted with bits of remaining glue around the edges. "How this man got it is the question. And where is my father?"

"I knew as soon as I saw you that you were related to the man in the photo. We thought it odd that Harlan bore no resemblance at all," Thorliff said, tapping his fingers on the table.

Haakan cleared his throat. "I think this is a job for the sheriff." He looked to Thorliff. "To where did you buy the ticket for Jeffers?"

"We gave him one hundred dollars in cash and a ticket to Chicago. We wanted him more than one state away. But who knows what he did after he left here. We told him if he returned to Blessing, we'd let the townspeople have him."

"Meaning what?"

"Well, we led him to believe that tar and feathering might be on his agenda if he returned, or some such mob mentality. After what he did—"

"I take it my name is not very popular here in Blessing."

"I'm sorry to say that you are correct." Thorliff reached for the envelope. "May I?"

"By all means."

Thorliff took out the papers and moved his chair closer to his father's. "Look at this. I think you'll agree that this has promise. And I think we could build a prototype here. Maybe go into production. Perhaps Hjelmer would be interested in being part of this too."

Ingeborg could see the wheels turning in her men's minds as they studied the blueprints.

Young Mr. Jeffers got up from his seat and stood behind them, leaning forward to point out special details. The discussion grew more animated.

"We need Lars and Andrew here to see this."

"You want me to go ring the triangle?"

"Please do, and wave them in."

"They'll think something is terribly wrong."

"Not for long. This could be something incredibly right."

Several hours later, the men sat around the table nodding at each other. Ingeborg could feel the excitement in the air, lifting the hair on her arms like before a lightning storm.

"I'd say we can draw up an agreement regarding this project, if you are willing to do that, or we can just shake hands like we do here in Blessing."

"Or both." Thorliff smiled at his father. "Knowing what a snake Harlan whatever-his-name-is, I want everyone protected."

"Good idea."

Haakan tapped his chin with one forefinger. "Did your father have a lot of money with him?"

"I don't think an inordinate amount. Maybe a couple hundred dollars. Why?"

"I don't know. The Jeffers we know didn't seem the kind to have enough cash to buy the store from Penny. And yet he did."

"Did you ever ask Penny how Jeffers paid for the store?"

Thorliff shook his head. "Didn't seem to be my business. Besides, I wasn't real happy with her for selling like that. Remember?"

"None of us were." Haakan turned to Ingeborg. "How about bringing us paper and ink, please? And give it to Thorliff." He inclined his head toward the young dark-haired man. "We don't want to try to read my chicken-scratching down the road."

After they'd all agreed on what to say, they made three copies, signed them, and placed them in three envelopes. Thorliff, Haakan, and Daniel Jeffers each took a copy.

"Now, I suggest you go to either Grafton or Grand Forks and talk with a sheriff regarding your father. Let them see what they can learn. Thorliff, you write out a description of Harlan Jeffers to send with him."

"Actually, I think I'll go along. There seems a certain justice in getting an artist's sketch as close as possible to the man we're looking for." He turned to Jeffers. "Come along. We'll get you set at the boardinghouse and catch the train tomorrow."

"Thank you, Mrs. Bjorklund, for the delicious cookies and pie and for keeping the coffee coming while we worked." He nodded to the others. "And thank you. I'm looking forward to working with all of you."

After closing the door behind them, Ingeborg sank into the chair by Haakan. "Uff da. Whoever dreamed when we got up this morning what amazing things God had in store for us? And Penny is coming home. God sure has been working behind the scenes to answer all these prayers."

35

"You really admitted it. Out loud. That you believe you are in love with Gerald."

Rebecca stared at the face in the mirror. Even though the glass was wavy, her eyes were clear. And purpose shone brightly. *"Why do you love him?"* That was the question someone had asked at the party more than a week ago and she'd not had an answer.

"I guess I've always loved him," she'd finally dredged up with all of them staring at her. "He's been my friend forever."

"Love is more than friendship," Sophie, of many experiences, had intoned.

"But doesn't it start there?" she'd asked.

"Not always, but friendship is good."

"Ellie loved Andrew forever," Deborah put in.

"He wouldn't allow anything else. He branded it on her brain." Astrid looked at Ellie with a smile.

"Are you saying I don't think for myself?" Ellie asked, sitting up straighter. "I do too, and remember, I almost made him not come back."

"That took terrible fortitude on your part."

"The way I look at it, Gerald would be easy to love," Ellie said. "He's gentle and kind."

"And spineless," someone dared to say.

That ugly word lay on the floor in the middle of their circle. The circle of friends who were either helping her or hindering her—she just wasn't sure which at that moment.

"What!" The word made Rebecca want to lunge at the speaker.

"If he can't tell his mother that you are the one he loves and she must accept that, then he's not the man for you," Deborah declared.

They all turned to stare at her.

"Guess that shoots the deer between the eyes." Astrid grinned at Deborah. "You don't say a lot, but when you do . . ."

"Weren't you even tempted to kiss Kurt?" Maydell asked, her elbows propped on her knees and her chin on her hands. "I mean, he sounds so romantic."

"I think he wanted to kiss me at the train station, but with Penny and everyone there, he just squeezed my hand."

"And did you get tingles up your arm?"

Rebecca thought back and shook her head. "I don't think so. I had gloves on."

Maydell rolled her eyes. "What about with Gerald?"

"When he looks into my eyes, I get all melty inside." She had admitted that.

"That's attraction, all right," Maydell had said.

Rebecca pinched herself so she could think of the present instead of the past. She didn't have time to spend staring in the mirror. Today was a new day, and perhaps Gerald would stop by the store before his shift on the switchboard started, as he had the last few days. There were definite advantages to living in town.

And what a relief to know she could stay. Penny had called her herself to make sure Rebecca knew.

"We can't move back into the store after living in Bismarck, Rebecca. So if you like it, you are welcome to stay. But if you're finding it lonely and want to move back with Gus, I understand too."

"I love it here, Penny. I'd love to stay." She hadn't added how much seeing Gerald every day meant to her too.

But he didn't come that day or the next. The furor over the young Mr. Daniel Jeffers had died down, her new order had arrived, and she'd found places for all the merchandise. Penny and Thorliff were working out the sale of the store. Today, since it wasn't so busy, she intended to fill out her own order for two tables and four chairs, her first real investment in her soda shop. She had located a supplier for the soda machine supplies and planned to order those soon. The company said to allow two to three weeks for delivery. That would give her time to get the store ready. And now that Dorothy had Maydell's help, she could use her evenings to work on it.

How she would run both her shop and the store during the day until Penny arrived was something she had yet to figure out. If, of course, she could get her own shop up and running that quickly. She was really hoping to open before school let out for the summer.

Mischief bounced down the stairs with her, hinting that it was time to eat.

"I know, I know. I kept some of that chicken for you, and Astrid brought me a jug of milk." With the advent of warmer weather, the iceman now delivered ice for her icebox, so she had a cool place to store perishables. One thing about Penny, she had ordered the newest items and then talked everyone else in Blessing into trying them. An icebox in the kitchen was easier than a springhouse like out on the farm.

She glanced out the kitchen window. Samuel Knutson had come and spaded her garden, and now when she had time, she would plant her peas, lettuce, carrots, and marigolds. She'd read an article that said marigolds kept bugs away from vegetables, besides adding cheer and color. One of these days she would bring some of the last potatoes in from the farm and cut them up to plant. How strange it seemed to have this little plot rather than the huge garden that she and Dorothy used to work together.

After having bread and milk for breakfast, she let the cat back in and went to open the store. Mrs. Geddick and Mrs. Solberg were chatting as they waited, and Rebecca caught something about "that poor boy."

"Who?"

"Why, Gerald Valders. He's had a terrible time with that malaria again."

"I see." No wonder he'd not been by. Why didn't he ask Toby to tell her? The thought got her back up. Why was she always the last one to know when he took sick?

She helped the women with their orders and sent them on their way with a cheerful good-bye and returned to her thinking. What could she take to him that might tempt his appetite? He'd told her once that when he was running the fever, he had no desire to eat.

At one o'clock she closed the store and, wrapping her bowl in a dishcloth, walked over to the Valderses' house. Knocking at the door, she caught herself humming. A robin hopped around in the grass and with a beady eye located a worm and pulled it out of the ground, then flew up to the tree. Maybe if Gerald sat out here in the shade and watched the world go by, he'd feel better. She knocked again.

When the door opened and Mrs. Valders barred the entry, Rebecca smiled and held up her dish. "I brought something that Gerald might enjoy. I thought I could peep in and maybe cheer him up."

"Peep into a man's bedroom, his sickroom, no less? Don't be so impertinent. That's the problem with all you young women; you have no sense of propriety."

Her cheek stung from the verbal slap. She held out the dish. "Well, at least tell him I'm thinking of him and hope he likes this. It is a new receipt."

Mrs. Valders took the dish. "I'll see." She started to shut the door, then added, "Thank you." The door closed with a click.

How rude! And she has the nerve to say I have no propriety? Rebecca spun on her heel and headed back to the store. The next time she saw Gerald, they would have to have a discussion. Of course, he might have no idea what was going on. His mother might not even give him a taste. As she marched back to the store, she realized an amazing connection.

Her brothers kept discouraging her suitors, and his mother did the same. All in the name of what they figured was best for the one kept in the dark. She felt like screaming from the back porch. Out on the farm she could have done that. Here in town, someone would come running to help. Especially after what had happened. Instead, she snatched up her spade and turned over two more feet on the south side of her garden. Pumpkins would be good to plant there. Maybe she could plant her ire too, but who wanted an ire vine? Surely it would grow like quack grass.

At least her bitterness against her brothers was no longer taking root inside. But now she was angry with Mrs. Valders again.

↬

April 1903

Two days later, still a bit green around the gills, Gerald brought her empty dish and freshly laundered dish towel back. "Thank you. It was delicious."

"I was afraid you would not get to taste it."

"Why?"

"Well, the way your mother acted, I thought she might just throw it out."

"No, that would be a waste, and one thing she does not do is waste anything." He gave a weak smile.

"If you'd like to sit on the back porch here, I'll bring out some lemonade. Or is it too early in the morning for lemonade?"

"That sounds wonderful. Lemonade sings of summer." He sat on the chair and reached down to stroke Mischief's ears as she rubbed up against his pant leg. "She's sure growing fast."

Rebecca poured two glasses and handed him one before she took the other chair. "I'm glad you are feeling better. I've missed you." Well, that surely was saying what she thought.

"Me too." He smiled into her eyes. "Missed you, I mean, not missed me." He paused. "That's not true. I really miss me when I'm in the throes of fever again."

"Will you always have these episodes?"

"That's what the doctors say."

Ask him! I can't ask him! "Do you ever think of having a home of your own?"

"Sometimes. But I so dread being alone when these episodes come."

"What . . . I mean, what do I have to do to be allowed to help take care of you? Marry you?" She hoped her tone sounded teasing.

"Ah, Rebecca, I can't think of anything I would rather have, but I've been doing a lot of thinking. Being ill gives one time for that." He leaned forward, staring intently into her eyes. "I will never put you in the position of losing someone you love again. It's hard enough when we don't expect it, but if we can protect those we love, we should. I will. So I'll never marry."

How could he admit he loved her and at the same time say he'd never marry her? Rebecca stared at him in shock. Never? Not because of his mother's influence but his own choice.

They heard a knocking, and Rebecca leaped to her feet as if spring propelled. "I have to open the store." She ran to the front door, flipped the *Closed* sign to *Open*, and welcomed in her customers. "Look around, and I'll be right back."

But the chair was empty, and Mischief had been put back inside. She crumpled. No one knew her better than Gerald. And if she couldn't have him, then she would be an old maid like she'd said so many months ago. But did she really want to marry someone who could die from malaria? First, when she was a little girl, a couple of babies had died, leaving her mother so sad, and then her mother grew big with disease inside her and died when Rebecca was nine. Her father died later of a broken heart, and the bull gored her brother Swen. The people she loved most died. Was she asking for more of the same thing in thinking of loving Gerald in spite of his misery? A burst of anger flared.

Why had he ever made her realize she loved him, then? *I was happy just being best friends. How do we go back?*

As if she had any choice in the matter now. She returned to the store with a wooden smile pasted on her face. She couldn't even escape to Bismarck, because Penny and Hjelmer were coming home.

❧

The next evening, after she'd replayed the conversation for the sixteenth time, she realized he had said he *couldn't* marry. He'd not said he didn't love her. He didn't want her to watch him being ill and maybe die. But wasn't that her decision to make? She paced back and forth.

Since she no longer had to go out to the farm every night, she walked next door to what used to be the dress shop. Miss Christopherson had given her the key several weeks ago. She unlocked the door and entered the one-room shop. Empty. Down to the bare floor and walls. The first step would be to paint the walls and floor. That would brighten it up considerably. She wanted to paint the outside too.

"Exploring the new shop?" Toby Valders asked as he stepped through the doorway.

"Yes. Now that Penny is indeed going to come back to the store, I will take over this space."

"It's not very big."

"No, it isn't."

"You'll need a counter with work space behind it." He moved and motioned a line about a third of the way from the back wall. "Here?"

"About. I know that I'm going to need a refrigeration room eventually, but I hoped to build it later as an add-on. For now I'll need a box to keep ice in so the canisters can stay cool."

"What else?"

"I ordered two small round tables with four chairs. I'd like to put up two booths: one in each front corner."

"A table attached to the wall with benches on two sides? High backs?"

"Yes. Have you seen such a plan?"

He nodded. "That will really take up all that area. You want display shelves on the walls? Mirrors?" He turned to look at the work area. "You'll need cabinets and shelves for glassware. Running water will be important."

"Running water? We don't have running water here in Blessing."

"We will soon."

"Penny had running water and an indoor privy and bath at her house in Bismarck."

"Thorliff said we're going to be building them a new house. Fast. They are ordering a Sears and Roebuck house. If you want help with this, we can do it in the evenings."

"I can't afford to pay much for help."

"Who said anything about pay? After all, it's all in the family."

"What?" Rebecca stared at him as if he'd lost any sense he'd ever had.

"Well, you know, when you and Gerald get married and—" He stopped.

She kept shaking her head. "Gerald told me he has no intention of ever getting married. That the malaria keeps coming back all the time, and it would be too hard on a wife and family. Besides—" She stopped. Why was she telling Toby all this?

"Besides?" He made beckoning motions with his fingers.

"Besides, he doesn't really love me, at least not enough."

Toby burst out laughing. "He's loved you for years. You gotta make sure he knows how you feel, you know?"

"Lead him on? Your mother already says I am too forward, improper, and silly. You want to hear the rest?"

"No. Ignore her. She means well. I just let it go right on over my head. Like a river flowing around a big rock."

"But it's different with Gerald. The malaria and all."

"True. And he's too kind and considerate for his own good. I just took him his supper. Why don't you go on over and visit with him while he eats."

"I can't. That wouldn't be proper."

"You two are entirely too concerned with proper." He studied the room again. "We'll start with painting. Surely you can run an account at the store, especially since you manage it."

"I-I guess." She followed him out the door and locked it behind her. "Thank you, Toby." Right now she could have flown right over the building. Someone else had offered to help, just as if she were starting on it in the morning. Or rather the evening. And the way Toby talked, Mrs. Valders was not nearly as much of an obstacle as she'd thought.

"You're welcome. And don't worry about Gerald. He'll come around. That is, he will if you really want him to."

She pondered that comment. Of course she wanted to marry Gerald—didn't she? This was obviously another time when she really needed to pray. And get definite answers.

36

Sunday morning as Rebecca packed a basket for a picnic after church, she heard a light knock at the back door. She gulped as she realized it was Gerald.

Inviting him in she caught a look in his eyes that she wasn't sure she'd ever seen there before. "What? Is there flour on my face?"

"You're beautiful."

She knew it wasn't heat from the oven that suffused her face. "Gerald, what's come over you?" She fanned herself with the dish towel.

"I think my eyes have finally been opened."

Could he see her heart about to leap out of her chest? She fanned again and started to say something, but nothing made sense.

"I was going to wait until after church and take you for a walk along the river, but I've waited so long that now I just have to say it."

"Say what?" If this was what faint felt like, she realized she'd better sit down.

"Please, Rebecca, I've loved you forever, and I want you to marry me." The words almost ran together, he spoke so fast.

She looked at him, then away and then back again. "Did you say *marry*? I thought you didn't want to get married, ever."

"Can a man not change his mind?"

"Depends on the reason why." She forced the words out despite her thoughts screaming at her. Why was she hesitating now? *Say yes!*

"Fair question after our last conversation. I began to realize that I was hiding behind my own selfish fears. I didn't want to love you so much and then have to leave you if I died. I told myself I was being unselfish, but really I was protecting myself from pain."

Rebecca forced back the tears gathering in her eyes. "What made you change your mind?"

"Toby."

"Toby?"

"Toby asked me if I could still live in Blessing if another man married you. He told me to go see Sophie. So I talked to Sophie."

"Sophie?"

"I asked her if she had known what would happen to Hamre, would she still have run away to marry him. She answered quite vehemently that love is too precious to waste a drop. You grab it by the tail and give it a good whirl and rejoice in every minute together. She said, 'I wouldn't have traded a minute with him. Garth and I feel the same way now.'"

Rebecca smiled, wishing she had heard that conversation.

"So, the question is: Will you marry me?" He covered her hand with his while his gaze held hers captive.

If one could drown in another's eyes like a romance story she'd read said, she was there. *Marry you? Of course I'll marry you.* She glanced down to see his fingers stroking the back of her hand. Turning her hand over, she clasped his fingers in hers. "Gerald Valders, I will be delighted to marry you."

"Thank you, God." He tipped his head back to look heavenward.

Mischief rubbed up against Rebecca's skirt. The robins sang in the trees.

All the world was singing. She leaned forward, he leaned forward, and they met in the middle, lips soft on lips. When her eyes drifted open again, she smiled. "I have one question."

"What is that?" He traced the curve of her cheek tenderly. "What?"

"Will we live with your parents?"

"Absolutely not. But I think you're in for a surprise there too."

"Nothing can be more surprising than this."

The church bell began to peal. "Shall we?" He offered her his arm.

As they neared the church, Mr. Valders came up to meet them. "A very wise decision. I can't think of anything better." He kissed Rebecca on the cheek while Astrid looked on dumbstruck and then went into the church.

Rebecca held on to Gerald's arm a little tighter. "They know already," she gasped.

"Well, they knew I was going to ask. I made it quite clear."

"And your mother's response?" Rebecca looked around nervously, expecting an attack.

"I'll admit she was struck silent for a moment." Gerald smiled. "But then she said, 'I'll need to get that receipt from her. It was quite good.'"

Gerald laughed at Rebecca's expression. "I told you there were more surprises." He leaned over and gently kissed her again. "Let's go in and thank God together for His mercies."

Rebecca nodded and, with flushed cheeks, entered the sanctuary to the smiling faces of family and friends. She and Gerald would be getting married! She wanted to run to the front and shout it to the entire congregation. In spite of all their doubts and questions, God had worked it all out. Lives could and did change. Even Mrs. Valders. An unexpected thought struck her as she sat down on the bench beside Gerald. She would be a Mrs. Valders. As the opening hymn burst forth, she took in a deep breath and stood, singing, "Holy, Holy, Holy, Lord God Almighty." *Only you will make this all come out right.* "All thy works shall praise thy name in earth and sky and sea." *Especially me.*

~ EPILOGUE ~

Late June 1903

COULD LIFE GET ANY more splendid than this?

Rebecca searched each inch of her soda shop to make absolutely sure there was not one thing out of place. The dishes were polished to a sparkle, the floor was painted in black and white diamonds, the mirrored walls on one side reflected the shelves laden with gift items on the other. Red-and-white checkered tablecloths adorned her two round tables, while a band of red-and-white diamonds decorated the backs of the two booths. She'd hoped to add another table and chairs, but Penny had encouraged her to leave room for customers to wait to be helped at the counter.

She turned at the tinkle of the bell that Gerald had hung over the door. Her heart leaped at the sight of his dear smiling face as he entered.

"Is everything all right?" He paused and surveyed the shop, mentally checking off the last-minute finishes. "The place looks great."

"What did you think of the sign?" She motioned to the banner outside that shouted *Grand Opening*.

"Everything is just right." His smile deepened. "Like you."

Her heart skipped a beat this time and then took off running. Could eyes kiss? It felt so to her. He slid his arms around her and rested his chin on her forehead. Her arms circled him as though they'd finally found a home. Tomorrow was the day. A wedding in the morning, and the party here at the Blessing Soda Shoppe afterward. The women of the town already had their spare tables and chairs set up under the trees in the back. The coming wedding and grand opening had been the buzz of the town for the last weeks.

The only thing that didn't get done was the permanent sign that would eventually match in lettering the new one on Penny's store: *Blessing Soda Shoppe*, next door to *Blessing Mercantile*. Penny had decided that her business needed a new name and a new look to cancel out the memories of the last few months.

"I love you, you know," Gerald whispered, his breath tickling the curls she'd so carefully arranged about her forehead.

"And I you." She leaned back in his arms. "I can't begin to tell you how much."

"We have a lifetime to do that."

She nodded and reached up to plant a kiss on his smiling lips. Brazen is what Mrs. Valders would call her, but right now Rebecca no longer cared. After all, even Mrs. Valders was coming around. She'd called Rebecca *Dear* at church last Sunday, an event that had caused more than one set of raised eyebrows.

"There is now a real door that closes," he said as he took her by the hand. "Come, I'll show you." He led her out the back door of the soda shop. Since Penny had invited Rebecca to live in the store for as long as she wanted, they had decided a door, instead of a curtain, between the store and their home would be a good thing. And Hjelmer was working on that now.

"How are the two lovebirds?" Hjelmer asked as he slammed another nail in the doorframe.

"Excited." Rebecca looked up at Gerald. "Your turn."

"That's a good word. Mine needs whole sentences."

"Well said." Hjelmer stepped back from his job. "Guess I haven't lost all the skills my father taught me." He examined his hands. "But

I sure need to toughen up some. Working in an office means blisters when you take on real labor. Sure feels good to be home."

"Rebecca?" Sophie's voice came from the soda shop.

"Back here behind the store."

Sophie came around the corner in such a rush that her skirt billowed behind her. "The girls are all at the boardinghouse waiting for you."

"Oh." Rebecca looked up at Gerald. "I forgot."

"You go have your party. I have things that need to be finished. I'll see you tomorrow at the church at ten sharp."

"Yes." His calm confidence helped still her butterflies.

The next hours passed in a whirl. The party where they all burned their lists. Spending the night at the boardinghouse at Sophie's request, waking to sun streaming in the window and a tap at the door.

"Your bath is ready," Miss Christopherson announced.

"In a real bathtub?"

Sophie had remodeled parts of the boardinghouse with inside plumbing, hot running water, and a bathtub that she could sell tickets for.

When Rebecca had luxuriated long enough in the water, Ingeborg and Astrid were there to help her dress in a gown made for her by Miss Christopherson. The cream fabric set the fire in Rebecca's hair to flashing. She smoothed down the front with gentle fingers. Never had she owned such a fine garment.

"You look so lovely," Ingeborg said. "I just wish your mother was here to see you."

Rebecca nodded, then dabbed the tears away with the tips of her fingers. "Me too."

"The buggy awaits," called a male voice from the hallway.

Rebecca hugged Astrid first, then Ingeborg. "How can I ever thank you for all you've done and been to me in my life?"

"You needn't worry. That's what family is for."

"They're ready inside," Haakan said moments later as he helped her out of the buggy at the church. "There's not an extra square inch of space in there." He kissed her on the cheek and whispered, "Your mother and father would be so proud of you."

Knute waved from the door. "Come on, or you'll be late to your own wedding."

Haakan tucked her arm through his, and the two of them mounted the steps, where he handed her to Knute and said, "I give you your father's blessing this day and forever."

Rebecca nodded, her throat too full to speak. She blinked and then took the handkerchief he offered to wipe her eyes. "Thank you." She sniffed once more and gave her elder brother a watery smile. "I'm ready."

Dorothy peeked her head out the door. "Hurry, so we get this done before Adam wants to eat again. I just nursed him, but all we need is a screaming baby in the middle of a wedding." She heaved a sigh and, after handing Rebecca her bouquet, kissed her on the cheek. "He's up there waiting for you."

Haakan held the door for Knute and Rebecca. The piano picked up the wedding hymn, and Dorothy started down the aisle, Sarah scattering flower petals in front of her.

Rebecca inhaled the fragrance of flowers, those in her bouquet and those decorating the church. Gerald and Toby stood at the front of the church, the smile worn by the groom bright enough to light the building, even without the aid of the sun streaming in the windows and setting a halo of light around his head.

Rebecca rolled her lips together to keep the tears at bay. While she knew everyone along the aisle was smiling at her, she could see only Gerald, her best friend and soon-to-be husband. When he took her hand, his smile promised the love he'd spoken.

"Dearly beloved . . ." Pastor Solberg started the ceremony with the beautiful age-old words. They sank into Rebecca's heart and mind. *Dearly beloved.* Dearly beloved by the man beside her, by her parents who waited in glory, and by God himself. *Dearly beloved.* She promised within herself to let Gerald always know he was her dearly beloved.

As the service progressed, they gave their vows, both clearly, both promising to love and to cherish. Gerald stared deep into her eyes as he slid the gold band onto her finger. *To love and to cherish. Dearly beloved.*

"I now pronounce you husband and wife. Gerald, you may kiss your bride."

Rebecca's cheeks wore roses as she and her husband turned to face the congregation. Everyone stood as Mrs. Solberg hit the keys again, this time in a joyful song, and they marched back down the aisle.

"The party will begin at the Blessing Soda Shoppe as soon as our women get everything set up," Pastor Solberg told everyone. "The Lord bless and keep us all under His mighty arms. Amen."

On the front steps of the church, Rebecca paused for the next ritual. She inhaled the fragrance of the flowers she held, snipped off one tiny piece to press in her memory book, and waited, listening to the tittering and teasing as the unmarried young women gathered.

"We're ready," someone called as she turned her back to the group.

"Throw to the left," Gerald whispered in her ear. She gave him a questioning look, shrugged, and tossed. The squeal of delight told her without looking who had caught it.

"Maydell?"

"And Gus is blushing."

Rebecca turned and surveyed her friends and family. For this was indeed her family. All of them. Dearly beloved. She hooked her arm through Gerald's, and they stepped down the stairs into their new life—together.

"I think I'll make your mother the first soda, Mr. Valders."

"I think you are one very smart young woman, Mrs. Valders."

NOV - - 2010

g Series!

As the prairie yields bountiful harvests, the Norwegian pioneers enjoy a measure of prosperity. Now their young daughters are seeking to fulfill their own dreams and aspirations—but each will need faith, courage, and perseverance to find God's plan for her future.

DAUGHTERS OF BLESSING by Lauraine Snelling
A Promise for Ellie, Sophie's Dilemma, A Touch of Grace, Rebecca's Reward

MORE MOVING HISTORICAL FICTION FROM LAURAINE SNELLING

Faced with the forbidding prairies of North Dakota, the Bjorklund family must rely on their strength and faith to build a homestead in the untamed Red River Valley. Through the daunting challenges of this difficult land, the Bjorklunds suffer tragedy and loss, but also joy, hope, and a love that remains strong.

RED RIVER OF THE NORTH:
An Untamed Land, A New Day Rising, A Land to Call Home, The Reapers' Song, Tender Mercies, Blessing in Disguise

A scandal and an inheritance, a secret past, and a dream of a future draw four women to the unknown wilds of the Dakotah Territory. As each leaves behind a measure of comfort and security, will she find the strength to adapt and flourish?

DAKOTAH TREASURES:
Ruby, Pearl, Opal, Amethyst